And when he hath the kernel eat,
Who doth not throw away the shell?
John Donne

PART ONE

The Collector

Gaius ... wasted no time in summoning regular legions and auxiliaries from all directions, levied troops everywhere with the utmost strictness, and collected military supplies of all kinds on an unprecedented scale. Then he marched off so rapidly and hurriedly that the Guards cohorts could not keep up with him ... Gaius showed how keen and severe a commander-in-chief he intended to be by ignominiously dismissing any general who was late in bringing ... the auxiliaries he required. Then, when he reviewed the legions, he discharged many veteran leading-centurions on the grounds of age and incapacity, though some had only a few more days of their service to run; and, calling the remainder a pack of greedy fellows, scaled down their retirement bonuses ...

Suetonius, *The Twelve Caesars* (Gaius Caligula), translated by Robert Graves.

1

The way Harry Griffin recalled it the first time the Inspectors asked him, he might possibly have been in the south of France back in the summer of 1973; but even if he had perchance happened to be there, to the best of his knowledge he certainly hadn't met Guy Magnus. When the Inspectors pressed him further, Harry gave his solemn assurance that even if their paths had happened to cross briefly – and this wasn't to be taken as an admission that they had – they definitely hadn't discussed Britton Trust.

His interrogators then put to him that Guy Magnus had told his own lawyer he had bought shares in Britton Trust that July on the recommendation of his old chum Harry Griffin.

Not so, Harry protested. Their relationship was by no means as friendly as Magnus implied. Guy had most likely been motivated by envy that a company in which Harry was a major shareholder was doing so well. He probably wanted to teach him a lesson.

How so? asked Harry's interrogators.

By taking Britton Trust over, of course, Harry replied, as if to ask, how else?

If Harry's replies seemed less than candid, he thought it only fair to take into account that he was being put at a considerable disadvantage, being unfairly outnumbered as well as unreasonably victimised. For the Board of Trade had seen fit to appoint a distinguished Queen's Counsel and a leading City accountant to carry out an investigation into the affairs of Britton Trust, and these members of the great and the good seemed to think that Harry Griffin could and should assist them in their task. It ran counter to the principles of natural justice, Harry told himself, to have to score his runs without first being told where the opposition had placed its fielders. Obliged to respond to a pretty unsporting line of questioning, in which the more detailed his reply the more penetrating the next question turned out to be, his eyes had sought inspiration from the mahogany bookshelves of the QC's

Inner Temple chambers, only to find them ominously lined with ranks of leather-bound volumes of the Statutes of the Realm. In the clammy air of an Indian summer heatwave, rivulets of perspiration trickled down his well-fed cheeks, making it increasingly difficult for him to sustain his habitual 'would-I-ever-do-such-a-thing?' expression. Under such adverse conditions the memory was apt to play one awful tricks, he excused himself.

Perhaps due to the cooler weather, by the time he next met the Inspectors, Harry's powers of recall had made a miraculous recovery. He realised he had been in the south of France that July after all, and though more than two years had gone by, he did seem to recollect a chance meeting with Guy Magnus. But of one thing he remained sure: the subject of Britton Trust had never come up; and even if it had, Magnus had been the last person he would have wished to own shares in so prestigious a company.

The Inspectors' next informant, though generally not the most reliable of sources, may have come closer to the truth. By now an unemployed stock-broker, his firm having had the misfortune to be hammered by the stock exchange, Ray Munster told them Harry Griffin had lost money all across the board and was heavily in hock. He owed money in Jersey, he owed money in London, his last firm but one was after him for a load of dosh; so he disappeared into Paris and wouldn't come home. That summer Harry and Guy had dined together regularly to compare notes on the celebrated chefs of the Côte d'Azur. Munster reckoned Harry would still have been smarting from the sale Guy had negotiated the previous autumn for Mallard, the company they'd taken control of together back in 1969. Harry had taken his profit on half of his stake too soon, shortly before Guy agreed the deal with Universal Credit that valued Mallard's shares at ten times their original cost. Guy hadn't stayed with his shares in Universal Credit, of course; he had this thing about cashing in his chips so he could put his winnings back on the table. Whereas Harry had accepted the share swap for the rest of his stake and had lost the lot when Universal Credit went belly-up, reported Munster with the memory for detail of a born dealer. After that, Harry had bombed on pretty much everything – except Britton Trust, of course. But as that company issued more stock for each of its acquisitions, his share stake had been watered down. Having started with a lot of bugger-all, Harry had wound up with bugger-all of a lot; and, added Munster sagely, he must have had a pretty good idea that this particular lot was a load of crap. So he probably wanted to get his own back on Guy – they were that kind of friend. Moreover, Harry was a pretty damn good salesman; he may even have slightly conned Guy into buying the shares in Britton Trust.

Slightly conned? Guy Magnus? The image was not one the Inspectors recognised from their researches in the City of London. If you were wise, you wouldn't try to outsmart the sharpest, least scrupulous of the whizz-kids of the early seventies. However, they did know from another of their victims that when Magnus had called his office from the south of France that July, he was in a flap. It was pretty obvious something was up, Danny Gilbert told them. Magnus hadn't just seen a mention in the papers and told him to check it out on a whim. He knew something. You could hear it in his voice. It was a pitch higher than usual, and his order was clear-cut: 'Buy Britton Trust!'

Danny Gilbert, whom the Inspectors judged to be a truthful if rather naïve young man, ran one of Magnus's many corporate vehicles. Though barely twenty years of age, he was well trained. So even when his boss had already made up his mind, he still went through the same drill: get out the Extel card, send for the company's last three years' reports and accounts, find out if there was anything more up-to-date at Companies House, check for directors' dealings. Next, analyse the balance sheet. This was an art form: for however thorough Danny Gilbert thought he'd been, Guy Magnus would always be several steps ahead of him. One day, Gilbert guessed, he'd put his finger on a business with under-utilised assets by dividing the sales per employee by the rate of depreciation on plant and machinery. Rephrase that: he probably already did.

Finally, Gilbert told the Inspectors, he'd look up the chart. The chart tracked movements in a company's share price. It told him all he needed to know about trading in its stock: its highs and lows, trends and support levels. Britton Trust's chart showed no discernible support. Whenever the shares crept over 200p, sellers came out of the woodwork. He had called Guy back.

'It's the worst chart I've ever seen,' he had protested. 'I don't think Westchurch should touch it.' Westchurch, Gilbert explained to the Inspectors, was the name of the company he was running for Guy. At the time it had been in the market for stakes in investment trusts, not run-down industrial conglomerates.

'Well, I'm telling you to buy,' Guy's voice crackled down the line.

'Listen, Guy, why don't you just enjoy your holiday? We'll talk when you get back. The shares won't run away.'

'I told you to buy them now,' Guy had insisted. 'Do as you're told, damn you, Danny.'

'I'd really rather not,' Gilbert had replied as firmly as he dared. From time to time Guy Magnus would treat him like a messenger boy; but he wasn't a boy any longer. After all, he would soon be twenty-one. And he had his twenty per cent stake in the company to protect. That should give him some say in the matter.

'Right, you little bugger!' Guy had slammed down the phone without further elaboration.

What, the Inspectors wanted to know, had happened next?

For a moment, said Gilbert, he had sat in thought, doubtless pulling at his sideburns as he did now in his attempt at accurate recollection. Then he had taken the chart up to the next floor where Nigel Holmes, who managed Guy's back office, was staring at an empty minute book.

'You wouldn't buy shares on a chart like this, would you?' he had asked half-heartedly, knowing Holmes to be an instruction-taker not a decision-maker.

'Guy wants you to?' asked the latter without looking up. 'I'd buy,' he said with uncharacteristic certainty.

Next Gilbert had tried Brian Proctor. 'What would you say to this chart, Brian?' he had asked with a touch more hope, on the grounds that Proctor was a giver, rather than a taker, of instructions. His loyalty had recently been rewarded with promotion to the board of St Paul's Property, another of Guy's corporate vehicles.

'Guy likes it, doesn't he?'

'He hasn't seen it.'

'I'd buy,' said Proctor, with characteristic obedience.

Gilbert hadn't bothered to show the chart to Larry Callaghan, as he had no days to spare waiting for Guy's father-figure to come to town from his accountancy practice in Norwich, let alone for him to offer an opinion. Callaghan's contribution to Guy's share dealings wisely excluded decision-taking, for the closest he ever approached to a clear choice was between minestrone and paté maison, a dilemma he would resolve after an interminable crisis of conscience by finally accepting the head waiter's recommendation of the prawn cocktail, but only on receiving his assurance that the prawns were fresh.

Instead, Gilbert had spent the brief intervals between adding to his stakes in investment trusts putting all possible constructions on Guy's last remark and assessing the likelihood of each. He had already woken up to the fact that Guy knew half the Britton Trust board and was a close pal of Harry Griffin, a major shareholder in the company.

But it was not until the following Monday that Gilbert found out exactly what Guy had meant. The contract notes that arrived on his desk that morning were from a firm of stockbrokers he had never previously dealt with, nor indeed had he heard of them. He learnt from the heading that its name was C D Ramper & Co, and from the reference that the partner who had dealt for Guy went by the name of Mark Penney-Stockes. According to the contract notes, not Westchurch but another Magnus company, Ludgate Investments, had bought 85,000 shares in Britton Trust on 8th July at an average price of just under 200p. And when Gilbert checked the chart – a point he stressed to the Inspectors – he saw that this had been achieved without so much as a blip to alert a wary market. It was as if the schools had broken up early and stock-broking fathers had sacrificed the life-long habit of a couple of weeks alone with their secretaries to build sandcastles with their kiddies on the beach.

But the Inspectors knew all of this, and were anxious to move on. Twenty million pounds had gone walkabout from a merchant bank. The Board of Trade wished them to find out whether Guy Magnus and his chums had stolen it, and if so, where they had hidden it and whether any of it could be recovered. Danny Gilbert would have liked to know as much, though he reckoned that if he ever saw any of his own money again it would soon be taken away from him. The men from the ministry also took more than a passing interest in complaints by Britton Trust's merchant bank that Guy Magnus had offered a director an improper inducement, and that a board chaired by a peer of the realm had been in breach of both its duty to its shareholders and the rules of the London Stock Exchange. These and related matters caused the Inspectors to interview a wide range of City luminaries, older and, they hoped, wiser than Gilbert; though they guessed that such a hope was likely to prove vain considering how readily these supposedly astute gentlemen had allowed so many millions to be lost.

But when the various versions of events had been told, checked, retold, rechecked, put into shape and set down in the omniscient manner of the great and good when engaged in matters of consequence with the benefit of hindsight, the Inspectors were forced to admit that their report was incomplete. It lacked a contribution from the principal player. For Guy Magnus had seen fit to refuse their many invitations to meet them, on the ground that as he had once instructed one of them on a personal matter, a conflict of interest was bound to arise. To his friend and colleague Dominic Arthur he was more candid: 'It would ruin the funeral if there was no corpse.' Or perhaps he had said, 'no murderer.' Whichever it was, as Magnus remained abroad there was little the Inspectors could do about it. They were unable to make their own assessment of the young man the other players seemed to hold in such awe, or to discover at first hand why he had been driven to risk so much on a single throw. The closest they came to his motivation was the suggestion from one source that Magnus nurtured a grudge his friend Harry Griffin had crossed him over a lunch bill, or a bet, or something of the kind; though how such a trifling matter could have affected his hitherto apparently infallible judgment was never explained.

But by this time the Inspectors had discovered for themselves that Guy Magnus and Harry Griffin went back a long way together: to the days of their connection through Tanquery Taylor Tealeafe, stockbrokers to the shady; to the time when Harry had made a spirited response to a challenge from Guy.

2

Responding to a challenge was no new experience for Harry Griffin. He had learned to respond to challenges from the time when a stroke of ill-fortune had cost his father his life. His mother Bernice's view of the relative merits of a balanced diet and pocket money had proved the first challenge among many.

As he grew up under his mother's frugal wing, Harry developed into the kind of friend one could rely on in time of need. True, the need would be Harry's; but his friends could rely on him to tell them all about it.

Harry's need arose because his grandfather had settled a modest fortune on him in trust, on the premise that you set up a trust for someone you don't. So rather than settle the capital on Harry when he attained his majority, the old man decreed not only that he was to receive his inheritance in ever-increasing tranches, but that these were to be released to him at ever-increasing intervals.

The first tranche, when Harry was sixteen, bought him a taste for alcohol; at seventeen he became a fan of fast cars; at eighteen he satisfied his thirst for knowledge of women; and at twenty-one he began to study the form and breeding of racehorses. Then, before he had a chance to reach his twenty-fifth birthday and make further progress in developing his lifestyle, he met Sybil Harris at a dinner party in Hampstead. Sybil did not take long to find out about his inheritance, fall head over heels in love with it and determine to marry him.

Once married, Sybil soon showed herself to be a discriminating woman. Nothing but the best was good enough for her Harry. His reputation required that his wife be both elegantly dressed and properly decorated. Folk could spot a fake, she explained. So Harry had to supplement his private income.

He had been looking for a job for the best part of an hour when, during a break after his first interview, he all but came to blows with a tall young man in a City sandwich bar over a roast beef with horseradish on rye for which both claimed to be first in the queue. Guy Magnus got the sandwich, of course; but with such aplomb that Harry felt obliged to offer him a drink after the close of business. They shared a further drink the following evening, and quickly found that in their attitude to what they sought in life and in their disdain for anyone who stood in their way, they had much in common.

The adopted child of respectable residents of the commuter belt, Guy Magnus had watched his father work steadily towards his pension as a servant of Her Majesty's Inland Revenue while his mother made a home devoted to their comfort. When still a fifteen-year-old schoolboy he had bought the *Financial Times* daily, followed the share movements on the back page, done a few dummy runs on paper, come up a winner every time, borrowed £100 from his father, found himself a stockbroker and within weeks turned a profit of £1,000. His father had done what any tax collector who intends to retire a tax collector would do. When Guy proudly presented him with the evidence of his success, he frowned, took the papers from him and included the gains in the family income tax return.

Already less than impressed by his father's lack of ambition, Guy now felt cheated by his lack of imagination. He knew his own career would be devoted to making money on the stock exchange. The university scholarship planned for him wasn't going to teach him how to avoid paying tax on what he earned. As soon as he passed his sixteenth birthday he brought grief to his doting mother by telling her he was leaving school and informing his stockbroker that he intended to come to work in the City forthwith. Did he have a job for him, or must he take his talents elsewhere? So Guy joined the ranks of the City's tea boys, until the sickness of a colleague – for which unusually he was not the cause but merely the opportunistic beneficiary – gave him the chance to impress his partner with the speed of his learning.

With a year's experience behind him, it did not take Guy long to see in Harry Griffin a man who could use his help.

'Can't give you any details, Harry, it's top, top secret, but if you punt your beer money on Whistler Blauer you won't go far wrong,' he was soon confiding. For if you bought a line of shares in the morning but failed to tell the world you'd done it, how could you be sure they'd go up before you sold them tomorrow? ... though Guy Magnus rarely had the patience to wait until tomorrow before he sold.

'I bought five hundred,' Harry told Guy when they met the following day; 'but the story must have been kept pretty tight 'cos they were marked down overnight. Should I buy some more, now they're cheaper?'

Guy had already taken his profit and had no more to gain. 'I'd sell,' he advised. 'Then short 'em,' he added, taking pity on his new friend. Harry raised his brows. It was plain he had much to learn. 'Sell more of them,' Guy elaborated.

'But if I've already sold them, I won't have any more to sell.'

'You don't need to have the shares to short them,' Guy explained. 'You just put in a selling order. Then you buy them back at a lower price before the end of the trading account. That way you don't need to deliver the stock certificate to your broker. He just pays you the difference.'

Harry did as he was told and recouped his losses. More than that, he had learnt his lesson about Guy.

Shortly afterwards, Guy accepted a job from Harold Antony, a partner in stockbrokers Tanquery Taylor Tealeafe, at £1,000 a year. Almost immediately a director of Highell Cappery, a merchant bank of some prestige, told him he was worth £1,500. Where a young man with less imagination would have done no more than grab the second job and forget his manners, Guy wept his apologies to Antony and said he could recommend someone to take his place, a brilliant young share dealer who would fit the bill at least as well as he. After all, he told himself, if it took two to do a deal, it would do no harm to know the fellow at the other end of the phone. Then he told Harry to take the job and challenged him to last more than ten minutes in it.

Though not overly keen to exert himself, especially for as long as ten minutes at a time, Harry nevertheless convinced himself that stockbroking sounded fun.

A small firm of doubtful repute, Tanquery Taylor Tealeafe had two senior partners: Harold Antony and Archie Laws. At half past nine on Harry's first day in his new job, Antony came to his desk and expounded the firm's policy. In order to avoid the possibility of serious losses, he said, their investment clients' funds must be spread across a variety of assets, of which sixty per cent should be equities, thirty per cent should be fixed interest bonds and ten per cent should be cash.

'Only an arsehole would have a policy as crass as that,' responded Harry bluntly. He had profited from his acquaintance with Guy, he had lasted longer than ten minutes in the job, and he felt entitled to pass on the benefit of his experience to his new boss. 'You buy what's going up and you sell what's going down,' he elaborated. 'That's an investment policy.'

Harold Antony's habitually pasty face turned purple and his body trembled. 'When you start a new job, young man,' he retorted, his overfed jowls working overtime, 'you don't start off by telling the partners how to go about their business, or the door you came in by is liable to be the door you go out by.'

Harry was unmoved. 'Crap is still crap, whether it's the first day or the last, and whether it comes from the backside of a partner or the backside of a donkey,' he replied.

Antony was on the verge of making their differences irreconcilable when he noticed a dealing slip on Harry's desk. The name of the buyer was Highell Cappery and the buying order Guy Magnus had placed was substantial. In the interests of the firm he held his peace.

The talents of an opportunist like Harry did not remain hidden for long. Tanquery Taylor Tealeafe found itself acting in a takeover battle on the side of the defending company. Harry was assigned to look after his firm's client's interests. He judged that the best way to do so would be to invite the opposition for a drink.

'Your offer's miles below the real valuation of the company,' he told an executive of the merchant bank acting for the bidder. 'Its balance sheet is way out of date. You'll have to come up with a better offer.'

'We couldn't go any higher without justification,' responded the executive. 'I don't suppose you'd let me glance over your shoulder while you're running through their latest property valuation? That way I could see if we could justify a few more pence per share.'

Harry considered the proposal carefully. Such a breach of client confidentiality was unethical. It contravened stock exchange regulations. It was probably against the law. Nevertheless ...

'I'm not a betting man,' he concluded his internal debate aloud, 'but I'm pretty sure such information must have a value. One would have thought that whoever provided it would merit a pretty decent reward.'

The merchant banker admitted that this was probably so and promised to consult his client over the appropriate value. To Harry's misfortune, the firm's telephonist misdirected the call to give him the predator's assessment of how much his information was worth to Archie Laws. Harry was invited to an interview in his boss's office, where he was confronted by the charge.

'But you know as well as I do our clients don't stand a chance,' he protested. 'Their earnings record is lousy. The only question is the price they go down at. I thought it'd be in everyone's interests to give the other side enough comfort to put a few more pence on the table. The shareholders will be happy; you'll get your fees; so where's the problem if I happen to make a few bob on the side for using my brains?'

Archie Laws said he was sorry, but Harry had to go. Harry said he was sorry too; he hadn't appreciated how scrupulous the firm was. Laws considered the merits of this response and the amount of business Harry was bringing in and concluded that the proper sentence for a man of his ability was a reprimand. Indeed, so useful did Harry become to Tanquery Taylor Tealeafe that after a short while he was invited to become a partner.

Meanwhile Guy Magnus had been asking himself what was the point of earning £1,500 a year, or even £2,000 a year, at Highell Cappery when merchant banking – or at any rate this merchant bank – was offering him less scope for share-dealing on his own account than he desired. So he moved on to Consolidated Finance, a growing investment bank. There he impressed his boss Lewis White so much that in next to no time he was managing one of the bank's largest investment funds.

Through one of its many takeovers Consolidated Finance had acquired a controlling interest in Commercial Holdings Investment Trust. CHIT owned a portfolio of some of the least exciting shares traded on the London Stock Exchange – so unexciting, in fact, that however hard White had tried he had been unable to find buyers for them without depressing the market. CHIT had no place in White's strategic plans. He told Guy to find a buyer for it, fast.

Guy could think of no one more suitable than his good friend Harry Griffin. 'A few tasty titbits in it, something to cut your teeth on,' he was soon telling him. 'You can have control of the whole shooting-match for half a million. Your partners should buy it. It's a golden opportunity. I'd do the deal myself if Lewis wasn't so sanctimonious about conflicts of interest.'

'What on earth would we want with an investment trust?' asked Harry, associating himself with his partners.

'It's authorised, so your dealing profits will be tax-exempt. You haven't started paying tax, have you, Harry?'

'Of course not,' replied Harry, his pride wounded.

'It has other uses as well. Suppose you have some shares you're fed up with and you can't push your clients into buying them. You stuff them into the trust. That way you share your losses with the other shareholders. Not to mention any expense claims your firm won't stump up for, you know the sort of thing: flowers for the girlfriend, lawyer's fees for the divorce – don't forget to give my love to Sybil, will you, Harry?'

Harry mentioned the proposition to his senior partners. In those days any investment vehicle that saved tax was regarded as good news, so they each took up some shares. Harold Antony happened to know an earl who for a modest honorarium would be happy to lend the board the credentials of his title and act as its chairman in the event of a conflict between the shareholders. Harry was surprised at how little effort it took to persuade his bankers to lend him the money to join them.

The commercial relationship between Harry and Guy was no one-way affair. As Harry's career as a stockbroker blossomed, he had the inspired notion that he should offer Guy the opportunity to follow his rising star.

'My job's to find businesses run by idiots who haven't a clue how to run them,' he replied when Guy asked him how he was doing. 'No client's as profitable as a business that's going down the pan. You see, no chairman whose company's losing money will ever admit it's his own fault. I help him buy another company so he can use its profits to hide his losses. When he makes a cock-up of that one too and his shareholders lose patience, I persuade some other fool to bid for him. That way I earn two fees. You know what, Guy: we should do more business together. I'll tell you what's going on, and you tell me how much you're going to spend on my advice.' These were, after all, the sixties, when dealing without the benefit of inside information was widely considered a dumb way to trade on the stock market.

Even before the coup that put his name indelibly on the City map, no one who crossed Guy's path had any doubt that he was going to be a star. Until then, however, his light had ostensibly shone for the benefit of others. That is to say, he made money for his employers as well as for himself.

Making money for his employers was not an activity of which Guy was particularly proud; but it was a necessary means to an end. For he was making so much money for the investment funds Lewis White gave him to manage that it took but a small step to tell himself that if he backed his professional judgment with his own money, he could profit himself as well as Consolidated Finance. While it was rash to deal on his own account unless he was confident of market support, what better assurance of such backing was there than to know that the funds he was managing took the same view as he did? That was the beauty of being a fund manager in the upbeat spring of 1969.

Guy overcame the handicap of his limited resources with the aid of the stock exchange settlement system he had described to Harry, whereby transactions were settled at the end of each fortnightly trading account. Just as he was able to buy back shares he had sold short, so was he able to sell the shares he had bought during an account before he had to settle with his stockbroker. When Guy won, the broker simply paid out the difference in price after deducting his commission. When Guy lost, which was rare, the fact that his broker was Harry Griffin was of considerable assistance, for Harry soon learnt to roll over Guy's account until the following settlement day – or indeed until it was once again in surplus.

Moreover, whenever Guy spotted a dealing opportunity but was not wholly confident about the outcome, he would tell Harry that the decision on which of his funds was to be the buyer would be deferred. Sometimes it might not be taken until after the shares had been sold, with the result that those transactions which turned out most profitable would be booked in their entirety to a buyer of whose name only he and Harry – but not, he hoped, Lewis White – were aware.

This is not to say that Consolidated Finance never won, for it generally came along in support of the unnamed buyer. Nevertheless, when Lewis White, a seasoned operator and a shrewd judge of character, objected that while Guy was entitled to buy and sell shares on his own account, he must decide at the time of dealing into whose portfolio the shares he had bought were going, Guy told himself that if he made profits for one employer he could make them for another. He asked himself, moreover, whether Lewis White had not put too low a value on his services. The calculation of his worth was simple. He usually invested £1,000 of his funds' money behind every £100 he punted on his own behalf. That year he had made £10,000 in dealing profits for himself. *Ergo*, he must have made £100,000 for Consolidated Finance. This being the case, his current remuneration was hardly an adequate reward for his efforts. When Lewis White failed to agree, he took these observations to his next job interview.

'In that case you shouldn't be working for somebody else,' he was told. 'You should be running your own business. If you do, I'll put some of our money behind you,' the highly-impressed interviewer added.

Guy did not take long to think about the idea. Something of the kind had been gestating inside him for some time. For prestigious as Consolidated Finance was in the investment world, and responsible as his position was, he did not own the company. He had, moreover, recently been asking himself whether to be working for others at the age of twenty-four was not in itself an admission of failure? A star that merely sat in its constellation and shone was no more than a dot on a celestial map. If he wanted to be treated seriously, to attract the interest of the astronomer, he had to shoot: to become a comet, a meteor. Free to fly, to burn, to generate energy, to leave his trail across the galaxies of the universe. For universe, read the City of London.

All around him in the City Guy saw the sons of wealthy families, educated at public schools and given three years to drink and play at Oxford or Cambridge before starting their careers on the bottom rungs of ladders owned by their fathers. They lived in a closed, charmed circle. Conned early on by one of the fathers into acquiring the finest shares in his portfolio, only to discover that everyone else knew they were about to become worthless, he had no intention of being similarly hotted by the sons. It was not long before the boot was on the other foot and Guy Magnus was climbing up a ladder of his own making.

Not surprisingly, Guy felt entitled to the rewards he achieved by his own efforts. For who, he asked himself, was more worthy of them: the sons of the ladder-owners or he? And who would make better use of them? He would strike out on his own, put himself to the test, and show the sons of ladder-owners his worth. He had learned all there was to learn from Lewis White. The time was ripe: the Labour government was on its last legs; the dragon of extortionate taxation would be slain and enterprise would again be fully rewarded. All he needed was a corporate vehicle through which to realise his ambitions. Without – for he had as yet accumulated no capital – having to pay more than he could afford to acquire it.

His search did not take long. Harry Griffin told him about Mallard, the smallest company quoted on the London Stock Exchange. Tanquerys had been asked to advise the board on raising new capital. Harry had proposed they make a rights issue, giving shareholders the right to invest more capital in return for more shares. But the directors' families, who owned more than half of the shares, had no desire to put any more money into the company. What did Guy think?

When Guy found out how little profit Mallard made and how small a dividend it paid to its shareholders, he didn't bat an eyelid. When he found out how much it would cost to underwrite a rights issue, he batted both. But he knew that the rapidly growing band of secondary banks was in hot competition for any proposition that offered a slice of the action, and would willingly lend him the money to finance a personal stake in his prey. So he suggested to Harry that he tell the Mallard board Tanquerys would be happy to underwrite their rights issue. If this resulted in the directors and their families no longer owning a majority of the shares, the brokers would ensure that the board retained control of the company by placing any newly issued shares the existing shareholders did not subscribe for into the safe hands of their clients. And what hands, Guy asked Harry, could possibly be safer than theirs?

When Harry Griffin had to tell the Mallard board the rights issue had been undersubscribed, but the sub-underwriters had saved the day and he, Harry, and his most trusted friends had added their own modest support out of confidence in the future management of the company, they were more than happy.

Until Guy Magnus went to see their chairman and told him, as casually as if he were asking him for a gin and tonic, that as he and his partners now had more shares than the directors, he would like a seat on the board and the management surrendered into his hands.

And Harry confirmed that was what he'd meant by confidence in the future management of the company.

Guy Magnus's star was ready to shoot.

3

Their bet – or was it the bill? – can be pinpointed to a glorious Indian Summer's day three months after Mallard became a done deal. At a quarter past one, under a sky so blue it seemed to deny the turning leaves would ever fall, a slim, fashionably dressed young man six feet one inches in height strode confidently into the entrance lobby of the Connaught Hotel and turned right along the oak-panelled corridor to the Grill. This haven of fine dining was one of the few venues, in London at least, Guy Magnus considered worthy of his new-found flair for hospitality; for the invitation was his, his reward both to Harry Griffin for having introduced the Mallard deal and to himself for having done it. An overweight Harry in an ill-fitting suit bustled after his host at a respectful distance.

Guy was elated by his coup. Here he was, at twenty-four years of age, enjoying the fruits due to a controlling shareholder of a public company. The Mallard family had not taken long to agree terms for their departure from the boardroom. This had been necessary because he had not bought the company for fun, but to make money; and the family directors had shown every prospect of getting in his way. For you made money nowadays by buying a company as a shell, stripping it of its assets and ramping its shares so you could use them to buy another run-down shell company that owned assets waiting to be liberated; and the Mallard family understood nothing of that.

But Guy was not content merely to make money. He had a deeper purpose: he knew his worth and he wanted it recognised. So as soon as his first deal was done he set out on a programme of self-education. Determined to broaden his horizons, it was not long before he made connections in the circles of the rich and cultured. He impressed all he met with his earnestness, a perception beyond his years, and a respect due to those who had travelled the road before – even if their fathers had owned the means of transport. Herein lay a paradox, for though Guy sneered at inherited wealth, he found no problem in cultivating the friendship of those who possessed it, and with his dry, caustic wit he never paid his new friends back with less than stimulating company. This was no hypocrisy, for he had an intuitive aesthetic sense and made a clear distinction between those who simply spent money and those who used it with discrimination and good taste. Alert and receptive, he absorbed his lessons rapidly. It was not long before he developed appetites of his own: for Schubert and Mahler, for haute cuisine and Dom Pérignon champagne.

And for works of art. The rising young artists whose names were being whispered in the circles he was beginning to move in would soon become the passwords of the cognoscenti in the galleries of Cork Street, and thereafter be noised abroad at cocktail parties like those of the more fashionable Mayfair couturiers. The gallery-owners would mouth adjectives of aesthetic provenance that their well-heeled clients did not understand, along with nouns of scarcity and value that they did. Guy became friendly with an art lover of impeccable taste. Through him he gained an entree to a select circle of owners whose expertise was not limited to representing the incomprehensible as art. With their help he surveyed the scene and narrowed his field of interest to four contemporary artists: Francis Bacon, Lucien Freud, and the rising stars David Hockney and R B Kitaj.

None of the four came cheap. That was partly why, on the pay-out of each profitable deal, Guy bought their work. But there was a difference between him and his rivals in pursuit of art ownership: in his case the instinctive good taste was there first. It was part of his charm that he made no secret of his joy over what delighted his senses. He would bubble with enthusiasm as he paid the asking price or outbid the room at auction. Paying top dollar gave him the comfort that he had purchased an article of high quality. Paying more than everyone else reinforced his sense of his own worth. A worth that deserved the reward of lunch at the Connaught Grill. He glanced quickly round the room to see if there was anyone he should acknowledge – or, more to the point, anyone who should acknowledge him. Disappointed, he consoled himself with the thought that they could be lunching later.

Harry was as excited as Guy about their rendezvous, but from different motives. He was as anxious as Guy for Mallard's success: his own participation in the underwriting had given him the largest share stake he had ever owned. To buy it, he had had to borrow from his bank far more than he could afford to lose. But such considerations did not overly exercise his mind, for Harry was a gambler and therefore an optimist. He was also more interested in the next deal than the one he had just put to bed. So he had accepted Guy's invitation to lunch partly on its merits – for good food, drink and company were never less than agreeable – but also as an opportunity to launch his next lucrative deal.

Harry studied the menu. He dithered between the salade de melon et pampelmousse nature and the poire d'avocat au jus de citron before selecting a Caesar's salad. He regretted his decision the moment Guy ordered the paté de fois gras truffé, but accepted a glass of the sauternes his host ordered to accompany his choice. He held his glass to the light, casting one eye on the refraction of the golden liquid through its crystal prisms while the other squinted at the date on the bottle's label.

'The fifty-nine, if my palate deceives me not,' he pronounced his unerring judgment.

'Nectar of the gods,' murmured Guy. 'Too fine for mortals. Less full-bodied and velvety than the forty-seven, but more honeyed and fragrant,' he recalled his manual. 'Yquem with the goose, Dom Pérignon with the crêpes. Always.'

Harry judged that any attempt to gain Guy's attention while he assessed the texture and flavour of his squab pigeon with wild mushrooms and its affinity to the 1961 Hermitage – for the claret of that wondrous vintage, Guy judged, was still too young – would be doomed to failure. While the rules of business were regarded by both as designed for the obedience of fools and the guidance of full-sized idiots, Guy's attitude to the rules of polite society had of late become rather more observant. Was this a business or a social lunch? Harry asked himself. In either case, the golden rule that the subject for discussion be not introduced until the host's spoon was well and truly poised over the pudding might well be sacrosanct. Safer to assume that small talk, or at least no more than medium talk, was the order of the day.

'What d'you make of the flurry of activity in Sydney? Think there's anything in it?' Provided no name was mentioned, Harry told himself, general business talk was not real business talk.

'Poseidon?' It was hard to tell from his dismissive tone whether Guy regarded the topic as one of scant interest or unpardonable ill manners. 'They won't find any.'

'Any what?'

'Nickel, of course. Not in viable quantities.'

'So you don't think they're a buy?'

'Of course they're a buy,' Guy sighed. 'I've sold twice already.'

Harry felt out of his depth. Unless, it occurred to him, this was Guy's way of making the point that as the company's shares had tripled in the past week, he'd missed the boat. 'Bit late, eh?' he said ruefully. 'Should've had 'em at six bob.'

'It's never too late,' Guy told him.

'At 20 shillings?'

'They'll triple again this week.'

Harry guessed that Guy's irony was turning to kidology. He must still have some to sell. 'Maybe I'll invest in a few,' he said without enthusiasm.

'You don't invest in shares,' Guy admonished him as if he had committed a sacrilege. 'How many times do I have to tell you? Shares are for buying and selling.'

Harry wondered whether Guy's candour was a signal that the time was ripe to fine-tune the discussion. He was, however, the guest. If they were to cross no man's land between the general and the specific, his host must play the intrepid subaltern and lead the charge. But Guy was forever peeping through his periscope without sticking his head out over the parapet.

Harry held his fire until the maître d'hôtel had completed his pièce de resistance with the pan, the match and the cognac, but once the sommelier had removed the Dom Pérignon from the ice bucket and popped the cork he could control himself no more. He leaned conspiratorially towards Guy, fingertips poised on the tip of his nose. Guy stared entranced as the face of his friend's tie slid gracefully across his plate, dividing the Red Sea of sauce. Rather than embarrass his guest, he decided to remain silent on the grounds that this would make for superior entertainment.

'I trust all goes well at Mallard.'

'It's about motivation, Harry,' Guy expounded his business philosophy. 'Money. My job is to make sure everyone has as much of it as he needs. The example has to be set from the top,' he said with disarming frankness. Guy had the ability to put essential truths into the proverbial nutshell. It had been the secret of his success from the day he acquired his stake in Mallard. Where others might have wasted precious time congratulating themselves on having gained control of a quoted company with a million pounds worth of assets for less than a hundred thousand of borrowed money, he had focussed on the future. He hadn't bought his stake in the company to prove he was an industrial manager. That had been Neville Macrae's job. When the family directors had resigned, the company's finance director had remained. That had proved a master-stroke. Where others might have sent the dour Scotsman packing out of a false sense of pride, Guy had instantly recognised in him a man who knew how to manage – his way.

Macrae had arrived at Mallard the previous year. By the time of Guy's coup he had had his fill of hearing how 'We've-always-done-it-this-way-and-it's-always-worked-so-far'. His Presbyterian mind wanted only to learn whether his new master was bringing anything new to the party. When he discovered that Magnus had no interest whatsoever in what Mallard made, but every interest in how its shares could be used to buy other businesses and liberate their assets, Macrae stayed for the ride. Set free, he was like a man possessed. Products were dropped, inventories liquidated, workers released onto the dole queue, vacated factory space turned into offices and leased. This gave Guy time to focus on his own area of expertise: share-dealing. And, in his spare time, rewarding himself.

'I expect you have plans,' Harry pursued his inquiries.

'I have plans,' Guy confirmed. But he was damned if he was going to tell them to Harry and have them returned to him down the market grapevine before he was ready to implement them.

'Don't forget I too have an interest in Mallard,' Harry reminded Guy of his fifteen per cent shareholding. 'I have a right to be consulted.'

Guy stayed silent. If he were to take advantage of opportunities to expand his new vehicle, he had to be in a position to act fast. Stakes in other sitting ducks were there for the buyer with cash in hand. Bids would be made, shares bought, control taken and assets sold. A boardroom was no place to debate such niceties. There'd be no point in debate anyway, once he'd made up his mind.

'There's been some gossip as to whether this year's earnings will cover the dividend,' Harry tried again.

'What dividend?' asked Guy, deadpan.

Harry ignored the question, less out of discourtesy than from ignorance of the answer. 'Archie Law's been following your latest deals. He's hellish impressed,' he revealed. 'It can't just be luck,' he rushed on as Guy inclined a modest head. 'You obviously know exactly what you're doing. It occurs to … ah, some of us, that if you had any particularly interesting project in mind, we'd be happy to consider increasing the level of our support.' He raised his glass of champagne as if to toast their next deal.

Guy twirled his fork. 'I was wondering when you'd come to the point, Harry. The tension was unbearable. You want a private viewing of my shopping list, don't you?' He raised an emphatic eyebrow to indicate that the question was not rhetorical but required a full and frank response, if not a grovelling confession.

The champagne bubbles hit the spot. As the tears welled in Harry's eyeducts, a mouthful of half-chewed crêpes regained the spoon from which it had recently departed. The obverse of his tie dragged back through the Red Sea of sauce, as if to defer the Lord's judgment on the Egyptians. 'Oh Guy, would I?' he splurted.

'You wouldn't be very smart if you didn't. I can't imagine why you act as if it's a state secret. I couldn't be more delighted if Tanquerys wanted to spend a few grand on the back of mine. It'd prove how sound your judgment is.'

'Well, ah, naturally I didn't want to put you under an obligation by telling you of our support, bearing in mind our exposure,' Harry improvised.

'No problem, Harry. I can arrange to settle my account any time you don't feel comfortable about it.'

Harry's expression showed his anxiety only too plainly. The meal had begun to resemble a five-day Test match which, after heading inexorably towards a draw for four and a half days, was transforming itself without warning into a humiliating rout.

'Though if you prefer to change the nature of your exposure and offer your support on a more structured basis, with an equity element,' Guy hinted amiably. He'd had enough of teasing Harry. It was time to do business with him.

'Would you … ah, who's in with you at present?' Harry replied cautiously.

'Just you and me, Harry. And our trusting supporters. Entry fee's fifty grand, by the way. Shall we drink to friendship?'

Harry nodded his assent. The way he felt he would have drunk to anything.

'The point is, Harry,' Guy went on as soon as the toast was completed, 'there have to be rules. As in, you break my rules, I break your arms.'

'What rules?'

'Rule Number One is matched deals. When it's my deal, Harry, you don't sell until I've found you a buyer. Don't worry: I won't let you down. But a seller can't take his profit until he's found a buyer, and if I don't know you're looking for one, there may not be one, may there?' he guided Harry through the argument step by step.

'I think I see what you mean,' replied Harry truthfully. Comforted that he was to be one of the select, he leant back. His tie followed obediently, adding a map of the Nile Delta to the fly of his trousers. 'When do we start?' he enquired.

'I thought you'd already done so. In future I suggest you cover your tracks more carefully. Shuffle your jobbers around, vary the amounts, make it look as if there's general demand. Incidentally,' Guy asked as if the matter he was about to raise was a topic of only marginal curiosity, 'did you know Traill Blazer is a sell?'

This was news to Harry. 'Where d'you hear that?' he asked. As far as he was aware, Traill Blazer was still on every stockbroker's shopping list.

'I decided this morning.'

'It's not a company we actually … er, have much of a holding in at present,' Harry pointed out with undisguised shame.

'Of course you don't. Let's mount a bear raid, you and me.'

Harry shook his head in disbelief. Nobody raided Traill Blazer. If you sold its shares short and they fell, you'd make a killing, as it would cost you less to buy them back before you had to deliver the stock certificate to your broker. But Jon Traill's fans were too loyal to permit disrespect to the master of the London Stock Exchange. They'd rally round and bid up Traill Blazer shares so his antagonist would put himself into a man-eating grizzly of a bear squeeze.

'I thought we should stick our fingers in and see how much honey we could suck,' Guy persisted. 'You could put ten grand yourself and fifty grand for the firm. While you're at it, you may like to point out to anyone you speak to, especially the office boy, as he probably has better contacts in the market than the rest of your people together, that one of Jon Traill's subsidiaries is on its last legs over a shaky mining venture in Zaire.'

'Where d'you hear that?' asked Harry. He prided himself on reading all the newspapers.

Guy ignored the question. 'I've put it about that its forestry arm bribed the wrong minister in Brasilia with enough dollars to repay the country's national debt but the rotten skunk flatly refused to pay his bribe back.'

'Who's going to believe us if we tell different stories?' objected Harry.

'Who'll believe us if we tell the same one? You know how jobbers love rumours. They may not believe them, but they mark the shares down just the same. One sniff of bad news and they can't *bear* to miss out on the action – excuse the dreadful pun. Come on, Harry, let's have some fun at Jon's expense.'

Harry knew better than to ignore what Guy told him. While his domestic spending and his income tax remained sky-high – and his wife and the Chancellor of the Exchequer had both set their hearts on them doing so indefinitely – there was a limit to how much money he could set aside to buy shares. Roy Jenkins was about to prime the pump ahead of a general election – but by then, predicted Guy, voters would be fed up with Harold Wilson's pipe. Conservative government, refreshed and raring to go, was around the corner. Good times were a-coming. By the time they arrived he must put together some capital if his boat was to run free before the balmy breezes of renascent capitalism.

But while the long-term omens were propitious, opportunities to buy shares profitably on a falling market were strictly limited. Fortunately no capital was needed to sell shares short. When Guy spread his rumours about a company, fund managers who held its stock would go into a funk and off-load even if they suspected the stories were false, scared to hang on lest the shares plummeted and their bosses accused them of being out of touch. Guy would then buy in the shares he had sold at a lower price, and pocket the difference.

But Traill Blazer? Harry hardly dared put himself the question. You had to go to Pamplona in August to find a bull in such unswerving form.

'It's high time you involved yourself in some grown-up action instead of playing with toys,' Guy warmed to his theme. 'Dealing in shares for others to make a profit – honestly, Harry! Search and destroy, that's what it's all about. What's more, it's about time you did something with CHIT. I didn't bring you the deal so you could keep your right hand busy'.

When the maître asked for their post-dessert orders, Harry settled for a coffee. Guy ordered an Armagnac from a dust-encrusted bottle. While he savoured it, he refused to permit talk of business. Instead he turned the conversation to the art of gracious living. Frank Stella and Brancusi passed his scrutiny; the Royal Academy Summer Exhibition was deemed an unmitigated flop. As he put down his glass for the last time, he glanced at the new Rolex Oyster which protruded from his butterfly cuffs and rose from his seat. 'Sorry, Harry, next appointment presses. Lunch was beta plus. Be a good chap and settle up for us, would you? I do so hate checking the bill in front of the waiters. Makes me feel I'm in a Turkish bazaar. I'll send you a cheque for my share. Pigeon post.'

'When are you ever going to pay for a meal, Guy?' asked Harry, half-serious.

'You show a million clear before me and I'll take you to lunch at Maxim's,' Guy replied, half-flippant, taking a final unrequited look around the Grill. 'I beat you and it's your treat.'

'Clear? I take it we're talking tangible, marketable and unencumbered,' Harry established the ground rules, listing qualities he reckoned were bound to be absent from any investment Guy was liable to acquire. The million must be in cash; or if in shares, it would have to be a stock whose price didn't blow around like an autumn gale. Nor could it be used as security for a loan, for when Guy took a profit he always put the proceeds straight back on the table as seed-corn for the next deal – or at any rate as collateral for the seed-corn.

'Naturally,' Guy confirmed, as if the affair was starting to bore him.

'Done!' Harry clasped Guy's hand before it could be stuffed into his jacket pocket. It was, he reckoned, a bet to nothing. 'First to show a million clear's the winner. See you at Maxim's, Guy. And don't forget to bring your wallet.'

4

The new decade brought fresh triumphs to Guy Magnus. How many budding tycoons can open *The Times* and see their own photograph gracing the Business Diary on the day they announce a takeover bid, let alone that such an occurrence should coincide with the day the *Financial Times* Ordinary Share Index fell to a year's low of 316? There had been a swing to Labour in the local elections, so Harold Wilson decided that June 18th was the best date to give the nation the opportunity to reward him with five more years in office. The opinion polls predicted a Labour victory, the leader of the opposition privately admitted that the battle was lost, and so far the stock market had endorsed their view.

'Fat chance!' Guy proclaimed confidently. 'I bet Harold forgot to check his *Charles Buchan's Diary.*'

Sure enough the England football team, whose victory in the 1966 World Cup was reckoned to have given Labour that election victory, decided that this time charity would begin at home and lost on penalties to West Germany on the Sunday before polling day.

'The country may forgive Sir Alf Ramsey some day, but not Harold Wilson by Thursday,' crowed Guy that Monday morning as he piled into the stock market. As usual he got it right, and the pollsters and a shell-shocked Edward Heath got it wrong – though Guy judged that if the opposition leader had kept his weather eye on the recovering stock market instead of on the morning clouds he might not so easily have been caught on the hop.

Before the general election Mallard's shares had risen so sharply that when they reached 54 shillings Guy announced a one-for-one scrip issue. He had given himself two years to make a success of his company; not that he ever contemplated failure. But two years was the longest he expected the bull market to last. After that analysts would be starting to think about the next general election – and President Nixon's re-election. If the situation in Vietnam worsened, Wall Street would have a touch or more of the jitters and the London Stock Exchange would soon catch the draught.

Guy was the first to acknowledge that he could not have achieved such rapid success without the help of Mallard's managing director. On one occasion his debt to Neville Macrae had been infinite. They had been walking along Oxford Street so deep in conversation that Guy failed to notice where the pavement ended and Orchard Street began. At that moment a double-decker bus had swept round the corner. Macrae had barely managed to pull him out of its deadly path.

'You've saved my life,' Guy told him. 'You'll live to regret it.'

Macrae was the tool Guy used to deal with Mallard – and the less Guy knew about the methods the Scot used to extract cash from that business and those it acquired, the happier he was. Macrae knew how to strip a business to the bare essentials, which as far as Guy cared was the point at which there was no business left. Cronic Footwear, which manufactured and sold shoes for the halt and lame, was a case in point. It could justly have been said that its production and sales were in balance – until Mallard bought the company. Macrae soon saw that the strategy which had dictated that Mallard make a rapid entry into the footwear industry demanded an even quicker exit from it. The most valuable shops – those that sold the most shoes – must be closed and sold. As a result, production was too high. The most valuable factory – the one which ran with the greatest efficiency – must therefore also be closed and sold. Production was now too low, so the fleet of vans that delivered Cronic's shoes to its shops was no longer needed. Faced with diminishing supplies, the less valuable shops sold fewer shoes than before, so they too would have been closed and sold had Macrae been able to find a buyer. Instead, he cut costs by laying off shop staff until only the under-manager was left – a manager being too expensive – and by turning off the lights in the shop windows.

Early in 1970 Macrae had returned from Scotland to report that Highland Timber was a dog, and a flea-bitten mongrel at that, and could never be turned into a cow. But in the small print of its accounts Guy noted that Highland Timber held shares in Woodland Industries and General Forestry Investments. Further research had revealed that though otherwise of no great consequence, Woodland owned shares in General Forestry. General Forestry was a considerable prize. With Harry's help, Guy had gained control over Highland Timber at modest cost. Guy had then announced that the company would no longer cut down trees but would combine with Woodland Industries to gain control of General Forestry Investments, whereupon the latter's commercial operations would be sold or wound down, its financial interests would morph into an investment holding company under the more appropriate name of Ludgate Investments, and its headquarters would relocate to the financial heart of the nation where none of the present directors would be required to report for duty.

Macrae became so busy shutting businesses down that he had no time to take care of integrating those Guy bought. This was where Larry Callaghan came in. Guy had come across Callaghan when he was an auditor to Consolidated Finance. Guy had asked him for help with his tax return and been so impressed with his expertise in tax reclaims that he persuaded him to do likewise for Mallard. A provincial accountant, Callaghan was slightly taller than Guy but not quite as slim, with a small pot belly that had developed with his mature years. A crop of white hair flew free as candy floss above his calm and friendly face. Where Macrae turned assets into cash, Larry Callaghan converted cash profits into paper losses, gains into reserves, gold into base metal, away wins into six-nil home defeats. Guy's claim that he could turn a sold pair of shoes back into leather and last was never seriously challenged.

Where Mallard bought and sold companies, Ludgate Investments bought and sold share stakes. Guy knew how to lay his hands on other companies' shares, but needed his newly acquired tax expert to set up their new home so as to stretch the credulity of the tax inspector without engaging the energies of the tax collector. Before long Callaghan was appointed to both companies' boards, and Guy was treating him as a confidant and father-figure.

In the post-election stock market hangover, Mallard's split shares soon fell from 27 to 14 shillings. But despite the market's apparent lack of confidence Guy remained optimistic. His conviction was not based on the headlines of *The Times*. 'Industry Expects New Deal?' he scoffed to Callaghan one morning. 'This is what it's really about!' he pointed to a report on how Robert Maxwell, who had lost his parliamentary seat in the general election, planned to buy back a company he had not long ago sold for a small fortune, but which he now claimed was worth next to nothing – presumably due to his brief absence from the helm. While the new government was busy settling docks disputes and drafting White Papers on industrial action, Guy reckoned it was hardly going to find time to interfere in the workings of the free market.

On February 15th 1971, the day the pound was decimalised, Mallard's shares rose rapidly past 100 of the new pence and never looked back. By now

Guy Magnus had earned a reputation as one of the City's brightest whizz-kids, and Mallard as one of its most exciting growth stocks. Its shares rose steadily as each takeover prey was consumed, chewed into little pieces and spewed out of its digestive system. By the first day of 1972 they were hovering around £2.50, and then they rose again.

For equities were on the move. Not even the state salvage of a sinking Rolls-Royce could halt their upward march. Nor, when the purchase of gold coins was legally permitted, did the alternative appeal of Krugerrands. As winter turned to spring, turnover on the London Stock Exchange rose to record levels and the *FT* Share Index scaled successive peaks as if they were but rolling uplands.

These were indeed heady, upbeat days. A pharmaceutical company led the way with an eye-catching advertisement on page nine of *The Times*. The model whose shapely body took up most of its space must have been caught unawares as she brushed her long blonde tresses, for it was apparent that no one had warned her to cover her naked torso when the camera shutter clicked. The next day's letters included one from a reader who hoped the delightful picture would have the same effect on the paper's circulation as it had had on his own. In Australia an ambitious young newspaper proprietor saw the ad and reckoned it was six pages too far from the front.

No sooner had the furore died down than a West End solicitor produced an envelope inscribed with a Will in which another model – recently widowed but apparently not by *The Times*'s letter-writer – had been bequeathed one shilling and four nude photographs of herself, while he inherited the residue of the Estate. When the police went in search of him they found he had relocated to Brazil. If the Swinging Sixties were not to be followed by the Sordid Seventies, an example must be set; and so it was. Shortly after, an Old Bailey judge who was not in tune with the changing times instructed a jury to find three magazine editors of Antipodean accent and unkempt coiffure guilty of obscenity, and sent them off to jail until a more socially aware Court of Appeal set them free.

Guy shared in the optimism that warmed the City air. As one finance house after another – for they were not yet described as "secondary" or "fringe" banks – reported profits up a quarter, a third, or even a half, he would analyse its accounts and take similar action. It would not do for Mallard shares to rise more slowly than those in Traill Blazer, Consolidated Finance or Universal Credit. How he set about achieving this would depend on the skill and ingenuity he knew he possessed. But of one thing he was sure: he must use whatever lawful means there were to achieve his ends – for nobody else in the City did otherwise. And when the law was not clear he felt no need to seek clarification, other than from a compliant source – for again, nobody else in the City did otherwise.

One late spring morning Nigel Holmes, the back-room manager of Ludgate Investments, answered a summons to Guy's office to find him studying *The Times* even more closely than usual.

'See what the Board of Trade Report says about Bob Maxwell? "Reckless and unjustified optimism in reporting the maximum profits any transaction could be devised to show. Stating what he must have known was untrue,"' he quoted.

'Awful, isn't it?' Holmes agreed, in the erroneous belief that this was the response his boss required. He scratched his prematurely balding scalp as he searched for a further helpful comment.

'How do you mean, awful?' This was the season hot pants were all the rage, and Guy had drawn the obvious inference that the unadorned truth was often far from palatable. 'Shareholders aren't interested in the truth. They want profits. From now on we're going to follow Cap'n Bob's example to the letter,' he ordered, failing to hide a boyish smirk.

So frenetic was the activity that Guy's centre of operations became known in the City as the Ludgate Circus. On the first floor of the town house he leased within sight of the dome of St Paul's Cathedral, Guy would sit either behind an immense rosewood desk surrounded by his telephones or with his feet up on a plate-glass and brushed steel coffee table he bought from Hille's stylish Mayfair showrooms. There he would scour the newspapers and Extel cards for dealing opportunities.

'Get so-and-so's accounts,' he would call to his secretary when his instincts told him something was afoot. Whenever his researches identified a sleepy board of directors he would buy a share stake, wake them up and offer them a choice: he would sell the stake either back to them or on to a rival, whoever offered more money and faster. The name Ludgate Investments soon struck such terror into its targets that the knowledge it was in the market gave it an immediate gain on its purchases. Guy was often able to profit from mere rumour without the need to put his hand in his wallet.

While Guy directed affairs from the first floor, Nigel Holmes and Brian Proctor, two equally overweight subordinates whom he nicknamed Dum and Dee, whose principal distinguishing features were Holmes's balding pate and Proctor's penchant for Gauloises, watched over the day-to-day operations from the floor above him. Holmes's tasks were to keep Ludgate's bankers aware of Guy's readiness to take its overdraft elsewhere and to check whether what his boss did was within the rules of the game. If it was not, Proctor was to make alternative arrangements so that both deed and rule were in near-perfect harmony. He needed a constant supply of Gauloises to help him achieve these tasks. On the third floor, under the eaves, sat Miles Leppard, the fund manager Guy had engaged to run Ludgate's eclectic portfolios of shares.

Blessed with such stalwart support, Guy was free to concentrate on creative dealing. Small investment trusts were his prey. The worse they performed, the happier he was: for the worst performers often held stakes in the very companies that were most vulnerable to the Magnus treatment. If Guy deemed that Ludgate Investments was short of liquidity, he might also buy their shares on his own account; and who could complain if from time to time he bought and sold first, before Ludgate had woken up? Not Holmes, nor even Proctor, for Guy would often suggest that they buy and sell second and third.

There was but one hitch in the frenzied activity of the Ludgate Circus. Guy might take the decisions, but someone had to be made responsible for them. There were, after all, documents to be signed, and Guy was chary of putting his name to any that might be the subject of future scrutiny. He accordingly appointed Miles Leppard managing director of Ludgate Investments. He also made him chairman. He even made him a director of Mallard. He told him what to buy and what to sell – and what to sign.

Regrettably, his confidence proved misplaced. For though Leppard was not usually averse to taking advice, when Guy decided that a property belonging to a company Mallard had acquired was surplus to its requirements, but at its low book value would fit rather nicely into his personal portfolio, Leppard asked why, if it was good enough for Guy, it wasn't good enough for Mallard's shareholders?

'You know fuck-all about what's good for my shareholders,' Guy exploded. *He* knew. They were doing very nicely, thank you very much. Their shares were going up. They should be only too delighted that the person who was managing their company was doing well too, especially as income tax was still too high to reward him with a decent salary. There was no place in the Ludgate Circus for spoilsports. 'I'm appointing Miles prospective former managing director,' Guy told Nigel Holmes. Then he gave the signatory's job to Giles Kane, a fund manager with less grandiose pretensions. For a trial period, he said.

It was at this time that Harry Griffin called him to warn of an amendment to the City Code: from now on anyone who bought fifteen per cent of a company's shares for cash must offer the highest price he had paid to all other shareholders.

'You know I never pay cash,' retorted Guy, not entirely in jest. Even so, he instructed Harry that in future he was to book his purchases of strategic stakes to those of his friends whose warehouses were abroad.

Ludgate's financial needs grew so rapidly that it had to make a series of rights issues. To ensure that the new shares were taken up, its largest shareholder, Mallard, always subscribed in full. The directors, especially those who were on both companies' boards, were happy to approve these investments, as they had developed the habit of respecting Guy's wishes. They sloughed off any doubts as to whether their decisions might involve conflicts of interest when Guy reminded them that Mallard's profits for the previous year had merely doubled. Its share price would rise faster if it remained in tandem with its more successful associate: for Ludgate's profits had trebled. The Mallard directors saw the benefit of Guy's strategy, for it was not by chance that they were all shareholders as well as directors, and their company's share price had begun to show disturbing signs of stability.

Unfortunately, by the end of 1971 Neville Macrae began to suffer from attacks of insufferable sanctimony not dissimilar to Leppard's. On the completion of Cronic's reorganisation Mallard had kept a thirty per cent stake, Macrae had been rewarded with a substantial shareholding and the remaining stock had been placed with investors not privy to Guy's thoughts on the future of the footwear industry. Told that Mallard was going to buy a private company from Guy at a price set by Guy, Macrae protested that the rules required him to obtain an independent valuation. He seemed, moreover, no more capable than Leppard of distinguishing between assets best left in the company's ownership and those that would benefit from a transfer to Guy's. It was when he objected to the removal of a painting of horses from Cronic's boardroom to the Ludgate Circus that Guy's patience finally ran out.

'Who was it that spotted it was a Munnings?' he challenged. 'For all you knew, you'd have sold it to a junk dealer for a tenner.'

'That's not the point,' retorted Macrae; 'Cronic's a public company.' Like Leppard, he argued that if the picture was worth hanging on Ludgate's wall, no doubt en route to Guy's private collection, it must be of equal value to Cronic. Guy explained that this could not be so, as it had been written down to a pound in the books and produced no profit. He'd be doing Cronic a favour if he took the picture off its hands at book value and saved it the insurance premium. Macrae was too stubborn to be suborned; but he failed to convince Guy.

'If you want the painting that much, you'd better have the whole bloody shooting match,' he told Macrae sourly. On any rational prognosis, he told Larry Callaghan, Macrae's disease was Cronic. As in terminal. 'He's okay for chopping things up but he hasn't a clue how to stitch them together. Investment banking needs needle-and-thread men like you, Larry.' So Mallard's shareholding in Cronic was placed, and Macrae was left to hoe his own patch.

To be fair to Guy, the mood prevailing in the City favoured his philosophy rather than Macrae's. Jon Traill, that renowned guru of the stock market, told his peers at the annual conference of the Institute of Directors that the relationship between management and ownership must change: company managers would only be properly motivated if they owned a stake in the capital of the businesses they ran. It was but a small step to the notion of taking capital from the businesses they ran, and Guy was not one for semantic nit-picking. His shareholders, he repeated, were doing fine. He knew how happy they were for him to share in their rewards, as he was one of them.

A love-hate relationship had been developing between Guy and Jon Traill. The love emanated from Traill's participation in financing the Mallard take-over back in 1969; the hate from Guy's selling Traill Blazer shares short a few months later. When Traill had called him a filthy beast for his disloyalty, *Private Eye* had refined the sobriquet to Caliban. Asked to comment on the announcement that Traill Blazer had insured Jon Traill's life for a million pounds, Guy said he would have Mallard insure his life for £10 million if only he could arrange to be around for the pay-out. Traill, he added gratuitously, was a skunk.

That winter the skunk pinched Guy's latest and best idea. Traill Blazer announced that it was setting up a new investment trust that would hold stakes in its satellite companies. It would, in effect, be selling its own shareholdings to buyers of the new units while their price was still high. The Dual Investment

Trust, Traill called it, and Guy knew why. It was because Traill had it both ways. He got cash in the bank and he kept control of the companies. Guy knew this was so, as he'd been planning to do the same with Ludgate Investments. Traill had stolen his thunder. He would have his revenge.

He picked up his phone and told his secretary to get the editor of *Private Eye*, on the line. 'It's not a trust, it's a swindle,' he told him after he had introduced himself. 'It's your duty to rubbish it.'

'Rubbish Jonathan Traill? Why would a respected organ like ours act in so partisan a manner?' Richard Ingrams sounded hurt, as if his integrity were in question.

'Because it's a dustbin, that's why.'

Thus was born the Dustbin Trust, and with impeccable timing: for that December unemployment passed the one million mark for the first time since the freezing winter of 1947, and within a month the miners would be on strike, the government would announce the Three Day Week and heating would be forbidden in offices, shops and restaurants.

Despite the anarchic state of the labour market, the stock market continued to prosper. Early in 1972 the *FT* Ordinary Share Index passed 500. City analysts described this as a psychological barrier. Guy said it was more of a magical milestone, for his confidence remained high. Mallard shares, which on New Year's Day had stood at 250p, passed 300p at a gallop in March and reached 340p in April. Even so, his envy was roused by the news that shares in the secondary bank Universal Credit had risen from 360p to 400p in a single day. He must redouble his efforts to keep the Mallard dice rolling. On May 1st he announced another scrip issue; but rather than allot one new share for every three or four held, in line with the prevailing custom, Mallard would allot two shares for one and undergo a reconstruction. Its share quotation was suspended with the price at 315p, pending publication of the details.

On May 20th, when the *FT* Index stood at 543.6, Jon Traill made a public prophesy that it would trade in the 650 to 700 range during 1973. When Traill played the oracle, his utterances moved markets. But his words only served to make Guy more sceptical.

'You can bet your last penny Jon's put in his selling orders,' he said, when Harry Griffin asked him whether he thought the bull market would ever end.

'How do you know?'

'Jon's an altruist. He believes in selling while there's something left in it for the other chap,' Guy responded sardonically.

Though Traill had made no one privy to what his true intentions were, Guy knew it was time to move on. The days of buying and selling businesses were over. The day of the financial conglomerate which traded share stakes was about to arrive. So when Mallard's shares were re-listed at the end of May, he announced that it was about to become a financial investment house. It would shortly – he specified no date – have £10 million in funds under management.

It was Guy's misfortune that this announcement was greeted by a nervous stock market. The perverse *FT* Share Index fell through the 500 barrier in as many weeks as it had taken months to climb from it. When Mallard returned to the market, the shares were immediately marked down from the adjusted price of 105p to 90p. By the end of June they had fallen to 66p.

They were not alone. Expectations of the high-flying Universal Credit had been so great that when its chairman announced a profit increase of 160 per cent and a scrip issue, dejected jobbers marked its shares down. Guy judged that increases less dramatic than the recent rise in the cost of a marriage licence from £2.25 to £5 would no longer be acceptable. The bull market was over. His two years were up.

It was on reaching this conclusion that he put in a call to Clive Salmon, the chief executive of Universal Credit, to congratulate him on his results. 'How ever do you keep it up, Clive?' he asked, when connected at last by a telephonist whose instructions were to make it discreetly known that her boss was engaged in international dialogue of high consequence. Guy knew the answer full well. Salmon's reputation as a masseur of accounts and window-dresser of balance sheets came hard-earned.

'Smart deals,' the reply came down the line. 'Do 'em all the time. Should do one together some day.'

Guy's instinct told him his call had been a good move. He offered Salmon lunch at the Savoy. To show he was under no pressure, he set a date in September.

It was time to prepare for his next takeover.

5

After his call to Clive Salmon, it took the whole of July for Guy to talk Mallard's shares back up to 80p. Once the bull market was over you had to sell companies, not buy them, for your shares to go up. Even then you needed the full resources of your fan club to fight the inertia of the stock market, and the capacity of Guy's followers for unquestioning loyalty was beginning to diminish.

At the end of the month he flew to the Cote d'Azur to recharge his batteries. As he sunbathed by the swimming pool of the villa he had rented in Saint-Tropez and read in his airmail edition of *The Times* that Traill Blazer was probably no more vulnerable than any other company in the financial sector, his unerring instinct told him the writing was on the wall.

'Time to clear the decks,' he decided a few days later as he perused a broker's circular in praise of Mallard's performance under his astute leadership.

'Time to cash in your chips,' he repeated as he watched black come up five times in a row in the Monte Carlo casino. 'Timing, timing, timing!'

He returned to a depressed City on the last day of August.

'What you got to offer me, then?' Clive Salmon asked him a few days later as they took their seats in the Savoy Grill. The chief executive of Universal Credit boasted himself a man of few words, believing that in fine speech lay weakness, in concision authority. 'Bristol Investment Trust? Been lookin' into it. You only have a third. Don't want the lot, but you're locked in. Cheese omelette, tomato salad, cup of tea,' he gave his order to the maitre d'hotel without changing his tone.

Guy guessed that if he sold his holding now, Salmon would bid for the rest of Bristol's shares and then sell the trust and make a turn. But Salmon was right: he no longer wanted to hold on to his stake in Bristol. To buy more shares and gain control would cost more than he was prepared to pay; to sell what he had would raise valuable cash.

'If you want it so much, Clive, bid me for it. Same for me,' he told the maître, turning from the temptations of the à la carte menu. Salmon would not be impressed if he were to indulge his love of caviar and vintage champagne.

'Pay you a fair price. Net asset value. Fifty-five pence,' Salmon offered. 'Cash.'

Guy leant back slowly in his chair and scrutinised his adversary. Slightly below medium height, a touch overweight, nondescript features, sparse blonde hair turning grey at the temples: Clive Salmon was the kind of man you could spend hours with and not recognise the next time you met him. His expression gave no clue to his thoughts; they must be divined from an assessment of his situation.

Guy gravely shook his head. 'Jon Traill's already bid me that,' he lied. 'I turned him down flat. Told him if he tried to put together a portfolio of that quality today, he'd drive the market against himself. He knew it was true,' he said, showing as much bravado as he dared. 'Even if we wanted to sell, which I'm not sure we do, we wouldn't take less than 60.'

'Right you are, young man. Shouldn't have tried it on. Old head, young shoulders. Last offer first, then. Fifty-eight. You deserve it.'

Guy knew Salmon was hell-bent on growth at all costs. Even with a purchase at a premium, the financier would massage his books to show a profit on the deal. But if he were taken for his last penny, would he be tempted back for the next one? Guy made up his mind. 'Split the difference and it's a deal,' he said quickly.

'Deal!' Salmon could scarcely hide his pleasure. He'd come prepared to pay up to 65p. 'You're a good boy, Guy,' he said. Business done, he managed a complete sentence. 'You've learnt the most important lesson of dealing. Always leave something for the other man. Our lawyers'll be in touch. How's business otherwise?'

'Business?' Guy affected not to care. 'I don't want to spend my life operating businesses. If you really want to know, I find them a bit of a bore. I'd be perfectly content to be left to get on with trading shares. But one has to accept the responsibility.'

This time Salmon failed to hide the gleam in his eyes. The two financiers talked on. They found they had much in common.

'We've done our job. Hammered out the framework,' Salmon summed up their labours as they stood to leave the Savoy Grill. 'Let's have our merchant banks put the flesh on the bones.'

Salmon's takeover of Mallard suited Guy's dealing philosophy down to the ground. As a director of Mallard, he couldn't sell its shares without announcing it to the stock exchange. In their place he'd own shares in Universal Credit. As he wasn't a director of that company, he was free to turn them into cash without making an announcement. The week before the deal was completed, Universal Credit had published its half-year results, declaring profits four times greater than for the same period the previous year. Its offer document for Mallard forecast more of the same. But Universal Credit's shares had fallen to 300p from last April's peak of 400p. Guy bet himself they'd never see that level again. He never held shares that had fallen and were about to fall still further.

As part of the deal it was agreed that Universal Credit would sell Mallard's shares in Ludgate Investments to Guy and his associates. The sale did not include Mallard's shares in Highland Timber, even though that otherwise defunct company also held shares in Ludgate. Instead, Salmon agreed to Guy's proposal that Universal Credit take an option to sell the shares in Highland Timber to him in three months' time, and swore on his mother's life to exercise it. Naturally this promise had to be kept secret, as the chairman of the London Stock Exchange had recently pronounced insider trading no better than theft, and Guy had no intention of being tempted into crime while he laid his plans for the future.

Guy's new business association brought an early reward. Salmon reckoned that a favour given was a favour owed, and repaid Guy by sharing his skill in window-dressing balance sheets. So he said that on January 31st 1973 Universal Credit would be delighted to lend St Paul's Property, one of Guy's companies, a couple of million pounds overnight. When St Paul's Property discovered it did not need the money after all, but the date happened to coincide with the last day of Ludgate Investments' accounting year, St Paul's obligingly passed on the same £2 million overnight to Ludgate. Ludgate's year-end balance sheet had never looked so healthy. At the end of March, Salmon suggested, Guy would return the favour.

Lest the question arise as to whether such acts of mutual support were in the interests of both Ludgate's and St Paul's Property's shareholders, Larry Callaghan insisted that the loans be formally approved by both boards. While as a director of each Callaghan was well able to speak for both camps himself, he insisted that a second director be present at each meeting to make up a quorum; or if not present in fact, at least so in spirit. St Paul's Property was represented by its managing director, George Ellison, whose compliance

Guy secured by granting him ownership of some of its shares without having to pay for them. And when Clive Salmon said he was well able to provide his own directors for Mallard, Guy's friend and lawyer Dominic Arthur duly resigned from that board and became available for duty at Ludgate Investments. Guy had met the affable Arthur socially and had soon found his professional advice helpful whenever he needed an opinion from which a less amenable lawyer might differ.

Though not bound to exercise his option to sell Highland Timber back to Guy three months' later, Clive Salmon did not hesitate in doing so, as he no longer had any need of the shares. The snag was that Guy was not personally in funds to the tune of a million pounds, and it had been decided that the option would have to be taken up by his private company, Westchurch.

'That's got the cash?' Salmon had presumed.

'Come off it, Clive; Westchurch has only a quarter of a million in capital.'

'How will I exercise my option, then?' Salmon had asked with a touch of concern.

'You're going to give Westchurch an overdraft,' Guy had replied unabashed, as if to ask whether Salmon of all people hadn't heard of gearing.

'You must be joking.'

'I was never more serious. It's a very reasonable suggestion. By the way, I want the Paris property development to come back to St Paul's. That will need financing too.'

'You know how it is, Guy,' Salmon wheedled. By now Guy had graduated to being accorded complete sentences. 'Even Barclays is telling its branch managers not to grant overdrafts to finance equity or property purchases.'

'So I'm doing you a favour, letting you fill a gap in the market.'

Salmon had been quick to turn the position to his advantage. He had become desperate to declare ever-higher profits to maintain the market's appetite for shares in Universal Credit, but achieving such profits in the normal run of business had become increasingly difficult. Only his close colleagues shared his knowledge of how little money his company was actually making. It had become necessary for him to find transactions out of the usual run, and to find ways to declare profits from them. Buying Mallard for shares and selling its assets back to Guy and his friends for cash was one way to achieve his ends. Lending them the money to finance the roundabout was the route to another.

'We'll only charge you four per cent for the money,' he had said with a wink. Then, after a moment's hiatus, 'And ten per cent of the loan as a facility fee.' Guy had immediately seen the point of the manoeuvre: Universal Credit would take the whole of the facility fee into profit in its current year's accounts.

Which is how Westchurch came to buy Highland Timber and its shares in Ludgate Investments from Universal Credit with Universal Credit's money.

'We must do another deal some time,' said Salmon as they parted, without much conviction. He made Guy promise to attend the opening of Universal Credit's new headquarters on Marylebone Road, the visible manifestation of its ceaseless drive for growth. The City would be represented in force; there'd be champagne, caviar, no expense spared, to ensure that each guest was kept happy as he awaited his personal guided tour of the heart of the bank's operations, equipped to handle its sophisticated credit controls with the very latest in computer technology.

Guy made a diary note to buy shares in Universal Credit that morning before leaving for the celebrations – and to sell them in after-hours trading. His timing, as ever, proved impeccable.

Meanwhile the sale of Mallard had cleared the decks. He was in a position to mount his own takeover bid.

6

It is time to return to Harry Griffin and to discover what he got up to after he had paid for lunch with Guy Magnus at the Connaught Grill. We will need to spend time, as the Department of Trade Inspectors did, learning what we can about CHIT and Britton Estates. This will of necessity involve the roles of their principal shareholders. Above all, we will need to discover the truth, or as close as we can get to it, of Ray Munster's assertion that Harry Griffin rather conned Guy Magnus into taking an interest in the future of that asset-rich company, Britton Trust. For if even the Inspectors found difficulty in getting to the bottom of this mystery, our readers will want to give it their most careful attention.

Harry had not, of course, wasted his time sending the lunch bill, or even half of it, on to Guy. Instead, he had treated the expense as a valuable investment. He had taken Guy's strictures to heart. And the more he followed his friend's advice, the more CHIT showed itself to be every bit as useful a vehicle as Guy had predicted.

Harry's working day at Grieff & Hammer habitually began with a review of the previous day's trading on the London Stock Exchange. Each day the changes in the share prices listed on the back page of the *Financial Times* told a different tale The uninitiated might marvel that the value of a public company could go up by £1 million today and down by £1 million tomorrow. Though Harry knew the answer – that jobbers were on the lookout for trade, speculators were after a turn, fund managers were taking profits or losses depending on whom their investment director had lunched with, or amateurs were trying to salvage their disasters – his guts told him it was a strange way to value businesses.

It was, however, a lucrative way to do business. Provided you knew which stocks to buy. And when to sell. To Harry, Guy Magnus's feel for the day-to-day rhythms and flows of the market was nothing short of miraculous. The stocks he bought went up faster than any other, while those he sold plummeted. The former was to be expected, in view of his following. Guy had only to give his broker a buying order for the world and his brother to want a piece of the action. Literally the world: for his admirers were to be found as far afield as Liechtenstein and the Netherlands Antilles. Indeed, so respected was the judgment of his fan club that before their stockbrokers executed their buying orders they would place similar orders for their private clients – and what client could be a more private than a wife or a children's trust?

But where you might expect Guy's selling orders to be followed by an avalanche of dumping by these avid fans, the market would suddenly become a model of orderly behaviour. It was as if nobody knew when he sold.

Harry was the first to admit his good fortune in being able to anticipate some of the purchases Guy was about to make. If pressed, he might even modestly confess that they were often in companies he had recommended. From his position at the head of Tanquery's corporate department he had an unique opportunity to assess the nation's growing army of entrepreneurs. And from the way in which they discussed their takeover plans with him, it was not hard for him to determine whether they were the sort of people Tanquery and its client funds should support. Harry's genius for keeping an open shell-like ear to the sound of the waves paid off handsomely, since sharing his assessments with Guy enabled him to check them out with an interested observer who would from time to time act on the information provided.

Harry's mistake was to buy from time to time without Guy's imprimatur. On one occasion he overheard two of Tanquery's brokers placing separate buying orders for the same penny stock. He asked one about the shares.

'It'll be a good little earner, sir,' he was told. 'The offer price last week was only fourpence ha'penny. There was heavy buying from Geneva, so I took a position. Then the Sunday papers quoted Guy Magnus saying he was making a long-term investment in the company, so I knew we wouldn't go wrong if we went long. Shall I put you down for 10,000, sir? The offer's 9p at the moment.'

At the end of the stock market trading account the shares had fallen to 6p. But Harry had taken Guy's advice about CHIT to heart. It was on such occasions that his new corporate vehicle found its first role, as a parking lot for his least lucky purchases. It took up the shares he had bought from the suspense account in which he had taken the precaution of housing them pending a final decision on their ownership, following the example set by CHIT's other directors. For Archie Laws and Harold Antony also made mistakes as stockbrokers that they wished to correct as company directors. CHIT was soon showing itself to be every bit as useful as Guy had predicted.

When he and Guy next met, Harry mentioned the matter.

'Which shares?' Guy asked. 'Oh, those,' he recalled when Harry repeated the name. 'I sold on the Tuesday. It was announced. You should read the papers.'

'But on the Friday you said you were buying them as a long-term investment.'

'The very point the *Telegraph* made. You must be psychic, Harry.'

'What did you tell them?'

'That what I'd said on Friday was the truth. I held them right through the weekend. Including bank holiday Monday.'

Having accepted Guy's recommendation and bought shares in Poseidon at 20 shillings, Harry heeded the advice of *The Times* a month later that the shares were "felt to have over-reached themselves" and cashed in his chips at 120 shillings. But when they passed 400 shillings at a gallop early in November, he felt ashamed of his faint-heartedness and went back into the market.

Harry was not alone as an investor in the wonder-stock. 'You haven't missed out on Poseidon?' he enquired of his secretary Sharon.

'I've been busy doing your typing,' Sharon excused herself as she passed him a pile of letters for signature. 'Who's Poseidon anyway, when he's at home?'

'It's an Australian mining company. It reckons to have made a big nickel strike in Western Australia.'

'What price are they now?'

'They opened at twenty this morning. I bought a few on my own account. The market's a bit thin, but I can still find you a few if you're interested.'

Sharon was a modest investor. From time to time she allowed Harry to buy penny stocks for her account. But twenty shillings! 'A pound a share?' she queried aloud, pursing her lips and sucking in her breath. 'Bit pricey for my taste.'

'Twenty *pounds!*' exclaimed Harry. 'And worth every bit of it, once they find what they're looking for. Guy Magnus reckons they'll be over a hundred by the year-end. I'll try to find you ten shares if you want. Don't worry, I'll leave your account open until you sell them. It's entirely up to you,' he added generously.

Sharon succumbed to temptation.

As the price of Poseidon shares rocketed, Harry reckoned his investment might even bring him his free lunch at Maxim's before next year was out. By New Year's Eve they were pushing £120. The price fell during the early weeks of 1970, but his confidence was renewed when they returned to their peak in February on rumours of a nickel strike, so he bought some more. However, in March the board's report on operations was delayed and panic selling set in, resulting in the shares falling to a quarter of their peak value. Caught on the hop, Harry found himself holding more Poseidon stock than he wanted. He was left to console himself with the thought that at a time when the *FT* Index was wallowing at its lowest level since the doleful days of 1967, not many shares were worth £30. In October, when the company announced that nickel production would definitely begin at Windarra in 1972, he went cautiously back into the market. But in December the board said it needed to raise £26 million to develop the mine, a sum it appeared not to have in its hip pocket, and the shares fell again.

By now Harry was monitoring the company's announcements closely. He was sufficiently encouraged by the next one, that Poseidon had 100 million tons of nickel reserves and intended to mine a million tons a year, that he bought again at £18 – 'to average', he explained sagely to Sharon.

'To average?' she queried.

'Well, initially I bought fifty at £20, so not much damage there. Then I went in again just before Christmas.'

'At a hundred pounds apiece, I'll be bound.'

'Ninety.' Harry hung his head. 'But if I buy some more now, my average will be below £40. They'll only have to double for me to break even,' he excused himself, without much conviction.

Sharon sighed. He'd probably bought the shares she'd sold.

On New Year's Day 1971, the City was as silent as a morgue. Envious of the extra winter break the work-to-rule electricians and striking firemen were taking, the airline workers had downed tools to prevent them taking their leisure-time abroad. Not to be outdone, the print unions made sure the public knew none of this by refusing to print the newspapers. As if in sympathy, everyone else had decided that New Year's Day would be an unofficial bank holiday. Rather than spend the day at home, Harry went to the office to review his strategy for CHIT in peace and quiet.

'That's novel,' he said as he walked through Sharon's office, noticing a new paperweight on her desk. She had said she would come in too so she could get on with her filing while no one was around.

'Selfridges were selling them off, so I picked one up as a memento.'

'It's an unusual colour. What's it made from?'

'Nickel.'

At noon Harry's private line rang for the first time that day. Sharon told him the caller was his wife. The absence of his *Financial Times* had made Harry irritable.

'Can't she see I'm busy?' he snapped before he took the call.

'Are you free to talk to me or aren't you?' Sybil enquired querulously.

'Sorry, darling; one of those days. The phone hasn't stopped.'

'I got through easily enough. I'm at Harrods. You couldn't come over could you? I want you to look at some curtains. They'll be in the sales next week.'

Harry's heart sank. It was not the first time it had plunged to his diaphragm. It did so every time he ran out of resources to maintain his wife's standard of living. Life with Sybil was like walking a neverending tightrope. Once she had finished saving in the sales more than he earned in the office, she would be after a new flat.

'I'm up to my eyes,' he lied. 'It's the only day of the year I can catch up.'

Sybil reluctantly accepted his promise to come to Harrods on Saturday.

CHIT's second benefit, as a payer of expenses, was becoming more apparent. Meanwhile he must write to Archie Laws to express his concern over CHIT's future. There were others who owned its shares, but they did so only because they knew no better. Laws, who owned a majority of the equity, knew better than most, but he had been heard to complain that as he made fewer dealing mistakes than Harry, he saw no reason why he should bear an equivalent share of CHIT's losses. He must manoeuvre Laws into putting pressure on him to buy his shares. The more of the equity he owned, the better would he be able to control the company's destiny. The letter must be drafted without delay.

'Sharon! Come here!' he called.

As he did so, the phone rang again. 'Happy New Year, Harry!' Guy's disembodied voice greeted him.

'And a prosperous one to you, Guy,' responded Harry.

'Are you alone? Sharon's not in, is she?'

'Not today,' lied Harry.

'Glad to hear it, Harry. Mine neither. It's the only day in the year you can chat to an old pal without the world and his brother eavesdropping.'

'Anything interesting going on at General Forestry, Guy?' Harry fished for inside information.

'General Forestry?' asked Guy, feigning disbelief over Harry's ignorance.

'Well, Ludgate Investments,' Harry corrected himself. 'I take it you still want me to bring any takeover prospects to Mallard in the first instance?' he asked.

'Of course. Mallard's an industrial conglomerate. It's for my long-term acquisitions,' Guy elaborated. 'For the time being, that is,' he added silently. 'Though I may want to put some of my purchases into Ludgate while I'm deciding what to do with them. I'll let you know at the time.' For Ludgate Investments had set up a subsidiary, a tax-exempt authorised trust. Whenever Guy found a prey too big for Mallard to swallow in one bite, Ludgate Investment Trust would take a position in its shares. When the market found out who had been buying, the price would shoot up. Being small, the investment trust would grow rapidly on the dealing profits. Anyone who happened to buy the same shares on his own account, as Guy frequently did, would do pretty well too.

'But,' Harry hoped Guy would not be cross with him for pointing out an obstacle, 'if the share stakes the authorised trust buys are large enough to be worthwhile, won't some of them cost more than fifteen per cent of Ludgate's capital? If an authorised trust does that, doesn't it lose its tax-exempt status?'

If anything made Guy impatient it was having someone tell him the basics. 'Silly boy! It buys the larger stakes through a fellow subsidiary, Ludgate Securities. Nothing to do with Investments. Don't tell me you don't do that with CHIT?' he sneered.

Harry could hardly have said he was shocked. Nothing Guy did shocked him. He was, however, concerned. Concerned that Guy should think he could get away with such a blatant device to circumvent the regulations.

'How is CHIT working out for you?' Guy enquired solicitously.

'Moving along nicely, thanks,' replied Harry non-committally.

'So it's making profits?'

'Naturally.'

'Mistake.' Harry waited for the reason. It was not long coming. 'Tax. I thought I told you not to join. Some people never learn.' The line went dead.

On his desk pad Harry wrote, "Commercial Holdings Investment Trust". Beneath them he wrote the letters, "C, H, I, T". He stared at them long and hard. Then he wrote beneath, "Conserve Harry's Increasing Treasury".

Disgusted by his lack of imagination, he tried a few more creative alternatives. But only when he came up with the unambiguous "Cut Harry's Income Tax" was he finally content.

Guy was no longer alone. Harry too had a corporate strategy. Though he had not yet put into practice his plans to exploit CHIT's second benefit, the day had pointed the way towards developing the third.

He called a tax counsel specialising in setting up offshore trusts.

7

When the Poseidon board admitted it was finding it hard to sell the nickel ore it had yet to mine, a stockbroker's circular said the shares were worth no more than £3.25. Fortunately for Harry Griffin, the market treated the comment with disdain and only marked them down to £11.50. The customarily phlegmatic *Times* said the company was "poised for a sustained recovery … the nickel is definitely there."

Though their shares continued to slide, the Poseidon board showed its optimism by announcing a one-for-twenty scrip issue; but even this unexpected windfall was cancelled when it was discovered that most shareholders would fail to benefit, as few apart from Harry held as many as twenty shares. Such an investment had been too rich for most private punters when it had cost £2,500. It was less exciting when it was worth only £130 and nickel production was to be deferred for yet another year.

During one of their periodic chats, Harry asked Guy for his view.

'Poseidon? God of the deep blue yonder, wasn't he?' asked Guy, frowning. 'Sounds like you dipped your toe in the water and got your head soaked in piss,' he added more pointedly.

So Harry's Poseidon shares found their way into CHIT's eclectic portfolio.

But for all its convenience as a repository for unlucky share purchases, a payer of expenses and a saver of taxes, CHIT had yet to prove the bonanza Guy had led Harry to expect. Its auditors exhibited an unhelpful lack of flexibility. The audit manager took a holier-than-thou view of the directors' use of company funds which, he claimed, belonged to the shareholders. He missed the point: Harry had no way of returning money Sybil had already spent; and in any event, without his willingness to act on the shareholders' behalf their funds would not be managed so profitably. The auditor then said the annual general meeting must be postponed, as the books for 1970 were in such a mess he couldn't produce the accounts. Harry replied that this was no problem, for Archie Laws had accepted his view that the company was going nowhere and had sold him most of his shares. As he now spoke for a majority of the equity, what was and what wasn't in the company's interests was up to him, and he didn't give a hoot whether the accounts were certified or when the meeting was held, if ever. When the audit partner asked him to produce his share certificates to justify his claim of ownership, Harry reflected on the offshore nature of the trusts that held his shares and said this could be a problem. The following day the senior partner called to inform Harry that the auditor had a duty to report to all of the shareholders, not just a majority. He then asked CHIT's stockbrokers to confirm Harry's assurance that none of the shares he owned were held as security for a loan. On receiving a reply that did not accord with Harry's, he said the company's report and accounts would have to be qualified.

It was at this tricky juncture that Harry met Jolyon Priestley, and the value of his shareholding began its inexorable upward march towards £1 million pounds.

Earlier in the year Harry and a like-minded young colleague, Andy Oakes, had decided that Archie Laws and Tanquerys no longer suited their free-wheeling style of trading. They had taken up an offer of partnerships in Grieff & Hammer, a more tolerant firm of brokers. It was on a miserable grey late autumn morning that Sharon, who had accompanied Harry in the move, announced that a Mr Priestley awaited him in his new firm's meeting room.

Harry asked Sharon to tell Priestley he would be with him in a few minutes, finished his coffee, folded his *Financial Times* and strolled the few paces along the corridor to the meeting room. Jolyon Priestley was well-known to him as a dealer in loss-making propositions. At their first meeting he had brought one: Watson's. Having recently sold his stake in a chain of loss-making dance halls, he proposed to make his next investment in a loss-making company that serviced the oil industry and happened to own four gravel pits in Sussex and an office building near Euston station. The only flaw in his plans was that the sale proceeds of his dance halls did not cover the purchase costs of Watson's. This, Priestley had told him, was a pity, as the company offered a unique opportunity for a profitable carve-up. Could Harry find him a punter for the difference?

Tall and slim, with receding ginger hair, Priestley had a shifty expression. Harry reckoned he slid like a snake. Despite the more relaxed atmosphere in his new milieu, he could bring to mind none of his clients who would make an ideal partner for the man. On further reflection, however, he had said he had an idea where some wise money might be sought, provided the deal was sufficiently attractive. He had suggested that Priestley come to a further meeting with more precise details as to how Watson's could be carved up. This was the further meeting.

'So you reckon we need a million to buy the company,' he said when Priestley had finished extolling Watson's virtues for a second time. 'What can you bring to the table yourself? How much did you get for the dance halls?'

'Well,' said Priestley after a lengthy pause, 'I got a pretty good price, actually. But I want to de-gear, of course. My bankers, Ernest Burke, aren't too happy about that. They want to lend me more, not less. As much as I want, in fact. But I'm a cautious kind of chap. *Reculer pour mieux sauter*, as they say.'

Harry nodded. He decided not to ask why Ernest Burke was being denied the opportunity to finance the Watson's deal. 'That still doesn't answer my question,' he said, and sat silently waiting for the reply.

'Actual cash, well, not actual cash,' Priestley confessed. 'But I've got another business. A good, sound, cash-flow business. I could consider putting that in.'

This business, it transpired, was the Norfolk Broads Company. It owned a stretch of the eponymous waters and allowed people who messed around in boats to do so between its banks at a weekly rate. If they had no boat of their own, the company allowed them the use of one of its own barges for weekly hire. Trade was, Priestley admitted, somewhat seasonal; but for that part of the year when it was busy – in years when the weather was anything like – it was a good, sound, cash-flow business.

'How much profit did it make last year?' Harry enquired cautiously.

'Actual profit? Well, not an actual profit, as such,' Priestley replied, averting his eyes. 'Not after paying my salary, that is. But it has assets.' By the time he had finished listing and attributing values to these, in particular one asset located neither in nor anywhere near to Norfolk, Harry could see why he reckoned they were worth double their book value of £100,000.

When he had completed his exposition, Priestley turned the tables. 'You won't take it amiss if I ask you what your clients can bring to the party?' he asked. 'No offence, of course.'

'None taken,' replied Harry. It was his turn to hesitate. But CHIT badly needed a fresh investor. 'To be perfectly frank,' he added, 'the firm's fully invested at present. But we too have a business. An authorised investment trust. Now I think of it,' he pressed on as if under the influence of sponta-neous inspiration, 'it occurs to me that our businesses might do something with Watson's together.'

They soon agreed that CHIT would buy Priestley's Norfolk Broads Company for shares and then bid for Watson's. A share exchange would avoid CHIT spending cash it did not have. While it would also dilute Harry's shareholding to less than fifty per cent, this was academic: for having failed to declare most of it to the auditors, he was unable to use his majority to exercise control. More important, the deal would solve CHIT's lack of man-agement skills; for Priestley would be bringing his entrepreneurial expertise to the party and his investment in the equity of the enlarged company would give him the incentive to make it thrive.

The two haggled. As he had paid Archie Laws 75p per share, Harry felt justified in valuing CHIT at 100p. Priestley accepted this, but argued for a ten per cent discount to reflect the value of his secret asset. They settled at five per cent. Priestley then asked to be put in funds in order to settle his outstanding personal commitments. It was plain he must put something more into the pot to cover this, so he offered the lease of his office which he valued at £15,000. Harry said he was pretty sure CHIT didn't need another office and offered £5,000. They settled at £10,000. It had been an amicable negotiation.

Harry called Sharon to see Priestley out. He watched her lead his guest along the corridor to the lift. Priestley stumbled as the door slid open and grappled with her to steady himself, apologising profusely as he regained his balance.

Sharon turned indignantly to Harry, mouthing words that could hardly have been mistaken by the most amateurish of lipreaders.

'Dirty old man,' read Harry.

He returned to his office and picked up the phone to clear the deal with Harold Antony, CHIT's next largest shareholder. While at first their rela-tionship had been sticky, Antony had eventually adjusted himself to Harry's investment philosophy. He had also reached the conclusion that Tanquerys was too narrowly based to contain his talents, as it dealt only with London-based investors. For though Antony dealt in UK stocks, his select group of clients preferred them to be purchased through such safe havens as Zurich and Geneva. He was accordingly setting up a firm of licensed dealers based in Switzerland, with facilities to deal on the London Stock Exchange. Antony suggested to Harry that if CHIT was on the lookout for opportunistic investments, it could do worse than make one in his Swiss venture. He proposed that it put in £10,000. They settled at £7,500.

The deal also had to be cleared with CHIT's chairman. The Hon. Beresford Beauchamp had been born ninth in line to the earldom of St Edmunds, and had joined the armed forces with no expectation of his future elevation. He had been promoted to the rank of colonel, and then posted to duties in the foreign service, before returning to take up a series of positions in the civil service. Meanwhile his cousins had died off one by one before the old earl had the grace to predecease them, so that when at last the old boy was promoted to the uppermost of all Houses, Berry Beauchamp found to his amazement that he had succeeded to the title.

The new earl had learnt of his fortune in a roundabout way: the offers of directorships preceded the obituaries by some forty-eight hours, the pro forma from *Burke's Peerage* by a week and the discreet contacts of the powers-that-be by a month; so Berry Beauchamp had plenty of notice to brush up his lordly guffaw and shuffle off to Jermyn Street to order the requisite wardrobe of dinner suits, dress shirts, black bow ties and patent leather shoes – to be paid for, it went without saying, when his lordship found convenient – before Jennifer put her Diary's seal on his social indispensability and the gilt-edged invitations began to pour in. Meanwhile, company letterheads were reprinted and the City career of Berry St Edmunds was launched. When Harold Antony and Archie Laws agreed to appoint a neutral chairman for CHIT, he was the natural choice. Taking the chair was a favour returned, though Harold Antony never enlightened Harry as to the nature of the original good turn.

Obtaining the approval of the Earl of St Edmunds to the various deals posed Harry no problem, for it transpired that the earl was to be chairman of Harold Antony's new venture too. He declared the whole idea a jolly good show, especially when it was agreed that CHIT would further broaden its business base by acquiring the public relations firm whose board he had joined shortly after succeeding to his title and which, though currently losing money, he vouchsafed would be profitable as soon as it was backed by CHIT's resources.

His lordship came to lunch at CHIT's head office to sign the board minutes approving the offer document for Watson's and the transactions he and the other members of the board had promoted. Harry was a contented host, because the earl soon proved to be not such a duffer as he had feared. During the smoked salmon his lordship hemmed and hawed, and during the roast pheasant he praised the cook roundly for hanging the wretched fowl for ten days rather than five; but the treacle tart brought out the best in him. When he had finished complimenting Harry on the crust being crunchier by far than the one served yesterday by Britton Estates, he admitted that, yes, he was chairman there too, for his sins, and in his view there was never any harm in seeing if there was common ground, what? It so happened he knew of a line of half a million shares in Britton Estates that could be had if the right noises were made. To judge from the noises he then made in the direction of Harold Antony, Harry was left in no doubt that as soon as Britton Estates had made an investment in Antony's new venture, the half a million shares would be safely deposited in CHIT's back pocket.

As he passed Harry the port, the Earl of St Edmunds sheltered his mouth with his hand and whispered conspiratorially, 'You should get together with our chap Charteris. Good man, Charteris. Only director we've got who knows anything about property. Do much property at CHIT, eh, Griffin? It's the coming thing. Get him on your board, if I were you.'

'I'm sure we'd welcome his counsel,' said Harry, knowing his arm was being twisted but that he had little option but to succumb with good grace.

So another lunch was convened for the end of January, and at the board meeting that followed the Earl of St Edmunds proposed, Harry seconded and it was unanimously resolved that Mr John Charteris be appointed a director of CHIT. The board then resolved, the earl and Charteris abstaining to avoid any possible conflict of interest, to take up the line of Britton Estates shares that had been overhanging the stock market for several weeks. At this agreeable juncture Charteris said he was sure his colleagues would be delighted if Jolyon Priestley would consider a reciprocal appointment to the Britton Estates board.

Finally, under any other business, the earl proposed that the company invest £10,000 in Harold Antony's new venture, only to be reminded by Charteris that this was what the Britton Estates board was supposed to be doing tomorrow. At this juncture the party broke up with much hand-shaking and back-slapping, and everybody went home happy.

8

In Budapest Richard Burton threw a fortieth birthday party for Elizabeth Taylor at which he pledged eternal love with a £1,000,000 diamond. In Guy's book you didn't lash out that kind of bread on a woman unless the writing was already on the wall. The moment he read of the gift he bet Harry a lunch at the Moulin de Mougins the marriage wouldn't last twelve months. Earlier that day Sybil had told Harry that diamonds were forever, and she wished he were capable of such a romantic gesture. So Harry had taken Guy's bet, telling himself it would give him his revenge for the unpaid lunch bill at the Connaught Grill.

In London Harry Griffin's young associate at Grieff & Hammer brought him a gift of even greater value than the diamond. He told Harry about Laserbeam.

Andy Oakes was short, round and persuasive. He was the kind of broker who never came to you with a straight buying proposition, for that yielded but one commission. His specialty was surefire buy-and-sell deals. That way he made two commissions. He told Harry he knew where a long line of shares in Laserbeam was to be had. All they needed was a couple of million and they'd have a twenty per cent stake in the company. It was a sure fire deal. They'd make a bundle on the turn.

'What does Laserbeam actually do?' asked Harry.

'It has a research project on the cutting edge of technology,' came the ready reply: literally, for the company was developing a process by which the cloth for men's suits would be cut by a computer-controlled laser.

'A research project? On the cutting edge of technology?' Harry parroted. 'What the hell are you frigging about with one of them for?' Shares, as Guy Magnus never tired of lecturing him, were for buying and selling, not for throwing a couple of million at an investment that would take forever to pay off.

Oakes was unable to contain his enthusiasm. 'The menswear manufacturers in Leeds would kill their grandmothers to get hold of it. Imagine, no more union problems with the cutters, no wastage of material: all you do is key the customer's measurements into the computer, and out comes the cloth ready to be made up.'

'I've never known you so keen on what a business actually did, Andy,' Harry observed sarcastically.

Oakes ignored the jibe. 'There are only three major players in the industry,' he continued confidently. 'Whoever winds up in control of Laserbeam will hold the others to ransom. It'll make a bomb in licence fees.'

'So Laserbeam will make money. Some day. So what?'

'So there'll be a fight over the share stake. Not so much to have it for themselves as to stop one of the others owning it.'

'And who's supposed to leave his couple of million on the table while you run the auction?'

'We won't run an auction,' Oakes grinned. 'We'll sell the stake on and let someone else hold the gavel. It's a one-way bet.'

'Which you're the only guy in town to know about?'

'I just happen to be the only guy in town who's spotted the opportunity.'

Harry set his scepticism aside to point out a practical objection. 'You still need to find a couple of million to buy the stake in the first place.'

'Maybe, maybe not. Suppose I've got a back-to-back deal?'

Harry detected from Oakes's tone that he was bluffing. 'If you've got one lined up, what do you need me for?' he asked.

'I did think of booking the deal in my own name,' Oakes hesitated, letting Harry work out the problem. 'but I thought that perhaps … CHIT?'

Harry thought for a moment. What if there really was a back-to-back deal to be done? But CHIT was in the middle of a rights issue. It was issuing shares to raise the funds to pay for Watson's, the Norfolk Broads Company and the earl's public relations business, not to mention shares in Britton Estates and Harold Antony's securities firm.

'CHIT's rather committed just now,' he said. 'On the other hand, maybe it is the kind of opportunity we shouldn't pass up without a closer look. If you and I … when will you need to come up with the name of the buyer?'

'Well, as long as we have a name on the contract note, we can always tear it up later if we change our minds. We're bound to have the sale wrapped up in the same account. Our names won't appear on the stock transfer.'

Harry considered the proposition carefully. The more he thought about it, the more he liked it. If he judged correctly, there could be a dealing profit of at least 50p per share on Laserbeam's current market price of 200p. On a million shares that came to £500,000, to be split two ways. 'I'd have thought an investment in advanced industrial technology might suit one of our client funds,' he pronounced after a brief hesitation. 'We can decide which when the deal's done – unless, of course, we happen to receive an offer in the meantime that we can't refuse,' he added in a throw-away tone.

'Fifty-fifty?' proposed Oakes.

'Fifty-fifty,' agreed Harry. But like Oakes he needed to distance himself personally from the transaction. And he had no authority to commit Grieff & Hammer to make such a purchase – for no partner could commit the firm so heavily without the agreement of the full partnership. 'Why don't we test the water by buying a few shares on personal account first?' he proposed. 'Then maybe I could talk to Jolyon about the deal.'

'Why not, indeed?' Oakes agreed. 'Harold may like to punt a few quid too.' He returned to his own office to test the water with Harold Antony.

Once he had confirmation that the water was fine, Harry called Jolyon Priestley to tell him of the proposition. 'The shares must be sold on to a gilt-edged buyer. We don't want the transaction to be queried,' he explained. 'You don't happen to know of anyone suitable, do you? Someone keen to do deals.'

Priestley confirmed, with the air of one surprised his credentials as a contact-maker should be in question, that of course he did. Only the other day his accountant had claimed more than a passing acquaintance with Paul Petrosian, the doyen of multinational dealers. This was good news to Harry, because once Priestley was on the hook CHIT would be waiting in the wings ready to pick up the pieces if anything went wrong. So when Oakes reported to Harry that the sellers of the shares had said it was make-your-mind-up time, Harry told him to set up a meeting with them.

He was impressed with Oakes's preparatory work, for they soon reached agreement to buy the Laserbeam shares. Oakes told the seller he was acting for a client of the firm and Harry said he was acting for another client of the firm. That Oakes's client was Harry and Harry's client was Oakes never arose. In any event, once the ritual bargaining stopped at a price 10p above Oakes's initial offer, hands were shaken and the contract was drawn up. Their unnamed clients would buy 1,150,000 Laserbeam shares at 230p, settlement to take place fourteen days hence.

Harry told Priestley to set up a meeting with his buyer. But he was less impressed with Priestley's preparatory work than he had been with Oakes's, for when the meeting with Paul Petrosian broke up after only a few minutes, the negotiations to sell the shares had not left the ground. Priestley's gilt-edged buyer observed that as far as he was aware the shares were already owned by somebody else, and he wanted to know who was this very special client of Grieff & Hammer who could deliver them to him at so much higher a price than he could buy them for in the open market. He did, in fairness, undertake not to talk out of turn to the shares' owners, and said he would be delighted if Harry were to keep in touch. But that was all.

'He's bluffing,' Priestley assured Harry in the cab back to his office.

'He can bluff till the cows come home,' Harry replied sanguinely. 'The more he overplays his hand, the higher our price will be.'

As the days passed and Paul Petrosian continued to overplay his hand, Andy Oakes told Harry that the time had come when the shares must be booked to someone. Harry asked Priestley how much cash he had in the kitty. Priestley shrugged. Harry asked Andy Oakes the same question. Oakes laughed. Harry didn't bother to ask the question of himself, for Sybil had just carried out an identical piece of research and had been disappointed with the result. Instead he debated which of his clients might like to make an investment in advanced industrial technology. No face sprang to mind, other than that of Grieff & Hammer's senior partner, whose response to a proposal that the firm invest £2.6 million in a company as unmarketable as Laserbeam was liable to make the peals of St Mary's sound like the tolling of the bells of doom.

'They'll have to be booked somewhere,' Oakes repeated.

Harry took the unwelcome news on board. 'If we don't have the money, the only place we can put them is CHIT,' he decided.

'If CHIT writes a cheque for £2.6 million, the bank will bounce it higher than the dome of St Paul's,' said Priestley with even more confidence than usual.

Harry thought about praying for an upsurge in orders for men's suits for Easter, but he was unable to persuade himself that the US cavalry was going to ride over the hills in time to boost the price of Laserbeam's shares before somebody had to pay for them. It was one thing for CHIT to buy the up-and-running Watson's for a million, or Priestley's office, Harold Antony's offshore securities venture and the Earl of St Edmunds' public relations firm for a few grand apiece; but £2.6 million for a minority stake in a company whose principal asset was an unproven research project was of an entirely different order.

'I don't suppose the money from the rights issue?' Oakes asked, without his usual confidence. The proceeds were due by the end of April, in time to enable CHIT to complete the takeover of Watson's.

'That won't make much of a dent in £2.6 million,' Priestley said. He turned to Harry and asked, 'Do you reckon they'd agree to take staged payments?'

'No chance,' Harry shook his head. 'And we can't buy the shares for CHIT, as the deal would have to be reported to the board.'

The others nodded. They had all seen the item on the agenda for next week's board meeting that had been circulated that morning: current status of investments. It wouldn't do to add another to the list. They scratched their heads searching for somewhere to lodge the Laserbeam shares – temporarily.

'I wonder whether I could get my friends at Ernest Burke to warehouse them for the time being?' Priestley thought aloud. What was a merchant bank for, he asked himself, if not to accommodate those who brought it business?

'If Andy tells Jamie they're for CHIT?' Harry asked himself out loud. Jamie Tulloch, a director of Ernest Burke, had shown himself in the past to be as amenable as he was affable.

'Or at any rate some of them. We'll tell him they can have a few for their clients while we do a deal on the rest,' suggested Oakes.

Tulloch's reputation proved justified. He readily acceded to Priestley's suggestion that Ernest Burke take delivery of the Laserbeam shares pending a decision on their final resting place. So when the resolution was put to the CHIT board that although a number of unprofitable investments had been made, particularly in Australian mining, these holdings should all be retained as they were no longer worth selling, Harry Griffin, Andy Oakes and Jolyon Priestley were able to hold their hands up without embarrassment. In any case, the directors soon had another matter to divert their attention.

'I wish to advise the board that I shall shortly be living in Paris,' Harry announced under any other business. 'I shall be opening an office there for Grieff & Hammer. We take the view that now we're about to join the Common Market, the future lies in Europe,' he linked his firm's decision grandly with that of the nation. 'May I propose that in view of his experience we ask Harold to advise us on setting up an overseas subsidiary for this company?'

While Harry's colleagues digested the implications of his announcement, it fell to Priestley to make a practical proposal. 'If I may be permitted to make a suggestion, Chairman,' he said, 'Harry is a substantial shareholder. Should he not appoint an alternate director to represent his interests in his absence?'

Harry nodded with well-rehearsed sagacity. A director's duty was, he said, to represent not one shareholder but the shareholders as a whole. Nevertheless, he would be delighted to recommend Mr James Tulloch, a director of Ernest Burke, to stand in his shoes and offer the benefit of his substantial financial experience should the board so wish. It was hard to resist the force of his argument, and in any event his colleagues were in no mood to do so.

The appointment was never confirmed, perhaps because the attention of the board of Ernest Burke began to focus on another matter. The disposal of the Laserbeam shares proved easier to talk about than to achieve. Jamie Tulloch found himself invited by his chairman to explain why the bank had spent £2,600,000 on a share stake in a company nobody had ever heard of, on behalf of clients whose identity appeared to be uncertain, but who at all events seemed either unwilling or unable to pay for their investment themselves. Did Tulloch have any thoughts on the matter? asked the chairman.

That morning Tulloch had read in the newspaper of President Nixon's reaction to reports of an attempted burglary in a Washington apartment building. It seemed to fit this case. 'It is a bizarre affair. I admit there may have been some technical violations,' he plagiarised the president shamelessly. 'I reckon the shares pretty definitely belong to CHIT – or if not now, soon. There's a mutual put and call option. I'm pretty sure it's morally binding. I'll have a word with Griffin and Oakes. Or Priestley. Something will be resolved.'

Having committed himself thus far, Tulloch was not easily won over to the notion that the Laserbeam shares could conveniently be left to fester in Ernest Burke's asset ledger. And when the Earl of St Edmunds was told of CHIT's morally binding put and call option, he was no more amused than the directors of Ernest Burke. He knew enough to be aware that in the absence of a board resolution not even the signatures of two directors could commit CHIT to buy the Laserbeam shares. But he also knew that Ernest Burke would not willingly keep them, that neither Harry Griffin nor Jolyon Priestley, let alone Andy Oakes, had the cash to pay for them, and that if CHIT refused to complete the transaction it could bring a messy lawsuit on itself. Win or lose, this would do his reputation no good. So CHIT must pay now for as many Laserbeam shares as it could afford, and it must pay later for the rest. Of one thing he was sure: Harry Griffin was too deeply implicated to deal with Ernest Burke on CHIT's behalf. Jolyon Priestley, he decided, was not. As Harry had suspected, the Earl of St Edmunds was not such a duffer after all.

Nevertheless, a far from chastened Harry enthused to Sybil that evening as they packed their boxes in preparation for their move to Paris, CHIT had at least truly become a Commercial Holdings Investment Trust. It owned businesses in the building aggregates and leisure industries, service companies in the public and private sectors, and investments in property and securities. It had offices at Euston and Bethnal Green, and it owned assets in Sussex, Norfolk and Scotland, not to mention places even farther afield. It had liabilities too; but the rights issue, in which Grieff & Hammer had shown its confidence as the principal underwriter, meant that these would be borne by an ever-growing army of shareholders. CHIT had doubled in size and had engaged expert management. It would soon hold a key stake on the cutting edge of technology.

Once he had sheltered his affairs in his new domicile, away from the prying eyes of the Inspector of Taxes, he'd soon show Guy Magnus who'd be first to have a million clear, Harry told himself contentedly.

9

'Gentlemen,' the Earl of St Edmunds addressed the board of Britton Estates on a drizzly October morning. The board meeting of CHIT, he knew from his diary, was after lunch. Pity it weren't the other way round. The CHIT people fed and wined their visitors with more ... respect. 'Gentlemen,' repeated the earl: 'main item on today's agenda, proposal for merger of the company with, er, Commercial Holdings Investment Trust. See from your briefing papers, comes recommended by our merchant bankers,' he consulted his own papers, '... er, Thruston Cutwell, supported by our stockbrokers, Tanquery Taylor Tealeafe. Need hardly add, seems a natural marriage.' He paused deliberately, without looking up. If the expected objection were to arise, it were better that it should do so now, and be dealt with promptly.

'Natural? Perhaps, chairman, you might care to elaborate.' Thomas Goodman's tone was deceptively bland. The senior partner of the company's lawyers, Goodman was nobody's fool. His well-cut suit hid an athlete's physique, his high forehead a forensic mind. His dark, alert eyes peered shrewdly at the Earl of St Edmunds over rimless half-moon spectacles.

The earl decided to take the high ground in order to defer confrontation until the territory had been thoroughly reconnoitred. 'Marriage,' he ignored the adjective in favour of the noun, 'an institution much maligned nowadays, but based on mutual respect and support. Commercial Holdings has given us no less. One word from our brokers when our shares were under pressure, and support us it did. Now its board proposes to make flesh of our ties, to bind its destiny to ours. I tell you, gentlemen, good marriages are made in heaven, and this is one of 'em.'

'I do not doubt your sincerity, Chairman,' Goodman interjected coolly; 'but do our business activities not differ somewhat? We are a property company. This paper says they own a variety of businesses as varied as oil services, gravel pits, financial services, public relations – though I seem to recall you once suggesting, Chairman, that we might become involved in something of the kind – and, if I understand it properly, boating?' Having reached this far, Goodman was unsure whether to be proud or ashamed of having failed to express his real opinion: that CHIT was a load of tat.

'Above all, its investment in Laserbeam offers the opportunity to reap the rewards of modern technology,' continued the earl, brushing off the interruption as no more than a display of ill-breeding.

'Whereas we know little about anything except property.'

'If I understand rightly, this is precisely the ground for the recommendation of our financial advisers. Diversification. No spread of interests to protect us if the property market turns down. Merger with Commercial Holdings would provide that protection in one fell swoop.'

'Look at its balance sheet. It's unhealthily short of working capital for its businesses, while we've been husbanding our resources to pay for our future developments.'

'Cash flow: that's what their trading companies provide, and what we lack. And once we're together, if we need a few bob we can sell a few shares from their portfolio. I say it's a jolly good merger. No, Goodman,' the earl waved an airy hand, 'heard your views; how about the others?'

The other directors had already gauged the sense of the meeting. They had in mind not only the views of their colleagues but the presence of the merchant bankers, stockbrokers and corporate lawyers lined up menacingly at the far end of the table. You didn't board a gravy train to tell the driver, conductor, signalman and chief steward they didn't know where they were heading. That wasn't how you got yourself invited on to the next gravy train.

'Point of order, Chairman,' insisted Goodman; 'do three directors not have interests that preclude them from taking part in the decision?'

The earl had come prepared. He deferred to the far end of the table, where Thruston Cutwell's in-house corporate lawyer adjusted his horn-rimmed spectacles.

'Those interests must be declared, no doubt; as to the rest, they may feel they shouldn't vote, but there's no reason why they shouldn't take part in the discussion,' the latter pronounced.

Goodman shrugged. If he had had the other directors on their own he might have persuaded them to vote the merger down, but in this gathering the odds were stacked hopelessly against him.

'All in favour of accepting the CHIT share offer?' asked the earl. He, Priestley and Charteris kept their hands below the table as all but Goodman raised theirs. 'Any against? Good to see a unanimous vote,' beamed the earl, ignoring the abstention. 'We will meet next as members of a united Britton Estates and CHIT board. I take it as a compliment to us that the CHIT board is to consider a resolution to name the merged company Britton Trust.' His tone left no doubt that unanimity would be achieved and the resolution passed without any unseemly display of indiscipline.

The CHIT board meeting that afternoon was less contentious. In the absence of a compliant alternate director from Ernest Burke, Harry Griffin had slipped back into the country to attend in person. Since the Laserbeam debacle he had reconciled himself to the idea that it was better to be a minority share-holder in a company with investments in Watson's, Laserbeam and Britton Estates than a controlling shareholder in a company which was unable to meet its commitment to pay a firm of stockbrokers in which he was a partner. When he read that weekend of the merger of Mallard with Universal Credit, his view was reinforced. If that incorrigible punter Guy Magnus was taking his money off the table, was it not time to plan the removal of his own?

Jolyon Priestley was equally keen on the merger. After Harry Griffin's departure for Paris, he had been left on his own to haggle with Ernest Burke over the terms on which CHIT would take up the Laserbeam shares. The merchant bank had insisted CHIT pay interest from the date of purchase and a special fee for its forbearance, and that it settle an outstanding fee account. Priestley had reluctantly handed over a cheque for £900,000 and taken delivery of a first tranche of shares. At this point CHIT had run through its entire cash resources, with the result that the position was still not fully unwound when the merger with Britton Trust was mooted. He hoped that as managing director of the merged company he could authorise payment for the Laserbeam shares from their new associate's carefully husbanded bank balances. Meanwhile he locked CHIT's chequebooks inside his private safe.

Each of the other directors had his own agenda. Harold Antony reckoned the enlarged company would have greater scope for playing the pan-European stock exchanges. Andy Oakes was so thrilled to earn an underwriting com-mission on the merger that he put up both hands. The Earl of St Edmunds was content not only that the good offices of one of the companies he chaired would help the other avoid embarrassment with its merchant bank, but also that in spite of having only half the number of lunches to attend, the other CHIT directors insisted he keep both honoraria on the grounds that the board he would be chairing was twice its current size.

'Should not such a matter also be considered by the board of Britton Trust?' he had asked himself, before satisfying his scruples with the answer: 'I think not. It is, after all, CHIT which is making the offer for Britton Estates. A resolution passed by that board will therefore suffice.'

Jolyon Priestley's troubles worsened when Thomas Goodman was appointed to the board of the merged Britton Trust. Wishing to learn more about its new partner, the lawyer asked to inspect CHIT's minute books. These contained little to enlighten him. There were no resolutions approving its acquisitions, nor even on the formation of its offshore companies. There was no reference at all to Laserbeam, and though he saw a cryptic report that interest was mounting on a loan from Ernest Burke, he could find no record of the loan's authorisation or its purpose. Further investigation showed this to be not the only unauthorised loan; nor had any been revealed in the offer document for Britton Estates. So when CHIT's shareholders had voted to approve the merger, they had been told of their company's assets but not of its liabilities. If he, as a director of Britton Estates, had no idea how much CHIT was worth, how on earth could they? He thought of asking its auditors for an explanation, but as there was no minute either of their appointment or of their predecessors' resignation he knew he would be wasting his time. Instead he wrote to the chairman setting out his concerns and asking for an interview.

Much saddened by Goodman's letter, which he felt obliged to regard as a threat to the unity of the board, the Earl of St Edmunds invited his colleague to his private office for a cup of tea.

'Know those CHIT chaps well,' he told him. 'Bright fellows, good traders, honourable men. Won't hear a wrong word against 'em. Shrewd judge of a deal, Griffin. Dashed sloppy with the paperwork, I'll grant, but straight as a die. Priestley: sharp eye for a profit, make a lot of money with him; just needs a clerk to keep the books in order. Antony and Oakes: jolly smart market operators, in the know when opportunities are to be had. What d'you want? Have the books apple pie and lose money? Keep your eye on the ball, old chap, not ...' he waved a lordly hand at Goodman's letter, '... on this stuff. I'll keep my eye on them. Trust me. No marriage can survive without trust.'

If Goodman was a good lawyer, he was also a loyal subject. A peer of the realm was not to be mistrusted. If not fully understood, he should be given the benefit of the doubt. For the time being.

When Goodman had departed, the earl called Priestley. 'No good leaving this Laserbeam matter where it is, old son,' he told him. 'Got to resolve it before Goodman kicks up another stink. You're stuck with a line of shares that ain't paying a dividend. Can't afford to carry it much longer, let alone pay for the rest of them. Don't have the cash; bank's not going to lend it to you. You three villains are going to have to do better. Any bright ideas?'

Priestley's mind had not been idle. 'Laserbeam owns the rights to a process with exciting prospects,' he said. 'If we own the whole company instead of a minority stake, we'll have a quality earnings base. Our shares will be re-rated.'

The earl considered this revelation. If Priestley was right and Britton Trust were to own Laserbeam entirely, the profits from Watson's, the Norfolk Broads operation, the public relations business, even the dividends from Antony's venture, might all be valued as if the company were a growth stock. That would be jolly good news for Berry St Edmunds. He fancied he was already a pretty successful company chairman; soon he'd also be chairman of a pretty successful company. However, his knowledge of Britton Trust's financial position told him it had no cash to buy the rest of the Laserbeam shares.

'We'd have to pay for it with shares,' he pointed out. Then he reflected further. 'But the market's already had a bellyful of our stock,' he observed less happily.

'By then the merger will be through, we'll have changed the company's name and we'll have mapped out a clear corporate strategy,' countered Priestley.

The earl fiddled with his pen as he stared at the darkening skyline. Unable to match Priestley's confidence in the market's reaction to yet another share issue, he nevertheless had no alternative plan. But he promised himself that next time the offer document would be more carefully prepared. He couldn't afford any more misunderstandings with Goodman. He would get the auditors in – after his return from the Algarve. Life shouldn't be all business and no pleasure, and the Cabo do Bimbo project was an ideal way to combine the two. His and Bertie Brimpton's own golf club: no members, a few agreeable guests and the rest holiday-makers paying green fees and villa rentals. As soon as the contract for the access road was signed, they'd exercise their option to buy the site. And as soon as Priestley had given it the once-over, Britton Trust would provide the finance.

The earl called his secretary on the intercom and told her to book flights to Faro for him and Priestley. Yes, First Class.

'On CHIT's account as usual, your lordship?'

'Britton Trust's from now on,' he corrected her. It was to prove an unfortunate decision.

10

On a late spring morning in 1973 Harry Griffin sat in Jolyon Priestley's office reviewing the shareholder register of Britton Trust. For the past year he had been content to remain in France to establish his tax domicile, though from time to time he may have returned on the boat train without having his passport stamped – to avoid confusing the authorities, he explained to his friends. Now there was no need for subterfuge, as he had no intention of staying in England for as long as the six months in a year that would put him back on the register of taxpayers. That would also have given his creditors time to find him. For Harry's cash flow troubles had refused to go away. Previously indifferent to whether she freshened her wardrobe in Bond Street or the Faubourg Saint-Honoré, Sybil had recently transferred her loyalty to the boutiques of the rue d'Antibes in Cannes without any discernible economy. She was spending as if her husband's fortunes were thriving when he knew they were foundering. As he read in his newspaper of the prime minister's strictures against the unpleasant and unacceptable face of capitalism, Harry made the heartfelt prayer that some of its rewards would rub off on him.

Harry's purchase of Archie Laws' shares had given him control of CHIT. But as each acquisition was financed by issuing more stock, his holding had been watered down. When CHIT offered its shares for Britton Estates the resultant company, Britton Trust, had nearly 7 million shares in issue. While his holdings in it, both declared and undeclared, had a stock market value of more than double the £500,000 he had borrowed to acquire them, they now comprised less than 8 per cent of Britton Trust's equity. He might be the largest shareholder, but that was all. The share register told him Priestley, Antony and Oakes each had a substantial stake; but even as a group the former CHIT directors owned less than a quarter of the company's capital. The former directors of Britton Estates held almost as much. As a result, the company was no longer under his, nor even his friends', control.

This would not have caused Harry undue concern had Jolyon Priestley been in sole charge of the merged company. Priestley had himself been led to believe that on completion of the merger he would be managing director of Britton Trust. However their new colleagues, wishing to provide a counterweight to his less-than-orthodox management style, had insisted on the appointment of a joint managing director. A bustling, nuts-and-bolts manager in his middle thirties, Alan Palliser was far too orderly an executive for Priestley's comfort.

Palliser's arrival had been as unwelcome to Harry as it had been to Priestley. Where the joint managing director should, like Priestley, have been on the lookout for lucrative deals, he had persisted in ruining Harry's visits to London with unhelpful queries on shares CHIT had taken up from him when his investments had turned sour.

'CHIT's ancient history. Your responsibility is for Britton Trust,' Harry had protested.

'As far as you're concerned, CHIT was for stuffing. The good was for you, the bad was for CHIT,' Palliser had persisted. As if this were not enough, he made heavy weather of Harry's loan account and constantly queried his expense claims, without taking into account the scale of his investment in the company.

Harry had objected to this unfriendly attitude; for such was his devotion to duty, he claimed, that even when he and Sybil unwound at Annabel's he never ceased to seek opportunities to develop Britton Trust's interests. As for the shirts and ties, did the board expect him to be unsuitably attired on duty? The flowers? To show no gratitude to his hostesses? The Diners Club account? Not to return corporate hospitality? In that case, retorted Palliser, the thirteen grand of expenses Harry had claimed must make him the most devoted after-hours director in corporate history. When Harry agreed this might well be the case, Palliser replied that he would ask the chairman to put the matter on the agenda of the next board meeting.

Harry felt entitled to ask whether CHIT had not taken over Britton Estates rather than the other way round. If Britton Trust was no longer willing to take up his unlucky share deals, repay his personal expenses and save him tax, of what earthly use was it to him? It was, to be frank, a load of crap. It was time to cash in his chips. On reaching this conclusion, he quickly revised his opinion. Britton Trust was an asset-rich growth company in which he owned a valuable equity interest.

He determined to clear the air with the chairman. The Earl of St Edmunds was a jolly good sort, not one to stop the other chaps on the board from having fun. He had proved extremely understanding about them parking broken-down shares without feeding the meter. It would be surprising were he not equally sympathetic on the minor matter of their expense accounts. Harry told Sharon to make an appointment with the earl at a time convenient to Priestley, Oakes and Antony, as he would be taking them along.

When the delegation arrived, the Earl of St Edmunds was contending with his own difficulty. The day after his return from the trip he had made to Portugal with Priestley, he had found the note from Palliser asking that the board discuss the matter of directors' expenses. Though the earl sometimes complained that his memory was beginning to fail him, it was not easy to forget an expense claim he himself had lodged not twenty-four hours ago.

'Dashed awkward,' he acknowledged the sensitivity of the issue when Harry had finished setting out his grievances. 'Don't want any misunderstandings. Must maintain harmony in the boardroom.'

'Couldn't agree more, your lordship. Trouble is, if there's any suggestion the board isn't united, the shares are bound to fall,' Oakes gave the market view.

'It may be too late to do anything about that,' added Priestley gloomily.

The earl considered the remark carefully. He had a substantial investment to protect. He had cashed in some of it when the merger took place, but he still owned over 250,000 shares in Britton Trust.

'If the board has no faith in my integrity, I might just as well resign and flog my shares to the highest bidder,' Harry said softly, as if to himself rather than as an open threat. 'You'd think major shareholders should be treated with more respect,' he joined his companions in his cause. He put pen to paper, listing their holdings. 'I mean, 2 million shares is hardly to be sneezed at,' he said when he had finished totting up the numbers. 'Worth four million quid at today's price.'

'Trouble is,' Priestley added, 'if you tried selling that number on the market, you'd have it run against you.'

The conversation was taking a turn Andy Oakes found impossible to resist. 'You wouldn't sell on the market,' he put the professional view.

'You'd place 'em,' agreed Harold Antony, his jowls shuddering.

'And get far more than two quid,' Oakes continued. 'Maybe two fifty. After all, you'd be providing a launching pad for a bid. There aren't many companies you can buy thirty per cent of in one hit.'

The earl felt it was time to inject a note of caution. He couldn't stop them doing whatever they set their minds on, but their enthusiasm was running a trifle strong for his taste. At the same time, he didn't want to be left out of the picture. 'Discretion, gentlemen. We have colleagues. Can't afford goings-on.' He paused before continuing just loud enough for the others to hear, 'Other hand, no harm putting out a feeler.'

Oakes put out a feeler. He wouldn't have been Two-Commissions Oakes if he put it out to anyone else but Lewis White of Consolidated Finance. Oakes reckoned White would spot a ready profit in Britton Trust. Ready profits were becoming harder to come by daily.

But when the two met, White's response to the price Oakes asked was uncompromising. 'Two fifty, bollocks!' he exclaimed. 'That's a selling price, not a buying price. They're only two quid in the market. Might bid you two twenty.'

Oakes rejected the figure without hesitation. 'I'd get that off Jon Traill. Clive Salmon will pay me two thirty.'

White was wise to the ploy. As Salmon was the best bidder in the market, Oakes had probably tried him already. 'Suit yourself,' he said. But Traill was another matter. 'We might go a penny or two higher to keep Jon out,' he added, 'but I'm not getting into a Dutch auction. Come back to me if you think again.'

'I like doing business with you, Lewis,' Oakes lied. 'Give me a piece of the action on the sale and I'll do it for two twenty-five.'

'Put it in writing,' White tested him. 'I'm not having you go away and use my bid as a marker for others to shoot at.'

Oakes hesitated for barely a second, took two sheets of Grieff & Hammer letterhead from his briefcase, placed a sheet of carbon paper between them and wrote for barely a minute. Retaining the copy, he handed the top sheet to White.

White stared at the letter in disbelief. 'You undertake to deliver 2,000,000 shares in Britton Trust in seven days ...?'

'Conditional on the agreement of the interested parties. Don't worry, it's a formality. I already have their word on it.'

'Does the Britton Trust board know about this?'

'Not as such,' Oakes admitted.

'Then you must report it immediately.' White made sure that Oakes was aware of his fiduciary duty as a director. As for himself, he had no intention of being caught red-handed lifting shares with intent. 'You must call a meeting of the board to inform them of the position. I'll attend,' he added. 'I'll call the chairman and suggest I be invited to join the board.'

Oakes feared the conversation was getting out of control. 'Tell him you're just taking a minority stake as a long-term investment and want to reassure the board as to your intentions,' he pleaded.

The next day's emergency meeting of the Britton Trust board was a far from happy affair. Oakes introduced Lewis White and presented the chairman with a copy of the letter he had written to him. The earl read it out loud, without giving any hint that he had prior knowledge of the matter.

'Bit of a bolt from the blue, Oakes,' he commented when he had finished. 'Didn't know you had so many. Sorry to lose you and all that. Shouldn't you have warned us?'

Thomas Goodman was growing angrier by the second. 'It's nothing short of scandalous!' he protested. 'You're proposing to hand over effective control of the company without a full bid. It's against stock exchange rules. If you proceed, I shall go straight to the Takeover Panel and register the strongest possible protest.'

'We're entitled to know the identity of the sellers, chairman,' said Palliser.

'Quite right, quite right,' agreed the Earl of St Edmunds.

Harry decided to come clean. 'You can hardly blame me for wanting to sell. It's become perfectly clear I'm no longer trusted by one of the managing directors,' he said in a tone which made it clear that such a slur was unwarranted. 'But you can't accuse me of selling control. I only have half a million shares.'

'I presume you're selling too?' Goodman pointed his finger accusingly at Oakes, his penetrating glare shaking the latter's confidence.

'Er ... ' Oakes looked round at Harry for guidance. Receiving no help, he turned towards Jolyon Priestley.

'Don't look at me,' said Priestley guiltily as the former Britton Estates directors stared at him. 'I mean, if it were considered in the best interests of the company, I might consider selling part of my holding – naturally I would, if the board wanted me to.'

The stares turned their attention to Harold Antony.

'Absolutely not. I haven't agreed to any such thing,' he said firmly. Then, more hesitantly, 'That doesn't necessarily mean I wouldn't be a willing seller – under the right conditions, of course.'

The earl looked round the table. There was a pregnant silence. The next move must come from him.

'Ahem,' he cleared his throat. 'As you'd expect, gentlemen, I am not a party to these undertakings. First I've heard of them, to be honest. Wouldn't dream of such a thing. Unless, as Priestley says – how d'you put it, Priestley? – best interests of the company and all that. Rely on me then, naturally.'

Lewis White could hardly believe his ears. He knew he'd have a struggle on his hands if he tried to enforce the terms of Oakes's letter. The man simply could not deliver what he'd promised. Nevertheless, the atmosphere of the meeting told him he should buy as many shares in Britton Trust as he could lay his hands on. Divided boards created profitable opportunities. Apologising for any misunderstanding he might have caused, he made a strategic withdrawal.

Though Harry Griffin, Jolyon Priestley and the Earl of St Edmunds soon decided there was more than one way to cook a goose and held on to their shares, their colleague would not have been even One-Commission Oakes, nor Harold Antony a man of his word, had Lewis White failed to receive some reward for his pains. Within a few days their combined efforts produced a million shares and Consolidated Finance held a fifteen per cent stake in Britton Trust.

Harry had been disappointed at the outcome of the board meeting. Even so, he knew that if he sold his shares to Consolidated Finance, Thomas Goodman would go running to the Takeover Panel. So he made his apologies to Lewis White and asked to be allowed to withdraw his offer. Having broken with his colleagues, however, he concluded that it was time to cash in his chips and sever his links with the company. But while the stock market remained in the doldrums, the sale of a substantial holding in one with such diverse and unattractive business interests as Britton Trust seemed an unlikely prospect.

Nonetheless, he had set up his marker. The board knew his stake was up for grabs. If the directors wanted the company to be proof against takeover, they had better make sure his shares were in friendly hands. And what friendlier hands could there be than their own? All they had to do was to come up with the cash. But how many of them could put their hands on a million pounds in ready cash or borrowing facilities? Harry knew there was only one.

John Charteris had missed the crucial board meeting, but bad news travels fast. It was not long before the call came.

'It's time we talked,' said Charteris tersely.

'Anything in particular?' Harry replied disingenuously.

'I'll be in your office tomorrow at ten.' Charteris spoke with the certainty of one who had already checked Harry's diary with Sharon.

The following day his erect figure marched into Harry's office on the stroke of ten o'clock. 'You wish to sell your shares. I'm in a position to buy some of them,' he said without waiting for the coffee to arrive, his pale face and tired grey eyes revealing signs of strain.

'It's all or nothing,' replied Harry. 'I'm not prepared to be locked in to a company whose board has no confidence in me.'

'Impossible.' Charteris was equally firm. 'I don't have that kind of money.'

Harry recognised a powerful argument when he heard one. If true, this one was unassailable, other than by Sybil. 'How many are you prepared to buy?' he asked.

Charteris had spent the night asking himself that very question. His bank had agreed to lend him up to half a million pounds, provided he pledged the shares he bought as security. Though he was not a poor man it was a tight deal, for the dividends on his total shareholding would only just cover the interest on the bank's loan. However, if he wanted Britton Trust to remain independent, he had little choice but to buy at least half of Harry Griffin's shares.

'I'll go as far as 200,000 at £2,' he offered, deliberately casual, smoothing his carefully parted grey hair.

'Not the number and not the price,' said Harry, smelling a wounded animal.

Charteris sensed there was a deal to be done. No longer was it all or nothing. 'How much do you want?' he asked. 'Bearing in mind that the higher the price, the harder it will be for me to justify the number.'

'You know what Lewis White was prepared to pay.'

Charteris frowned, his bushy eyebrows almost meeting. 'That included a premium for control. In any case, his offer's no longer on the table,' he pointed out.

'Two twenty-five is the lowest price I'll take.' His bet with Guy Magnus flashed through Harry's mind. It gave him a useful pretext. 'And I won't sell fewer than 450,000. Less than a million pounds and I'm not interested. If you haven't got it, you've no business being at the table.'

Charteris shook his head. 'Too bad,' he said, and began to rise to his feet.

Harry saw he had gone too far. 'I'm not saying I *will* sell fewer,' he changed his tune; 'but if you make me a sensible offer, the least I can do is to give you the courtesy of considering it.'

'They're 205p in the market,' Charteris replied. 'I'll offer you 210 for 250,000 shares. On two conditions,' he added. 'First, you and Oakes must resign from the board. Second, you'll have to agree not to sell the rest for twelve months. There'd be no point otherwise.'

Harry weighed up the proposition. His seat on the board was of minor importance: once his colleagues learned of Oakes's dealings with Consolidated Finance, his position had no longer been tenable. Half a million pounds was more than tempting: it would clear his loan account with Britton Trust – provided he said nothing to Sybil. He'd still be stuck with over 300,000 shares for the next twelve months, though; and other than through Harold Antony he'd know little of what was going on with his residual investment. He weighed up the chances of selling his entire stake.

Charteris guessed from the silence that he was almost there. Had Harry an alternative? Was there another buyer? He reckoned not.

'What if the company receives a bid?' Harry asked, confirming Charteris's hopes.

'You won't be able to accept it.'

'That's absurd. Suppose the board were to recommend acceptance?'

'That would be different. I would be out too.'

'If you want the conditions, you'll have to pay me 220,' Harry tried.

Each looked down the barrel of the other's gun. It was apparent that both would have to give something away to allow the other to leave the table with honour.

'Two fifteen?' they asked as one, each relaxing as the other nodded unsmiling acceptance. The deal was done.

Harry spent the return trip to the Cote d'Azur thinking through the implications of their agreement. If he was to cash in the rest of his shares, a bid would have to be made for the company. Then all he'd need to do for his obligation not to sell his shares to lapse would be to wait until the board recommended the highest offer. And when that happy occurrence materialised, he would be a real millionaire. Ahead of Guy.

But how to put Britton Trust in play? It was a question that was to exercise Harry's mind greatly during the coming weeks.

11

It had concerned Guy Magnus not a jot that once he had completed the sale of Mallard to Universal Credit he would no longer have anything to do with the company he had developed from a shell to a highly-valued industrial holding company. His plans for the future left no room for sentiment. Whenever he had pulled off a deal for Mallard the profits had gone to its shareholders. He had benefited only to the extent that the value of his own shareholding had risen. But no amount of clever dealing was going to keep a share price going up when the stock market was on its way down. Public companies, like shares, were for buying and selling.

True, most of the vehicles Guy chose to keep were also public companies; but their shares were more tightly held than Mallard. Ludgate Investments was smaller and his stake in it proportionately greater. St Paul's Property was smaller still. Each served its purpose, for Ludgate owned twenty per cent of St Paul's, and St Paul's owned ten per cent of Ludgate. This suited Guy, for while each held shares in the other he could keep control of both. As for Westchurch, which was even smaller than St Paul's, that was not a public company at all; for Guy believed that certain investments were best suited to private vehicles whose value was not affected by the vagaries of market sentiment and whose activities were not bound by its petty rules and regulations.

The complexity of these arrangements posed Guy no problem, for his flexible mind worked best in an environment of labyrinthine cross-shareholdings. His corporate organisation was designed to cope with any proposition that presented itself. Depending on its size, nature and relative attraction, he would determine whose shareholders it suited best: those of Ludgate, St Paul's or Westchurch. Or indeed those of his smallest company, Bijou, in which only a select few had shares, for Guy guarded his privacy jealously. Westchurch was his favourite: he would use it to acquire investments that were too good for Ludgate or St Paul's, but too large for Bijou.

While he supervised the growth of his corporate pyramid, Guy needed to find an enthusiastic dealer who was bright enough to identify the right investments for Westchurch. As he gazed out of his office window in search of inspiration, a high-flying aeroplane flew out of the bright November sun, cutting a twin powder trail across the clear blue sky above St Paul's Cathedral.

'Got it!' exclaimed Guy.

Danny Gilbert had been a mere seventeen years of age when Lewis White took him on as a junior at Consolidated Finance. However, White had become so impressed by Danny's keenness and his eye for a deal that before long he had put him in charge of the investment fund Guy Magnus had previously managed.

Since then their paths had crossed but once. Back in 1969, having tucked Mallard securely under his belt, Guy had gone in search of further prey. Not every foray had been successful; but failure exacted a fearsome price. On one occasion his researches had identified a run-down aircraft manufacturer which owned a runway that would enjoy an enhanced value as a private housing estate. Its shares stood at 30 shillings in a tight market. Guy called his broker and put in a buying order at 31 shillings and sixpence. When no shares were offered, he asked why.

'Danny Gilbert's broker has been in the market offering 32 and 6. He's picked up everything going. Gilbert must have got wind something was up,' he was told.

Guy called Danny Gilbert. 'You little bastard! You've no right to interfere in my deal,' he screamed down the line. 'Those shares are mine. I want them, and I want them now.'

When Gilbert refused to oblige on the grounds that it was a free country, Guy called his switchboard operator to his office.

'I want you to call Consolidated Finance and keep calling them on every line we have, and keep all the calls open until they come up engaged,' he ordered her.

'But that will jam their switchboard,' she shook a professional head.

That suited Guy fine. No one hotted him and survived. While Consolidated Finance spent the day waiting for the post office to repair its switchboard, the runway was vacant and ready for take-off. By nightfall it was ready for takeover. Once a would-be counter-bidder had been bought off with the part of the business that made the aircraft – but not the part that enabled them to take to the air – its fate was sealed.

When his telephone rang three years later, Danny Gilbert was busy recording the details of a share purchase he had just agreed. Danny was smart, enthusiastic and fresh faced. A helmet of thick brown hair covered his ears and neck and fell over his forehead in a tidy fringe. Since his early run-in with Guy Magnus he had become Consolidated Finance's most successful fund manager, responsible for a fund running into millions. When Danny Gilbert dealt, brokers listened and jobbers moved prices.

Told that Guy Magnus was on the line, Gilbert's antennae went into overdrive mode. Guy Magnus headed a number of small quoted companies. While these hardly met the investment criteria for inclusion in his fund, if Danny heard news that could make money for himself as well as for Consolidated Finance, that was okay by him – and by Lewis White, provided Danny made up his mind right away where to book the deal. White reckoned you didn't keep sharp dealers happy by paying them a good salary. You kept them happy by giving them a couple of telephones to keep in touch.

'Danny Gilbert,' he answered neutrally.

'Get your backside over here right away, Danny Gilbert,' replied Guy.

Not generally disrespectful to his elders, Danny reckoned that on this occasion a sharp response would be well-merited. He had deals to do. 'Fuck off, Guy Magnus,' he replied.

'What motor d'you fancy most, Danny Gilbert?' asked Guy.

Danny had been about to put the phone down, but his interest in the subject matter got the better of him. Conscience wrestled with temptation. It was an unequal battle. He already had an Aston Martin. He blurted out a truth which had recently been developing into an all-consuming aspiration: 'Porsche Carrera?'

'You've got five minutes to be in my office and you'll have one,' Guy stated firmly, slamming his phone down.

Danny's backside leapt from its swivel chair as if electrocuted. Yelling 'Call of nature!' at his nearest colleague, he hit the ground running. He'd think as he went. Unwilling to trust the lift, he scampered helter-skelter down the fire stairs. Gresham Street and Cheapside passed rapidly beneath his suede moccasins. He skirted St Paul's Cathedral at a gallop, thrusting tourists aside without regard to age, sex or photogenic appeal. As his heart thumped, he thanked God the road to Ludgate Circus was downhill and he knew Magnus's address. He dived across Fleet Street, leaving a couple of articulated lorries to interlock as they skidded to avoid him, raced into the secluded courtyard and through the front door of the elegant town house, took the stairs three at a time and crashed into Guy's office a full twenty seconds ahead of schedule.

'What kept you so long, Danny Gilbert?' asked Guy, feigning puzzlement at his visitor's apparent lack of urgency.

'Shit, Mr Magnus, did I make it?' was all Danny could gasp in reply. His decision to think on the way had been set aside.

'That depends,' said Guy. 'I only buy motor cars for people who do things for me. Like make money. Fancy the idea, Danny? And call me Guy, for God's sake.'

Danny was by now twenty years old, but this was still an age when the breath could be caught without the onset of a heart attack. His chest might be heaving but when his future prosperity was under consideration he could handle a simple question.

'Not sure,' he panted. He really meant 'No', but he was by nature an inquisitive young man. 'Got a job already.'

'Of course you have. But if you work with me you'll also be making money for yourself,' Guy qualified his opening gambit.

Danny pricked up his ears. He looked cautiously at Guy, interest mingled with suspicion. He was well paid; Lewis White looked after his brightest stars. Whereas Guy Magnus had a reputation. Ambitious, ruthless, unprincipled were the more complimentary epithets Danny had heard. It would be painful to get on the wrong side of him. On the other hand, he also had dynamism and charm, and was younger than you'd expect of so successful a man. It might be fun to be on his team. If nothing else, you'd learn from him. There was a limit to what you could learn at Consolidated Finance. Danny resolved to listen more.

'We'll start by building stakes in investment trusts. Ones that sell at a discount to NAV.'

Danny was unimpressed. All investment trusts sold at a discount to net asset value. Guy would have to try harder.

'Then you tell your friends to subscribe for shares at a premium.'

'If only they were that stupid.' Danny's scepticism turned into scorn.

'Wouldn't you if you had good reason to believe the trust would grow?'

'*If* I had.'

'And if you and everyone else bought its shares, wouldn't it?'

Danny thought about the proposition. 'I suppose.'

'And while it remained at a premium, its value would carry on growing. Exponentially. It would build up its share-buying potential.'

Danny was listening carefully now.

'And give you fire-power in the market.' Guy calculated he had told Danny enough about his strategy to whet his appetite. Having baited the hook, he must cast the fly. 'I've set up a private company, Westchurch. I want you to run it, Danny.'

The fund Danny managed for Consolidated Finance was as big as many a company. His expression told Guy he would have to try harder – much harder.

'Whatever Lewis pays you, I'll up it by fifty per cent.'

Danny carried on listening.

'And I'll give you twenty per cent of the company. So you'll deal in whatever takes your fancy and end up with twenty per cent of the profits.' Now he had Danny's full attention, Guy elaborated. He would deal in whatever took his fancy and Danny would have twenty per cent of those profits too. Losses were not mentioned.

Danny asked a few questions to show he was no pushover. That told Guy he was on the hook. At last Danny ran out of steam and sat in silence.

'What colour, Danny Gilbert?' Guy broke in after a while.

Danny stared at him uncomprehendingly.

'The Porsche, silly boy.'

'Oh, that. Red, I suppose.'

Guy picked up the telephone and asked for Lewis White at Consolidated Finance. 'Hi, Lewis,' he drawled. 'Thought I'd let you know Danny Gilbert's been round here … Looking for a job, of course. Said he was leaving you … What do you mean, when? Now, of course … What notice? … Listen, Lewis, if you heard what he said about you, you wouldn't want him within a hundred miles of you … Coming to us? Wouldn't touch him with a sterilised bargepole … Not at all, any time, Lewis. Bye.'

Danny found himself grinning. Then his smile disappeared. 'I want it in writing,' he insisted. 'I want a contract with everything you've promised me. And I want a put option on the shares if I leave – they'll be unsaleable if you have the majority. Or I'm going straight back to Lewis to tell him it was all a pack of lies.'

'I'll be happy to give you one, provided you stay with me for at least two years. I'm giving five per cent to Larry Callaghan,' Guy added casually. His trusted accountant would be keeping an eye on how Westchurch's profits were declared to the Inland Revenue.

Guy passed several stapled sheets across the table and pointed to a dotted line on the last page. 'Sign there,' he ordered. 'I've done so already. You share this office with me. Our secretary's through that door, the kitchen's at the end of the corridor. Nigel Holmes and Brian Proctor are one floor up; don't touch any of Brian's foul Gauloises; they're poison. Giles Kane's on the top floor doing Ludgate Investments. For the time being, anyhow.'

Working with Guy was even more fun than Danny expected. The agenda was driven by events; the more unexpected they were, the better.

'It's a scandal,' Guy declared a week after Danny's arrival. 'If nobody else'll do anything about it, I'll have to myself.'

He put down *The Times*, picked up the telephone and told his secretary to get him the curator of the Royal Academy. When he had been connected he said, 'I've just read the story about the calotype photographs. I want to come and see you right away.' He pushed the newspaper across his desk to Danny. 'Can you believe people are so mean-spirited?' he asked rhetorically as he rose purposefully from his chair and left the room.

Danny read the article. Its contents were hardly the stuff of the newspapers he usually read. The Royal Academy had been trying to sell some albums of photographs made by the calotype process in the 1840s. They were to have been auctioned by Sotheby's, but when *The Times* published a letter of protest they had been withdrawn. Now, it was reported, the Royal Academy had offered them to the National Portrait Gallery for £30,000 provided the money was raised without a public appeal, but had been turned down as the latter had no funds available. So what? thought Danny.

If he was unclear why Guy had been so cross, it did not take long for Danny to find out. By noon Guy was back in the office.

'I did it,' he said, dismissing whatever he had done as a matter of routine.

The following day Danny picked up Guy's copy of *The Times* and read that an anonymous charity had paid the entire £30,000 into the National Portrait Gallery Trust Fund. He saw he would have to read *The Times* regularly if he were to keep abreast of what his public-spirited boss was up to.

To Guy, the issue was simple. When Mallard had merged with Universal Credit, he had put part of the proceeds into a tax-exempt charitable trust. He was often asked for a donation to one cause or another. It was good to be in a position to help someone you might some day want to help you. The calotype photographs, being among the first ever produced, had to be saved for the nation. He'd found a way for the nation to help him save them. To share one's generosity with the tax man added much to the pleasure of giving.

Meanwhile he had found a dealer for Westchurch. Danny Gilbert was in for an exhilarating ride.

12

A few weeks after he sold his last shares in Universal Credit, Guy Magnus took delivery of the purchase he made with the proceeds. Every new home owner has his furnishing priority, and this was Guy's. He ran his hand over the rim of its oval cavity: it was smooth and cool to the touch. He had positioned it in the centre of the entrance hall, where his guests would form their first impression of his new home. As he had taken possession of the four-storey Queen Anne house a stone's throw from the Chelsea Embankment only that morning, it looked as if it had been laid waste by bailiffs.

Guy glared at the flock wallpaper, bare to the point of insult. There was work to be done. As he surveyed the walls he raised his hands to his eyes, forming frames with his fingers and thumbs. His beloved Kitaj drawings would add to the tone of the hall, but the pair needed a neighbour: the Ben Nicholson? Above the drawing-room mantelpiece his most treasured possession, Francis Bacon's blood-curdling Cardinal, would strike awe into his visitors as they passed through the tall double doors. He made a mental note to tell John Kasmin to find him a top Hockney: a double portrait, or a Splash? And a Lucien Freud male nude for the study, to declare his emancipation to his most intimate guests.

Guy had no doubt of his ability to select what was finest in contemporary British art; but to put together the collection he had in mind would cost money – real money. Cashing in on Mallard had been a well-timed move, but he had had to share the winnings with the other shareholders. So he was not yet really wealthy. He had little in the bank – you didn't put your money in banks, that wasn't what banks were for: they were there to lend you money. How else could he have purchased the forty-nine year lease on a street as fashionable as Cheyne Walk. And the small amount he did have was needed to buy furniture. To be in a position to buy the paintings he wanted, he needed to make himself rich – extravagantly rich.

In the meantime he had no seed-corn left to plough into his next business venture. Now Mallard had been sold, must he achieve his ambitions through Ludgate Investments? Or should he make use of his financial talent on a wider playing field? To such a question there was but one answer; for Ludgate had outside shareholders. He held a mere ten per cent stake through St Paul's Property and a further four per cent through Westchurch. Ludgate might give him firepower in the stock market, but that alone was not going to make him rich. Not extravagantly rich. He needed to create another vehicle better suited to making his fortune.

But it was not the creation of the corporate entity that posed Guy his greatest problem. Once he had identified his prey, structuring the vehicle with which to acquire it was child's play. Nor was it a matter of scale: in the current climate merchant banks were queuing up to lend you the money to buy any size of company you fancied. Provided you offered property as security. For where shares were paper, and their value could go up or down, property was real. Its value was rising steadily, and as supply was scarce and demand almost limitless, there was no reason why that should ever end. His next major challenge, he concluded without surprise, was to find an under-valued, property-rich company.

Guy stood back to savour once again the perfect proportions of his new possession, his eyes lingering over its rounded rim and shiny hollow interior with the pride of ownership. He slid his right hand inside it to caress the greenish patina of its polished contours. He was almost tempted to rest his haunches in its welcoming bowl: but he knew he mustn't. Even if the piece was pretty durable, it wasn't every day you went out and bought yourself a Henry Moore.

Just as he was setting himself his research task for the coming week, the telephone rang.

'Guy? How are you doing?' asked a voice he had not heard in months. From the poor quality of the sound it was apparently a fair distance away; from the tone, its owner was doing none too well himself. 'This is Harry,' followed the unnecessary announcement, so mournfully that Guy knew he had but to wait a few moments to be told of his friend's current need.

'I'm doing fine, thanks, Harry,' he replied to Harry's question without returning the courtesy. He was not in the mood to waste his breath on a question he knew was about to be answered. If Harry had emerged from seclusion, it was for a reason. He would soon be told what it was. 'Where in heaven's name are you?'

'I'm in Monte Carlo,' Harry confessed.

'You must be having fun, Harry. Weather nice?' Guy indulged in polite conversation while he waited to hear what it was that Harry was dying to tell him.

'No one around.'

'Sounds ideal for a second honeymoon.'

'Sybil's mother's in hospital. She's back in town looking after her father. I'm down here on my own.'

'What, no Sharon?' Guy took unfair advantage of his friend's misery.

Harry ignored the jibe. He had other things on his mind. The hour he had spent on the flight to Nice planning how to put Britton Trust into play so he could sell the shares he had not been able to sell to John Charteris was, he hoped fervently, about to bear fruit. But he knew he must proceed with care.

It was when he read of Universal Credit's latest results during his cab ride to Heathrow that Harry's lateral-thinking mind had turned to Guy Magnus. Having sold out to Clive Salmon, Guy would be on the lookout for the next turn of the wheel. Suppose his friend Harry cast his line on the waters? All that was needed was for Guy to nibble at the bait and the buoyant takeover market would do the rest. Either Consolidated Finance would make a full bid itself, or Lewis White would sell the 2 million shares he had bought on to someone else who would.

The more he thought about it, the more Harry saw an elegant symmetry in his strategy. It had been Guy who had put the investment in CHIT his way, though he must have known it was a dog; and it had been he, Harry, who had converted it into the holding in Britton Trust, of which he still owned more than 300,000 shares. Moreover, he'd have no need to take up Guy's challenge, the challenge of their bet, as Guy would take it up for him. How neat, if Guy himself were to be the catalyst of his victory; if it were his greed that brought Harry his first million and a free lunch at Maxim's. It needed no advanced mathematics to calculate that 325p per share would do the trick. If he played his cards right, the lunch bill he had picked up at the Connaught would be as good as a blue-chip investment.

So on his return to the apartment he had rented overlooking the harbour of Monte Carlo, Harry had put his thoughts into action and made his phone call.

'Don't suppose you'd fancy a long weekend down here yourself?' he asked.

'What for?' Guy replied. 'Loads to do here, people to see, deals to be done.'

From Harry's silence, Guy guessed he must have struck a raw nerve. Harry was doing no deals. But Harry lived for deals. He was never out of touch with the market for longer than an extended weekend, for fear of missing one. Something had gone wrong.

'Tell me about them,' Harry said at last.

'Do your own deals, Harry,' Guy twisted the knife.

Harry saw he would have to change his tune. 'I'm giving the stock market a break for the time being,' he said. 'Prices are still a bit hot for my liking. Thought I'd check up on a few property deals while I'm down on the coast. I've made a few interesting connections,' he added unconvincingly.

'Found anything good?' Guy was interested in all kinds of deals.

'Do your own deals, Guy,' Harry riposted; but his heart was not in it.

'So you don't have any,' Guy taunted him. But he guessed it might be fun to see what Harry was up to. 'I suppose I could drag myself down while the decorators are in,' he conceded. 'Yankee'll drive me – he'll give anything to watch the Monaco Grand Prix. I'll get out my Michelin and plan a route. I've been wanting to check out the *nouvelle cuisine* and see how the 1970 Romanée-Conti is developing.'

'Super!' Harry enthused. 'I'll ask Jolyon to lend me the *Gay Dog*.'

After he had put down the phone, Guy spent a few minutes asking himself about Harry's reason for making the call. Harry never called without a motive. If he didn't reveal it at the time, it was because he was weighing up your reaction before he did so. What was Harry weighing up his old pal Guy Magnus for now? Not a property deal; that wasn't his style. Harry was a share dealer. But there might be a property element to it. Could Harry be selling shares in a property company? He'd merged CHIT with one, Britton Estates, so he knew something about them. Of course, that was it! Britton Trust! The Earl of St Edmunds's company!

Guy wondered whether Harry knew that Harold Antony had taken him to a cocktail party given by the earl a few months ago. It should have been a high point in his social diary; but partly because he was not far short of a gate-crasher and partly because of the unhappy combination of rococo heirloom and Pall Mall leather with which the earl had furnished his flat, only a short walk from his own new house, he had found the affair something of a disappointment.

The earl, Antony had told Guy when he collected him, was a useful chap to know in the City. He had the ideal qualities for a chairman: he was good news at the top of a letterhead while not an intruder in the upper realms of management. Berry St Edmunds was, indeed, the sort of chairman who was glad to know that such matters as marketing, administration and finance were taken care of by others. They had taken him on board at CHIT and had not been disappointed. He was doing a fine job at Britton Trust, too, and at Antony's new securities firm. If Guy ever had need of a non-executive chairman for one of his companies, he could do a jolly sight worse than the Earl of St Edmunds, Antony had declared. Provided, of course, he was prepared to reward him generously with what he called his honoraria, liberally spiced with perquisites and larded from time to time with offshore capital gains.

Across a crowded sea of heads, Guy had spotted this corporate paragon surrounded by his admiring guests: the dark brown hair plastered back from a receding hairline, the nose fleshy, the toothbrush moustache more military than aristocratic. So this was Antony's chairman, and Harry Griffin's too. As he cast a shrewd eye over his host, Guy sensed the earl was rather pleased with himself; he was talking too much, listening too little, and continuously looking over his admirers' shoulders to see if someone more important was coming through the door.

'The line descends from George the Fourth, through his favourite mistress when he was Prince Regent,' Antony had informed Guy, his multiple chins jutting proudly as if such a pedigree were bound to rub off on a peer's business partner.

'I bet he doesn't pay his taxes,' Guy had guessed correctly. Harold Antony's clients rarely did. But there was no point in being holier-than-thou, for neither did he; why should he, or they, if the fruits of their transactions never landed where the provisions of the Exchange Control Act held sway?

After a couple of glasses of inferior sherry, Guy had decided not to join the throng attempting to touch the earl's hem. If he were to be useful, it were best they were properly introduced and their meeting held under less public auspices.

'How well do you really know him?' he had enquired of Harold Antony as they prepared to leave the party. As they went out of the entrance door it was just starting to rain.

In answer, Antony arranged with the earl's chauffeur to run Guy down the street in the earl's Rolls-Royce. 'Berry always changes for dinner,' he had said as they parted, without elaboration.

Guy noted the point. He too enjoyed the formality of a black-tie dinner, even when the party was limited to a few intimates. Antony had been happy to pass on an invitation to the earl. It took no more than a couple of dinners for Berry St Edmunds to succumb to Guy's cultured charm. On the second occasion, during a leisurely dinner at Claridges, he was even good enough to concede that the flattering comments Guy made about the company whose board he chaired were probably true. Like many proud chairmen, he proved his point by inviting Guy to visit one of the jewels in his crown, Watson's, where Jolyon Priestley and the managing director, who went by the name of Tim Cummings, were happy to show him round. Whatever other matters the four discussed privately on this occasion will for the time being remain, as the earl insisted they must, confidential.

Odd chap, the earl; probably less stupid than he looked, Guy had concluded after his visit to Watson's. Why on earth did the City permit these inbred idiots to take the chair of public companies? Why would the possession of a hereditary title somehow make them any more capable than everyone else? Or more honourable? For all the earl appeared to know about Britton Trust, the company might as well be in ruins. Why, Guy asked himself, had a peer of the realm from the wrong side of the sheets with next to no experience of the financial world any greater right to run a public company than the adopted son of a collector of taxes?

Guy scribbled a note to himself to look up CHIT's offer document for the company and to have a chat with Harold Antony. Best be prepared before his rendezvous with Harry Griffin.

13

In every corporate battle there is an *éminence grise*, a spider at the centre of the web, a fixer who comes out smiling whatever the outcome. However honourable his intentions may have been – and who, when he had earned the confidence of a peer of the realm, would doubt his word on such a matter? – Harold Antony was to find himself, *faut de mieux*, in such a position.

When Harry Griffin and Andy Oakes handed in their letters of resignation at the July board meeting of Britton Trust, they were not the only departures from the boardroom. Thomas Goodman pointedly remarked that the last thing the company needed was a spy in the camp. It was not much good the two of them resigning if Harold Antony was going to report everything that went on straight back to them.

'Don't believe he'd do any such thing. Man of honour, Antony,' opined the Earl of St Edmunds, following the aristocratic custom that if you have anything good to say about a man you say it to his face.

Antony expressed his own view by falling on his rusty sword. He had, he said in the press release that announced his resignation, acted in good faith. How dare his ungrateful colleagues criticise him for doing what any licensed dealer was duty-bound to do: to act on the instructions of his clients and to buy whichever shares they wished to own? However, his health was not as good as it might be. He wished to devote his remaining days to his family and his charitable affairs.

Privately, Antony was less than cheerful at the outcome of events. Had it not been he, he asked himself and his wife Rhoda that evening over his third scotch, who as broker to Britton Estates had saved the day when the market in its shares was sliding away by suggesting to CHIT's board that they might do worse than buy half a million of its shares? Both the Earl of St Edmunds representing one side, and Harry Griffin on behalf of the other, had thought it a brilliant idea. If the deal had ultimately resulted in the merger of the companies, that was because both sides had wanted it. If the two camps had subsequently fallen out, the blame could hardly be put at his door.

Now he was no longer a director of Britton Trust, to whom did he owe his loyalty? To the board that had shown such mistrust of him? Or to his friends: to Harry Griffin and Andy Oakes, whose careers he had nurtured; to Berry St Edmunds, to whom he was a trusted investment adviser; and to Guy Magnus, whose ambitions he had always encouraged? To what better purpose could he devote his energies than the achievement of their respective objectives: in the case of Harry, Andy and Berry, the realisation of their investments in Britton Trust, and in Guy's case the acquisition of the next vehicle on the upward path of his City career?

Was it his fault, Antony would ask himself in later years, if he had taken the view that a young man with the cheek to turn down a job and then put a friend forward in his place was bound to go a long way; so far, indeed, that he was worthy of an introduction to the backers who had helped him to buy into Mallard? Must it be accounted a sin to have kept in touch with that young man, to have done deals with him, to have brought him into his circle without discriminating between peer and commoner? And if all this had resulted in a mutuality of interests, and he had happened to find himself rewarded for his efforts, where was the harm in that? He was, he assured himself and Rhoda, worth every penny.

Rhoda Antony was even less happy than Harold at the turn of events at Britton Trust. Her husband had incredible flair for business. Admittedly the odd deal may have cost Tanquerys money; but he had been let down by his sloppy colleagues. They were unworthy of his wise counsel. She told Harold so, and he felt bound to agree with her. In any case, what counted, Rhoda knew, was not how much you made for your firm, but how much you made for your wife and society's appreciation of the manner in which she spent it. Her Hampstead salon was a focal point for a select circle of celebrated personages who met to praise her French chef's cuisine, her Impressionist paintings, her exquisite jewellery and Harold's firm's gold pages in the right charity brochures. A skilled practitioner in the art of scanning the minutiae of Sunday book reviews, concert programmes and art exhibition catalogues, to glean the essence from which cocktail party droppings are distilled, Rhoda Antony was, Harry Griffin had once said, a society hostess self-trained to a hair, without an ounce of surplus culture. She had not yet fully forgiven Guy Magnus for having labelled her guests a Barbizon landscape: all background with nothing up front; but she accepted that Harold had faith in the young man's ability and had made plenty of money on his back.

So when Guy asked him what he made of Britton Trust, Harold Antony was open with his views. It was, he said, the kind of company someone smart was going to make a lot of money out of. It would have been immodest to add who he thought that smart person might be, but Guy drew his own conclusions.

And when Guy called Harold again in August and sat down to go through the figures, and then asked him to find up to half a million shares in Britton Trust outside the stock market, Harold did as he was requested. Whether he also suggested to his agent in Geneva, the compliant M. le Fen, that he book a few in the name of his married daughter is unknown, for the Swiss are jealously protective of their clients' identity; but Harold Antony was the sort of person who ate from both ends of the candy bar.

As the Board of Trade Inspectors were to discover later, for the first four weeks after his return from the south of France at the end of June Guy Magnus had already been playing cat-and-mouse with Britton Trust shares. While he carried out his researches, his stockbroker Mark Penney-Stockes continued to siphon shares from their unwary owners, five and ten thousand at a time, with the circumspection of a laboratory technician sucking a sample of strychnine through a leaky pipette. The instant the price touched 200p he would withdraw from the market as silently as he had entered it, to return a day or two later as the price fell back. By the end of July Ludgate's holding had crept up to 200,000 shares without so much as a ripple disturbing Danny Gilbert's chart. A sterling crisis, two increases in Minimum Lending Rate and the fall of the *Financial Times* 30-Share Index to a 1973 low might as well never have happened. Guy took greater interest in the White Paper on warehousing and insider trading. The government was proposing to put a stop to the practice of buying shares through your friends so you wouldn't have to announce your holdings in the companies you were stalking. And to buying your own companies' shares with the benefit of privileged information. It would never work, said Guy – not if he had anything to do with it.

A few days later, on 1st August, Guy overheard Danny confirming the thirtieth purchase of Britton Trust shares.

'Stop!' he ordered.

Danny stopped. Reinstated at Guy's right hand, he had been kept so busy by the activity of the past month that he had lost his capacity for independent thought.

'Change of plan! We're going to buy in our own names. You're first in the chair, Danny. Tell Mark to book the next 80,000 to your account.'

'Money?' Danny gulped.

'You deal with the principles, Danny, and leave me to look after the details.'

Danny obediently booked 6,000 shares in his own name. He continued to deal with the principles all week.

'See what *The Times* is saying about Universal Credit?' Guy asked him the following morning, grinning wickedly. *'It's probably in a position to take the write-off in its stride,'* he read aloud. *'The bank's customers have received loans amounting to £2.7 million, secured on the shares of the parent. If foreclosure took place it would find itself in the extraordinary position of owning its own shares.'* Stuffed up his own backside, your friend Clive Salmon,' he scoffed. 'You should take care what kind of people you associate with, Danny.'

By Friday night Danny owned 30,000 shares in Britton Trust. He passed the weekend proudly telling himself he'd just spent 60 grand he didn't have. It might not make him rich, but the thought made him feel it.

The following Monday Guy changed plans again. He told Danny that Larry Callaghan wanted to buy 20,000 shares. Although Larry was not around to confirm his wishes, Danny was too fully engaged in his dealings with Mark Penney-Stockes to query Guy's veracity.

Two days later Guy strode briskly into the office after a breakfast meeting with a friendly chartered surveyor and scrapped the battle orders once more.

'It's going too slowly,' he said. 'I'm bidding now. What price are the shares this morning?'

'I had to pay 203 for Larry's,' Danny told him.

'Britton Trust must be an even better business than I thought. I'm going to call Mark and tell him to bid two ten. No, two twelve, to be sure to drag 'em out.'

Danny booked 2,500 shares to his own account before Guy had a chance to reach Penney-Stockes. He continued to bid for the small parcels from sellers who were happy to take the highest price they'd ever seen, while Penney-Stockes made Guy's presence felt amongst the larger holders. By the following Wednesday they had accumulated 400,000 shares and the price was touching 225.

'You see, you have twenty per cent,' Guy told Danny. 'And Larry has five. Exactly as per our agreement.' For when Guy had engaged Danny and allotted him twenty per cent of Westchurch's share capital, it had been agreed that this arrangement would also apply to deals they did outside the company. Larry Callaghan's talent for corporate tax management also came in handy; but as he brought no deals and little capital to the party, he had to settle for a more modest share. This was a source of some comfort to Larry, for he was more than twice as old as Danny, and Guy's failure to mention losses had not passed him by. Guy kept the remaining seventy-five per cent of Westchurch for himself.

Danny nodded obediently and rehearsed his speech to his bank manager, for the stock exchange account was coming to an end and his shares would soon have to be paid for: 'Excuse me, Mr Barclay, but would you happen to have a spare 160 grand lying around in your vault that I could borrow to buy a few shares? Till when? Will some time next year do?'

'Don't worry,' Guy read his thoughts. 'You have friends at Universal Credit. Clive Salmon thinks very highly of you. By the way, did you see their shares were down twelve yesterday? Don't let it worry you; by the time they want their money back I'll have the long-term finance in place. '

The phone rang and 5,000 more shares offered themselves for sacrifice. Before Danny could book them Guy had already yelled 'Stop!' again.

'Change of plan?' asked Danny superfluously.

'Westchurch's turn. Use the money we set aside to buy Dominion,' Guy ordered. 'And St Paul's had better raise some cash. Most of the loose holders must be out by now, so it's back to Plan A. Take it steady and bid just below the market. Make the shareholders think they'll have to hurry if they don't want to miss out at this level.'

The winkling out of Britton Trust shares began again in earnest. In a succession of small purchases Westchurch acquired 250,000 shares and St Paul's 40,000. At the end of the third week in August, Danny took a sheet of graph paper, drew an oblong building and divided it into 672 bricks: one for every 10,000 shares in their target. He blocked out seventy-eight of them, wondering as he did so how large a stake Guy had in mind to build before he made his usual threats to the board.

As he studied his drawing, it occurred to Danny that his building looked suspiciously like a warehouse.

On his way back from lunch that afternoon Danny felt the urge to stretch his legs before he got down to work. The town house that Guy had leased as his headquarters lent itself to leg-stretching. Guy knew his shareholders would want him to work in amenable surroundings, so his offices had been elegantly furnished with partners' desks, Regency chairs, comfortable settees and stylish coffee tables, and the walls were hung with tasteful prints – not of ancient maps of far-flung counties or red-jacketed huntsmen leaping over hedges on graceless horses, of the kind that adorn countless lawyers' waiting rooms, but of works by contemporary artists. And Guy knew his shareholders would also wish his meals to be regular and his diet healthy, so a room had been set aside for dining and a kitchen had been installed next door.

Danny had noticed a recent arrival on the staff. Charlotte had a Cordon Bleu diploma: Guy would settle for no less. She was blonde, rosy-cheeked, buxom of torso and tight of skirt. Danny was happy to settle for no more. He reckoned she must know of the important place he occupied in the Ludgate circus hierarchy and that she would show him appropriate respect. As a matter of courtesy he should introduce himself to her properly. He found her, wooden spoon to full, scarlet lips, sampling a red coulis she hoped Guy would send back to the kitchen so she could take it home.

'I'm Danny Gilbert. Welcome to our circus,' he introduced himself cheerily.

'Hi, Danny Gilbert. I'm Charlie. Welcome to my world,' she replied without turning round.

'Guess what, Charlie?' Danny posed the unanswerable question.

'Mm,' Charlotte replied, licking her lovely lips.

Danny took one look at her exposed neck – for a Cordon Bleu cook is trained to put up her blonde tresses before she blends a raspberry coulis – and decided to treat her response as consent. He came up silently behind her, placed his lips on her neck, his hands on the softest, roundest parts of her body, and squeezed gently. Charlotte reckoned it was no bad thing if her 'mm' had been loosely interpreted. She held the coulis on her tongue while she checked that it tasted exactly as intended, and then turned to Danny open-mouthed so he could have a lick. Danny thought it tasted delightful. Seeing Charlotte with the wooden spoon in one hand and a sieve in the other, he helpfully undid the buttons down the back of her dress and placed one hand on her spine so she could keep her balance when she swooned at his kiss, while he used the other to unclip her bra. Despite his support, Charlotte was unable to remain upright for long; and because of his lack of it, neither was Danny.

'Hurry up, before the soufflé rises,' she urged.

Spoon and sieve were soon deposited in unhygienic manner on the floor alongside Charlotte's panties and Danny's trousers, the fly of which was by now covered in raspberry coulis. Danny was so aroused he knew it would be impossible to slip back to his office to fetch one of the condoms he kept in the bottom drawer of his desk – for Danny kept condoms in all sorts of places where they might come in handy – without alerting whoever might be wandering along the corridor to his advanced state of excitement. Guy's secretary was forever wandering along the corridor at the wrong time. He gave Charlotte a questioning look. Fortunately she was able to give him comfort.

'Don't worry, it's already taken care of,' she told him.

Danny glanced down at his member, astonished that she could have achieved such a feat without his cooperation, or at least his knowledge. Its condition was as he expected: rigid, unprotected and ready for fun.

'Silly! I mean me. I'm on the pill,' Charlotte explained, grasping hold of the object of her desire and pulling it and the body to which it was attached towards her. So receptive was she that Danny made light of his entry, and the two were soon pumping away with the fervour that only uninhibited youth can muster.

It was in this state that Guy found them when he decided it had taken unacceptably long for his dessert to arrive.

'You filthy beast! What the hell do you think you're up to?' he screamed when he had recovered from the initial shock.'

'Charlotte was making a sauce for the soufflé. I was trying to have sex,' Danny confessed. He had been brought up to believe that if you were caught with your hands where they had no business to be but owned up honestly, you might be chastised but you would generally be forgiven. He pulled his underpants and trousers over his exposed parts, and tried vainly to wipe the coulis from the fly as he awaited his fate. It was not long coming.

'To think I trusted you! You're fired! Get out of the building this instant!' yelled Guy.

A crestfallen Danny rose slowly to his feet, his hand struggling with a zip whose working parts were by now clogged with the fast-drying raspberry coulis.

'Not you, silly boy! The soufflé's got nothing to do with you. I mean you, Charlotte!'

14

Guy's researches were revealing more each day of the treasures hidden behind the modest façade of Britton Trust's published report and accounts. One pleased him so much he was unable to keep it to himself. One afternoon towards the end of August he marched into the office to find Danny Gilbert colouring in his hundredth brick in honour of their millionth share.

'Guess where I've been?' he asked him, a broad smile lighting his face.

Danny shrugged his shoulders.

Guy gave him a clue. 'I've been with Don Corbishley.' Son of a minor peer, Old Etonian, ex-Guards and a member of Boodles, a man of generous dimensions, appetites and conceit, and a purveyor of boundless hyperbole, Corbishley represented everything that Guy most despised and most aspired to emulate.

'The Savoy?' Danny guessed. As it was nearly four o'clock, it seemed a reasonable assumption.

'Oxford Street,' Guy surprised him. Ordinary people, lots of them, shopped on Oxford Street. Bond Street and the Mayfair art galleries were more Guy's style; Sloane Street and Old Brompton Road came a close second.

'You've found a property?' Danny guessed again.

This time he was right. An estate agent with the ability to make the same property yield multiple commissions, once Corbishley sank his teeth into a building he never let go. If he was offering one to Guy, it was because he had the next buyer but three on the hook. But St Paul's Property had no money to spend. It was putting every penny it could lay its hands on into shares in Britton Trust. No way could Guy be contemplating a major property purchase at a time like this.

'And what a property!' Guy continued to confound him. 'Corner site, Dunn's in the ground floor shop and four floors of offices above. You know Dunn's: tweed suits and silly hats. Anyhow, Britton Trust owns the freehold. It's sitting on a gold mine and the directors don't even know it. They have it in the balance sheet at four and a half million. Don reckons the shop alone's worth more than that, if you take into account how much the rent will go up when the present lease comes to an end. Refurbish the offices and the sky's the limit.'

'How does he know when the leases end?' Danny asked.

'He doesn't, but he reckons that if rents in Oxford Street keep going up at the present rate, the longer the better.'

Danny sighed and carried on colouring in his bricks.

On the last day of the month Guy came in bearing an even broader grin. 'You're not going to believe this,' he said. 'You know I gave Harold Antony authority to buy up to half a million shares. Well, he called one of their directors, Archie Laws, while he was on holiday in Italy. Apparently Archie's not been too chuffed with the way things have been going on the board. Said he might have a parcel to sell if the price was right. A hundred and twenty-eight thousand, it turns out. I bid him two forty, and a Corniche on the side. He asked for two fifty and took two forty-five. Didn't seem interested in the car,' Guy added, feigning pique.

Danny sucked his breath. 'You can't do that, Guy,' he said. 'It's against the rules.'

'Whose rules? You think the old boy masonry doesn't find ways round the rules when it wants to keep an outsider off its patch? Archie must reckon his pals will see me off if I make a full bid, and wants to cash in while the going's good.'

'You're not going to make a bid, are you?' Danny asked anxiously. Guy didn't make bids himself. He solicited them from others.

'I'm thinking about it.'

'But if you did, and he accepted the Corniche, you'd have had to offer the equivalent value to all the other shareholders.'

'Another 15p a share! If only I could get away with that!'

Guy spent much of the following week with Harold Antony. Then, on Friday morning, he asked casually, 'You still talk to Lewis, don't you, Danny?'

'I suppose so,' Danny replied without much enthusiasm. Lewis White was the wrong man to try to interest in a Rolls-Royce.

'That block of a million shares he bought in June. We need it. Ask him if he'll take a profit, would you?'

Danny sighed and picked up the phone. At the other end White did not hesitate. Since buying the Britton Trust shares he had become increasingly aware of the perils of being locked into an expensive investment. While two million shares might have given him a powerful lever in the company's affairs, one million did not. They hadn't even offered him a place on the board. As he watched the shares rise, he realised someone was building a stake. When Danny called, he knew who it was. To compete with Guy Magnus would drive the shares higher than he was prepared to pay. He was left with a stark alternative: either to make a full bid and risk an uncertain takeover battle, or to sell out and take a profit. And he reckoned that what he knew, Guy knew too.

'Shares are for buying and selling,' he told Danny. 'Tell Guy to make me an offer. One I can't refuse.'

Danny reported White's response with foreboding. Until this moment he had felt comfortable with their position. It fitted in with Guy's habitual strategy. Their fifteen per cent holding would put the fear of God into the directors of Britton Trust. He could trade the stake on, either to them, to Consolidated Finance or to one of the more aggressive property companies. But doubling up on their bet at the extortionate price Lewis White was apt to demand was a high-risk strategy. Trained by White, Danny's thoughts followed the same route as his mentor but with a different conclusion. Two million shares would give Guy too powerful a lever; for if the Britton Trust board refused to parley with him, as well it might, he would be reduced to the last of the alternatives: selling the stake on. But what if there was no buyer for it? It was all very well for a major player to roll the dice for a couple of million, but the stakes were very different for Guy Magnus. And, it followed, for Danny Gilbert.

Was Guy bluffing? Danny asked himself. Was he feigning interest in Consolidated Finance's stake in the hope that Lewis White would offer to buy theirs? What did his boss have in mind?

Guy was on an altogether different tack. He was asking himself whether, even with Consolidated Finance's stake in his pocket, he would be ready to launch a full takeover bid for Britton Trust. For though a third of a company's equity was usually a solid enough base for success, he doubted whether it would suffice in this case. There were a number of large shareholders, and the attitude of some of them was uncertain. Harry Griffin would be in no mood to make his life easy, and Andy Oakes was a seasoned campaigner. Both would sell out in the end, but each was smart enough to drive him into a corner if he made the first approach. Needing the acceptance of a majority of the equity for the bid to be successful, he needed to be capable of gaining it without their help. If the board were to recommend an offer he'd be home and dry; but that prospect was a long way off.

What of the other directors? Between them they owned over a million shares. He wondered which way they would jump. From what Harry had said, there were two camps. A divided board was a vulnerable board. He took out the latest annual report and ran his eye down the list for the umpteenth time. Where, he asked himself, would he find the weakest link? The Earl of St Edmunds? It was time to find out which way the chairman would jump. John Charteris, who, according to Harry, had built Britton Estates? Doubtful. Britton Trust was an asset play, and Charteris's past said he'd know his property values. Thomas Goodman was a lawyer: he wouldn't overstep the line. Alan Palliser? He was too recent a recruit to have had time to become disloyal, and in any case his shareholding was too small to be of much help. Jolyon Priestley sounded more promising. The word from Harry, who ought to know, was that he was a snake, and heavily in hock. If nothing else, he might be persuaded to disclose how the land lay with the others. Guy checked the shareholding against Priestley's name. The joint managing director was listed as the owner of 365,000 shares. He would invite him to lunch – of the kind that never comes free.

But although he managed to satisfy Priestley that lunch at Claridge's the following Monday was not to be at his own expense, Guy was doomed to disappointment at its outcome. He had taken a suite at the hotel for an indefinite period. The course he was set on required him to be available in prestigious surroundings and in a position to offer hospitality at all hours. His new Chelsea home was not conveniently located, nor was its redecoration finished. No matter: if his shareholders knew the importance of the work he was engaged in on their behalf, they would willingly agree to their company paying for his comfort. While he had not yet decided which of his companies' shareholders were to be the beneficiaries of his present labours at the time he stepped into the hotel restaurant, he felt he had already done enough for Ludgate's for that company to pick up the tab.

But despite Guy's liberal hospitality, and however hard he was pressed, Priestley insisted that he was not a seller of his shares in Britton Trust. 'It isn't that I wouldn't if I could, as it were,' he made his position as plain as he was able.

'You mean you've already sold?' Guy asked in an attempt at clarification.

'Not at all,' replied Priestley, squirming uncomfortably.

'You've still got them, then?' As he tried to tie his guest down, Guy recalled Harry Griffin's description.

'Yes. Well, no. Not exactly.'

'They're not security for a loan?' Guy guessed.

'No way!' Priestley sounded mortified by the suggestion. 'Listen, Guy, they're not for sale,' he said, looking away. 'When they are I'll be in touch. Can we just leave it at that?'

At least the fellow was not off-side, Guy told himself. It was worth asking a few more questions. 'What about the rest of the board?' he tried.

Priestley hesitated. It was a pertinent question. If there was one subject that caused him endless irritation, it was the rest of the board. The atmosphere in the boardroom had never been the same after the merger with Britton Trust and the arrival of Alan Palliser as joint managing director.

It had not been long before Palliser discovered the nature of the Norfolk Broads Company's secret asset, of whose special value Harry Griffin had been so easily persuaded by Jolyon Priestley. For though Priestley had managed to convince the auditors of that company, and subsequently those of CHIT, that the transfer of a canal boat to the Mediterranean was justified by the need to test-market product diversification, he was less successful when Britton Trust's more rigorous auditors took stock of CHIT's assets. They made the unexpected discovery that the canal boat in question boasted a twenty-foot saloon, a fully-equipped galley and bar, a master cabin and six guest berths in addition to the quarters of the captain and crew, a sun-deck and a speed-boat. Moored in the port of Monte Carlo, the *Gay Dog* was certified seaworthy for extended cruising.

When the auditors had reported their findings to Palliser, he asked Thomas Goodman for his opinion as a lawyer. Goodman's advice was that if the *Gay Dog* was not required for genuine business activities, the proper course was for it to be sold and the proceeds paid in to the company's account. He said he would raise the matter at the next board meeting.

However, when the Earl of St Edmunds saw the item on the agenda, he took the view that what Britton Trust needed most was a contented, united board. Having praised the auditors for their vigilance, he proposed that the running costs of the company's southernmost asset be deemed a proper charge against its entertainment account. When the room finished resounding to 'Jolly Good Ideas' and 'I'll Take Septembers', his resolution was duly passed.

The earl had felt this to be an opportune moment to report on the visit he and Jolyon Priestley had recently made to the Algarve. Unhappily the project they were recommending for board approval proved less to their colleagues' taste. It seemed there were fewer golfers than sailors round the table.

'Don't suppose the expenses to date should be repaid by whoever incurred them?' the earl had offered grudgingly, hoping for dissent.

When no one demurred with this view, Alan Palliser proposed that he and Priestley, who was not present at the meeting, deal with the matter.

'The chairman did seem rather upset,' he said when the two met.

'If I were you, I'd destroy the board minute and forget all about it,' advised Priestley.

His advice had not been welcome, and relations between the joint managing directors had remained frosty ever since. Palliser had taken an increasingly unsympathetic view of Priestley's own expense account, with the result that after the unholy bust-up that led to the resignation of Harry Griffin together with almost half the board, Priestley concluded that his days with Britton Trust were numbered and he had better leave the company before it left him.

Hearing he was available for hire, Priestley's friends at Ernest Burke had offered him a position in a new venture that seemed to give freer rein to his entrepreneurial skills. Out of habit, Priestley had proposed an equity participation. In return they had enquired whether he intended to put up his stake in cash.

'*Actual* cash? Well, not actual cash, as such,' he had admitted. 'But I've got shares. Good, sound, asset-based shares. I could put them in.'

Priestley's prospective partners had been full of understanding. No one worth his salt had actual cash nowadays. Indeed, Ernest Burke's new venture was designed specifically to take advantage of non-cash opportunities. Its shares were to be issued at a par value of one pound. At the time of their discussions, shares in Britton Trust stood at 200p. The calculation was not complicated. The parties signed an agreement that when Priestley took up his position on the board of Ernest Burke's new venture, he would trade his 200,000 Britton Trust shares for 400,000 of its shares.

Should he report the agreement to the Britton Trust board? Priestley had been faced with a dilemma. If he failed to do so, he would be in breach of the stock exchange regulation that a company must report a director's transactions in its shares within five days. But if he did so before he was ready to hand in his notice, his colleagues might no longer invite him to participate in their more sensitive discussions. And that would put him in breach of his understanding with Harry Griffin that he would keep him fully posted on the company's affairs.

While Priestley agonised over his dilemma, the price of Britton Trust shares began to rise. The higher they rose, so did the answer become clearer – until at last they had risen so much that it was blindingly obvious. He had not delivered his share certificates to his prospective employers; *ergo*, the transaction had not taken place. Accordingly, his board had nothing to report to the stock exchange, and it followed that he had nothing to report to his board.

The entry of a third party into the arena made what had become clear more confused than ever. His agreement with Ernest Burke meant that if he sold his shares to Guy Magnus, both his present and his future employers would instruct their lawyers to issue him with a writ. Furthermore, the sharp rise in Britton Trust shares meant that the deal he had struck was no longer fair. To himself, at any rate. Priestley asked himself how he might reconcile fairness with duty, and came up with a Solomonic judgment: he would remain friends with everyone – with the Earl of St Edmunds and the board of Britton Trust, with Harry Griffin, with Ernest Burke, and with Guy Magnus. Where confusion had reigned, all would once again be in harmony.

He saw he could no longer delay in answering Guy's inquiry about the rest of the board. 'Things could be better, I suppose,' he muttered through a spoonful of sticky pudding, as if hoping this would muffle any clarity in his response.

'Split?' Guy asked. 'No clear direction?'

Priestley pondered how to avoid appearing disloyal to those who remained on the board while remaining loyal to those who had left it. 'You could say that,' he finally admitted. 'Too much of an asset company. I'm a trading man, myself.'

'Are the others all as strong holders as you?'

Priestley tried to recognise himself in Guy's description, but gave up. 'I reckon the chairman might be the weakest,' he answered the rest of the question.

'I wouldn't mind meeting your earl,' said Guy disingenuously. 'Do you think you could fix it for me?'

'Harold Antony's the man for that. He handles his share dealings. They're pretty close. The earl's chairman of his broking firm too. D'you know Harold?'

'Mm, may have dealt with him once or twice. I might give him a call. It wouldn't hurt, though, if you put in a good word for me with the earl at the same time.'

Priestley guessed from his host's expression that the good word wouldn't hurt him any more than it wouldn't hurt Guy Magnus.

As Guy checked the bill and took up the unaccustomed role of paymaster, he told himself his guest had paid handsomely for his lunch. The fact that he couldn't – or wouldn't – sell his Britton Trust shares today was evidence that he believed their value to be higher than their market price. As an insider, Priestley would know.

15

While the deal you expect to do with ease often fails to come off, the one you reckon will prove impossible may fall like ripe horse-chestnuts in a November gale. Ahead of the meeting Danny arranged with Lewis White, Guy had been pessimistic. Their former boss was not, he felt sure, going to do them any favours. In the belief that he had something they needed desperately, he would demand a king's ransom for Consolidated Finance's million shares in Britton Trust.

When he and Danny confronted Lewis White in the boardroom of Consolidated Finance's City headquarters, Guy decided to lay his cards face-up on the table. 'You paid 225p. I'll bid you 250. You'll make a quarter of a million turn.' He sat nervously, as one does when dealing with a former boss, his hands twisting beneath the table. He expected his offer to be rejected out of hand.

'Two fifty, bollocks! That's a buying, not a selling price,' White responded predictably, but to Guy's sensitive antennae without much conviction. 'They're almost that in the market.'

'Only because I've been buying.'

'Bid me 275 and I may be willing to talk.'

Guy pulled a long face to hide his surprise. The number was lower than he had expected. 'You taught me, Lewis,' he said; 'I'm a dealer. If I don't get what I want, I'll sell our holdings on to the highest bidder. You have three choices. Either you hang on and watch your profit disappear or you make a bid yourself at 275, if you think that's what the company's worth. I might even take it myself.'

'You said I had three choices.'

'Or you accept my offer. I'll go another five pence, but not a penny more,' Guy added, determined that the concession not be seen as a sign of weakness.

White argued for the obligatory five minutes before he conceded. Guy said he would settle in a fortnight. White said payment must be this Friday or the deal was off. Guy argued for the obligatory five minutes before he conceded. The deal was done and contract notes were exchanged.

As Guy left the room, White heaved a sigh of relief. Earlier that morning he and his colleagues had had a brainstorming session with Consolidated Finance's chief economist. Inflation was up to nine per cent and earnings were rising even faster; price rises would soon accelerate. There was a penalty to be paid for that. Interest rates, already at a peak, would go up again. This was no time to hold on to £2,500,000 worth of unsaleable shares – unsaleable to anyone but Guy Magnus. He had spoken briefly to Clive Salmon, but even he had shown no interest in them. Ominously, Salmon had sounded as if he wasn't interested in anything at present, not even the spate of IRA letter bombs going off all over town.

Meanwhile, as they settled into the back seat for the return journey to the Ludgate circus, Danny was telling Guy he could have done the deal at 250. 'I know Lewis. I could see it in his eyes,' he said.

'You may be right,' Guy conceded. 'But you didn't see what was in mine.'

Danny was silent for a moment, then said: 'If you had to, you'd have paid him 275?'

'You're learning, Danny, you're learning.'

Guy wrapped himself in a cocoon of concentration as his driver Yankee Tate crossed the City. Once inside the Ludgate circus he marched swiftly to their office, leaving Danny scurrying in his wake. He had made up his mind. 'Clear the decks, Danny!' he announced dramatically. 'We're making a full bid!'

A tremor of excitement coursed through Danny's body. Was this the big one Guy had talked about? Then fear took over. Spending £4 or £5 million to accumulate a third of a company's equity was risky enough, but good business if you sold the stake on at a profit. Spending it as a launching-pad for a full takeover bid was altogether another matter. A £15 million matter.

'Guy, this business about me having twenty per cent,' he began tentatively.

'Silly boy. I told you to leave the details to me.'

'Yes, Guy,' Danny said meekly, still far from happy.

Guy knew the course he was about to embark on was fraught with uncertainty. Once the purchase of Consolidated Finance's holding was completed he would have accumulated over 2,300,000 shares: almost thirty-five per cent of Britton Trust's equity. But that still left him more than a million shares short of victory. If the board united against him, and Harry and the other former directors held out for a ransom higher than he could afford, he would be in for an almighty battle. It was, however, a prospect he relished, for the rewards far outweighed the risks. Britton Trust, he was by now convinced, was a veritable goldmine of undervalued businesses and properties.

Once he went public with his offer the City fathers would watch his moves closely. All share purchases would have to be declared to the Takeover Panel. If he paid more for any single holding than the level of his bid, he would have to increase his offer to all shareholders to that price. But there would be some shareholders who would only sell if he paid them more than his bid. There always were. Even if he managed to split the board and acquire some of its holdings, he would be hard pressed to gain the shares he needed to win without those greedy fellows. He needed a few tricks up his sleeve.

As Yankee Tate drove him back to Claridge's that evening, he took his first step towards dealing with the problem.

'Fancy a punt on a sure thing, Yankee?' he asked, turning the tables.

A dashing racing driver who had been forced into premature retirement from a promising Grand Prix career by his team owner's inability to replace his cars at the rate he destroyed them, Yankee Tate had been nicknamed for his predilection for mammoth accumulating bets. He was the one person upon whose judgment on the science of probabilities Guy could absolutely rely.

'Where's the catch, sir?' he asked through the driving mirror, even more suspicious than usual.

'Catch? In your case, cash up front, I suppose.' Guy proceeded to describe the principles of stock market investment.

Yankee soon caught on. 'I give you the money, you give me the shares, but you don't tell me what odds I get for winning. What kind of deal is that, sir? It's out-and-out gambling,' he protested.

Guy felt bound to admit this was true. Unless, he explained to Yankee, you happened to know something the other punters didn't.

It was a lesson Guy had learnt from Tate himself. On their first extended drive together – to Scotland, after he had completed the takeover of the Highland Timber Company, so he could introduce himself to its directors – he had accepted Tate's proposal of a two shilling four-way accumulator of which the last leg was a 6/1 shot against the next hitchhiker being a woman. Shortly afterwards they passed a broad-backed, ruck-sacked, athletic-looking, unmistakably male figure. Except that when they stopped to pick it up, they found it had a smooth-skinned, red-lipped, bright-eyed, rather pretty face and a throat without the least sign of an Adam's Apple.

'What on earth do you make of that, Yankee?' Guy had asked, unable to hide his chagrin.

'Fifty three quid and fourteen bob, sir,' Yankee had responded.

Guy had adjusted quickly to his driver's narrow perspective. 'Will you take a cheque?' he asked hopefully.

'Will I fiddle, sir? Even if I trusted you, sir, I don't have a bank account. I wouldn't leave my cash with them buggers, not where the tax man can find it.'

'You were jolly lucky,' Guy had pronounced the following morning as he handed Yankee a wad of bank-notes and some coins. 'You have to admit it. Be honest.'

'Totally honest, sir? You want me to tell you what I really think, sir?'

'I would ask if I didn't.'

'I think that's what happens to silly buggers who go for a pee while their driver's filling up the tank with petrol, sir.'

Yankee's artless response had rung an honest bell.

'He has more horse-sense than the rest of you put together,' Guy told the directors of the Highland Timber Company the next day when they invited him to join the board and he proposed that Mr Ian Tate also be elected a director. This appointment had an important benefit, for the company's Articles of Association provided that no director could be dismissed except by the unanimous vote of the rest, and Guy reckoned he was going to need one loyal supporter. For he was about to announce that Highland Timber would no longer be cutting down trees, and that its name would be changed and its headquarters moved to offices near to St Paul's Cathedral, in the financial heart of the nation. He had then invited the newest member of the board to provide down-to-earth counsel on the chances against the services of any of its executive directors being required for duty there.

'Twenty-five to one, sir,' Yankee had solemnly proffered his assessment, and it was too early in the day for him to be referring to lunch.

As that worthy steered round Hyde Park Corner three years from the day he had been appointed to his position of authority, he eyed his master carefully through the driving mirror.

'There don't seem to be many rules, sir,' he observed shrewdly.

'Only three you need to remember,' Guy told him. 'Rule number one is that shares aren't for papering the walls. They're for buying and selling.'

'Got it, sir!' Yankee beamed, happy to learn that shares possessed qualities similar to his master's half-used car tyres.

'Rule two is that I can tell you when to buy a share, but not when to sell. If I told everyone when to sell, I'd never get out myself. Last one out's a sissy.'

Yankee guessed that if that was what the last one out was, there must be an advantage to being the first one in. And when he heard that Harry Griffin held a stake in the company he was to buy shares in, not even he could resist the appeal of a modest flutter. 'I'm not saying how long I'll hold on to them, though, sir,' he warned. It gave him no comfort that his master was setting the bets, if not the odds; but he concluded that although at first sight the punt on the sure thing sounded like an offer to drop his wages down one of those stand-and-do-it-down-a-hole-in-the-floor jobs favoured by the Frogs, the use of special knowledge did seem to change the odds in his favour.

'You've got rule three!' Guy told his pupil proudly. 'Never fall in love with a share. Dealing in shares is like dealing with a woman: if you don't want to land yourself in trouble, never date on your first screw.'

If anything made Yankee cross, it was being told when not to overtake on the inside. 'Catch me being a sissy!' he shook his streetwise head.

Guy had one more loose shareholding to wrap up before he was ready to launch a takeover bid for Britton Trust. But just as Consolidated Finance's stake had proved easier to acquire than he had anticipated, so did this one prove more irksome when he came to deal with it the following Friday morning.

Pat Crisp was a share dealer with a gambler's instinct and an eye for stocks that suddenly became popular without any obvious explanation. He may have spotted the increased trading activity in Britton Trust shares during July. Or perhaps loose talk had put him on the track. In any event, he had beaten Mark Penney-Stockes to the draw. Generally happy to share his thoughts, his purchases and his profits with his long-time ally Guy Magnus, on this occasion he had bought 100,000 shares without a word to him until after the deed was done.

'Come on, Pat, we're supposed to be friends,' Guy tried to cajole him. 'Hand them over, and no more nonsense.'

'Why should I?' Crisp asked, trying to keep a straight face. 'I'm building a stake. With these as security, I can borrow 150 grand. That'll buy me another 60,000 shares. I'll borrow another 100 grand on the back of those and buy myself 40,000 more. A few more days, a few more deals, and hey presto!'

he grinned, stretching out his arms to show the palms of his hands. 'I'll be mounting a bid of my own.'

Guy's anger boiled over. It happened whenever a friend tried to hot him. 'You dirty little rat!' his voice rose. 'You knew I was in the market. You had no business buying the shares outside our agreement. They're mine. Give them back to me right away, or I'll break every bone in your lousy little body.'

'Cool down, Guy. All I want is my little joke. And a fair price, of course.'

Guy relaxed. Pat was willing to deal; but at what price? 'You can have the same price I paid Lewis White,' he offered. As evidence he passed over his copy of the contract note with two cheques clipped to it, ready for delivery at noon, one from Westchurch, the other from St Paul's Property. Neither company could have bought all of the shares without exceeding the ten per cent ceiling above which its holding must be declared to the stock exchange.

'Don't even bother to show it to me,' replied Crisp. 'You wouldn't be in such a stew if you weren't going to make a bid. My shares are yours, but I won't take less than the price you end up paying for the rest.'

'In that case you'll have to wait until I make the bid and take your chance with everybody else,' Guy tried.

'No way. If you want to be sure of me, you'll have to do the deal now and undertake to give me a top-up when the dust has settled.'

Part of Guy wanted to reject Crisp's proposal; but the more shares he had in the bag by nightfall, the more comforted he would be. Moreover, buying Crisp's on the terms proposed was against the takeover rules. That added considerably to their attraction. What were friends for, if not to assist with such transgressions? However, both Westchurch and St Paul's had reached the ten per cent limit: if they overstepped it and failed to advise the stock exchange, it would impose sanctions.

'Bijou will take them,' Guy decided. 'On one condition. Payment. Danny has accumulated 200 grand of Dominion Equity & Bond. You take them off our hands and deal them on, and we'll offset their value against whatever you paid for your Britton stock.'

'Sorry, Guy, but Dominion's not my thing. I don't mind seeing if I can find a buyer for you, though. How much do you want for them?'

'Two hundred,' replied Guy. That was the average price Danny had paid, but Dominion shares had fallen since then. If Westchurch had to sell them at arm's length the loss would hurt him, for he owned seventy-five per cent of Westchurch. But Ludgate, of which he did not own seventy-five per cent, had been prepared to pay generously for Westchurch's holding. Even so, Guy wanted to recover as much of Ludgate's loss as he could.

'Bit rich,' Crisp queried the price.

'Danny says they're worth it.'

'I'll do my best. But I want half of whatever I get over one eighty.'

Crisp rose to leave. Guy gestured to him to sit back down. The meeting was not yet over. He had suffered an indignity he could have done without.

'Answer me two questions, Pat. Do you have any sisters?' he asked.

'One,' Crisp replied hesitantly. He was fond of Alison, and his mistrust of Guy was based on experience. He braced himself for the next question.

'Have you ever screwed her?'

Crisp grinned. This was more like the Guy Magnus he was used to. 'Not yet,' he replied.

PART TWO

The Takeover

All that (Gaius) accomplished in this expedition was to receive the sur-render of Adminius, son of the British King Cunobellinus, who had been banished by his father and come over to the Romans with a few follow-ers ... In the end, he drew his army in battle array facing the Channel and moved the arrow-casting machines and other artillery into position as though he intended to bring the campaign to a close. No one had the least notion what was in his mind when, suddenly, he gave the order: 'Gather sea-shells!' He referred to the shells as 'plunder from the ocean, due to the Capitol and to the Palace', and made the troops fill their helmets and tunic-laps with them ... Then he promised every soldier a bounty of four gold pieces, and told them: 'Go happy, go rich!' as though he had been excessively generous.

Suetonius, *The Twelve Caesars* (Gaius Caligula),
translated by Robert Graves.

16

Guy Magnus settled into the Chesterfield armchair. The suite he had taken at Claridge's while the builders created havoc in his new home had been furnished with comfort and longevity in mind, rather than good taste. That should suit the guest whose arrival he awaited. He pressed the bell and asked the butler whether the champagne was on ice.

'The vintage is the one you ordered, sir.' Claridge's floor butlers were used to nervous guests. If they didn't ask about the condition of the refreshments, they found some way to enquire about one's discretion. How few knew what it took to be a gentleman! A real gentleman knew what a butler was for. He was there to make his master appear a gentleman, whether he was one or not. For such an exercise in dissimulation, discretion was a prerequisite.

As he sat waiting, Guy reviewed his position. Other than picking up the odd loose line of stock, he had stayed out of the market for Britton Trust since the end of August. It had been essential to avoid bidding up the price prior to his negotiation with Lewis White. It was also vital not to alert Britton Trust's directors to his plans. Even on the coming Friday, when his purchase of Consolidated Finance's holding was due for completion, he need not make a public announcement, as he would be acquiring the shares outside the market. He would divide them between Westchurch and St Paul's, so neither had a holding large enough to have to be declared to the stock exchange. As far as the stock market was concerned, the price of Britton Trust shares remained 235p. To all but a few sharp-eyed professionals any activity must be seen as steady investment demand.

'Your guests, sir,' the butler broke into his reflections.

Guy rose to greet the men who came through the door. Harold Antony, limping tight-arsed, led the way, doing his manful best to overcome the chronic hypochondria from which he was plainly suffering. Jolyon Priestley sidled in at the rear, low to the ground and as close as possible to the door-frame, as if hoping to remain anonymous. Behind them a straight-backed, middle-aged man wearing an immaculately tailored navy-blue pinstripe suit stepped confidently through the door. He peered at Guy. It was understood that he would not make his previous acquaintance with his host known to Priestley, but in any case he was making a pretty good job of having forgotten him.

Harold Antony made the formal introductions.

'Berry,' the shambling character corrected him loudly enough to make his dissembling obvious. 'Still can't get used to this titular nonsense,' he harrumphed.

Guy glanced towards at the butler and spotted the flicker of a wink. A champagne cork was extracted with a gentle exhalation of air and the elegant tulip glasses were soon filled with frothing bubbles. With an inclination of his head the butler put the idea into Guy's mind that his guests should at least be offered a seat.

'Do sit down, Harold, Jolyon, er, Berry,' he invited them, cursing himself for the uncharacteristic nervousness which had prevented him from observing due precedence. 'Caviar?'

'Never touch the stuff. Weasel's droppings,' the earl pronounced judgment as he dropped into the Chesterfield armchair and made himself comfortable.

'A glass of Krug, then?'

'Champers makes me fart. Don't have a drop of scotch, by any chance?' the earl enquired.

'Neat, water or soda, sir?' asked the butler, unfazed.

'Water, no ice,' replied the earl scornfully, forbearing to describe the effect of soda on his intestinal system.

The four sat down and exchanged views on the prime minister's weekend diatribe against the prophets of doom.

'He says there'll be no going back on his policies,' Guy commented; 'I only hope he means it.'

'Mustn't let himself be put off by these ruddy letter bombs,' opined the earl. 'String 'em up if I found any of the buggers lurking round my garage.'

The earl and Guy found themselves in political harmony. It took an intervention by Harold Antony to bring them to the agenda.

'I believe Guy would like a confidential word with you about Britton Trust, Berry,' he said.

The earl turned quizzically towards Harold Antony as if to ask whether he was aware of the protocol in these matters. He was still on his first drink and the chap was threatening to talk trade. Then he remembered his brief: that was what he had come here to do. This was not a social occasion.

'May I compliment you on having put together an exceptionally interesting company, Berry?' Guy began, more as a statement than a question. 'As you know, we've made a substantial investment in it, and we'd very much like to increase it. We were wondering, in fact, whether you and your colleagues would consider accepting an offer from us for some of your shares, if the price were right. Above the market, of course.'

The earl coughed. He'd hardly sat down and the chap was talking terms. But he was a guest, and his mother had taught him that a gentleman best put his host at ease by playing his game. 'You after the lot?' he asked brusquely.

'Not our style,' Guy replied. 'We've bought a few hundred thousand, and as we like the look of the company we thought of buying another half a million or so, to make it worth our while helping you with your further development.'

'What makes you think you could do that?' The earl swirled his tumbler.

'You have some very good property. We have a lot of expertise in the field, both here and abroad. If we put our people together with yours, I'm sure we could come up with ideas that would provide a lot of added value.' Guy swirled his own champagne flute in response, though he knew better.

'Since we merged with CHIT we've had a good many industrial companies to look after as well,' the earl corrected him, indicating Priestley as the culprit. He peered out of the Georgian window as the Brook Street traffic grew heavier in the rush hour.

'I know. Laserbeam's a jewel. You must be proud of it. Watson's too; it's in a growth industry. But can your management develop these businesses on its own? Do you have the right kind of experience on your board now three of your directors have resigned? Our industrial management team has an first-rate track record.' Guy took a deep draught of champagne and spluttered as the bubbles caught in his throat.

The earl recognised that Guy had found his weak spot. Charteris knew about nothing but property, Goodman was obsessed with his so-called fiduciary duty, Palliser was buzzing around like a blue-arse fly moaning about expenses and Priestley was no better than a used car dealer. Meantime cash was running through Laserbeam like claret through a weak bladder, Watson's had become an over-manned bureaucracy servicing a ragbag of unwanted products and Norfolk Broads was a sleaze racket.

'Your shareholders have had a pretty good run,' Guy continued, recovering his equilibrium. 'You'd be doing them a favour if you brought us in. If they don't like it, they can always sell in the market. But if we don't get what we want and take our profit, their shares will be back below two hundred in no time;' then, as if musing to himself but audibly enough for the earl not to miss a word, he added, 'If you manage to achieve a higher price for them than they expect, they should be grateful. If you happen to get a little extra for your pains, so what?' Seeing a quizzical look on the earl's face, he went on: 'We're thinking two fifty at a pinch.'

The earl had bought cheaply into Britton Estates and CHIT, and his Britton Trust shares had risen far higher than he had expected. Two months ago 200p had looked a fancy price; now, if he got 250p or better, he'd be sitting pretty. However, he knew the rules. If he didn't know their precise wording, he knew the general sense. And there were strangers present. He turned to Priestley and Antony.

'Look here, should we be talking like this?' he asked. 'I mean, duties of directors, and all that.'

'At this stage any discussion would be regarded as exploratory, Berry,' Antony reassured him. Priestley nodded his accord, though sufficiently briefly that the gesture might subsequently be deniable.

'Capital gains tax?' the earl muttered, just loud enough for Guy's ears.

'You're an expert at offshore arrangements, Harold,' Guy said in the tone of one changing the subject. 'I hope you haven't been keeping your secrets from your own chairman.'

Antony studied a sliver of toast, loaded it with a heavier than usual helping of caviar, and filled his mouth so as to prevent it from uttering an indiscretion.

'I suppose, in principle,' the earl began, but failed to finish.

The hesitation was enough for Guy. 'We haven't finalised our intentions yet,' he said. 'We've a few more people to speak to, a few more investigations to make. I suppose all I'm really asking for is an assurance that in principle you don't oppose our interest in your company. And that you wouldn't be averse to selling your shares to us, given the right offer.'

The earl took a long draw on his weak scotch as he formulated his response. Perhaps it was time for another merger, or better still, a full takeover. There was surely no harm in manoeuvring in that direction.

'Put it this way,' he said when his glass was empty; 'Every company has its price. Every man, for that matter. Gentlemen, I have a dinner engagement.

Have to go home to change. No need to get up, Priestley. Why don't you hang around in this very nice suite and see if you can't persuade this interesting young man what an exceptionally valuable company Britton Trust is? Arrange a visit to Watson's for a start. Cummings'll be delighted to show him round.'

As the earl marched from the room, Guy asked himself what kind of a world he was living in. Here was a chairman of a public company who owed his appointment to the fact that his ancestor had slept with a king, while he, Guy Magnus, might just as well owe his high-flying ambition to the possibility that his natural mother had slept with a Polish airman. He doubted whether the earl was even aware that Britton Trust owned a property in Oxford Street, while he, Guy, probably knew more about the value of its assets than any member of its board. Not for the first time he asked himself which of the two was better suited to own and run Britton Trust.

'Well, Jolyon,' he turned to his remaining guest; 'where shall we begin? With the top management? With you, Jolyon?'

17

This, Guy told himself as he strode confidently through the ornate double doors of the Berkeley Square offices of Ulster & Cayman the following afternoon, was his scene. The long-established Ulster & Cayman Bank had merged with Lyndon Meyham, the fastest growing of the new breed of boutique merchant banks that had sprung up and flourished as a result of the property boom. Lyndon Meyham had made loans where the clearing banks had feared to tread. It had developed such expertise in evaluating property risks that it had moved into the property market as an investor. It had then developed such expertise as a property investor that it had moved seamlessly on to the acquisition of property companies. But though its directors believed they had bought Farranwide Properties at the bottom of the market, they soon found themselves on the brink of financial disaster. Before it became too late they managed to impress the less astute directors of the much larger Ulster & Cayman Bank with their expertise in property affairs, and the two banks had merged. They had later sold Farranwide at the peak of the market to an even larger property company, whose own demise was still twelve months into the future.

Lyndon Meyham had been a success story and its leading lights, 'Whirling' Sam Dervish and Sidney de Deyler, were City folk heroes. Such heroes were they that they had no need to work in the Square Mile but held court in Mayfair, where West End property dealers in search of money could conveniently beat a path to their door. By contrast, Ulster & Cayman's head office in Gresham Street was a quiet and envious place. Its managing partners Charles Cassels and Stephen Cornelius, who operated from there, didn't know a deal from a deck of cards, according to Dervish. The bank's chairman, Sir Anthony Winchester MP – a distinguished parliamentarian but, unlike Britton Trust's chairman, from the lower house – was a recent appointment as a neutral peacemaker. He would have liked Dervish and de Deyler to join their colleagues over coffee each morning to discuss the business of the day, but Dervish had pointed out that the City was as near to Mayfair as Mayfair was to the City, and Westminster was just around the corner. Sir Anthony knew, moreover, that banks grew rich lending money at a profit. So when Dervish and de Deyler told him that as they had provided the bank's free capital by selling Farranwide, Mayfair rather than City was entitled to decide how the proceeds were loaned, he found himself stuck for an argument.

Guy Magnus was announced by a long-legged receptionist with blue eyes and straight blonde hair of the kind who passes the job interview before a word passes her lips. He found Dervish and de Deyler seated at opposite ends of a mahogany table whose very length determined the magnitude of their office building; for few Mayfair properties had met their required specification, having not been built on the scale of a City block. A set of Regency dining chairs stood sentinel along both sides of the table; not one dozen – for they would have been set so wide apart that it would have seemed as if the bank was short of cash – but two dozen. The search for a Persian carpet to adorn the parquet floor – more than twice as long as it was wide – had covered three continents.

Guy was shown to a chair two places to Dervish's right; de Deyler remained in the far distance, a shadowy figure against the bright light of the window, from where he was able to take notes of the discussion without surveillance.

'Let's do business. What can we do you for, Mr Magnus?' Dervish cut short the civilities, his small brown eyes searching his visitor's face for a weakness. He was a man in a hurry. The sale of Farranwide Properties had brought in almost £100 million. If this was not entered into the loan book before his City colleagues bent Sir Anthony's ear, Mayfair might have £50 million to lend at best. He and de Deyler had been debating the matter that very morning. They had agreed they had a problem, but had been interrupted some way short of a solution. If Guy Magnus was wasting their time, he had better not do so for long.

Guy returned Dervish's gaze. The balding banker looked shrewd, tough, cool. 'Twenty million,' he replied confidently. He hadn't read Mein Kampf but he knew the gist. Plead for £2 million and you'd be treated as a schoolboy. Demand £20 million and you were a serious businessman, if not a national hero.

'Shouldn't be no problem,' said Dervish, as if it didn't matter what the money was for.

De Deyler, curly-haired, round-faced and blue-eyed, raised his eyebrows at his partner. 'What you got in mind?' he corrected any such impression.

'I don't want to bother you if you can't do it right away,' Guy replied. 'We'll be making a takeover bid in the next few days. We must have the finance in place before we make an announcement. We'll need to issue an offer document shortly after.'

'Why go elsewhere?' Dervish asked rhetorically. 'I'll tell City branch to put its corporate finance team on the job.' His tone spoke for the inferior role of City, implying that when he gave the order its managing partners would jump.

'May we know the name of the lucky company?' asked de Deyler, as if he were a father interrogating a prospective bride.

'My private company Westchurch will probably be making the offer, but I haven't made up my mind whether to set up a newco for the actual acquisition,' replied Guy disingenuously.

'The target company,' de Deyler pressed. He was clearly an equal partner to Dervish, the foil to his sabre.

'Oh that?' Guy sounded as if that were a detail to be sorted out later when everything else had been arranged. 'I'm buying Britton.'

It was de Deyler's turn to raise his eyebrows and Dervish's to shrug.

'Trust,' Guy completed. He handed a copy of the company's most recent accounts to Dervish and sent another sliding down the table towards de Deyler. The two exchanged glances and pushed the document to one side.

'What about yours?' Dervish asked, holding out his hand.

Guy passed a sheaf of papers to each. 'Pro forma,' he said. 'In draft.'

De Deyler leafed professionally through the pages. 'Your company is worth barely a million,' he pointed out, gratuitously as far as Guy was concerned.

'We have resources,' Guy countered.

Dervish wondered whether he should call the meeting to an end there and then and send his visitor away with a flea in his ear. A company worth £1 million was proposing to bid for another with a valuation of £9 million, and was asking to borrow £20 million to do so. Magnus had a hell of a nerve to put so bizarre a proposition on the table.

But Dervish knew it cost nothing to listen a little longer. Guy Magnus had earned a reputation for finding deals that made money. He was no fool: he must have spotted plenty of scope for uplift in Britton Trust's balance sheet; it would be interesting to know how much. Its assets were mostly in property, which had risen dramatically in value during the past two years. Dervish knew without looking at the balance sheet that they would be included at original cost. Before its merger with CHIT Britton Estates had occupied the floor above theirs. Any merchant bank worth its salt knows all there is to know about its neighbour. If it judges that others might show an interest, it might even make a friendly investment in its future.

'What price are you thinking of offering?' asked Dervish, flicking an invisible piece of fluff from his black jacket.

'Two fifty-five a share for starters. We may have to go up to two seventy-five to win.'

At the far end of the table de Deyler banged his calculator. 'That's eighteen and a half million, Sam,' he told Dervish sombrely when he had finished. No way was the bank going to lend Guy Magnus, or anyone else for that matter, £20 million against a bid of eighteen-and-a-half.

'It has a net asset value of over £25 million,' Guy countered. 'That's nearly £4 a share. If we pay eighteen and a half, you'll have plenty of margin.'

'Twenty-five million, eh?' Dervish looked at de Deyler. They must be sure that the bank would recover its money if the deal went wrong. But if they were satisfied that the value of Britton Trust's assets more than covered their loan, and if they held its shares as security against repayment, little could. 'How long would you need the money for?' he asked sceptically.

'A year at most,' Guy replied confidently. 'We'll sell most of the surplus assets within six months.'

'What say we have a valuation carried out and lend up to sixty per cent of net asset value, Sam?' de Deyler suggested cautiously. 'Subject to repayment of half within six months,' he added.

'I'd get seventy per cent from the Bank of England for this deal,' Guy argued fearlessly.

'I thought you said you had your own resources to bring to the party,' Dervish reminded him.

'We've already bought over a million shares for cash,' Guy set out his hand. 'We're buying another million today,' he played his joker.

De Deyler was impressed. 'How sure are you that you'll go unconditional?' he asked. 'Fifty per cent's still a long way off if the board doesn't recommend your offer. The directors have some pretty hefty holdings. You could wind up with egg on your face.'

'You don't need to lose any sleep over that,' Guy assured him. 'I've already got the chairman on-side.'

Had they underestimated their man? Down the length of the table Dervish and de Deyler exchanged signals which agreed that might well be the case. And homes had to be found for the £100 million they had in the tank.

'If you can prove to us you're right about the assets, we'll lend you £15 million, half to be repaid after six months,' said Dervish, meaning it.

'I'll want at least seventeen and a half,' replied Guy, equally firm.

'At three per cent over base rate, on our usual fee terms,' Dervish continued. 'Don't try to push us further than we'll go,' he warned as he stood up.

'I wouldn't dream of it, Sam,' replied Guy. He knew that for the time being he should leave matters as they stood. He had been offered a million pounds more than he had hoped for, and the battle was not yet joined. 'I'll come back to you as soon as we're ready to proceed with our offer.'

18

'By Hand and Secret, eh?' The Earl of St Edmunds squinted at the envelope Harold Antony had handed him and fingered it gingerly. 'Understand by hand, but secret?' He held it to his nose and sniffed it. 'Better not watch me read it, eh, Antony. Second thoughts, probably wrote it yourself anyway. Better hang about, case it blows up in me face.'

Harold Antony blushed, in so far as the tightening of his temples might be construed as a display of embarrassment. He screwed up his eyes as he watched the earl read the letter he had dictated and Guy Magnus's secretary had typed on Westchurch's letterhead.

'Thirty-five per cent of the stock, bum, bum, two fifty-five – not exactly generous, eh? Incumbent upon us ... fine turn of phrase, our friend Magnus ... considerable property expertise, bum, bum, entrepreneurial skills ... what's this? Britton Trust's proven managerial abilities, must tell Priestley and Palliser that, their jobs don't sound safe for a minute.' He chuckled quietly at his own witticism. 'Laserbeam a fine established company, there's a laugh! bum, bum, continue improving the return on capital employed – wonder where he gets this stuff from ... exciting future for Watson's, exchange of views ... I'll say, if they don't wake their ideas up in a hurry – record of industrial relations excellent, he says, bum, bum, wishes to discuss the future of the company with the board. My obedient servant, eh? Well, well, what are we to make of all this? I ask meself.' The earl peered at Harold Antony through his heavily magnified reading glasses as he awaited the messenger's reply.

'You should seriously consider what he says, Berry,' Harold Antony took up a holding position. 'Two fifty-five a share puts a value of over £17 million on the company. That's a pretty full figure in today's market.'

'Might be, if it was his last word. But it ain't. Sighting shot. Knows he's not going to win in the market – got whatever he can from there. So he wants to talk to the board. Knows we hold the key. Someone had better tell your friend Magnus that if he wants to buy Britton Trust he'll need to offer a jolly sight more than two fifty-five.'

Antony saw his role as a messenger was being transformed into that of an intermediary. He took the message back to Guy, who was unperturbed. 'I expected it,' he said. 'We'll have to pay £20 million in the end. I'm not worried; it's worth at least £30 million.'

Guy spent the first days of the following week preparing for a more serious meeting at Ulster & Cayman. The financing agreements must be negotiated in detail and an offer document prepared. The bank had to carry out due diligence investigations. Its managers would require a good deal of information to satisfy themselves on the financial standing of the acquiring company.

Meanwhile he must explain to his partners how he planned to structure the deal. Larry might otherwise be too old-fashioned and fastidious to go along with his plan; Danny too inexperienced and naïve.

'Here's what we do,' he explained when they were seated around the Hille coffee table in his office. 'Larry, get out your chequebook and write out a cheque for a fiver. Make it payable to MGC Investments Limited. You too, Danny. No, not five, you fool: your share's twenty per cent.' Seeing Danny's bemused expression, he took out his own cheque book and proceeded to write. 'Here's mine for seventy-five. I trust myself,' he said blithely. 'Or do you want me to change it into a hundred and take all the profits?' he said when they still hesitated.

'Why don't you use one of the other companies?' asked Danny.

'Ludgate couldn't,' Callaghan pointed out. 'An investment trust can't put more than fifteen per cent of its funds into any one investment. St Paul's could if it could raise the finance.'

'Surely you don't expect me to share £10 million profit with St Paul's shareholders?' asked Guy, incredulous.

'What about Westchurch, then?'

'Better, but not best. The gearing's the key. Just do as I tell you.'

Larry knew that if Guy had worked out how to structure the deal, it could not be bettered. He nodded to Danny. They scribbled obediently passed their cheques across the table to Guy.

'You'd better not ask me for any more,' Callaghan told him. 'You still haven't paid me back for the Mars Bar you made me buy you last week.'

'Now we have a £100 company,' Guy ignored the cynicism, pinning their cheques to his and putting them into his wallet. 'All we're short of is £20 million and we'll be bidding for a £30 million company. What percentage of £100 is £10 million profit, Larry?'

'Ten million per cent,' replied Callaghan without hesitation. 'Before tax, that is,' he qualified his answer.

'Now that's what I call gearing,' added Danny, getting the idea.

'Nobody in his right mind is going to lend us £20 million,' Callaghan spoiled the party.

'Ulster & Cayman will,' Guy corrected him, smiling smugly.

Larry Callaghan rolled his eyes, then shrugged his shoulders. Why should he explain that banks required a safety margin on their security when Guy knew it already? If his fiver humoured the boy, it was a small price to pay. He felt sorry for Danny, though. Twenty pounds was a big night out for a kid like him.

'Banks will lend you whatever you want nowadays, as long as you convince them you don't need it,' Guy told them. 'We have a meeting with Dervish on Thursday at ten. He wants to see a pro forma balance sheet for Britton Trust. It mustn't show a net worth of less than £20 million, Danny. And for Ludgate. Last July the accounts showed £8.3 million: I want you to get it up to £10 million, Larry. Let me have them both on my desk by six o'clock on Wednesday.' He was smiling no longer.

Danny spent the following days with his head well down over the Britton Trust balance sheet. If its shareholders would have been excited on Wednesday evening by the news that their company's value had jumped to £18 million, they would have been delirious on seeing Guy's adjustments the following morning.

It was a quarter past eleven when Guy re-entered Ulster & Cayman's offices with his partners, walking slowly so as not to show concern that he was late.

'Sorry, Sam,' he apologised as he sat down; 'some guys are the very devil to shake off. I told them you had first refusal, but they wouldn't listen. The City's so desperate to lend money nowadays, it'll offer any terms.'

Dervish had spent twenty minutes waiting for whatever traffic was holding up Guy to dissipate, the next twenty-five swearing he would never do business with the ignorant bastard again and a further half an hour cooling down from a fever that had reached a pitch from which it could no longer climb.

'Let's do business,' he said brusquely.

Guy handed him a copy of the amended Britton Trust balance sheet, sent

Danny on a mission to the far end of the room with one for de Deyler, and passed the rest to the bank's corporate finance team lined up on the other side of the table.

Dervish picked up the figure on the bottom line. 'Twenty point six million, eh?'

'That's the worst scenario,' Guy explained.

'And the best?'

'I'm not prepared to say. A cautious businessman never banks on more than the minimum. That way he's never disappointed.'

'Twenty-two? Twenty-four?' Dervish pressed him.

'Conservatively?' Guy inclined his head soberly. 'Let's just say that you're going to be very pleasantly surprised, gentlemen.'

Dervish and de Deyler exchanged glances down the length of the table.

'Maybe we were a little shy,' Dervish acknowledged. 'On a bid of £20 million we could possibly go to £16 million.'

'I knew all along you'd suggest that. We'll be delighted to accept,' Guy conceded magnanimously. 'Larry, why don't you take it from here?'

While Callaghan took it from there with de Deyler and Ulster & Cayman's head of banking, Guy discussed takeover strategy with Dervish and the merchant bank's head of corporate finance. Danny conveyed messages between the groups. Most were routine, but one seemed more important than the others.

'Guy, they're asking Larry where the other £4 million's coming from,' Danny interrupted his chief's discussions in a whisper.

Guy turned to Dervish. 'Say if you feel we're asking enough from you already, Sam,' he said; 'but while you're funding Westchurch, we ought in fairness to give you first refusal on financing the expansion plans of a couple more of our companies,' he suggested casually.

'Tell me about it,' said Dervish.

Guy passed him copies of the latest accounts for Ludgate Investments and St Paul's Property, with Larry Callaghan's note on progress since the year end. 'Ten million's small beer today for an investment trust,' he said. 'The minimum size should be 20, but we're more conservative than most. We'd rather take it up in two stages: two and a half million for each company for the time being, and the same again in six months' time when we see how the stock market's going.'

'How would the money be invested?' asked Dervish. He looked out of the ceiling-high window across the square to demonstrate the level of his interest in the reply.

'If interest rates weren't on the way up, Ludgate would lock some away in long-dated gilt-edged; but in present conditions we'd put £2 million into equities and leave the rest in cash so we're in a position to take advantage of any weakening in the market. St Paul's is looking at an extremely promising property proposition,' Guy replied.

'We may be prepared to lend up to £4 million, but certainly not five,' Dervish said sagely. 'That would keep the gearing of both companies within safe limits.

Guy acknowledged the older man's prudence, smiling inwardly. He turned to Danny and whispered to him to take the message back to Callaghan that Westchurch could now provide the balance of the finance for the takeover from its own resources. Then he turned back to Dervish to negotiate their respective shares of the profits and to set up a further meeting for the following week.

'De Deyler couldn't see how a £1 million company could possibly have cash resources of £4 million,' Callaghan said on the return journey. 'I couldn't help him. You're better at explaining things than I am, Guy.'

'Tell him we're bringing in partners,' replied Guy. 'It's a good job we have friends.'

'Friends?' asked Larry and Danny with one voice.

'Wouldn't you call Ludgate and St Paul's friends?'

19

Guy Magnus needed more friends than Ludgate and St Paul's. Under the rules of the London Stock Exchange, a forty per cent holding in a company's equity would trigger an unconditional cash offer for the rest of its shares. Recent market purchases had brought their holding in Britton Trust to the threshold of this limit. He was not yet ready to take the irrevocable step of exceeding it.

But even the most careful calculations can go awry. Unaware of a purchase Guy had transacted through another stockbroker, Harold Antony had erroneously calculated that picking up another 7,500 shares would still leave his client below the limit. Made aware of the problem, Guy told Antony to cancel the sale; but the jobber refused to take back the shares. What should Antony do? He decided to hold the shares in his own name for twenty-four hours, on the grounds that as Guy had not agreed to take them – yet – he could not be termed his client – yet.

Guy saw the issue from a different perspective. He had his friends' fortunes to look after. What greater fortune could they have than that they should happen to buy Britton Trust shares and perchance profit from their foresight? Likewise his employees. Was it not apt, he asked himself, that he reward the loyalty of his speculating driver by directing him into the path of a sure thing? So loyal, and indeed so trustworthy, was Yankee Tate that Guy's brokers, Grieff & Hammer, had readily offered him credit. Lack of dealing experience might have put Tate at a disadvantage had not one of its partners, Ray Munster, come up with the idea that he be authorised to act on Tate's behalf 'with discretion'.

Guy was confident his bid would succeed. He owned forty per cent of Britton Trust's equity, and he had friends. Financial backing to buy the rest would shortly be confirmed. The directors, who owned fewer shares than he, had agreed to see him that afternoon. They couldn't possibly turn down an offer valuing their company at £20 million. Its latest balance sheet showed less than half that figure, and last year's profits were only just over a million.

Because his confidence was so high, he was surprised at his cool reception when he entered the Britton Trust boardroom. It was perhaps as well that the earl not present, for their earlier meeting was best left unknown. In the absence of the chairman, the tall, angular figure of John Charteris, his face gaunt and serious, his eyes piercing and bushy-browed, his grey hair carefully parted, had taken the head of the table. On his right Jolyon Priestley shared folders and computer print-outs with a younger man who, Guy guessed, must be Alan Palliser. On Charteris's left sat an inscrutable Archie Laws. The much-vaunted Thomas Goodman was nowhere to be seen.

For his part, John Charteris saw Guy Magnus as tails on the coin of which Harry Griffin was heads: an unwelcome intruder while he and his remaining colleagues were trying to sort out the company. He waved him to the bottom of the table in the manner of a General Secretary of the Communist Party of the Soviet Union about to inform a prospective former member of the Politburo of his fate.

'We've read your letter, Mr Magnus. Have you anything to add?' he asked. In accordance with custom the accused was being offered an opportunity to admit his guilt and make a full recantation before sentence of death was pronounced.

'Anything to add? I'd have thought it's self-explanatory,' said Guy. 'You have a fine company. I represent its largest shareholder. We plan to make an offer for the rest of the shares and to develop the company to realise its full potential. We seek the board's recommendation. The more you help us, the easier it will be to justify paying the best price to your shareholders.'

Or the more you know, the less you'll offer, thought Charteris. He had an uneasy feeling about the earl's absence. He'd have preferred Thomas Goodman to be by his side; but everyone was entitled to a holiday. 'The view round this table is that you're trying to buy our company on the cheap, Mr Magnus. As for developing its potential, the record of your previous acquisitions could hardly be described in such terms,' he added sardonically.

Guy chose to ignore the jibe. 'We believe a full takeover to be in your shareholders' interests,' he said. 'We've already made their shares worth over 250p. Provided we have your recommendation, we're ready to offer more.'

Charteris stared down the table, poker-faced, and allowed a lengthy silence. 'Do you have a specific proposal to put to us, Mr Magnus?' he asked finally.

'Two seventy-five without your recommendation, two ninety-five with it,' Guy responded confidently. 'Provided you can satisfy Ulster & Cayman as to the company's value.'

'Impossible,' Charteris responded just as forcefully.

'Impossible?' Guy asked, nonplussed. He had not expected so unequivocal a rejection. 'Impossible to do what? To satisfy our bank on value?'

'Impossible to accept your price. Britton Trust is worth far more than that.'

Guy was gratified to have his valuation endorsed by so informed a source. 'If we turn our backs your shareholders will never see £2 again,' he said.

'We shall have to see,' Charteris said calmly. He knew he could ignore the threat. Magnus had spent £5 million buying thirty-five per cent of Britton Trust. He least of all could afford to see the price drop so far.

You smug shit, thought Guy; I can see you're going to have to be bought. 'May I make a suggestion?' he asked. 'Why don't you sleep on my proposal and we'll meet again tomorrow? That will give you time to decide on a price you can recommend to your shareholders. If I agree, we'll shake hands and save a lot of money. If not, the merchant bankers and lawyers will make the money instead.' He stood up. 'Mr Charteris, may I have a private word?'

Charteris eyed Guy suspiciously. He felt uncomfortable about leaving the room with him; the boardroom was not exactly a haven of trust nowadays. 'Not if you have anything to say that I cannot repeat to my colleagues.'

'We don't have to leave the room,' Guy said smiling, and moved to the window. Charteris rose and followed him. 'I don't know what the fuss is about,' Guy continued when they were out of earshot. 'I know your company's worth more than two ninety-five a share, but why should the other shareholders get it? It's the directors who put in all the work. You more than anyone.'

'What are you trying to suggest?' asked Charteris in an ominous tone, straightening his long frame.

Guy looked into a steely pair of eyes. 'Come off it, John,' he said; 'We're both men of the world. I've already looked after your chairman.'

Charteris felt his pale cheeks burn. 'Kindly regard this exchange as at an end. And this meeting,' he said firmly. He returned to his place, picked up his papers and strode from the room, leaving his colleagues to straggle out after him.

Jolyon Priestley showed Guy to the lift. 'What the hell was that all about?' he asked.

'The man's a lunatic,' Guy shook his head in disbelief. 'He refused to listen to a perfectly sensible proposition. How can you do business with a man like that?'

'Now you can see how difficult it's been to do a straightforward job here,' Priestley nodded sympathetically.

'When it comes to the crunch, I want to know you're on-side, Jolyon. I'll see you all right,' Guy said reassuringly.

'You have my word on it,'

That, thought Guy as the lift took him down, gave him no comfort at all. But, he told himself as he walked through the back ways of Mayfair to Berkeley Square, he must shrug off negative thoughts.

'I've come straight from Britton Trust,' he told Dervish when he was seated in his usual place at the right hand of the master. 'It's go at two ninety-five.'

'The board will give its recommendation?'

Guy thought of giving a positive affirmation, on the grounds that Dervish had not specified which board, but as the point was one that could be verified, he settled for something less.

'Not yet,' he admitted. 'But there's no doubt the company's worth a bid of £20 million,' he changed his ground.

'We calculate it's going to cost you £20.6 million,' Dervish pointed out. 'You have to provide five per cent for fees on a deal of this kind.' Not even Guy Magnus would expect a merchant bank to work for nothing.

'In that case it'll cost you £16.5 million,' Guy replied, taking care to avoid any mention of the £4 million to be loaned to Ludgate and St Paul's. Not even Dervish could renege on an offer to finance eighty per cent of the cost of the bid.

A frenzied signal came down the table from de Deyler.

'You're a wealthy man, Guy. A man of means,' Dervish recalled.

'Some,' Guy acknowledged humbly.

'Able to see this thing through if anything goes wrong.'

'Naturally.'

'We must have your personal guarantees.'

'From all three partners,' de Deyler clarified the point. Then he apologised and left to make a telephone call to Britton Trust's property advisers. It would be prudent to make one last check before a final commitment was made.

'Tell me, Everard,' he was soon asking the firm's principal: 'I know you act for Britton Trust, so I probably shouldn't be asking you this, but – can I put it this way? – you wouldn't advise against lending, for argument's sake, £16 million against an offer for the company, would you? If such an offer were made, that is.'

Everard Sellars considered his position. His firm had recently completed a revaluation of Britton Trust's properties. It owed a duty of confidentiality to the company. However, this duty was properly owed not to the company's directors but to its owners. Would he not be failing in his duty to its shareholders if he refused to give advice which would be to their ultimate benefit? If this advice also proved beneficial to the company's future owners, and they were to reward whoever had given it with the next round of fees, so much the better: for did he not also owe it to his partnership – and through it to himself – to maximise his firm's fee income both now and in the future? There was a neat symmetry in the reconciliation of his duty to his clients and his duty to his firm. Its dictates required no complex casuistry but the simple pursuit of well-motivated intuition.

'Advise you against? You understand that I'm their adviser, not yours?' he made sure that de Deyler understood his professional position.

'But if you were advising us?'

'If I were advising you and not them? Let me put it this way, Sidney: no, I wouldn't advise you against.'

'So their shares are undervalued?'

'Undervalued? You could say that, Sidney, but don't quote me.'

'We're safe, though.'

'As houses.'

'Thanks, Everard. I feel much better now about the whole thing.'

'The whole thing? I'd better not ask what whole thing, Sidney, or you'd be revealing a confidence. We must talk again – it's high time we did some business for you.'

Everard Sellars put down his telephone and reflected for a couple of seconds. It was all the time he needed. He told his secretary to fetch the files of the Britton Trust property revaluation. While he waited for them he picked up his *Financial Times*, checked the previous day's closing share price. When the files arrived he jotted down the salient figures and made some calculations. It was too soon to make the telephone call he had in mind, but when the time came he must be fully prepared.

Meanwhile de Deyler returned to his boardroom to find Dervish and Guy wrapping up an agreement on Ulster & Cayman's fees. Depending on how long it took to repay the loan, the bank would earn up to a million pounds.

'Congratulations, Guy,' said de Deyler; 'I can tell you, you've got a good deal here. Straight from the trainer's mouth. What's the situation, Sam?'

'We're ready to go,' said Dervish. 'City's sending a formal letter to the Earl of St Edmunds by hand first thing tomorrow morning and announcing the offer to the stock exchange at ten. Tell them to draw up the facility letter and the personal guarantees, would you, Sidney? We're only the brains factory,' he explained to Guy. 'City office is the paper mill.'

Guy found it hard to refrain from asking which was the bread basket.

20

At half past eight next morning Pat Crisp called Guy to tell him he had an offer for the shares in Dominion Equity & Bond. Ludgate Investments had to take a loss, but Guy congratulated himself on his foresight: better that Ludgate's shareholders take the knock than Westchurch's.

At half past nine Ulster & Cayman's City office called. Its letter had been delivered to the Earl of St Edmunds. The earl had agreed that the Britton Trust board would meet Guy at eleven, but asked that once again his own apologies be accepted. The earl was a man who left no footprints.

At ten o'clock Ulster & Cayman called again to confirm that the offer had been announced by the stock exchange. Britton Trust shares, which the previous afternoon had miraculously been marked up to 294p, had risen by another penny on the news. The market seemed to think the bid would be enough.

Guy's line was soon buzzing with calls from stockbrokers asking how they could help; and from City reporters asking Guy to help them. What, they wanted to know, was Britton Trust when it was at home? And why did he want to acquire it? They seemed unconvinced by his response: to help it make money. It was a blessing when the clock reached a quarter to eleven and he was able to refuse the last call.

The Britton Trust boardroom was more subdued than the day before. In the nature of such gatherings, directors who own shares calculate whether to try to hold on to their positions or to sell out; directors with jobs hope either to make a favourable impression on the bidder or to be generously rewarded on their departure; some few, perhaps conscious of the presence of legal and financial advisers, prepare to do their duty by the shareholders.

Be that as it may, John Charteris was even less communicative than on the previous day. 'I see your bid is 295p per share even without our recommendation, Mr Magnus,' he observed icily.

Guy felt himself on the defensive. Was Charteris implying that the board's endorsement was worth a further 20p? 'Naturally we'd prefer an agreed take-over,' he responded. 'Contested bids are messy. We're offering a knockout price to avoid one. We have forty per cent in the bag, so a counter-bid's out of the question. Why don't you recommend our offer and we can all go home?'

'You're still ten per cent short,' said Charteris laconically. He left the statement hanging on the air.

'We've had promises,' replied Guy as briefly. He would have liked to nod towards the chairman's seat, but Charteris was occupying it. He would have liked to nod towards Priestley's too, but the latter was still something of an enigma. As it was, he nodded towards the window, as if to imply that the world outside was forming a queue to sell to him.

'You'll need more than promises,' said Charteris, a note of asperity in his voice. 'Acceptances is the word. You won't get any while the share price is above your offer. The shareholders will either sell in the market or hold out for more.'

The old boy was roused, Guy thought. Better an opponent in a foul mood than one who kept his cool. 'Persuade me you're worth more,' he challenged.

'We'll see your offer document first, and then decide whether to include a property valuation in our defence,' Charteris replied.

The other directors might as well not have been present. Their eyes either swung from side to side as if watching a Centre Court final, or fixed on their merchant banker to see what could be gleaned from his expression, or in Priestley's case stared down at an empty jotter pad. Their merchant banker's expression gave little away, for there was little behind it. He and the lawyer seated next to him were, Guy saw, no more than middle-rank messengers reporting back to senior luminaries who wouldn't be seen dead making a personal appearance at a sub-£50 million bid. There was nothing to be gained from prolonging the meeting.

'Well, gentlemen,' he said as he rose to leave, 'in the end these matters are decided not by the directors, but by the owners of the company: the shareholders.'

He spent the afternoon with Larry Callaghan and Danny Gilbert in Ulster & Cayman's corporate finance department, helping to draft the offer document. From time to time a lawyer or accountant would seek clarification of their intentions for the Britton Trust businesses.

'Don't worry,' Callaghan would tell him after consulting Guy; 'Just give a general reassurance – no, that won't arise. The chairman's on our side.' For the earl, in conveying his apologies for his inability to attend the morning's meeting, had not felt precluded from offering Guy a time and venue later in the day for a less public rendezvous.

As the three were about to leave at the end of the afternoon, a manager from the banking department walked into the room where they had been working.

'We've drawn up the loan facility letter,' he said, handing Guy a document. 'You'd better sign it while you're here.'

Guy read the document with meticulous care. Every word was important. *The lesser of £16,500,000 and 80% of the total consideration payable* – yes, that was right, – *offer of not more than 300 pence per share – the facility to be available for twelve months – must be reduced to £8,250,000 within six months – secured by the deposit with us of all shares acquired by you in Britton Trust – the personal guarantees of Messrs. G. Magnus, L. Callaghan and D. Gilbert.*

The manager handed him the personal guarantee agreements.

'Come over here, would you, Larry?' Guy called across the room as he signed the document. When Callaghan was seated, he passed him the facility letter and awaited his comment.

Callaghan's middle finger passed steadily down the pages until it came to a halt at the relevant clause. 'Not from me,' he objected. 'No point. Wouldn't be worth the paper it's written on. I couldn't guarantee £16,500, let alone £16,500,000.'

'True,' Guy agreed. 'Family man, house under mortgage, boys at public school. I'll tell them.'

'I don't think you should ask Danny to give one either,' Callaghan persisted. 'It's up to you whether you're feeling suicidal enough to give one yourself.'

'Check the rest of this through, would you, while I have a word with Danny?' Guy picked up the copy he had just signed and one other document, left the room and found Danny Gilbert putting on his coat.

'Sign these, Danny,' he ordered, putting the documents down on a low table.

'What are they?' Danny asked.

'We have to sign a copy of the facility letter, agreeing to its terms,' replied Guy. 'Don't worry, Larry and I have checked it out.'

Danny skimmed the first document. It seemed all right, so he signed his name below Guy's.

'You'd better sign that one too, while you're at it,' Guy said, pointing at the other document.

'What's it about?' asked Danny.

'It's in the facility letter you just signed. We're giving guarantees.'

Danny saw Guy's signature and the vacant space opposite Callaghan's name. 'Is Larry signing?' he asked.

'He's got a family to look after. Anyway, he only has five per cent.'

Danny scratched his head, uncertain about Guy's reasoning. 'Why do they want it?' he persisted.

'Silly boy, you don't think they're going to lend us all that money without personal guarantees, do you?'

Danny saw the logic in that. Of course they wouldn't. This was a man's world; it was time he stopped acting like a child. He signed.

'Can't wait, gotta put on my glad rags and go meet an earl,' Guy grinned at him as he left the room. Danny grinned back. Life with Guy Magnus was fun. Some day he might even get to meet the famous earl himself.

Guy whistled as he strolled along Cheyne Walk an hour later. The sky was darkening earlier now, but the evening was clear and the lights of the riverside buildings shone brightly in the early autumn dusk. As he approached the apartment building where the Earl of St Edmunds lived, he slowed his step, savouring the anticipation of the deal to be done and the person he would be doing it with. Then he gathered himself, crossed the pavement and rang the bell.

Harold Antony was there already, embarking, it appeared, on at least his second scotch. Guy refused one, his eye having lit on a decanter with a promising pale amber hue. When this was offered as a last resort, he managed a 'May I?' of apparently equal reluctance. He was soon sipping appreciatively at a fine, nutty amontillado, far superior to the one the earl had offered at his cocktail party. A recording of Gustav Mahler's *Das Lied von der Erde* was playing on the earl's out-of-date hi-fi system.

'Kathleen Ferrier?' he asked. The ageing sound confirmed what the photograph of the woman in the pale blue dress on the sleeve peeking from the rack had already told him. 'Christa Ludwig's good, but Ferrier was rather special.'

The earl beamed. He was plainly flattered.

'Berry and I have been talking,' said Antony. The introduction was unnecessary, but it helped him feel less uncomfortable with his position. 'What kind of time did you have with the board this morning?'

This was not, Guy realised immediately, the *non sequitur* it sounded. The two must have been briefed on the meeting: but by whom? By Charteris? Not if he could keep control of the information for twenty-four hours. By the bankers? They had little enough to report.

'Much as I expected,' he said non-committally.

'Reception pretty cool, eh?' The earl was not guessing. His informant must have been Jolyon Priestley.

'Pretty cool,' Guy acknowledged.

'They've got shares,' the earl commented shrewdly, forbearing to add that he was one of their band.

His meaning was not lost on Guy. 'They want the best price. Who doesn't?' he observed. 'The trouble is, if everyone gets the best price, it no longer is the best.' There was a lengthy silence. Each sipped at his drink. 'If the total price we can afford is £20 million, that's no reason why everyone should be stuck with 295p,' Guy elaborated.

Harold Antony poured himself another whisky as if the decanter were his own. 'I see your point,' he said on the way back to the settee, as if in casual reference to a matter of little moment. There was a further silence. Guy determined not to break it. 'You mean,' Antony finally got the message, 'that if there were to be another quarter of a million in the kitty, there's no reason why everyone should have 5p more. After all,' he added as if in justification, 'you bought most of your shares for less than the price you're offering.'

The Earl of St Edmunds stared at the ornate cornices of his ceiling. 'Don't suppose the boys were much bothered about their own jobs,' he brought the subject back to the morning's meeting.

'Will you be wanting to keep any of them on, Guy?' asked Antony pointedly. 'There's something to be said for an element of continuity – provided they observe strict loyalty to you and your business plans, of course. But will you be wanting to do all the barking yourself?'

'Not my style,' Guy replied truthfully. 'But I suppose we could pay the non-executives off, buy the chairman a new Rolls-Royce and pay him £30,000 a year.'

'And be in for the same deal as before,' completed Antony.

'I'm concerned about job security for the staff,' said the earl briskly, as if to point out that as each item on the agenda was resolved it was time to move to the next business. If his credentials as a company chairman happened to be enhanced by this show of efficiency, not to say compassion, so much the better.

'All taken care of,' Guy replied dismissively.

'Guy has an excellent record,' Antony confirmed, nodding his head to the earl. 'Second to none.'

Guy stared at him hard, indicating that he should stop while he was ahead. He did so.

'Well, that's that, then,' the earl made clear his satisfaction with the outcome of the exchange of views. 'Can't ask you to stay for supper: not dressed.'

Worse, I'd unbalance the table, Guy told himself, as in the absence of any other manservant he allowed himself to be shown out by Harold Antony.

21

As befits an occasion when the board of a public company is about to commence the most important meeting of its brief life, this time the chairman was present. At the Earl of St Edmunds' side sat a director of the corporate finance department of Britton Trust's merchant bank.

Grover Seagull was Thruston Cutwell's most brilliant product. The cut of his Savile Row suit bore witness to his distinction; the waves of his brown hair ascended in layers to match his Olympian aspirations. Not yet thirty years old, he had flown high above his peers for almost a decade; if not in their opinion, at least in his own. Such detractors as he had based their dissent on the discovery that the companies he defended from unwelcome take-over bids had proved without exception to be managed by sharp, dynamic entrepreneurs, while those his clients attacked were soon shown to be run by sleepy village idiots.

Lest this view be judged less than objective, let it be affirmed that it was founded on empirical fact. For just as the eponymous birds select the tastiest fish from just below the surface of the sea, so was Grover Seagull picky about the clients he accepted. A sleepy village idiot with the temerity to enter his office complaining of an unsolicited approach for his company would find himself shown out in a hurry, whereupon Seagull would pick up his telephone and invite a sharp, dynamic entrepreneur of his acquaintance to prepare a counter-bid. Should the entrepreneur demur, he would be relegated to the village idiot division without waiting for the end of the season. The rest of the City fed on Seagull's droppings.

Grover Seagull's colleagues had been somewhat surprised when he announced not only that he had accepted the defence of Britton Trust, but that he would be attending on the board in person. They reckoned without his greatest quality: flexibility. Even the most moribund company could, he calculated, be successfully defended if the predator were sufficiently unpopular. Guy Magnus's popularity had been on the wane for sixteen months, ever since the stock market turned down and he sharpened up his practice of selling shares he did not own.

Moreover, Seagull was flirting with the novel notion that if you failed to defend a company from takeover but nevertheless nominated the ultimate winner, your campaign would be accounted a brilliant success. While this strategy might not earn you a glowing reputation among vulnerable companies, there were others whose directors knew their days of independence were numbered, and cared for no better outcome than that their conqueror was not their most hated rival.

There may have been one final, clinching factor. The chairman of Britton Trust was a peer of the realm.

Be that as it may, Grover Seagull was at the Earl of St Edmunds' right hand when he declared the meeting open, read the minutes of the last meeting and moved to matters arising. The first of these was to report that following the receipt two weeks ago of a letter from Mr Guy Magnus which he had brought to the board's notice the following day, a number of meetings had taken place. He must now inform the board that Magnus and others acting in concert had yesterday made a public offer for all of the shares in the company that they did not already own. With their approval, he proposed to ask Mr Grover Seagull of the company's financial advisers Thruston Cutwell to report on the matter and advise the directors of their fiduciary duty.

Seagull stood to carry out his task. He had developed a style of presentation that favoured upright rhetoric. If it were helpful for a speaker to see his audience from a point of vantage, how much more did the reverse apply? Looking up to him in expectation he saw ranged the Earl of St Edmunds and his colleagues. Other than the earl he knew no one by name; but his ignorance was of no importance, for they all knew him.

'The company's shareholders have received an unconditional offer of 295p in cash for each of their shares,' he announced, as if the news had only just reached the newsreader's earpiece. 'This is not the usual practice. Offers are generally conditional on the bidder receiving acceptances for over fifty per cent of the company's shares. However, stock exchange rules require that where a bidder already holds over forty per cent, he must make an unconditional cash offer for the rest at the highest price he has paid.

'The shareholders are, I have no need to tell you, the owners of the company. When an offer is made, the directors may advise them what action is in their best interests, but the final decision rests with the owners. You are, of course, owners yourselves in so far as you hold shares, and you are obliged to inform the other shareholders of how you intend to deal with them. You have a number of possible courses of action. You may advise your shareholders either to accept the offer or to reject it, you may try to get it improved or solicit a counter-offer, or you may ask the Secretary of State for a referral to the Monopolies Commission. No chance of the last. The first question I have to ask, chairman, is this: what action does the board believe is in the best interests of the shareholders?'

'We wish to reject it,' Charteris set the tone before the earl had a chance to reply.

'Too low,' the earl followed him.

'Are those your grounds too?' Seagull turned to Charteris.

'That goes for Thomas Goodman too,' Charteris replied. 'I have his proxy.'

'What do you think your shares are worth?' asked Seagull.

'May I, chairman?' said Alan Palliser, opening a folder. The earl nodded. 'Asked Palliser to do some sums after the first letter. Tell him, Palliser.'

'On my calculation, our net asset value is £31.8 million,' Palliser told Seagull.

The banker whistled under his breath. 'After tax?' he asked.

'Before. Even so, that's £4.73 per share.'

'That can be a bull or a bear point,' Seagull said. 'It shows Magnus is bidding cheap, and it may convince the shareholders to hold out for more. It also makes it look as if management may not have made the best use of the company's assets. The shareholders may wish to know whether they're being fully utilised. If they think they're not, they're liable to become impatient.'

'If they wait until Monday, they may get their answer,' Charteris riposted. When Seagull raised an eyebrow, he continued: 'We've had an approach for Laserbeam. They seem pretty keen. Palliser and I are meeting them on Monday. If they offer us a good enough price to sell, it will make us more valuable and less vulnerable.'

'You want to defend, then?' Seagull summed up. There was a murmur of assent. 'Well, ultimately your influence on the other shareholders may be measured by the number of shares you control yourselves,' he moved to the next stage. 'My understanding is that at present you account for 1.6 million shares: twenty-three per cent of the equity. Magnus has almost forty-one per cent. That leaves thirty-six per cent outside the two camps. Do you have any shareholders outside this room you can rely on for support?'

'Cummings, managing director of Watson's, has 80,000,' the earl spoke up gruffly. 'Told me so at the AGM.'

'Good. Any more you know of?'

'Harry Griffin can't sell his holding for twelve months unless the board were to recommend an offer,' answered Charteris, sounding pleased with himself. 'That's 310,000 that Magnus can't lay his hands on.'

Seagull was jotting numbers down on his pad. 'You're still looking at thirty per cent out there, and Magnus needs less than ten per cent to win,' he declared the result. 'The good news,' he continued, 'is that the shareholders won't accept while the price in the market is above his offer, and he's not allowed to buy any more without increasing his bid to the highest price he pays.'

'Meaning that if the price remains above 295p ... ?' Charteris asked for clarification.

'It doesn't mean you're safe from him, but you certainly won't go down at that price. Are you agreed, then, gentlemen, that you wish to reject Magnus's offer?'

The earl went round the table naming his colleagues. When each had confirmed his agreement, the earl added his own.

'In that case, I advise you to pass two resolutions,' Seagull said in a tone that made it clear he sought not permission but acquiescence. 'The first,' his tone became official: 'That the price offered for the ordinary shares of the company is significantly below the directors' estimate of the underlying net assets of the group and shareholders be advised accordingly.' While the earl put the resolution formally to the board and obtained its approval, he turned to a colleague who had been sitting in silence at his side and muttered: 'Usual press release, shareholders to take no action until they hear further from the board, etcetera, etcetera,' When the earl indicated that the board had done its duty, he resumed his formal manner. 'Do we have an up-to-date list of the directors' holdings?'

Palliser took another sheet of paper from his folder. 'May I, chairman?' he asked. On receiving the earl's approval he handed it to Seagull.

'Would you kindly pass this round the table? Would each of you kindly check that the number of shares set out against your name is correct?' Seagull requested.

The list went slowly round, each director taking covetous note of his colleagues' holdings as well as his own. Priestley alone gave it a cursory glance.

When it had gone full circle, Seagull ran his fingers along his waves and wet his lips. 'Second resolution, if I may suggest: That the directors present affirmed that their holdings listed in this document would remain in support of the board.'

'And that this support would not be withdrawn without prior notification to the board,' Charteris added, looking meaningfully at his colleagues.

'That's it,' Seagull confirmed.

'In favour?' the earl recovered his role. Each director gave his assent. 'Against? None. Declare the resolution carried. Next business?'

'Forgive me, chairman,' Charteris broke in again. His association with the cautious Thomas Goodman had not been wasted. 'Would it not be appropriate for the list to be appended to the resolution and for each of us to add his signature? I find such a practice often assists the memory.'

'Far as I'm aware, all present are honourable gentlemen. Word their bond,' the earl protested.

'If no director would break his word, how could he have any objection to saying so in writing?' asked Charteris.

'I think you'll find that the practice is sound,' Seagull confirmed.

'Quite so,' the earl conceded.

With the aid of the earl's secretary, Seagull's colleague produced a document for all to sign. As it was being passed around Priestley could be seen staring at the window as if hoping it might offer a way out.

Once the signatures had all been gathered, Charteris made his apologies to the chair, left the boardroom, went to his office and called his stockbroker. He was told that Britton Trust shares were still quoted at around the opening price of 295p, and that to buy in any volume in such a narrow market he would have to bid higher. If he did so, Magnus would be prohibited from coming into the market without increasing his offer, as a bidder must offer all shareholders the highest price he has paid.

'Yes, that's fine,' Charteris confirmed his buying order: 'Ten thousand shares at 300p.'

If Guy Magnus wanted a fight, he, John Charteris, was ready to give him one.

22

The Englishman's weekend is a sacred affair. His family hearth is a haven of tranquillity, its atmosphere of peaceful domesticity broken only by an expedition with his sons to a Saturday afternoon sporting event while his wife and daughters replenish the larder and their wardrobes, and by their joint visit to church on Sunday – unless father should happen to be so exhausted by the previous week's labours that he needs to restore his energies at the golf club. Woe betide he who disturbs the time-honoured habits of the Englishman at leisure, for he will be made to suffer guilt-ridden remorse for such time as the injured party fails to return the compliment – generally the following weekend.

Unless there is business in the offing. Then the Englishman reminds his wife he has mouths to feed, requests her to make the usual apologies to his sons, his daughters, the vicar and his regular fourball partners, retires to his study saying he is not to be disturbed, takes his seat in front of his bulging briefcase, picks up the telephone and calls a friend.

'Grover,' he greets him; 'Everard here. Got a moment?'

'For you, Everard, as long as you want,' replies the unmarried and much relieved Grover Seagull, for his study telephone has not rung for at least ten minutes and he is about to toss a coin to decide where to place a call of his own. He does not bother to add that he will always give Everard Sellars as long as he wants, as Sellars never calls other than to propose mutual business, and he calls on evenings and weekends more often than weekdays, for that is when he knows he can catch Grover Seagull unprotected by a secretary.

'Good meeting on Thursday, Grover?'

'Much as expected.'

'Our property revaluation of you-know-who's probably a bit low by now. I was wondering whether you wanted it brought up to date. Don't worry about the costs. If you win, we'd make it an armchair exercise to keep the fees down. If you lose, Magnus will pay.'

'But it's only a few months since you did it.'

'Yeah, I know; but that was on a professional basis. Arm's length, willing-buyer-willing-seller. Not the best for a defence. We can stretch it if you want.'

'How much?'

'Depends how much you need, and whether you want to win or to lose.' Seagull was silent for long enough for Sellars to guess the answer. 'You want to lose, but not to Magnus, right?' he asked.

'You always were a smart bastard, Everard.'

'It's obvious. You can't defend the board at this level, but the more you make Magnus pay up, the less likely it is he'll use you to break up the business.'

Grover Seagull knew there was no point simulating. 'And you know as well as I do, that it's a property break-up not a business break-up,' he said. 'So you want to be there at the other end when it's all over. That's why you want to know what I'm up to. I'll be straight with you, Everard. I was about to draw up a shortlist and start phoning round. You can save me the bother. You know better than me which property companies are still buying.'

Everard Sellars did not need to be told this was true. On the other hand such information was too valuable to be shared. 'You want a counter-bid, don't you?' he asked rhetorically. 'But you don't want to solicit one yourself – sign of weakness. You want me to get it for you. What time will you be in the office on Monday? … Me? Half past seven as usual.'

On Monday morning William Fleischman was in his office as early as Everard Sellars. Fleischman was a man of wide commercial interests – so wide and varied, indeed, that one or other of them seemed to attract almost every deal that was to be done. He had left Fleischman & Sons, the City's most prestigious merchant bank, to create the space in which to do these deals, but on such friendly terms that it had remained his financial adviser. The name Fleischman on a financial deal was like a hallmark on silver plate: it conveyed a judicious mixture of probity and piracy.

Everard Sellars treated Fleischman with greatly more respect than he had Seagull. 'I'm calling to ask your advice, sir,' he said when he had introduced himself. 'It seems that an unwelcome approach has been made to Britton Trust. A fine old British company – the chairman's the Earl of St Edmunds – with substantial property interests. That makes it rather vulnerable in the current market. Guy Magnus – you may have heard the name – has made a cheap bid for it … How do I know it's cheap, sir? Our firm has just revalued the properties. Frankly, sir, Magnus's offer is not at all popular, but because the company is rather – should I say, exclusive? – nobody knows enough about it to make a counter-bid, though we happen to know there's plenty of scope for one. It occurs to us, sir, that City Star,' he named a property company on whose board Fleischman sat, 'might be interested in making a white knight bid, but none of us knows the best way to approach them. That's why I'm taking the liberty of seeking your advice, sir. As I say, I have a very good idea of the value of the assets, and any help I can give to make sure the company ends up in safe hands…'

The message was one Fleischman had heard a thousand times. His success derived from the fact that it was one he rarely ignored. 'Provided the matter's dealt with in the strictest confidence,' he said carefully.

'You have my absolute assurance on that, sir,' Sellars promised.

'Give me five minutes to brief Philip Alexander. Then call him yourself. He'll want to see the valuation figures before he decides whether City Star wants to take an interest. That shouldn't cause you too much difficulty,' Fleischman finished, barely suppressing a throaty chuckle.

Sellars used the five minutes to call Grover Seagull. 'In the strictest confidence, but I mean absolutely the strictest,' he told him, 'you may be hearing from Fleischman's – or from City Star direct. It seems they're pretty much up to speed on Britton Trust on the assets side. They may need a bit of guidance on the liabilities, though. Any help you can give …'

'Leave it to me,' Seagull replied. When Sellars made his excuses as he had another call to make, he took the opportunity to pass the time of day, naturally in the strictest of confidence, with his equivalent at Fleischman & Sons.

For the remainder of Monday and the whole of Tuesday, while the rest of the world debated what to do with the shadow chancellor's marital kit should he ever be in a position to carry out his threat that when he had his way there would be howls of anguish from the rich, heads were down, strict confidences were exchanged and numbers were crunched in a variety of offices of the City and West End. By Wednesday William Fleischman was ready to make his own telephone call.

'Long time no speak, Sam,' he began cheerfully.

Sam Dervish felt a sense of impending doom. When William Fleischman sounded cheerful something had gone wrong, and he was about to tell the fellow at the other end how he was going to put it right.

'Nice to hear from you, William,' he lied. 'What can I do you for?'

'Britton Trust, Sam,' replied Fleischman in a tone that brooked no refusal. 'Britton Trust, William?'

'You heard me, Sam. Your boy Magnus is making a most unpopular figure of himself. Word is, if he gets this one he'll never live to tell the tale. His friends won't be much loved, either. If I were you, Sam, I'd tell him the game is up.'

'Come on, William, you can't talk to me like that. We go back. Anyway, who's to say he'll listen to me?'

'He'll have to, Sam. He's using your money.'

'It's not as easy as that. We've exchanged facility letters. We're legally committed.'

'Let me put it to you this way, Sam. City Star's prepared to offer Magnus three twenty for his shares. His average buying price is two forty. He has two choices. Either we do things the nice way and he gets a couple of million profit to console his bruised ego, or we do things the nasty way and bid him up. If we have to do that we'll win anyway, and he'll live to rue the day he ever heard the name Britton Trust. Got the message, Sam?'

'Got it,' Dervish acknowledged. 'And I'll pass it on. Good to hear from you, William. Better than meeting at funerals.' As he put the phone down and picked it up again to call Guy Magnus, he changed his mind. Funerals were more fun.

'William Fleischman's a load of hot air,' Guy told Dervish when he put the proposition to him. 'He knows City Star won't bid against our forty per cent; they'll lose if they do. Either that, or they'll have to bid a darn site more than three twenty. Tell William to go fuck himself.'

'I can't tell him that, Guy. Nobody tells William that.'

'And nobody tells me when to buy and when to sell. Not even William Fleischman.'

Guy replaced his handset and proudly told Danny Gilbert of Fleischman's offer and what he had said he could do with it.

Danny felt dizzy. A fat six-figure sum had apparently been in his grasp, and now it had being whisked away from him. You could buy your own cordon bleu cook for less than that, freehold. 'You're making a terrible mistake, Guy,' he said. 'You've thrown away the best deal you've ever done. You've turned down a sure £2 million pound profit for a shot in the dark. Why on earth did you do it?'

'Three reasons, Danny. First, Britton Trust's undervalued. Why do you think City Star wants it so much? They've got hold of the property values from somewhere – they wouldn't have made us the offer unless they were sure of them. If they're willing to pay us 320p for our shares, it's because they know they're worth 400p.'

'Four quid a share? But that's £27 million!' Danny was incredulous.

'As it happens, they're on the low side. I told you Britton Trust's a gold-mine. It's worth a minimum of £30 million.'

'You can't be serious,' Danny objected. 'How do you get to that?'

'Pass me that envelope, Danny.'

Danny obliged and watched mesmerised as Guy proceeded to cover it with abbreviated names and numbers in his scrawled hand. As he did, he gave a running commentary.

'Start with the net asset figure in last March's circular: £8.8 million. Laserbeam stood in the balance sheet at £9.8 million, but this time last year they said it was worth £12.2 million. It's worth a million more by now. That gives an uplift of three and a half million. Trading properties are in the balance sheet at £4.8 million. The merger circular said they were worth £8.3 million, but values have gone up a third since then, so now they'll be worth £11.1 million. Add £6.3 million to the total. Now for the real surprise: Don Corbishley's done an armchair appraisal of the investment properties. What d'you think it throws up?' Guy smiled the smug smile of one who knew the answer.

'You tell me,' Danny threw the ball back.

'Eleven million surplus,' said Guy.

'Where the hell does he get that from?' Danny asked. Everyone knew that property values had been rising, but this was ridiculous. Corbishley was a bullshitter.

'Don's been looking more closely at the Oxford Street property. The upper floors are full of corridors and poky offices. We get the tenants out, take down the partitions and make the floors open plan; then we get planning consent to add two more floors. That will double the letting space. Rents in that location will soon be £20 a square foot. Don reckons we'll get half a million a year out of the building. He values it at £9 million, but he's sure it'll fetch more on the open market.'

Danny was finding it hard to keep up with Guy's new-found property expertise. Guy interrupted his thoughts by asking him how much he had got to so far. Danny checked his running total.

'Twenty-nine point six million,' he said.

'Good. Now add an uplift of £2.2 million for Watson's Euston property, say half a million for Norfolk Broads, half a million for the majority stake in Wallis, and what do you come to?'

'Thirty-two point eight million,' Danny said, visibly impressed. Then he hesitated. 'But you haven't made any allowance for corporation tax on the trading properties,' he pointed out. 'You have to make one if we're going to sell them.'

'I've made that calculation. You have to take off £3.1 million. But add a million back for the warrants we won't have to provide for. That gives you,' Guy looked at the envelope and announced triumphantly, 'Thirty point seven million! Told you so! The bargain of a lifetime! Now for the other reason to buy: look at the gearing. The company's got fixed term borrowings of £23.5 million against gross assets of over £50 million. When the assets go up ten per cent, our £10 million surplus will become £15 million. I'm afraid you're going to have to learn how to live like a millionaire, Danny.'

'You said there were three reasons,' Danny said numbly.

'If I give up now, no one will ever treat a bid from me seriously again.'

'They will if you walk away netting £2 million profit on the deal.'

'Not when I bid for Marks & Spencer, they won't. They'll say I'm only in it for the turn.'

'Marks & Spencer?' Danny's brain was reeling.

'You think I'm in this as a game, Danny? Why shouldn't I own Marks & Spencer? Or any other company, for that matter? It's only paper.'

'Isn't that playing at God?'

'If it takes God to bid for Marks & Spencer, why on earth not?'

'Because shares are for buying and selling. You're breaking your own rules, Guy.'

But Guy Magnus was already on his way.

23

Guy's judgment proved right, if not for the right reasons. No sooner had he rejected City Star's offer than Isadouros Holdings announced its intention to bid 325p per share in cash for Britton Trust. The previous day the City Star board and Fleischman & Sons had calculated that a bid worth up to 330p in shares and loan stock would be in order. But to have a realistic chance of beating Isadouros, they would have to offer 340p. This was too rich a price. They resolved to stand aside and await events.

City markets react sensitively to world events. When the news came that Egyptian and Syrian forces had attacked Israel while its citizens were at their Yom Kippur prayers, the financial institutions Isadouros's merchant bank had lined up to underwrite his offer postponed their decision on whether to back the bid until the desert sand had settled. When Iraq nationalised United States oil interests and the president told Americans to turn their heating down, they put their discussions on the backburner. The chairman of Isadouros Holdings made his excuses to the Earl of St Edmunds and said he hoped they would do business together some other time.

Harry Griffin had been following the newspaper version of these events from his Monte Carlo tax haven with growing interest. Three hundred and ten thousand shares at 325p each came to £1,007,500 in anyone's book. For all Sybil's efforts to reduce his fortune before he made it, even Guy would find it impossible to deny the value of a cheque for that amount drawn on a City bank.

The question exercising Harry's mind was which of the competing merchant banks was to have the privilege of drawing the cheque for him to show Guy before he reserved the best corner table at Maxim's. Would it be Ulster & Cayman? Harry doubted it. Guy had served his purpose by putting Britton Trust into play, but once the City brethren had made up their minds to unite against an outsider, they seldom lost.

His contacts in the Britton Trust boardroom had also kept him informed of the identity of the company's new suitors. Would the cheque be coming from Isadouros's bankers? Though the choice was out of his hands, Harry had already reached the conclusion that even if that company was more popular in the City than Guy Magnus, it was less popular than City Star.

Or would Thruston Cutwell frustrate all their plans and force him to wait a full twelve months for his reward while Sybil made millionaires of the shopkeepers of Paris and the Cote d'Azur? And what would be the value this time next year of the load of crap he knew Britton Trust to be?

By the first days of October Harry had resolved to come to the aid of City Star, less on the grounds of Alexander's popularity than in the hope that he might be persuaded to make an even higher bid.

'You're on to a good thing there, I can tell you, sir,' he told Alexander when the latter's secretary finally gave up the battle to shield her boss from Harry's calls. 'You won't believe the hidden assets in the company. When I was on the board I kept telling the others to have the balance sheet properly valued, but they kept bleating about conservative accounting and such garbage. I reckon the asset value's up to a fiver a share. Tell you what: Berry St Edmunds will do whatever I tell him. I can get him to recommend you at three thirty-five if you want, and I'll promise you my 300,000 … Guy Magnus? I'll speak to him on your behalf. He's an old mate of mine. If you want his shares, you only have to ask.'

Phil Alexander refrained from telling Harry to get lost, for if City Star were to proceed with a bid every 100,000 shares was going to count. But he made it clear that his financial advisers were in charge and Harry should stay as far from the action as possible. Even so, he was more influenced by what Harry told him than he was by political events. So when the government announced that the next phase of its pay policy was to be more flexible and City Star's shares rose sharply in the resulting euphoria, its board resolved that its interest in Britton Trust should be just as flexibly, not to say aggressively, pursued.

The Britton Trust board was also undergoing a philosophical reorientation. Isadouros's dramatic appearance and equally rapid departure from the scene had coincided with a loss of interest on the part of the would-be purchaser of Laserbeam. Nothing is more apt to persuade a father to solicit proposals for the hand of his daughter than to see her jilted twice during the week after he has paid the bill for her wedding gown. So last week's order to repel all suitors was replaced by an open invitation to any white knight who could ride a horse and demonstrate reasonably honourable intentions. According to Thruston Cutwell, who were so informed by Fleischman & Sons, Guy Magnus's suit of armour was rusting badly; but City Star's shone like its name. Intensive discussions on the value of Britton Trust were once more being pursued, and a firm offer was expected early in the week. So Ulster & Cayman dispatched its offer document to the shareholders on the very day its directors were most susceptible to a fresh approach.

The headlines that day were dominated by the resignation of Vice-President Spiro T Agnew on being fined for income tax evasion. The international telephone lines were humming with calls to tax advisers. In the excitement the board of Britton Trust may be forgiven for having failed to notice when they were preparing their advice to their shareholders that the offer was made on behalf of Guy Magnus's new corporate vehicle.

The cheques Guy, Danny and Larry had drawn in favour of the bidding company MGC Investments had been torn up and replaced by smaller amounts. To them were added £20 cheques from Ludgate Investments and St Paul's Property and a fiver from a recruit who went by the unlikely name of Kenneth John Peel, whose credentials in keeping the books of £100 companies, Guy assured Danny and Larry, were impeccable.

'MGC?' queried Danny Gilbert.

'Magnus, Gilbert, Callaghan, of course,' Guy replied. Then he explained to Danny how their £100 company was going to buy one for £20 million.

'That's magic!' Danny enthused when Guy finished.

'Ma-Gi-Cal,' Larry Callaghan corrected him. Thus was their new company renamed, and Magical Investments Limited took up its space in Guy's parking lot of corporate vehicles.

'If we want to increase our borrowings to £20 million, Ludgate and St Paul's will have to add their financial resources to Ulster & Cayman's,' Guy added drily, as if the idea were his own. His wry grin betrayed him. It had, in truth, been Sam Dervish who had forced the issue.

'We're a bit bothered about your plan for Ludgate to lend our £4 million on to Westchurch,' he had told Guy on the telephone the previous Friday.

Guy had not been pleased. Merchant bankers were not supposed to make an agreement and then go back on their word. But showing his displeasure would have achieved nothing.

'I don't know what you're worried about,' he argued as he made ready to compromise. 'It's a twelve month loan. We'll be in and out in no time.'

'It's the City boys who are nervous,' Dervish explained.

'Would they feel more comfortable if St Paul's shared the loan?' Guy asked innocently. 'That way you'll only be lending a couple of million to each.'

Dervish relaxed. With both companies providing security in addition to the assets of Britton Trust, 'I'm sure they'll see reason in that,' he agreed. He moved on to the next point. 'But if we're going to lend a couple of million each to Ludgate and St Paul's, and they're going to lend the money straight on to Westchurch, surely they're both entitled to be treated as risk-takers and have a share in the profits?'

Guy hated to see his stake in the deal watered down, but he would have hated even more to upset Dervish, particularly as he was about to explain that the money was to be lent not to Westchurch, but to a new company.

'I've been thinking along similar lines,' he said. 'The deal will be cleaner in a new vehicle.'

Dervish had been about to ask for further particulars of the new vehicle when his other line rang. But in any case the issue was peripheral: it was the City boys' job to tie up the loose ends. More important, there was competition to be defeated. It was his duty to see off City Star. It was academic whether Guy's new vehicle was a £100 company when everyone knew the deal was a *matzah* pudding and the bank's fees would amount to £1 million. The prize lay partly in that and partly in the prestige it would win for Mayfair in its running battle with City.

'Let City have the details,' he told Guy. 'They're the ones who have to get the document right.'

Guy was not unduly concerned at investing £40 of his money into Magical Investments, as he had a windfall profit of £250,000 from which to pay it. For while the other Britton Trust shareholders would have to wait for their money until six weeks after his offer went unconditional, he had decreed that Westchurch was to pay Danny, Larry and himself the offer price of 295p in cash for the 400,000 Britton Trust shares they had bought last August, and to accept the offer from Magical Investments in their place. Danny and Larry had no argument with this strategy: it was better than hanging around for their money like everyone else. Danny did suggest, tongue in cheek, that rather than write a cheque for his £10 subscription he take it from petty cash; but Larry said this would foul up the books, so Danny had to conform.

The Britton Trust board meeting called to consider the offer document from Ulster & Cayman was even more tense than usual. Each director knew that Magnus needed only 625,000 shares for victory; each knew how many his fellow-directors owned; and each suspected that colleagues only sign resolutions promising to stand united when they are about to break ranks. Since their last meeting mutual suspicion had turned into cancerous mistrust.

In the absence of Grover Seagull – for even an earl is entitled to only so much of a high flyer's time – his assistant reported the withdrawal of interest from Isadouros Holdings but said that the bank was once more engaged in discussions with Fleischmans acting for City Star. One school of thought held these were at an exploratory stage, another that they were substantive negotiations.

'Don't follow,' objected the Earl of St Edmunds. 'Sounds easy enough to me. Either they're going to bid or they ain't.'

'With respect, my lord, it's not as simple as that. They've asked for further information. Our lawyers are considering what we can give them without being under an obligation to give it to Magnus as well.'

'Magnus seems happy enough with the information we've given him.'

'He's only bidding 295p, my lord. City Star's advisers want to work out how much higher they can go.'

'So it's not whether they'll bid, but how much?' the earl pressed.

By now the rest of the board was growing increasingly attentive. Something was in the air. The chairman was not usually so astute, nor in such combative mood.

'They say if they can't bid well above Magnus, there won't be any sense bidding at all, as he's already got forty per cent,' replied Seagull's assistant. He lacked his mentor's age by a couple of years, his coiffure by a couple of inches and his tailor by a couple of hundred pounds, but he had the makings of the in-house style. 'Their only chance of winning will be if they can justify offering ten per cent more than him, and if they have your recommendation. Even that may not be enough.'

'Don't know about the rest of you,' the earl looked around the table, 'but it seems to me they'd better make up their minds. Don't like all this uncertainty. Bad for the businesses. Management wants to know where it stands, eh Palliser?'

Alan Palliser concurred. All round Britton Trust's businesses capital investment decisions were being delayed.

'If we sit around contemplating our navels while City Star debates what to do and they decide not to go ahead, we'll fall to Magnus at 295p, sure as whisky comes from Scotland, eh Priestley?'

Jolyon Priestley also agreed, even though 295p would suit him fine were he free to take it.

'What alternative do we have?' asked John Charteris, partly to himself.

'Go tell Magnus it's not enough. Tell him there's a counter-bid coming our way. If he wants us badly enough he'll have to pay more.'

'Not if I have anything to do with it.' Charteris said sharply. His curtailed exchange with Guy Magnus was still on his mind. Had the earl indeed been looked after?

The earl looked round for contributions to the debate. He was met by an embarrassed silence.

'Can't go on waiting for ever,' he said eventually, failing to specify whether the culprit was City Star or his recalcitrant colleagues. 'If no bid's been made by lunchtime tomorrow, I shall feel free to talk to Magnus myself.'

'You can't do that,' Charteris told him. 'You're not entitled to commit the board to anything it hasn't agreed. Our present position is to reject the offer. That's all you're authorised to say.'

'No intention of committing the board to anything,' replied the earl. Every man was entitled to speak up for himself. Including the chairman. Seeing that the business of the day had been concluded, albeit inconclusively, he declared the meeting closed. He would have stayed to lunch but circumstances favoured a tactical withdrawal. He retreated to his office to call Harold Antony, and was soon accepting his suggestion. 'Friday at seven? Jolly good idea, Harold.'

Meanwhile Seagull's assistant was reporting to his master. Seagull was not at all pleased by what he was told. He made two telephone calls: one to William Fleischman, the other to Everard Sellars. As a result of the first, Fleischman & Sons's corporate finance team worked through the night on its report. By nine o'clock next morning the document was on Philip Alexander's desk. The merchant bank recommended a bid at 330p, worth £22 million. Alexander was putting together a paper for his board when a call came through from Everard Sellars.

'Think you ought to know rumour has it a certain peer may be tempted to sell his birth-right to a certain beast,' said Sellars cryptically. 'Time you got your skates on,' he added more succinctly.

Alexander obliged. As a result, when the Earl of St Edmunds arrived at his office shortly after eleven o'clock, he found John Charteris waiting outside the door with the managing director of City Star.

'I thought I ought to take Mr Alexander's call. We didn't know where you were and it did seem rather urgent,' Charteris apologised after he had made the introductions. 'I trust it's not an inconvenient time.'

'Not at all,' said the earl drily. 'Been hoping he'd drop by.'

'I wanted to speak to you face to face, so you'd know we mean business,' said Alexander. 'My company wants to make an offer for yours. We know the bid from Magnus is unwelcome, both in principle and on terms. We hope you don't feel the same way about us as you do about him.'

'Don't much matter how I feel,' said the earl. 'Between you and me, just as happy to see it go to a big firm like yours as a chap like Magnus, but can't say our shareholders will care whose shilling they take. He's made an offer, we've rejected it. You want to make one, we're ready to hear it. Bit pushed for time, though.'

Did the earl mean he had another engagement? Or was time running out on City Star? Alexander worked on the assumption that there was no time to waste. 'We're ready to make an offer valuing the company at £22 million,' he said. 'One share of ours for one share of yours, plus a top-up of £1.10 in convertible loan stock. As our shares stand at 217p in the market, that makes 327p per share.'

'All paper, no cash,' the earl objected.

'It will be underwritten for cash at 315p. Provided you're willing to meet two conditions: either you guarantee acceptance from a majority of your shareholders, or you persuade Magnus to sell us his stake and go away.'

City Star's price was a good one. The earl doubted Magnus would match it. But the discussions through Harold Antony were progressing nicely. 'Can't speak for Magnus,' he said truthfully.

Alexander saw he had made a false step. 'What I mean is, if we come to an agreement with him, we won't need you to guarantee fifty per cent,' he explained. 'It would be up to us to pick up the rest – with your recommendation, of course.'

'We'd be bound to recommend 327p,' Charteris intervened. 'It's much higher than Magnus's offer, and far better than you'd get in the market.'

'Yes, we'd have to recommend at that level,' acknowledged the earl. 'Don't mean we wouldn't withdraw it if we got a higher offer.'

'No dice,' Alexander told him firmly. 'We're not going to waste our time in a bidding battle. If you can't get us majority acceptance, you can forget the whole deal. I'm prepared to go our board for approval, but we won't make the offer until you're in a position to deliver.'

The earl chewed on that for a few seconds. 'How can we be sure we're not wasting our time?' he asked.

'To make things clear, let me put it the other way round: as soon as you can deliver, we'll make the offer.'

'Got the message,' said the earl, unhappy that it had been given in front of a witness. 'Well, Charteris,' he sighed, 'seems we have to get everyone together again this afternoon.' He consulted his desk diary. 'Better tell 'em half past three.' He had never thought that being chairman meant having to be at the office all day. He used the short time before lunch to make a telephone call of his own.

'Spot of bother,' he told the party at the other end of the line. He described the meeting which had just taken place. Then he waited for the reaction. 'Got it,' he said when this had been made clear. 'Got it, old boy. See you Friday.'

24

At half past three the Earl of St Edmunds saw that for all his disapproval of working afternoons as well as mornings, it was in his interests to do so. With so much at stake, it would be improper to allow Charteris to take the chair on a resolution he had himself proposed, albeit with the help of Thruston Cutwell.

'Charteris's resolution,' he announced. 'Offer that hasn't been made to be one we'd recommend to shareholders if it were to be made? Can't say I much like the sound of it.'

'If I may, chairman,' Charteris took over: 'it seems perfectly proper to me. Our duty to our shareholders is to maximise the value of their shares. If we don't pass the resolution, they can get 295p from Magnus, but not more. If we do pass it, we may get them 327p from City Star.'

'Three fifteen cash. Hypothetical anyway,' objected the earl. 'City Star says we have to deliver fifty per cent. No chance we'll get 'em, my opinion. Magnus has over forty, so we have to get 'em out of less than sixty. Don't have 'em in this room, so what're the chances? Slim to invisible, if you ask me.'

'We have twenty-five per cent if we include Cummings,' said Thomas Goodman. 'Griffin's desperate to sell. He'll lob his in as soon as we make a recommendation. That'll take us to almost thirty. We know where most of the rest are. All we have to do is start phoning round, and we'll soon have them in the bag.'

The earl frowned. The meeting had just begun and it was already slipping out of control. 'Magnus's offer's on the table, unconditional, in cash. He'll pay more for our recommendation,' he argued. 'City Star won't make up their minds. If we can't find 'em fifty per cent, they won't even make an offer.'

'If Magnus doesn't get fifty per cent, the shareholders will get nothing,' countered Charteris. 'It's our duty to try for a better price if we think we can get it.'

'You have a stake in the company, Priestley,' the earl turned for help. 'Want to risk losing a bird in the hand when the one in the bush has no wings?'

'Certainly not, chairman,' Priestley agreed, on the grounds that this seemed to be a fair description of his deal with Ernest Burke.

'You want to lose a nice fat bird that can't escape once you've cast your net over the bush for a skinny old crow that's flying around in the wide blue yonder?' asked Goodman.

'I should say not,' Priestley continued to make himself agreeable. The less he argued, the less the chance they'd find out he was 200,000 shares short.

'I move we put it to the vote,' proposed Charteris, secure in the understanding he had reached with a majority of his colleagues. Serve the earl right for telling him to convene the meeting.

Out-manoeuvred, the earl knew the vital thing was to remain in charge. Let the others try to get their fifty per cent. When they found they couldn't, they'd turn to him for salvation. He hoped he wouldn't have to wait long; Magnus's cash would come in more than handy. 'Allow me to move we accept Charteris's resolution,' he offered magnanimously. 'Second, Priestley?'

'Seconded,' said Priestley obediently.

'In favour? Everyone? Excellent. Passed unanimously.' The earl looked at his watch. 'Goodness, time flies. Never get much wiser after four o'clock. Move we adjourn and meet again in the morning.' If Charteris and his gang were going to start phoning around in search of shares, it would be useful to keep tabs on how they were doing. 'Always good to see unanimity on the board,' he said as he left.

It was always good to see unanimity on the board, Philip Alexander told himself the following afternoon. That way he could get on with his job of running City Star. He patted Fleischmans metaphorically on the back for the quality of its report. No essential information had been omitted and no unnecessary padding included; a straightforward recommendation. The board had agreed to everything, and now he was to implement the chairman's suggestion: that Magnus be offered a sweetener. He was welcome to Britton Trust's operating businesses; City Star was interested only in its properties. He told his secretary to find out where Guy Magnus was and to get him on the phone right away. He was connected so quickly it seemed as though his call had been awaited.

'I thought I'd call as a matter of courtesy,' he told Guy, anxious to start on the right foot. 'We've decided to make an offer for Britton Trust, and you're their largest shareholder. I have their chairman's approval to a meeting between us. There may be common ground. Can we fix a time for me to come round to you? … Right away would be fine. Look forward to meeting you shortly, then.' Alexander made a brief call to pass on the news to John Charteris and then left his West End office for the City.

In the Britton Trust boardroom, Charteris gave a thumbs-up to his colleagues as he heard Alexander's news. During the afternoon he and what his absent chairman uncharitably called "the gang" had set up a barrage of telephones. The room had taken on the character of a party agent's action room on election night. Each director had a canvass list in front of him, the calls to be made by size of shareholding.

'Not much good, don't suppose?' the Earl of St Edmunds had betrayed his hopes when he entered the boardroom.

'You'll be pleased to know the shareholders are expressing solid support for the board,' Thomas Goodman told him happily. 'Always good to see unanimity amongst the owners! They reckon we've got them a pretty good price.'

Seagull's assistant, seated in front of a thick pile of continuous computer sheets which listed the company's shareholders and their holdings, was acting as coordinator. 'Magnus's offer is irrevocable for three weeks. We can afford to take our time,' he said, repeating what his boss had told him shortly after dawn.

'We should be close to home by tonight,' said Charteris. 'The resolution to commit our own holdings seems to have swung it with the shareholders.'

The earl thought quickly. If that were so, he had better put the target out of range before it was too late. 'Resolution? Ah, yes. Can't say I regard myself bound by that any longer,' he said, loudly enough to be audible but discreetly enough not to attract attention. One didn't announce one's thoughts in such a way as to start an argument. 'Circumstances no longer the same,' he added, as if in explanation.

The earl returned to his own office to arrange his next appointment. The chap he was to see said he would be engaged until seven. Infernal nuisance the way one spent one's time sitting around for folk who couldn't organise their lives. As he did so, the telephone rang. It was Philip Alexander from a call box in the City, wanting to pass on the news of the City Star board's decision.

'Good show!' responded the earl.

'What are the chances you'll muster the shares?' asked Alexander.

'My chaps assure me there'll be no problem,' the earl told him truthfully.

'Might take a little time to obtain written confirmation from all the share-holders,' he added cautiously and with equal truth.

Five minutes later the chap the earl was to see welcomed the guest with whom he would be otherwise engaged. It was good to deal with substantive nego-tiations instead of trivial queries like the one he had just dealt with. Brian Proctor, the Ludgate Circus operations manager, had asked Guy for author-ity to pay an invoice for £20,000 submitted by someone named Matthew Crisp "for services rendered". Guy had scribbled his initials on Pat Crisp's father's invoice and told Proctor to pass it to Nigel Holmes for payment to an account in Jersey: he was too busy to tell him himself.

'I don't know what I can do for you, Mr Alexander,' Guy said as the latter sat opposite him at his desk. It was a moment to savour: Mohammed coming to the mountain. 'We want to acquire Britton Trust ourselves.'

'I can't understand why,' Alexander countered. 'You want it to strip and make a turn. We're offering you your profit with neither the effort nor the uncertainty.'

'If I accept your offer, I'll lose credibility when I go after the next deal. This time I'm in deadly earnest. We're going ahead, and we're going to win.'

'The shareholders will have to decide that, and we're prepared to offer them a good deal more than you. The board has agreed to back us, and it says it will deliver fifty per cent of the equity. You can't win; you haven't got the shares.'

'With respect, the boot's on the other foot,' Guy told him. 'You've done your maths wrong. We already have too many for you to win.'

'What makes you think that?'

'The promises we had before today put us near,' Guy said. He had decided to play his cards close to his chest, but not too close. There was no point naming names until Priestley's shares were in his hands. 'Now we've secured the support of another party, we're home and dry,' he added, applying the same rule to the Earl of St Edmunds. 'You're too late, Mr Alexander, too late.'

Philip Alexander felt sure Guy Magnus was bluffing. If he wasn't, why had he agreed to meet him? He wanted to keep City Star from bidding, so he was pretending to have found a seller, hoping they would think he had dealt with Harry Griffin. But Alexander knew that without the board's recommenda-tion that was impossible. He must lay his own false scent. 'You may be right,' he said, dropping his shoulders in apparent submission, 'but neither of us can relish a messy fight. We'd prefer to come to an accommodation with you.'

'What kind of accommodation?' Guy asked suspiciously.

'Tell us which parts of the company you want, and we'll negotiate a deal with you. We're only after the properties. If we do decide not to bid, I wonder how you'd feel about selling some of them to us?'

Was City Star about to throw in its hand? Guy felt an adrenalin rush. If he played his cards right, he would see off one major player and be left free to deal with the other: Thruston Cutwell. By then Britton Trust would be defenceless. It would be a moment to savour: the moment he became a major City player. His instinct told him to take care; but his judgment told him to take the bait. Not to do so would leave him in conflict with a powerful enemy. He would win, but at a greater cost. He must not show a too weak a hand, though.

'I'd have to think about that,' he said without enthusiasm. 'I suppose it wouldn't hurt if you let me have a list to consider, showing the properties you want and what you'd be prepared to pay for them.' No harm, he thought, in having a free valuation from professionals.

'I'll send it to you this evening by hand,' Alexander offered; he had already told his lieutenants to start preparing one for himself. 'What time are you leaving the office?'

'I have to leave shortly,' Guy told him. 'Send it to me at Claridge's.'

In the taxi back to Mayfair, Alexander reflected on their brief meeting. He remained convinced that Magnus was bluffing about the promises of shares; his reaction to the list of properties would provide the proof. At the very least, giving him something to think about would slow him down. Back in his office he gave instructions for the handwritten list to be typed and dispatched without delay.

At precisely twenty-five past six City Star's messenger and the Earl of St Edmunds left their respective offices and headed for Claridge's. Each had less than half a mile to travel, but only the messenger had a hot Friday night date. By half past six City Star's shopping list was in Guy's hands and he was debating its contents with Harold Antony. Meanwhile the earl, meandering along a more circuitous route, was pausing to examine the latest models on display in the Mercedes-Benz showrooms and some more dated ones hanging about in the Shepherd Market doorways. When his odyssey was incapable of further extension without attracting the attention of the local constabulary, he passed the ten minutes before his expected arrival at seven o'clock nursing a scotch and water in the hotel bar.

'Good to see you again, Magnus,' he greeted Guy a short time later, as if he were a long-lost friend. 'You too, Antony. Things are moving fast; damned fast. Good job we arranged to meet. Board wants to deal with City Star.'

'How do they think they can win?' asked Antony.

'By handing over fifty point one per cent on a plate. Reckon I have to take them seriously. I mean, what do I do if they're so close all they need is Priestley and me? Turn down 315 in cash? Look a bit odd.'

'Look at this, Berry,' said Guy, handing the earl on City Star's shopping list on its letterhead. 'They're not serious. All they want is a few of your properties.'

'I say!' The earl stared at the paper in disbelief. 'Going behind my back: not on, is it?' he asked all and sundry, shaken that dishonour and deceit could so infest the boardroom of a public company. Neither Guy nor Harold felt any inclination to disagree. 'That case, no interest to me, nor to Priestley if I read him right. Want a clean deal, that so, Antony?'

Harold Antony agreed that it was.

'Then sell your shares to me,' proposed Guy.

'Got to have a reason, or that would look odd too.'

'They're using you to try to twist a deal out of me. Isn't that enough?'

The earl considered the question. His eyes lit up behind the thick lens of his glasses as he found the answer. 'Money! Got to get the shareholders more money! That should do it, eh? Wouldn't match their price, would you, Magnus?'

'It's not a real price; it's a device while they try to squeeze me.'

'Three ten?'

'Not a chance; we've pushed the boat out far enough. Though I see what you mean about helping you justify your actions. I suppose we might find a penny or two, if we really have to,' Guy seasoned his firmness with a hint of flexibility.

'Three pounds. Got to have £3. Show them I'd tried and won.'

Guy felt his heart pound. Five pence a share – just £350,000 – and he was practically past the winning post. 'Is this a firm offer to sell, or another ploy?' he asked. The earl looked hurt but said nothing. 'You've got to make your mind up,' Guy pressed the issue. 'We can't have any more hanging around.'

The earl looked for encouragement to Harold Antony, who nodded.

'In that case we'd better get on with it,' said the earl. 'Subject to everything being in order.'

'In order?' queried Guy.

'I mean, all shareholders getting the same,' explained the earl. Guy looked at him quizzically, and then at Harold Antony. 'The same £3. All other things being equal,' the earl elaborated.

'Yes, they'll all get £3,' Guy confirmed. 'I'll have to get formal approval, but as far as I'm concerned it's a deal. On one condition,' he added, determined to catch the moment. 'I'm not prepared to hang around while City Star plans its next bit of jiggery-pokery. You must sell me your shares tomorrow, or all bets are off.'

The earl nodded. Missing an autumn bag on Bertie Hampton's shoot was a damnable nuisance, but it took a distant second place when £800,000 was at stake. 'Want Cummings's 80,000 while you're about it?' he remembered to ask. 'You know, the chap from Watson's I introduced to you? Close to Priestley. Promised I'd let 'em both know when the time came.'

'I'd be delighted.'

'What about Priestley? You want his too?'

'I think we can accommodate Jolyon as well,' Guy conceded graciously.

'Better ring him,' said the earl.

Guy went over to the telephone and dialled Priestley's number. The earl half-raised his eyebrows and took the receiver from him.

'Make-your-mind-up time, Priestley ... Three hundred pence. You on? ... Tell Cummings, will you? My place, tomorrow morning ... Eleven o'clock?' He turned to Guy, who nodded. 'And don't forget to bring a pen,' he muttered down the line.

25

Guy Magnus hummed. The melody was apt: the haunting Abschied from Das Lied von der Erde that he had recognised on his last visit to the Earl of St Edmunds. He was on his way there again, to buy 700,000 shares in Britton Trust. Once they were his, he'd have the fifty per cent of the company's capital he needed for victory. And he wouldn't have to pay a penny over 300p. He wouldn't even have to plead with Harry Griffin.

The earl's concession to the weekend was to answer his own front door in a pair of old brown corduroy trousers. Harold Antony was reclining comfortably on the Chesterfield sofa and Jolyon Priestley was perching uncomfortably on the edge of a chair – not Chippendale, Guy noted, but a presentable reproduction of the period. As cramp had not yet set in, it seemed likely that Priestley's had been the more recent arrival.

'Harold and I have covered the territory,' the earl said, his conspiratorial tone telling Guy that he had no need to raise private matters in public. 'I'm ready to go. Priestley here can speak for himself.'

'I thought Cummings was going to be present?' Guy queried.

'He says he promised his wife to spend the day with her and the kids,' Priestley explained.

'He'd better get his priorities in order if he wants to keep his job, and if you two want to sell me your shares,' said Guy, annoyed. Without Cummings' shares he'd be left teetering on the brink. If he was going to spend a couple of million, he wanted to know the thing was done and dusted.

'I'll tell him to get over here right away,' said Priestley. 'He'll be twenty minutes,' he told Guy after a brief phone call. He sat down again, his fingers and feet twitching nervously.

'I've filled in Berry's contract note,' Harold Antony told Guy. He knew from long experience that the way to complete a sale is to present the seller with paper and pen and nothing else to write but his name.

'So everything's agreed?' asked Guy, trusting that Priestley would regard the query as a no more than a reference to price, which as far as he was aware it was. Priestley decided that whatever else was being implied was none of his business.

'Absolutely everything,' Antony confirmed. '300p, isn't it?' he added superfluously.

'Settlement on completion at the end of November, same as everyone else?' Guy checked. Having paid him for his own shares, Westchurch would be clean out of cash until Ulster & Cayman settled the acceptances on behalf of Magical Investments.

'The 29th,' Antony confirmed.

'Well, let's get on with it, shall we?' Guy turned to Priestley, whose twitches had by now developed into an advanced stage of the shakes. 'Bit early for a drink, Jolyon.'

Priestley shook the only part of his body which had hitherto remained more or less immobile: his head. 'Guy?' he said weakly.

' Jolyon?' Guy gave the only possible reply.

'Guy, I don't think I can actually, as it were, perform today.'

'I do feel most profoundly sorry for your wife,' responded Guy solicitously.

'No, seriously, Guy: I don't think I can sell yet. I haven't given notice to the board. I was going to on Monday.'

'What notice? You don't need to give them any.' A director reported a sale to his board after the event, not before. Guy looked to Antony for confirmation.

'We signed a resolution.'

Guy looked to the earl for an explanation. He was the chairman: he should know what the board had agreed, and he seemed ready to sign without further ado.

The earl shrugged, as if disassociating himself from his colleagues. 'Don't look at me,' he said; 'I gave notice yesterday.' He turned to the window, failing to return Priestley's questioning glance.

'It would appear that the directors resolved to stick together and not to sell without giving notice to the board,' Harold Antony explained in a tone which said that such an act of collective suicide would not have taken place had he still been one of their number.

Guy's annoyance was about to develop into anger, but a ring of the bell saved its object. Cummings soon joined them, excusing his earlier absence.

'Signed anything stupid lately?' Guy asked him.

'I don't think so.' Cummings showed manifest concern at the question.

Had he been right to let Priestley push him into the sale? He owed his job to him, he had bought his Britton Trust shares with a loan guaranteed by him, but he had given Alan Palliser his word that he would support the board. Recently, however, Palliser had been putting him under more pressure than he could happily handle. Palliser had complained of mismanagement, accounting chaos and unexplained "favours" at Watson's; even Priestley had described the last as unfortunate occurrences. There was disagreement between them as to whether the matters at issue should more accurately be described as mistakes or irregularities. Cummings had been hoping that a new owner would need his help to run the business and would be inclined to wipe the slate clean. From the sound of Guy Magnus's voice it seemed more likely that he had been called in for an awkward exchange of views.

'Not on the board. Not a signatory,' the earl answered the question for him.

'Thank God for that. I was beginning to think I was wasting my time,' Guy sighed. The postponement of the transaction with Priestley was irritating but unavoidable; if the other two were wrapped up, his position would be virtually unassailable.

Antony filled in another contract note and gave it to Cummings, who watched the earl sign his, took the plunge and followed suit. Both passed the papers back to Antony, who folded them and put them carefully into his pocket.

Guy stared out of the window, his eyes following the hardy rowers in their close season training as if the transaction were of minor importance. He knew by heart the number of shares on the contract notes and how many more he needed for victory, but he still made the calculation to satisfy himself that Priestley's would take him over the top. 'Monday, then,' he said to Priestley crisply. It must not sound like a question.

'Monday,' promised Priestley.

'I've been drafting a press statement for Berry,' Harold Antony introduced a new topic. 'He'll need to explain what he's done and why. We want to pre-empt anything the board may say and to persuade the other shareholders to fall into line before City Star wakes up.' He passed his draft to Guy, who looked it over.

'Better get a second opinion,' he said, shaking his head. 'Which PR firm do you use?'

'Vereker Associates,' Priestley told him.

'I know "Venom" well,' said Guy happily. He searched his Filofax for the number and dialled it. 'Ian Vereker? Hello, Guy Magnus here ... well, thanks; and you? Good ... Ian, I believe you act for Britton Trust. I'm with the Earl of St Edmunds. He needs your help. Can you come over to his place? ... Now, of course. You have the address? ... Good man. See you soon.'

The Saturday morning traffic on the Embankment was light. Ian "Venom" Vereker, a wizard in the abstruse art of corporate public relations, was with them inside ten minutes.

'Ian, the earl and I have reached agreement over Britton Trust,' Guy put him in the picture. 'I've agreed to increase my bid to 300p on the basis that he accepts it for his own shares and agrees to recommend it to the rest of the shareholders. Harold Antony has drafted this press statement. He's his broker. We need you to finalise it and issue it on the earl's behalf.'

Vereker looked to the earl for confirmation and received it. The room was silent as he read the draft. 'One or two points,' he said when he had finished: 'It says, Berry, you didn't believe any other bid could succeed, as Magnus already had forty per cent. That presupposes there are still sixty per cent out there. Suppose there were a higher bid?'

'We'll have over fifty per cent on Monday,' Guy pointed out.

'But we have to explain Berry's thinking before he agreed to sell to you,' Vereker spelled out the relevant issue.

'All this uncertainty. Not good for anyone,' explained the earl.

'Damaging to the company. Management, staff, customers, etcetera and so on,' Priestley elaborated.

'Good note to start on.' Vereker wrote a few lines. 'Shareholders too, I expect. You say you won't sell your stake, even to a higher bidder, Guy?'

'Absolutely not,' Guy confirmed.

'So it's reasonable to say, Berry, you thought another bid would be, let's say, unlikely to succeed? And you wanted to resolve matters as quickly as possible, in everyone's best interests?'

'Absolutely,' the earl echoed Guy's certainty.

'And you believed you had negotiated the best price you could get?'

'Wouldn't sell my shares if I didn't believe it.'

'And the best assurances you could get for the continuity and development of the businesses?' Vereker went through his checklist of standard phrases, noting them down in abbreviated form as he did so.

'My duty,' the earl stated with all the firmness necessary to ensure that even a public relations man understood.

'And as chairman of the company you urge the shareholders to accept the increased offer, which you believe to be fair and reasonable,' Vereker quoted from the manual of good takeover practice as he scribbled "f & r" on to the page.

'Sounds about right,' agreed the earl.

Vereker went over to a small table and wrote out a fair copy of the statement he had drafted. With the addition of a sentence from Guy emphasising the financial power and commercial experience of Westchurch, it soon became an approved announcement. Vereker left to arrange its release and the others dispersed. From his window the earl watched Guy depart with Harold Antony, and Priestley and Cummings go their separate ways, Priestley slowly along the river bank, his chin sunk on his chest, Cummings jumping into his car to rush home and make peace with his wife.

It had been a fine morning for shooting game, noted the Earl of St Edmunds regretfully as he contemplated the river, its flowing waters reflecting the weak autumn sun. But if all went well, come the end of November his debts would be repaid and his kitty replenished, he would have a new car to go with his old job, and the game would still be there if Bertie Hampton had anything to do with it. Bertie was such a lousy shot.

26

Drained by the tensions of the week just past, Guy spent Sunday morning listlessly reading the unflattering newspaper comments on the Earl of St Edmunds's press release. His antennae told him the mood in the Britton Trust camp was turning ugly; but the earl's problems were not his to resolve.

Lunch was a sorry affair: all his favourite restaurants were closed, so he had to eat alone in the hotel. Even when the body was replete, the mind lacked stimulus. The art galleries and shops were closed. As he sat alone in the sitting room of his suite, he felt it was a poor way to celebrate his coming triumph. Then Harold Antony called.

'I've been talking to Berry,' he reported. 'He tells me he hasn't slept all night worrying what the board's going to do to him tomorrow. Seems he's been getting some pretty irate calls from Charteris and Goodman. He's scared stiff about his legal position.'

'It's a bit late now. He should have thought of that beforehand,' Guy smirked.

'Anyway, I've recommended a lawyer to him. The three of us are meeting for breakfast.'

'For breakfast! That'll be a new experience for Berry.'

'Seriously, Guy, I'm rather concerned about the situation. Maybe we should get together to review things.'

'I could come over to you later, if you want,' Guy offered, pouncing on the opportunity. 'I'm at a bit of a loose end, actually,' he admitted. 'Rhoda couldn't find me some supper, could she, Harold?'

'You know she's been dying to feed you.'

'Tell her not to cook. Just bread and cheese. I'll bring a bottle of wine.'

Guy began to feel less unhappy. He ordered a bottle of 1959 Cantemerle from room service; better not waste a Mouton Rothschild if the wine was going to be disturbed by the car journey. It was Yankee Tate's day off, but he was happy to drive himself.

By the time he had negotiated the byways of Marylebone and the foothills of Hampstead, Guy was in fine mood. Harold had been a terrific support from start to finish. He had found half a million shares, he had dealt with the earl, and as a former director of Britton Trust he had provided matchless intelligence about the other side. He deserved a treat to go with his self-invited guest; a half-share of a bottle of wine was hardly an adequate reward for someone who had pleased Guy Magnus.

As Rhoda greeted him at the door of the Antony home a few minutes later, Guy realised that he did not owe Harold alone. For behind every Harold there stood a Rhoda. Harry Griffin had once described her as a woman without an ounce of surplus culture; but Harry was not an impartial observer as far as the Antonys were concerned. Guy knew that while her husband suffered his ailments audibly Rhoda made no complaint, tolerating his late evenings at the office, the business calls when he came home, the weekends catching up on his paperwork, even this intrusion into their Sunday evening together, when she would no doubt have submitted to a maternal urge to provide her guest with a three-course dinner in place of Harold's customary TV supper. Despite all this, Rhoda would always be immaculately made-up, manicured, coiffured, dressed and bejewelled in readiness for the moment Harold needed her on his public arm. Guy owed Rhoda too.

He followed his hostess into the hall. He noted she was wearing a gold bracelet on each wrist but no watch. 'Got the time, Rhoda?' he asked.

'A housewife doesn't need a watch to know what time it is,' Rhoda replied, smiling graciously. 'Supper will be ready in a jiffy. Harold's decanted a bottle of wine, but I'm sure yours is just as nice.'

Harold, or if not he, Rhoda, had taken Guy at his word. The dining table was loaded with crusty French bread, at least a dozen cheeses, and slices of apple, grapes and celery. Next to them sat a decanter, and next to the decanter a dusty bottle with its numbered Mouton Rothschild label stared at the place Guy was to sit.

'You should try the Brie de Meaux first, or the camembert with a slice of pear,' advised Harold. 'They're beginning to run nicely. Go for the stronger flavours later.'

As he tasted one delicious cheese after another, Guy checked on the state of the campaign. 'Now we have Berry's and Cummings's shares in the bag, I make it we hold forty-six per cent. We're only a quarter of a million shares short. Jolyon's will see us home.' He looked to Harold for confirmation.

'Provided there's no problem with the transfer of Berry's shares.'

'He signed the contract note. They're ours.'

'I think that's right, but the board may challenge it.'

'On what grounds?'

'That it's contrary to Takeover Rules. Directors are prohibited from selling shares if they would lead to a transfer of effective control.'

Guy knew the rules; the question was how to circumvent them. 'You didn't say anything about that yesterday,' he pointed out. 'In any case, it doesn't give us control. I don't see why the position should be different now we have forty-six per cent from when we had forty?'

'Once the lawyers stick their fingers into the pie, you never know what they're going to bring out. Try the Banon. It's my favourite *chèvre*.'

Guy did as he was told and took a slice of Livarot as well. 'Powerful stuff,' he commented. The pungent smell and strong flavour brought him back to sterner matters. 'You don't suppose … Harry?' he changed the subject when Rhoda excused herself and left the room.

'I keep trying, but he doesn't want to know. He's fully aware his shares will take you over the top. The way I see it, he just wants to squeeze a higher price out of you.' Antony's tone showed the dim view he took of Harry's meanness.

'He's always been a greedy son-of-a-bitch.' As if to show he knew what he was talking about, Guy took a mouthful of Mouton Rothschild to wash away one strong taste before he replaced it with another, from a chunky slice of Roquefort.

'So why don't you …?' Antony left his question unfinished.

'If Harry thinks he can get a special deal out of me, he can forget it. I'm going to show him I can win without him. You know, you've done a terrific job for us, Harold. We'd never have got the earl without you. You deserve something for all you've done.'

'I'll be billing you for my commission as we agreed,' Antony played a straight bat.

'If there's one talent I have, Harold, I'm a pretty fair dealer.'

'One of the best,' Antony felt bound to agree.

'It occurred to me, Harold, if you want to put some of your money with me and I were to invest it for you with my own.' Guy broke off as Rhoda re-entered the room. She glared threateningly at Harold, who in turn frowned at Guy in a manner that told him the subject was shelved for the time being. Guy turned to his hostess with barely a pause for breath. 'Rhoda, you've always spoiled me rotten. No cooking for you tomorrow night. I'm taking you both to the Mirabelle.'

When they had finished eating and Harold and Guy had taken their plates into the kitchen, Rhoda excused herself again, as if exhausted by the rigours of playing hostess, and left them to their men's talk. Harold led Guy into a drawing-room overflowing with Regency furniture and paintings which showed taste and expense if not the passion of a true collector. Gold-framed photographs of Harold with politicians, Rhoda with illustrious musicians and Harold and Rhoda with minor Royals stood on each flat surface. In a corner of the room Guy noticed a piano whose lack of distinction made it look out of place.

'Do you mind me asking what sort of a piano this is?' he asked.

'It's a Broadwood,' Antony told him.

'Didn't Beethoven have one?' Guy recalled.

'He composed on one.' Antony tinkled the keys modestly, as if to show he was familiar with, but would not presume to imitate, the composer's highly personal technique. 'Not like this; his was a fortepiano. He came to London in 1807 to see what John Broadwood was up to. Broadwood made one expressly for him and shipped it to Vienna. Ludwig hammered it to death – but that's another story.'

'Are Broadwoods the best pianos?'

Harold knew Guy had a way of finding out when he was lied to. Honesty, or at least modesty, was the best policy. 'Not today,' he admitted. 'They're perfectly respectable, but they're not the best.'

'What's wrong with them? How would you rate this one, for example?'

'Well, it has an agreeable action, but the tone's a bit dull for some tastes. It's a reasonable choice for us. After all, Rhoda's not exactly a professional.'

'If I was thinking of getting a grand piano for my new house,' Guy hypothesised; 'How should I go about choosing it?'

'It depends on who'd be playing it, on the quality of tone and how much you're prepared to pay.'

'I'm not asking you for financial advice, Harold.'

'Well, it depends on the kind of sound you like. Tastes differ,' Harold evaded the issue once more.

'I want to know what make I would buy if I wanted the best,' Guy pressed.

'The best? I'm no expert, but many of the world's great pianists play a Steinway. Rubinstein won't touch anything else.'

'What makes a Steinway so good?'

'Its tone, primarily. Their finest grands have such brilliance and power. But you have to be a good pianist to get the best out of them, because they have such a fast action. That requires pretty special technical control.'

Guy was close to gaining the knowledge he wanted, but he needed to apply the ultimate test.

'If you were buying a piano for Rhoda today, Harold, and money were no object, which one would you choose?' he asked

'Oh, I'd definitely buy a Steinway,' Antony said without hesitation.

'Right,' said Guy decisively, with the satisfaction of one who has at last found the elusive last item on his Christmas shopping list; 'In that case she's got herself a Steinway.' He marched from the room and through the front door without so much as a word of thanks to Rhoda. His mouth agape, Antony followed Guy as far as the porch and watched him climb into the driving seat of his Mercedes.

'Eight thirty at the Mirabelle,' Guy shouted as the car leapt from the kerb.

27

To say that the remaining directors of Britton Trust regarded the upper echelons of Her Majesty's house of peers as worth no more than the chorus of The Beggar's Opera would have been to risk an action for slander from the National Union of Bums, Tramps and Parasites. While Grover Seagull was at the Takeover Panel protesting against the sale of the Earl of St Edmunds' shares and Philip Alexander was telling the City Star board it was a dirty rotten trick, John Charteris, Thomas Goodman, Archie Laws and Alan Palliser took their places in an inquisitorial ring round the boardroom table and faced the man who sat at its head. At the far end an uncomfortable Jolyon Priestley sat alone, hoping to vanish into anonymity.

'I wish,' the earl began uncertainly, 'to make a brief statement.' He took from his pocket the handwritten sheet of paper his lawyer had given him at the end of their breakfast meeting and read, 'You will have learnt from the announcement published in the weekend press that on Saturday last, 13th October, I entered into a contract to sell my shareholding in the company to the interests of Guy Magnus. I retained 500 shares, a holding which qualifies me to remain a director. The price paid by Mr Magnus was 300p per share, a price which I consider to be fair and reasonable and which he is now obliged to offer to all the shareholders. The reason for my sale, as you will have seen in the announcement, was that I wished to bring to an end the uncertainty surrounding the approaches to the company. It is my duty as chairman to give the board a lead, and that is what I have done in the interests of the company's staff, its customers and its shareholders. I urge all of you to follow my lead.'

'What else did he give for your treachery?' Goodman interrupted spitefully.

'Wasn't offered a penny more than £3,' protested the earl.

The air was rank with disbelief. 'Not on the contract, I'll bet,' Palliser was heard to mutter.

'How many pieces of silver was it worth?' asked Laws.

'I say old chap, that's hardly fair,' the earl protested angrily.

'What about your agreement to give us notice?' asked Charteris.

'Gave you it on Friday.'

'You did what?' Charteris was incredulous.

'Said I regarded myself as free to talk to him.'

'Bloody great difference between talking to him and selling your shares to him behind our backs,' said Goodman. 'At best it's a disgraceful breach of faith, at worst a deliberate breach of contract.'

'Matter of opinion,' the earl refused to concede the point.

'What about City Star's offer?' asked Palliser, no more friendly than Charteris or Goodman. 'How could you ignore a better price for the shareholders?'

'Haven't made an offer; not likely to either. Too busy trying to buy a bunch of our properties from Magnus.'

'Don't tell me you fell for that,' Goodman sneered. 'Any fool can see it was just a ruse to string him along while we got our act together.'

'Could have been misled,' the earl half-admitted, dropping his eyes.

'What happens if we don't follow your lead?' asked Palliser.

The earl knew he could only be chairman while he retained the confidence of the board. 'I'd resign,' he replied. Then he thought again. Perhaps he shouldn't resign. Once he had, it might be difficult to regain the position. 'Not immediately, of course, but eventually. In my own good time,' he qualified his answer.

'There's no time like the present,' commented Charteris sharply.

'Perhaps a vote of confidence would be in order,' Goodman followed up.

'I say, hardly necessary,' protested the earl.

'I move a vote of no confidence in the chair,' Charteris ignored him.

'Seconded,' said Goodman.

The earl looked round the table for support. Jolyon Priestley looked round with him. Seeing none, he remained silent.

'No point in a vote,' the earl observed. 'Know when I'm not wanted. You have my resignation, effective now.' Mustering as much dignity as he was able, he rose from his chair and moved symbolically to one at the centre of the table.

'I move that the board appoint Mr John Charteris to be chairman of the company,' proposed Goodman, as if according to a planned script.

'Seconded,' said Palliser without hesitation.

For a moment Charteris seemed genuinely moved; then he took up the chair vacated by the earl. 'Gentlemen, I'm honoured,' he said. 'I may not be here for long, but on the other hand if we all pull together, I just may be. I propose we take a ten minute adjournment.' He glanced meaningfully at Goodman and received a nod in return. The two left the room deep in conversation.

The earl went over to Priestley, who stood uneasily by him, uncertain of what the others would make of their association. Rather than join them, they left one by one for the washrooms.

'May I take it the rest of us consider ourselves still bound by the resolution we signed on 30th September?' asked Charteris when the meeting reconvened ten minutes later.

Each of the other directors in turn solemnly confirmed his agreement. Except one. Charteris looked Priestley calmly in the eye. Priestley felt an emptiness grip his stomach. He could prevaricate no longer.

'I, er, wish to give notice that I, um, consider myself free to deal in the shares, er, listed in my name,' he said hesitantly.

Goodman picked up the nuance. 'Listed?' he enquired.

'Well, my shares, I mean.' Having reached the ledge beneath the summit, Priestley decided the view from the peak was not worth the extra yard of pain.

'Are you selling them?' asked Goodman.

'Selling them?' Priestley repeated. Was he selling them? he asked himself. 'No, I'm not selling them,' he answered with care.

'Then why won't you pledge them to the board?'

'Well, I'm going abroad tomorrow for a few days. How do I know what's going to happen while I'm away? I want to keep, um, a measure of flexibility.'

'Do you remain in support of the board?' Goodman pressed him.

'Er, yes, of course.'

'In that case, why don't you give us your proxy so we can count them towards the fifty per cent we need for City Star?' Goodman persisted. The pause while Priestley hesitated was enough. 'You can appoint the chairman as your alternate. Don't you trust him?' 'John Charteris, I mean,' Goodman clarified his proposal.

'No, not at all, I mean, of course I do,' agreed Priestley, trapped.

'May I suggest through the chair,' asked Goodman, determined to retain the initiative, 'that the company secretary be asked to prepare a proxy form for signature by Jolyon Priestley?' As in jolly bloody un-priestly, he muttered to Charteris, who winked back.

'All right by you, Jolyon?' asked Charteris.

'No problem,' said Priestley uncomfortably.

'I propose a subcommittee of the board be appointed to handle the company's defence,' said Charteris as the papers were being prepared. He and Goodman had agreed it was essential to keep as much intelligence as possible from the traitor in their midst.

'You'll chair it, I hope?' Goodman came in on cue.

'If you will join me. And one of the managing directors, I suggest. You'll be away, Jolyon. Pity,' Charteris added gratuitously. 'How about you, Alan?'

'Can't say I think much to the way things are being done around here,' complained the earl stuffily. 'Undemocratic. Don't look like there's much trust any more. I'm off.' He rose and shuffled from the room.

Charteris grinned at Goodman. Goodman grinned back. They hadn't had as much fun since they'd left school.

The earl stormed down to the garage, got into his Rolls-Royce and turned on the ignition. The engine purred into life. He slipped the gear lever into reverse and waited for the limousine to edge backwards. And waited. He checked the instrument panel. Revs okay, petrol okay, oil okay, electrics okay. Everything was okay. It seemed like minutes before he decided to get out and see what was wrong. He stood back from the car and looked at it. His eyes blinded by frustration and rage, he stamped out of the garage, back up to his office and picked up the phone. This time he did not wait long. He knew a dead line when he heard one. He stomped back down to the ground floor, out of the front door, across the street to a nearby telephone booth and picked up the receiver. The conspiracy seemed to have widened to include the General Post Office. As he stepped from the booth, the skies opened and with a fine disregard for precedence the entire resident, working and tourist population of the West End of London simultaneously waved its collective hand at the hitherto empty taxicabs and jumped in. An hour later a thoroughly soaked and disconsolate Earl of St Edmunds picked up his home telephone, prayed to the god of peers and dialled Guy Magnus's private number.

'Bastards took the wheels off my car, Priestley's wobbling and I've been sacked,' he listed his protests in the order they occurred to him. 'Don't know how I'm going to get around,' he moaned, close to tears.

Guy played the card of friendship. 'I'll send my driver over right away,' he offered. 'Don't bother to tell him if you don't like the way he drives,' he added some practical advice. Yankee never took any notice. 'Was it Charteris?' he asked.

'And Goodman, I expect.' The picture of the conspiratorial duo was fresh in the earl's memory.

'I shall write to the board this minute and request their removal as directors for mistreatment of company assets,' Guy told the earl, confident in his coming victory and forgetful of his own expertise in this particular form of dereliction of duty. After a few pleasantries he put down the phone. Then he picked it up again to call Priestley. The earl's reference to wobbling sounded ominous.

'Jolyon, I need to get myself up to speed before we meet at the Mirabelle,' he said. 'Can you come round to Claridge's after work? Save you having to go home, and you can get in your first round of champagne … Half past six, quarter to seven? … Cummings? Tell him you have to go somewhere on your own and to meet us there at half past eight … While you're at it, see if you can't rent a car with fixed wheels for the earl, would you? He'd lose his head if he knew how to loosen the nuts …'

Once he had dealt with the earl's transportation needs, there was nothing to do but to go shopping before anyone else came to him with his problems. Thanks to Westchurch, whose settlement department had paid him for his Britton Trust shares with uncharacteristic promptness, Bond Street was his for the taking.

Meanwhile Jolyon Priestley returned to his office, where he sat deep in thought. He might have described the process as a debate with his conscience; others might have argued that such a euphemism was out of place. He might have claimed that he had not lied; they might have said that neither had he told the truth. What was not in dispute was that as Charteris now had his proxy, he could conceal his deal with Ernest Burke no longer. He must report it to someone. Charteris was hardly the man: he would be angry. Goodman would be worse: he would be scathing. Palliser? Palliser would tell Charteris and Goodman.

Priestley made himself a cup of coffee, delaying the wretched moment as long as he could. Then he dialled Grover Seagull's private line at Thruston Cutwell.

Seagull's secretary was somewhat surprised. 'I thought he was with you, Mr Priestley: he left for Britton Trust half an hour ago. Hasn't he arrived yet?'

Priestley called Britton Trust. There the telephonist told him that Seagull was in a meeting with Charteris, Goodman and Palliser. She offered to put him through right away, and did so before he had time to object.

'Grover, I wonder if you could advise me on a personal problem,' asked Priestley when he was connected.

'Fire away,' Seagull said tersely. He had crossed town in response to a call from Charteris, who wished him to confirm that Thruston Cutwell would continue to finance his share purchases and would go into the market itself in support of the board. He had not expected to be asked to change nappies.

'My shares. You see, before all this began I split my holding ...'

'Go on.'

'Well, I transferred 200,000 to one of Ernest Burke's funds.'

'You did what?'

Priestley repeated his confession. 'I had to – for tax reasons. I'd have had to pay capital gains tax if I sold for cash, so my accountants advised me to exchange them for their shares,' he lied on the hoof and without shame.

'When did this transaction take place?'

'Beginning of August, I think.'

Seagull threw his free hand in the air in exasperation. 'Did you report the transaction to the board?' he asked.

'Um, not exactly.'

'What do you mean, not exactly?'

'Well, not at all, actually. Didn't think I'd have to. It was only a transfer from one pocket to the other. They're pretty much under my control,' Priestley assured him.

'How do you mean, pretty much? Either they are or they aren't.'

Priestley instinctively chose the option that would cause least grief. 'They'll remain in support of the board,' he said. 'I'm a major shareholder of the fund. Jamie Tulloch will do as I ask.'

'You had more than 200,000. What about the rest?'

'Those are still mine.'

'And remain pledged to the board?'

'Of course.'

'You asked for my advice,' Seagull sighed. 'You'd better tell John Charteris what you told me. We'll record it as a formal report to the board of the disposal of 200,000 shares – at the beginning of August. I'll pass him to you now.' He handed the receiver to Charteris and turned to Goodman. 'It's

Jolyon. Thank God he's still on-side,' he said. He drew a line through the figure of 365,000 shares against Priestley's name on the computer print-out, wrote "Ernest Burke 200,000" on one line and "Priestley 165,000" beneath it, and put a tick against each. With them he was confident they could satisfy City Star's requirement. Without them ...

The subcommittee went back to work. The earl's defection had made its task more difficult, but by no means impossible. It agreed to issue a press statement that an offer worth 327p per share would be made if the board could commit fifty per cent of the company's equity to the bidder, and that it was close to its target. Charteris reckoned they were three and a half per cent short and counting. His stockbroker called to say he had picked up 30,000 shares, the latest purchase being at 318p. While the price remained above his offer price of 300p, Magnus would be kept out of the market.

Meanwhile Priestley put down the phone and whistled under his breath. Pretty close call, he told himself. Charteris had been frosty but restrained. One down, one to go. He put on his coat and headed for Claridge's.

28

As Jolyon Priestley was shown into Guy's suite by the butler, he found its occupant on the telephone to the Ludgate Circus.

'Tell the *FT* that Ludgate and Westchurch have bugger-all to do with one another,' he was instructing. 'And the *Telegraph* that you hear what Britton says with … amusement and amazement; and if there's an offer, let's see it.' He put down the phone and nodded to the butler to pour the Dom Pérignon. 'When do we do the deal with your shares, Jolyon?' he asked as their glasses were refilled a few minutes later, hoping the second glass would give Priestley more confidence than the first appeared to have done.

'There appears to be a slight problem with them,' Priestley admitted.

'You can't go back on your word now,' Guy replied. The menace in his tone told Priestley the statement was not intended as a question.

'They'll be yours, just as I promised, Guy. Honestly. But I can't commit them all to you yet.'

'All? Explain,' Guy demanded.

'It's Thruston Cutwell,' Priestley explained, comforted that he had stuck to the truth so far, even if he was about to make a modest diversion from it. 'I'm in the middle of a property deal with them,' he invented. 'If it were small I'd let it drop, but it's a big one.' As he spoke, the size of the property grew in his mind. 'Pretty important to me, actually. I can't afford to upset Seagull by selling my shares at this stage.'

'At this stage?'

'Until I've exchanged contracts on the property.'

'When are you expecting that?'

Priestley had hoped not to have to deal with the detail. 'Listen, Guy,' he said, anxious not to upset him, the board of Britton Trust and Thruston Cutwell all at the same time, 'you may still be able to buy most of the shares.'

'Most of them?' Guy stared at him in disbelief.

'I had to transfer 200,000 to Ernest Burke,' Priestley confessed. 'Back in

August,' he added, as if the qualification would gain him absolution. Seeing from Guy's expression that it did nothing of the kind, he went on hurriedly, 'I'm sure Jamie will sell them to you if I ask him to.'

Guy calculated. He had counted on securing all of Priestley's shares. If the loss of 200,000 was grim news, that of the remaining 165,000 could be his death knell. He must make Priestley see that his payout depended on Ernest Burke selling. 'They'd better. You say you can't sell me those you've kept until I've won,' he spelt out the reality of his guest's position. 'But the board can't get fifty per cent, and City Star won't make a bid without it: they'd look stupid in the City, losing to me. So if you want your money, you'll have to make sure Jamie does as you say, won't you, chum?'

Priestley thought fast. Was there a deal which would suit both sides, and him too? He would need to make his mark when he started his new job. 'As it happens, Jamie could be interested in buying Watson's from you,' he tried.

'I can hardly discuss selling a business until I own it,' Guy said, alert to the opportunity. 'You'd better tell Jamie to sell me the shares right away if he's serious.' He picked up the telephone and passed it to Priestley.

Jamie Tulloch was still at his desk. After a few minutes' conversation he agreed to meet Guy the following morning.

'When do you expect your property deal to be completed, so you can put in your acceptance for the shares you still own, Jolyon?' Guy pursued his enquiries.

'Don't lean on me, Guy,' Priestly pleaded.

Guy's receptive antennae picked up the hint that Priestley was still hiding something from him. 'You haven't committed them to the board?' he asked.

'No, Guy, honestly I haven't. They'll be yours.'

'Then you've sung for your supper,' Guy smiled. He was within an ace of victory: it was so close he could pick up its scent, and it smelled good. He took up a small package and rose to his feet. 'Let's go, partner,' he said. 'It's eight fifteen. Mustn't be late for dinner.'

Guy greeted each of his guests as they reached the bottom of the stairs and entered the bar of the Mirabelle. Rhoda Antony received a special hug. When they went in for dinner he placed her on his right, Melvin on his left, with Harold Antony, Jolyon Priestley and Tim Cummings opposite. Rhoda sat on the velour-upholstered chair and looked around her. The ruched cerise curtains were drawn back to reveal a brightly-lit garden. Beyond arches supported by spiralled columns a row of wives and mistresses in little black dresses and gold Grima bracelets posed on the banquettes opposite prosperous entrepreneurs and socialites. Rhoda was happy she had chosen a low-cut Balenciaga gown and ruby necklace.

As the maître d'hôtel placed her table napkin on her lap, Rhoda noticed a gift-wrapped package on her side plate with a card attached. She looked round the table to check that everyone else had one too. No one had.

'What do I do with this?' she asked Guy.

'Open it?' he responded helpfully.

Rhoda did as he suggested, starting with the card.

'To the long-suffering Rhoda, with love from Guy,' she read. She opened the package and inside found a box embossed 'Les Must de Cartier.' She opened it. 'My goodness, Guy, what on earth is this?' she asked, fearing to touch its contents.

Guy extracted the offending item and examined it carefully. Then he placed it round her wrist and closed the fastening. 'It appears to be a wristwatch,' he deduced.

'What on earth for?' Rhoda asked, a trifle lacking in grace.

'Well, I was thinking about how I'd disrupted your weekend, inviting myself to dinner, and how I'm always phoning Harold at home and interrupting his private life. They don't sell them in London yet, so I had it sent over from Paris. They're all the rage there. Anyway, I love giving presents. Melvin and I are always giving presents, aren't we Mel?' His friend Melvin's nose was too deep in the wine list to make a decipherable response. 'You won't believe the fabulous day I've had,' Guy went on. 'I've been shopping. To celebrate our victory,' he added as if by way of explanation. 'I bought a couple of glorious Kitaj oils at Marlborough Fine Arts. Then I went to Asprey's and bought myself a clock. Set me back twenty-five ...' he said proudly.

'Twenty-five pounds? It must be a nice one,' Rhoda commented politely. He must, after all, have spent many times more on her watch.

'... Thousand,' Guy clarified. 'It was made in 1695 by Thomas Tompion. In those days clocks were the leading edge of technology, rather like computers or space travel today. He numbered all his clocks, you know. Mine's considered to be a very important example. It's a repeating "grande sonnerie", with incredibly pretty peals. It has an ebony case with a delightful statuette on top and lovely ormolu mounts. Incidentally, Harold, can you take a six foot one?'

'A six foot one?' Harold Antony was unhappy with the question, especially in front of Rhoda. He was, after all, exactly five foot six.

'At home, dummy!'

Antony caught on. 'Yes, we can take a six foot one,' he confirmed, taking care to use the plural.

'Good. A very pretty model's coming to you from Chappell next week.'

Rhoda blinked, but rather than cross-examine her husband in public on the part he played in Guy's moral or religious proclivities, she picked up her menu. She took one look at the prices on the crescent-shaped listing of hors d'oeuvres and asked herself whether she shouldn't go for something less modest.

'I always find it difficult to choose between the caviar and the foie gras. You can rely on the Mirabelle. They only serve Beluga and Strasbourg here,' Guy commented from her side.

Rhoda thought it discreet to compromise. She asked him if he minded her ordering smoked salmon, pleased to see that it now cost more than a pound. In the old days anyone could afford to eat well, but prices were shooting up, thank God, so you didn't have to dine with riff-raff who didn't dress for dinner. For the main course she accepted with alacrity Guy's recommendation that she choose from Les Plats des Gourmets, for which no prices were shown, as the Entrees listed beneath were all less than £2. As for the osso buco and tête de veau at under a pound, she could well do without them.

'The poulet à l'estragon's for two. Shall we try that?' Guy asked Melvin. 'Or do you think we should wait till we go to Père Bise?'

'That sounds nice,' Rhoda told Harold; but by now her husband's gastric juices were salivating for a juicy tournedos Rossini, on the grounds that it was the only dish visibly priced at over two quid and he was damned if he was going to let Guy off lightly. From their choices it was clear that Priestley and Cummings felt the same way, so Rhoda settled for the carré d'agneau en croûte. While the others were ordering, Melvin Cecil was in conference with the sommelier, emerging after several minutes with the proposal, warmly endorsed by Guy, that they try a magnum of the Château Cheval Blanc – the 1947, naturally.

Guy turned back to Rhoda. 'If we want the soufflé au Grand Marnier, we have to order it now,' he pointed out. 'Make it six,' he told the maitre d'hôtel over his shoulder.

Once they had taken care of the serious business of the evening the celebrating began in earnest. Guy was upbeat to the point of euphoria. He was about to clinch the deal that would set his career on an unstoppable upward path. Thanks were due to those who sat around him, and he was happy to offer them; though in truth the triumph that was to come was his alone.

'I can't tell you how much it means to me to have you all onside,' he said raising his glass. 'Especially you, Jolyon.'

'You know I'd be with you all the way, if it was just up to me,' Priestley replied. 'I'm sure Jamie'll do the right thing with the shares Ernest Burke holds. You can depend on me for the rest.'

'Got the time, Rhoda?' Guy asked two and a half hours later, finishing his last glass of his beloved Dom Pérignon just as she put down her spoon after her last delicious mouthful of soufflé.

Rhoda looked down at her wrist and smiled gratefully. 'Late,' she replied. 'Time for Harold to take me home,' she added, reminding herself to keep a close eye on next week's deliveries. Who or what in the name of heaven could this six foot one be?

29

Jamie Tulloch put down *The Times*. It told him City Star was a likely counter-bidder for Britton Trust if the company's board could procure fifty per cent of the shares plus one. Yet Jolyon Priestley was asking Ernest Burke to sell the stake he had owned — in truth still owned until the paperwork was complete — to that brazen pedlar Guy Magnus, whom *The Times* had reported as having said he thought highly of Britton Trust and very highly of Laserbeam, when the only thing he thought highly of was buying stakes in cut-price companies and threatening to bid for them if their boards refused to give him a swift and generous turn. Something fishy was going on.

Had this been a normal dealing situation, Tulloch would not have thought twice: he would have turned the Britton Trust shares while the market was bidding 320p for them and let Magnus do the worrying. His directors were keen for cash. Six hundred grand showing a one-third margin would suit them fine. Britton Trust wasn't their cup of tea, not by a long chalk: it was a highly geared hodgepodge of enterprises of dubious provenance. But if a higher bid really was in the offing, he had better hold on. Last night Priestley had sounded overanxious for the deal to be done. Better check the story out before it was too late.

Tulloch called Priestley's office, to be told that his quarry was going directly from his home to the airport. He persuaded the girl to give him Priestley's home number. It rang for almost a minute before the phone was picked up.

'What is it, Jamie? I'm going to be late for my flight as it is,' Priestley said impatiently.

Tulloch expounded his problem as succinctly as he could.

'City Star will never get its bid off the ground,' Priestley told him. 'Magnus is your only chance. He's already close to fifty per cent and I've promised him the rest of my holding, so he's home and dry regardless. He's only doing you a favour because I'm a friend. Be a good chap and do the deal, would you?'

'His bid of 300p will stay on the table,' Tulloch demurred. 'It can't do any harm to wait and see whether City Star comes up with anything higher.'

Priestley thought fast. 'You're thinking small, Jamie,' he said. 'The big hit is to use your bargaining power to get Magnus to sell you one of Britton Trust's goodies outside the market. You may even be able to get your hands on Watson's if you ask him nicely enough. Put you right in the heart of the North Sea oil bonanza. Can't stand here chatting, got a cab waiting. Call me at Heathrow if you have any problems. I'll be in the first class lounge in Terminal Two, with Grover Seagull.'

The North Sea oil bonanza! If Priestley was with Seagull, this had the ring of truth. Tulloch spent the time before Guy Magnus's arrival gleaning as much information as he could about Watson's. By the time his visitor was announced, he was left wondering whether Magnus thought more or less of this company than he did of Laserbeam.

'I want to make my position clear from the start,' Guy was soon telling him. 'We've won already. I've told Jolyon I'm prepared to buy your shares, but only on my terms.'

'What terms are those?' asked Tulloch nervously.

'There's a Panel technicality to sort out. We need a clearance that its ruling on the Earl of St Edmund's sale isn't going to be challenged. Our deal will have to be conditional on that. We're not prepared to risk our money buying your shares and then find we're still short of a few thousand.'

'But you said you'd already won,' said Tulloch in disbelief.

'Clearance is a formality.'

'What about City Star?'

'They're well short. They've no chance.'

Tulloch reckoned it was not worth betting against Guy Magnus. He might need his cooperation to solve one of his own problems. 'We may be prepared to consider a sale, but I'm not sure exactly when we could deliver. We haven't actually completed the purchase from Jolyon yet,' he admitted.

'What exactly is the problem?' Guy phrased his question with care. He didn't ask why there was a problem: when you dealt with Priestley, there was always some wrinkle or other. The question was, what particular twist had he come up with this time?

'The stock exchange has insisted we hold an EGM to approve the issue of our shares to him. We have to give three weeks' notice to the shareholders.'

'When does it expire?'

'November 5th.'

'I'll buy them conditional on that,' Guy offered. 'You can put it on the contract note.'

'You'll have to pay on completion,' Tulloch said firmly.

'When I said I'd only buy on my terms, I meant it,' Guy countered. 'We're fully committed until the finance comes through from Ulster & Cayman. If Jolyon wants you to sell us his shares now rather than accept our offer and wait for the end of November, you'll have to fund our purchase yourselves.'

Tulloch loved it. Magnus had such effrontery. He'd graciously allow you to sell to him at lower than the market price, so long as you provided him with the money to do it. 'We haven't agreed to sell to you yet,' he pointed out.

'Jolyon has. That's because he's smart. He knows that if he doesn't, he won't be on our mailing list when we get around to making disposals,' Guy pointed out. 'Are you smart, Jamie?' he enquired blithely.

'I have my moments.'

'Everyone wants Watson's. I'm not surprised. I tell the press it's Laserbeam I'm after, but Watson's is the jewel in the crown. I haven't made up my mind yet whether to sell it privately, as Jolyon has asked, or to put it on the open market and let the bidders wind the price up.'

'I have to consider what's best for us.'

'Another 20p on 200,000 shares... mm, that would bring you in a dealing profit of £40,000. You're right, Jamie; I don't suppose Ernest Burke would know how to make £40,000 out of Watson's,' Guy said, his voice laden with sarcasm. 'And I'm sure Jolyon won't object if you upset his plans.'

Tulloch knew when he was beaten, but he was still smart enough to check his bargaining position. 'Give me five minutes and I'll see what I can do,' he said. He went into his secretary's office and told her to call the VIP lounge at Heathrow Terminal Two and get them to bring Jolyon Priestley to the phone.

'At first Magnus didn't want to know, but I toughed it out,' he was soon reporting to Priestley.

'I'm not saying we won't sell; in fact, I'm pretty sure I can swing it with the powers-that-be,' Tulloch told Guy on his return. 'But it would help if you let me have a memorandum with your assessment of Watson's and your asking price. I need to show them it's not just idle talk.'

'No problem; I'd rather sell to my friends than to anyone else,' Guy assured him with total frankness; buying from his friends was an entirely different matter.

As Guy Magnus and Jamie Tulloch prepared the contract note for the sale of Ernest Burke's shares, Jolyon Priestley was relating part of his conversation with Tulloch to Grover Seagull in the VIP lounge at Heathrow.

'That was Ernest Burke,' he told him. It was an unnecessary piece of information. Seagull's intuition told him the origin of any telephone call received within thirty feet of him. 'In total confidence, Magnus has agreed to sell them Watson's.'

'If he wins,' Seagull made the qualification.

'If he wins,' Priestley acknowledged.

'Which he won't, provided you all stick together. Ernest Burke aren't monkeying around with your shares, are they?'

'Absolutely not. They wouldn't dare to without my say-so.'

'Which you won't give.'

'Which I won't give,' Priestley agreed.

'In which case he can make all the promises he likes, but if he can't buy in the market and we can, it's only a matter of time before we get the fifty per cent we need.'

'TAP regrets to announce a short delay in flight 206 to Lisbon, due to the late arrival of the incoming flight,' a loudspeaker interrupted their dialogue.

'TAP, Take Another Plane,' commented Seagull sourly. His vanity had already suffered a blow when the incoming call had proved to be for Priestley rather than for himself, and now he had to sit it out in this anodyne waiting room at the wretched airline's pleasure. 'I need to call the office,' he retaliated. It was important they knew at base camp that he had Priestley under surveillance and could personally vouch that Ernest Burke's shares were still in his right pocket. On such attention to detail was a rising merchant banker's reputation made.

Seagull made his call. His efforts were to no avail. While he was in Lisbon with Priestley, Ernest Burke sold Guy Magnus its Britton Trust shares, conditional only on the approval of its shareholders, who were conveniently available for consultation just along the corridor. And Guy bought the shares with Ernest Burke's money. Had Priestley been able to sell him the balance of his holding at the same time, Guy told himself, the deal would have signalled victory. As it was, he mused, looking at the back of Yankee Tate's head as the latter drove him back to his office, it was time to look to his insurance.

30

It was twelve noon: the ideal time for a meeting between City folk who will shortly be breaking into their crowded schedules to snatch some light refreshment. The conference room at Thruston Cutwell was packed to bursting-point. The campaign had reached the stage where, on the insistence of the absent Grover Seagull, the professionals had taken charge. Along one side of the table executives of the merchant bank took centre stage. John Charteris alone was permitted to sit in their midst, while the rest of the Britton Trust directors were relegated to the far end of the table. On the opposite side the pecking order differed. In the centre, as befitted the managing director of a major property company, sat Philip Alexander. Pinstriped executives from Fleischman & Sons, City Star's merchant bank, covered his flanks.

Even John Charteris had by now reached a state of traumatised acquiescence in the proposals put forward by the Thruston Cutwell team. For the past week he had accepted that an independent future for Britton Trust was no longer on the agenda, but he was still fighting for the best price for its shareholders and a secure future for its employees. Since the Earl of St Edmunds' treachery these twin objectives had at first receded, then drawn tantalisingly close; finally it seemed they would be achieved. City Star had been cautious, in his view unduly so: had they made up their minds and struck last week, they might already have won the day. But by dint of argument, persuasion and at times even threats, the board had at last gathered pledges for over fifty per cent of Britton Trust's share capital. And now, as its chairman, he was presiding over its final act of capitulation. The prospect was one that filled him with little joy, but he had the satisfaction of knowing that he had carried out his duty. Being himself a substantial shareholder, and having bought over 50,000 more shares during the past three days, he had the added consolation that with this would come a well-earned reward to his purse.

Seagull's assistant passed the list of pledges across the table to the

Fleischman executive at Philip Alexander's right hand. 'We make the total just over 3.4 million,' he reported with transparent satisfaction. 'Fifty point five per cent.'

Alexander held back the smile that had been waiting to emerge. William Fleischman might have identified the opportunity, but it had been he who had insisted that Britton Trust do its own dirty work. His strategy had been proved right. How often did the opportunity arise to bid for a company only when victory had already been guaranteed? He had saved City Star a mountain of costs and possible humiliation. His reputation in the City would gain a well-earned boost.

'Check the numbers against the register,' he instructed, determined not to relax until the job was complete. 'I don't want any mistakes at this late stage. No offence,' he said conciliatorily to Charteris.

While schedules were compared, ticks made in a different coloured inks and numbers listed, totalled and reconciled, Alexander went painstakingly through his checklist with the Thruston Cutwell team. City Star would offer shares and loan stock worth 330p per share. Fleischman & Sons would underwrite the offer for 315p in cash to anyone who lacked confidence in City Star's stock. They agreed the date for acceptances, the date for settlement and the names of the City Star representatives who would join the Britton Trust board. As they reached the end of their list, the two Fleischman executives delegated to deal with the arithmetic were on the point of completing their task.

'We seem to be a hundred out,' reported one.

A flush came to Alexander's cheeks. A hundred thousand shares meant one and a half per cent off the total. 'That leaves you one per cent short,' he accused Charteris.

'Not a hundred thousand: one hundred. One, zero, zero,' the Fleischman executive clarified.

Alexander relaxed. One hundred shares would be easy to find. Even without them City Star was home and dry. 'All we need to do now is write out the agreement. An hour should do it.' He permitted himself the postponed smile as he checked his watch. 'One o'clock.'

'We've laid on sandwiches upstairs,' Seagull's assistant came in on cue.

'Let's deal with the nitty-gritty on a full stomach,' Alexander proposed. He didn't want any more alarms.

Along the corridor from Jamie Tulloch's office there was an atmosphere of quiet contentment. The meeting with the Takeover Panel had been a breeze. A couple of chaps had admitted that as far as they were concerned the whole affair was a bit of a bore. They knew Ernest Burke wouldn't sell its shares to a bidder unless it thought it was in its interests to do so. It was entitled – it was its board's duty – to do the best deal for its own shareholders. So why, the Panel chaps asked their most awkward question, was Ernest Burke asking them for clearance? Did they think they might have done something wrong? No, they were just being extra careful and double-checking. If they didn't know what they were doing, they shouldn't be in the job in the first place, thought the couple of chaps. Go away, fellas, and waste somebody else's time, they said, stifling their yawns. One o'clock. Quick beer, then back for the next one.

'Now all we have to do is hold Ernest Burke's EGM and bank Magnus's £600,000. Hm, one o'clock. Not a bad morning's work,' summed up one of the fellas along the corridor from Jamie Tulloch.

'We'd better put out a press release,' his colleague brought him back to earth. 'Put it on the record. I'll tell Charles the good news.'

Across the City in Ulster & Cayman's Gresham Street head office, Charles Cassels heaved a sigh of relief. 'That was a pretty close shave,' he said to Stephen Cornelius, his joint managing director of its corporate banking division. Ever since the merger with Lyndon Mayhem they had fought a running battle with the Mayfair office. Dervish and de Deyler had been acting as if the money from the sale of Farranwide Properties was theirs to lend by right, and had been lending it by left and centre too, to people Cassels wouldn't have lent a bus fare; but their chairman, Sir Anthony Winchester, had closed his ears to their warnings.

By nature relaxed and genial, as each day of the bid went by Charles Cassels had become increasingly worried. If asked why, he would have put it down to mistrust. Mistrust of Guy Magnus and all his deeds. Magnus wouldn't do anything the straight way if he could find a tortuous alternative. He couldn't imagine what had persuaded Dervish and de Deyler to let the man through the front door in the first place, though to be frank he had grown to feel much the same way about the bank's own merger with those two devious operators.

'What do we hold with those shares?' he asked Cornelius.

'Over forty-six per cent,' came the reply.

'I can't say I'm happy about the way this affair has gone,' Cassels admitted. 'We're getting more flak every day. I don't remember a nastier bid battle. The sales by the earl and Cummings stink to high heaven. There hasn't been a deal that didn't have some kink to it. We may have got away with the Ernest Burke shares for the time being, but I bet they'll come back to haunt us.'

'Unless you make peace with the other side,' said Cornelius thoughtfully, stroking his fashionably long dark brown hair.

Cassels rubbed his receding hairline. 'You think I ought to try?' he asked.

'Can't do any harm. We've nothing to lose.'

'You're probably right.' Cassels checked his watch. 'One o'clock. I'll call them when I get back from lunch. We'd better issue a press release. Put Grover Seagull on the defensive. Make him believe he can't win.'

'Shit! I don't believe it!'

'The dirty rotten bastard!'

'No wonder he's fled the country!'

'Fucking left pocket!'

'Bloody great wank-hole in it, that's all!'

John Charteris listened to his colleagues' reactions to the lunchtime press releases with half an ear. However bitter their feelings, they were of no avail. If Ernest Burke had sold Priestley's 200,000 shares to Guy Magnus, that was bad enough: it would be almost impossible to find the holdings to replace them. But Charteris calculated further. If Priestley had defected to the other side, the board could no longer count on the shares he still held in his own name. Why he hadn't cancelled his proxy and sold them to Magnus was anyone's guess; but without them the board was back at forty-five per cent. It was only a matter of time before the remaining shareholders realised there was not going to be another bid and sent in their acceptance forms to Ulster & Cayman. Was Magnus on the brink of victory?

As he reached his conclusion, a young woman's head appeared round the door. 'Excuse me, gentlemen, but I have Charles Cassels of Ulster & Cayman on the line,' she announced. 'He was asking for Mr Seagull, but I said he was abroad – I didn't say with whom. Then he asked to speak to whoever's in charge of the Britton Trust defence in Mr Seagull's absence.'

'You did right,' Seagull's assistant praised her. Cassels must want them to concede defeat. 'Keep him on hold for a couple of minutes. Then put him through to Mr Green,' he instructed her. The delay would give him enough time to brief the head of corporate finance, who had requested to be kept fully in the picture in Seagull's absence. Frank Green worked on the principle that you never knew whether your highest flyer was going to be shot down in flames, let alone be enticed away by a predatory eagle.

Green heard Cassels through without interruption. Things were getting out of hand, Cassels told him. They'd known each other long enough to see it was getting too hot for their health. They must meet to lower the temperature. If not this very minute, as soon as possible.

Green hesitated. He read weakness in the message. When someone was in a too much of a hurry, you let him stew. But matters were coming to a head; if he failed to act and they went wrong, the blame would be his. 'Four o'clock? Couldn't you make it half past?' he bargained without conviction. He conceded that he would play away, and then capitulated by being on time.

'Come in and sit down, Frank,' Cassels welcomed him rather too heartily. 'We've got to cool down some hot heads, you and me.'

'Our chaps have been sorely tried,' Green rejoined.

'Not by us. It's Magnus who's been the villain of the piece.'

'You've been happy to take his shilling and do his bidding.'

'Oh, that's not entirely fair,' said Cassels, sounding as if he was pleading a cause with which he was not in complete sympathy.

'The offer document went out in your name. You allowed them to accuse the Britton Trust board of incompetence. Made it sound as if they should be lined up against a wall and shot. Those chaps are pretty sensitive about their reputations, you know. There's talk of writs being issued.'

'Madness!' commented Cassels. 'Make the lawyers rich, not them.'

'I know. But there's the question of whether connected parties have been paying over the top. There've been lots of dealings above 300p, and only a few of them are ours. I don't believe anyone would take the risk without an inside track.'

Cassels's experience told him Green was right. But even though he had expected the issue to be put, he was caught without a ready answer. 'These things can never be proved,' he replied lamely, aware that Green would spot his unease.

'If there's been buying at above 300p and the shares have gone to Magnus, there's going to be one hell of a fuss. Our chaps are bound to ask for a thorough investigation,' Green pressed.

'So what would the Panel do? Tell him to pay everyone else the difference?'

'It was you who asked to see me,' Green reminded Cassels. 'I take it you have a proposal?'

'I was actually wondering whether the directors would worry a little less about their precious reputations if they got a little more money for their shareholders,' Cassels flew a tentative kite.

Green saw a payoff for his visit and grabbed at it. 'How much do you have in mind?' he asked.

'I'd have thought 5p a share would be about right.'

'Their reputations are worth more to them than that,' responded Green scornfully.

'What price would you put on them?' asked Cassels with a hint of sarcasm.

'If you measure it by what we reckon Magnus's friends have been paying for the shares, I'd say at least 20p.' Seeing a blank wall of refusal in Cassels's eyes, he added: 'But if we're going to set a price we can both live with, he'll have to go at least half way to the bid City Star was prepared to make.'

Cassels caught the nuance: *was*, not *is*, prepared. 'How much was that?' he asked.

'Three thirty. Magnus'll have to offer at least three fifteen to tempt them.'

'Out of the question,' Cassels said peremptorily.

Green shrugged. Cassels had made an offer the Britton Trust board would not countenance. In return he had stated his case. For the moment neither was able to go further. 'I shall report what you say, Charles, but I don't expect anything but a raspberry in return,' he said with resignation as he rose from his chair.

'At least they can't say we didn't try, Frank,' replied Cassels, sounding even more resigned. He buzzed his secretary. 'Get me a copy of the increased offer document for Britton Trust, would you? They're going out to the shareholders in tonight's post,' he told Green. 'The least I can do is to give you a copy to go home with, so you'll have something to read when the football's over'.

31

Thursday was no day to admit you had watched the football, unless you were a Scotsman, a Welshman or an Irishman. On the day every Englishman was in mourning and every Englishman's wife was secretly celebrating the nation's failure to qualify for the World Cup finals, the stench of protests, refusals, withdrawals and resignations polluted the air of the City of London.

The protests went from Fleischman & Sons to the Takeover Panel. The same old arguments were rehearsed: by selling to Magnus, the Earl of St Edmunds had prevented shareholders from receiving a higher offer; he had dealt with the benefit of inside knowledge; he had been bought off at a price for his own shares, it was said, of 400p.

Once again the chaps at the Panel refused to take sides.

The withdrawal came from City Star. If the most the Britton Trust board could procure was forty-five per cent of the company's shares, there was no point in making an offer that was bound to fail.

The resignation came from Jolyon Priestley. If he was no longer trusted in the Britton Trust boardroom, there was no point in his remaining a director.

Only Guy Magnus remained unaffected by the atmosphere of doom and gloom which accompanied England's sporting disgrace. He was too engrossed in cashing in his chips. His insurance chips.

'I don't want to sound inquisitive, but how many shares in Britton Trust did you say Mr Munster bought you, Yankee?' he enquired of his loyal chauffeur.

'I can't say I rightly recall, sir,' Yankee replied.

'I've no right to know how you invest your savings, but would I be right in saying the number was not a million miles from 42,500?'

'You'd know more about that than me, sir.'

'Not at all, Yankee. But if you should happen to own that precise number and I should happen to find you a buyer for them, what would your reaction be?'

'What would he offer me for them, sir?' Yankee asked humbly.

'He's only allowed to pay you 300p per share.'

Yankee calculated rapidly. A hundred and twenty-seven thousand five hundred pounds. For a moment he thought he'd won the Irish sweepstake. Then he saw the grin on Guy's face and reality dawned.

'How much did I pay for them, sir?' he enquired.

'A hundred and thirty-five thousand pounds, give or take,' Guy replied. His expression was stern.

Yankee calculated again. He bore the implicit censure stoically.

'I suppose you're going to stop the seven and a half grand out of me wages, are you, sir?' he asked.

'You've done a lot of overtime recently, Yankee,' Guy observed. 'Let's just call it quits, shall we? You sign here.'

Yankee Tate was not Guy Magnus's only servant, acquaintance or friend to make a loss through an ill-timed investment in Britton Trust. Such had been their loyalty that while John Charteris was squeezing 50,000 shares out of the market, they had bought more than twice that number. In the case of Johnny Price this had been a particularly magnanimous gesture, for even though Price had paid up to 326p per share for his 25,000 share speculation, he sent in his acceptance form without demur. Despite his disappointment that his associates had acquired fewer than 200,000 shares, Guy repaid their loyalty by forgiving them for not having bought more, and hoping that their losses might somehow be made good.

But when all the numbers had been added together by Guy's office manager Nigel Holmes, double-checked by Danny Gilbert, triple-checked by Larry Callaghan, and divided by the number of Britton Trust shares in issue by Guy, the total still only came to 49.3 per cent. They remained 40,000 shares short. And in view of the constant stream of protests to the Takeover Panel, even Guy had to accept that for the time being the market was closed to Mark Penney-Stockes. It seemed that both sides were destined to remain short of victory, leaving everyone a loser.

Guy cursed. But he adamantly refused to accept defeat. He called Harold Antony, Ray Munster and all the other firms which had so far not resigned as his stockbrokers.

'Sorry, Guy, there are no more loose shares in the market,' they all excused themselves. 'We've been through the register a thousand times; there's not a breath of a chance ... Yes, we have tried the board, but no one will listen, not even with City Star out of the running ... No, we couldn't possibly do that; all the share certificates will have to be authenticated ... No, Guy, not even 50,000 ... Sorry, Guy, but no.'

Guy called Jolyon Priestley.

'Look, I'm not my own man,' Priestley excused himself. 'The shares are in Ernest Burke's hands ... No, they belong to me, not to them ... No, I can't sell them; I've appointed them to advise me and they say they need time to come to a considered opinion ... No, they won't release them on my say-so ... Sorry, Guy, but no.'

In desperation, Guy made his last throw of the dice. He called Harry Griffin in Monte Carlo.

'Sorry, Guy, Harry's in bed,' Sybil excused herself. 'He's practically on death's door with the 'flu ... He asked me to tell you he's still bound by his agreement with John Charteris – didn't he mention it? ... Sorry, Guy, but no.'

Not even the article in *Private Eye* telling the world – or those few of its inhabitants who read that notorious rag – how the vile Caliban had skinned Clive Salmon when he sold him Mallard, could brighten the weekend for Guy. He had forced the standard-bearer of the establishment, City Star, to retreat. But at the point of victory over its trumpet-major, Thruston Cutwell, he had faltered.

Sunday was worst of all. The *Sunday Telegraph* had the gall to allege that connections of Guy Magnus had been improperly buying his prey's shares for 330p at a time when that was City Star's rumoured offer price.

'Anyone with the slightest knowledge of me knows I only buy shares when there's a profit in them,' the target of their criticism complained to Harold Antony.

On Monday *The Times* picked up the story, suggesting that his offer might have to be increased to 330p following purchases at that price the previous Friday by parties acting in concert with Guy Magnus.

'Anyone with the slightest knowledge of my friends knows they would never dare to buy shares in a company I was bidding for,' he complained to Danny Gilbert.

That same morning John Charteris accompanied by Grover Seagull went to the Takeover Panel with the allegation that Guy had admitted to 'looking after' the Earl of St Edmunds.

'Anyone with the slightest knowledge of my character knows I look after all my friends,' Guy complained to Larry Callaghan. 'Is it a crime to lend a chap a car when his own is out of action?'

While he was digesting these trifles, the Department of Trade announced an inquiry into share-dealings in Universal Credit.

'Clive Salmon?' Guy was incredulous. 'I don't believe it. He's usually so careful. But I suppose anyone with the slightest knowledge of Clive ...'

By Tuesday morning the war of words had reached such a level that Guy could hardly wait for the battle to be over. He conceded that *The Times* was justified in commenting that the Britton Trust board had not come well out of the matter, for it was still failing to advise its shareholders to accept his offer. But its criticism of the share sales by the Earl of St Edmunds and Jolyon Priestley seemed to imply that no man was free to look after his own interests without the prior consent of the press. As for its insinuation that whether Guy Magnus had paid sufficient regard to the spirit of the Takeover Code might be another matter, since when, he asked, had the harlots of Fleet Street earned the right to be the arbiters of honourable conduct?

Despite the forces ranged against him, Guy refused to give up hope of victory. Determined to avoid any hint of defeatism, let alone bad manners, he asked his lawyers to advise him on the correct procedure for a company takeover. Did one simply march through the door and start calling the shots, or were there legal niceties to be observed? He did not wish to act improperly, he explained to their ill-concealed astonishment. It was best practice, they told him, not to ask for board representation until share control had been definitively established.

Unbeknown to Guy, at that very instant another legal nicety was engaging the attention of the Britton Trust board.

'I have received a letter from the Earl of St Edmunds,' John Charteris was reporting. 'He's asked for a copy of the minutes of the board meeting at which he claims to have given us notice of his intention to sell to Magnus. The minutes say he stated he would consider himself free to *talk* to Magnus if no bid came from City Star by the following morning. No mention of *selling*. Any objection to sending him the minutes?'

'They make the position abundantly clear,' Goodman agreed contentedly.

'I feel bound to say I've been shocked by the earl's action, not to mention Priestley's unseemly haste,' said Archie Laws in firm but measured tones.

Charteris had been waiting for Laws to show a sign of resolution. Priestley had left the board of his own accord; if the rest of them were unanimous, they could now get rid of the earl as well. *Carpe diem.*

'I propose the removal of the Earl of St Edmunds as a director of the company by the signing of a memorandum to that effect by all the other directors, as provided in the company's Articles of Association,' he said formally.

'Seconded,' Thomas Goodman supported him on cue.

'Can't happen too soon as far as I'm concerned,' Alan Palliser concurred.

Archie Laws wavered. 'I should hardly have thought it necessary to go to quite such lengths,' he objected.

'But you said you were shocked by his conduct,' Charteris reminded him.

Happy to condemn by word of mouth, which was subject to denial, Laws was wary about the permanence of marks made by the pen. 'I don't feel I should agree to condemning a man without a trial,' he said.

'Where do we go from here?' Charteris sighed to Grover Seagull, who was once more in attendance.

Seagull had been waiting impatiently for the board to come down to earth. He had spent long enough in its defence. It was time to lose with his reputation enhanced and to walk away with his bank's fees.

'To be perfectly frank,' he said, 'you've lost anyway. You have no other bidder and Magnus has acceptances for over forty-nine per cent. All he needs is for one more holding to fall. The only thing in your favour is that he must be feeling nervous. The question is, can we use that to squeeze a higher offer out of him?'

'If we're dead in the water, how on earth can we?' asked Charteris.

'If the decision were entirely in his hands, I doubt whether we could,' replied Seagull. 'His weak spot is Ulster & Cayman. They're putting the money up, so he has to listen to them. They know he's played dirty and they must be worried about their reputation. Last Wednesday they asked if you'd take 5p more to stop crying foul. We said we thought your number would be more like 20p, and nothing came of it. How d'you feel about us seeing if they still want to deal?'

'Not brilliant,' Charteris admitted. 'I hate giving up.'

'Come on, John,' Goodman tried to comfort him. 'We've done our duty by the shareholders. Let's go the extra mile and walk out with our heads held high.' He looked round his colleagues. Their expressions told him they felt like Charteris but thought like him.

'I couldn't do it. It'd make me sick,' Charteris made the further admission.

'Let me talk to them for you,' offered Goodman.

'Would you?' Charteris accepted the offer before it could be withdrawn.

'Unless someone else would rather do it.' But Goodman had no need to fear of a queue of volunteers. He was suddenly as popular as the private soldier whose favourite fatigue was sluicing the urinals.

'Not a penny less than 315p, though. Promise?' asked Charteris.

'I'll see what I can do.'

'I'll fix a meeting with Charles Cassels,' said Seagull before anyone could change his mind. He could talk business with Charles. He left the boardroom and found a telephone. Cassels heard him through in silence before he spoke.

'I'm not sure I'm your man, Grover,' he said thoughtfully when he had digested the proposal. 'We've been handling the bid, but the deal with Magnus was done by Sam Dervish's office. They're the ones to talk to Magnus. If this chap Goodman is such a hard nut, why don't we put him in a room with Sidney de Deyler? If anyone can sort him out, he will.'

'Good idea,' Seagull acknowledged gratefully. Each had reached the point where the battle had been fought to a standstill but their invoices had yet to be submitted. Where winner pays all, a nil-nil draw is not the best result from which to send in your bill for transfer fees.

An hour later Goodman was sitting diagonally opposite the place Guy Magnus had sat six weeks earlier. He stared out of the window and waited for Sidney de Deyler to begin. The latter had hoped to be spared that dubious privilege, but as host he had no alternative.

'I understand your board would like to negotiate a settlement,' he began. 'I'm not sure on what basis. We reckon we'll be home and dry by tonight.'

'In that case there's nothing for us to talk about,' Goodman replied brusquely. 'My brief is that you offered 305p last Wednesday. You'd hardly have done so if you didn't think you needed to. We turned you down, which we'd hardly have done if we thought we'd lost.'

'The situation's changed. Now we're on the point of winning,' de Deyler argued. 'Even so, we'd rather settle things amicably if we can. Life's too short ... can we find a way to do business?'

'That depends on how realistic you're prepared to be. We know Magnus's friends have paid up to 330p. We'll shout our heads off for a Panel enquiry, and when we've proved it you'll have to pay the same price to everyone.'

'Not when, if. Magnus denies all knowledge. He says he can't help it if his fans buy whatever he touches as if he were Midas.'

'You think they'd pay more than he bid without a side deal?' Goodman was derisory. 'Do me a favour!'

'We put that to him. He freely admits to telling everyone how much profit he's going to make on the deal. He says his followers must have bet on a City Star bid, and reckoned he'd be prepared to go higher. Prove him a liar.'

'In the end the evidence is circumstantial and the Panel will make up its own mind whose word to believe. In the meantime, the kerfuffle won't do your bank's reputation any good.'

De Deyler's expression showed that the point had gone home. 'We could argue all day,' he said, 'but it boils down to whether we can agree a price. I'm willing to try at 310p, but I can't force Magnus to accept.'

'You mean you have no authority to settle? Then what am I doing here?' asked Goodman, feigning anger at his time having been wasted.

'I believe I could persuade him to accept that figure.'

'There's strong evidence that his friends have paid over 320p, probably 325p. The other shareholders are entitled to the same.'

De Deyler shook his head. They fenced for twenty minutes. Each knew a deal would have to be struck eventually, but he must not be too eager to make the proposal lest the other force a penny or two more out of him. When they finally shook hands each was convinced he had squeezed the best bargain available, but knew he would have had to settle for less if faced with a brick wall.

'It's less than my colleagues believe the shareholders are entitled to, but I'm willing to recommend it if you'll do the same,' Goodman conceded reluctantly.

'You pushed me further than we were prepared to go; but if we're putting up the money and that's what it's going to cost us to bury the whole thing, then it's got to be done,' agreed de Deyler.

32

'Three fifteen! You must be out of your fucking minds!' Guy exploded when Charles Cassels gave him the news.

He had spent the morning in a state of growing euphoria. The more he analysed his position, the more certain he was that not even the accusations in *The Times* could prevent his victory. Who else but he was capable of masterminding a campaign in which a £100 company took over one worth £30 million for £20 million, all borrowed? Now it no longer mattered if Harry Griffin still refused to play ball. Harry had played a tight game, hoping for a private deal. He would have done one with anyone else, for the extra cost of the shares bought by Yankee Tate, Pat Crisp and the exceedingly generous Johnny Price, and the watch and piano Rhoda Antony so richly deserved, were petty cash against the profit on the shares he had bought before the battle got under way. But Harry was a special case. Nobody hotted Guy Magnus. Three hundred pence had been his price all along. In the end he would have had Harry's shares for exactly that. He'd seen off the combined forces of the defending board, its merchant bank and an opponent willing to bid 30p more. Now he needed the owners of but a few thousand shares to accept his offer, and there was no other bid on the table. If he could see that, so could Jolyon Priestley. It would only have been a matter of time before the snake kicked in the balance of his shares rather than give up £500,000. But now, behind his back, Ulster & Cayman had given away a juicy slice of the fruit he had fought so hard for.

'You're completely out of your skulls!' he repeated. 'An extra 15p! You've thrown a million of my money down the drain.'

'Our money, Guy, not yours,' Cassels corrected him.

'Checkmate next move, and Sidney chooses this moment to knock over his bloody king and resign. He's taken £1 million profit off the deal. That was my million to give away, not his!' Guy all but screamed.

'It was the best Sidney could do, Guy. You must take it or leave it. You want them to keep running to the Panel every day until they get you? They'll turn over every last one of your pals' deals until they can prove a concert party, and then you'll be made to pay the highest price they find. That'll cost you at least £2 million more, not one. Don't expect us to be around to lend it to you.'

Guy fell silent, but only for a moment. 'If you want to put in the extra million, that's down to you, Charles,' he said; 'but don't expect us to give you any more of the profit.'

'Let's get things straight, Guy, shall we?' Cassels said firmly. 'The bank's already gone as far as it prudently can. We have a legally binding commitment to lend you £16.5 million, but that's as far as it goes.'

'You have a morally binding commitment to lend us eighty per cent of the purchase price,' Guy argued. 'If Sidney goes off and negotiates a higher price, you ought at least to lend us eighty per cent of the difference.'

Cassels knew he had to succumb, if for no other reason than that Guy Magnus had no more chance of producing another £1 million than Sidney de Deyler had of persuading the Britton Trust board to accept 300p per share. Time had marched on and had taken its hostages.

'We'll increase your facility by £750,000,' he said abruptly. Seeing that Guy was about to protest, he repeated the figure and wrote it on his memo pad. The protest never left Guy's lips.

'We've fixed a meeting for half past three at their place, to get their answer,' Cassels told him. 'You're invited.'

'Before we take a formal decision on your offer, we think you may wish to read the press statement the board intends to issue at the end of this meeting,' John Charteris addressed Guy Magnus coldly. In the absence of Thomas Goodman, his colleagues had not been idle. On the assumption that his negotiations with Ulster & Cayman would seal their company's fate – for they would either obtain a higher price or lose anyway – they had drafted a statement to their shareholders recommending acceptance of the Magnus offer. In the light of recent press comment, they wished to issue a justification of the manner in which they had conducted the company's affairs. Each director had put in his rancorous pennyworth. As a result the draft had grown like Topsy, so that by half past three the statement read like prosecuting counsel's opening speech in the trial of Guy Magnus, the Earl of St Edmunds and Jolyon Priestley for conspiracy to misrepresent, defraud and enrich themselves at the expense of the Britton Trust shareholders.

Guy read the draft with growing annoyance. 'This is a most extraordinary document,' he said angrily when he had reached the end. 'It's nothing but lies, half-truths and misrepresentations. I shouldn't be surprised if some of them are libellous.'

Cassels had been reading over his shoulder. 'Contested takeovers often wind up in the odd feather being ruffled,' he tried to calm Guy down.

Guy refused to be conciliated. 'If you dare to send it out, I won't answer for my actions,' he snapped at Charteris.

Charteris had already been counting the cost of his recent forays into the stock market for Britton Trust shares. He had been forced to pay more for some of them than the 315p he would receive from Magnus if the board went quietly. He did not fancy spending even more money on legal bills. He nodded resignedly as Grover Seagull whispered urgently into his ear.

'The board reserves its rights,' Seagull said out loud; 'but you have our assurance that provided we reach agreement on your offer, the statement in this form will not see the light of day.'

'On behalf of our client,' Cassels came in on cue before Guy had time to intervene, 'we offer 315p for each share in Britton Trust that we or our clients do not currently own, on condition that its board commits itself to recommend the shareholders to accept.'

Seagull turned to Charteris. 'Is your company's board in favour of such a recommendation?' he asked formally.

Charteris's slumped shoulders gave his answer. Those of the remaining directors came equally reluctantly, but with a sense of inevitability. They had lost control of Britton Trust. The takeover battle was over.

As if in sympathy, a few hours later and three and a half thousand miles to the west, a president finally agreed to surrender his tapes.

PART THREE

The Settlement

Gaius, nevertheless, wrote an extravagant dispatch to Rome as if the whole island had surrendered to him, and ordered the couriers ... (to) make straight for the Forum and the Senate House, and take his letter to the Temple of Mars the Avenger for personal delivery to the Consuls ... He now concentrated his attention on his forthcoming triumph ... to distract attention from his inglorious exploits, he openly and vengefully threatened the Senate who, he said, had cheated him of a well-earned triumph – though in point of fact he had expressly stated, a few days before, that they must do nothing to honour him, on pain of death ... So, when the distinguished senatorial delegates met him with an official plea for his immediate return, he shouted: 'I am coming, and this' – tapping the hilt of his sword – 'is coming too!' ... Within four months he was dead.

Suetonius, *The Twelve Caesars* (Gaius Caligula),
translated by Robert Graves.

33

He who dares, wins; he who wins is entitled to the spoils. The day after his victory, Guy Magnus went to Britton Trust's head office to claim his. His frame of mind, euphoria at his triumph countered by despair at the attempts of others to destroy its fruits, was not helped by his experience when he arrived there.

He announced to the receptionist that the new owner of the company had arrived and requested that the board prepare to receive him. Unfortunately for him, John Charteris knew the rules; or at any rate he was in the same room as Thomas Goodman, who certainly did. While the Britton Trust board had recommended his bid to its shareholders, Magical Investments did not have title to over fifty per cent of its shares. It would not own them until Ulster & Cayman paid for the acceptances in four weeks' time. On Charteris's instructions, Guy was shown the door. In fairness, he could only have known the rules had he been listening when Ulster & Cayman's lawyers briefed him on the point; but he found legal niceties boring and other matters had been on his mind. Red-faced, he departed.

During the day a sufficient number of acceptance forms arrived at Ulster & Cayman's offices for Charteris to persuade Goodman that enough was enough. It was conceded that Guy could nominate two directors to act on his behalf pending final settlement. The following day he deputed Brian Proctor and Nigel Holmes to full-time duty as directors of Britton Trust, with a mission to report on the books.

Meanwhile Guy busied himself tidying up the loose ends of the ownership of the shares they had bought. Ludgate Investments and St Paul's Property had each borrowed £2 million from Ulster & Cayman and loaned the money on to Westchurch so it could buy shares on behalf of Magical Investments. Magical must buy these shares from Westchurch. Having borrowed £17,250,000 from Ulster & Cayman towards the £22,500,000 the acquisition was now going to cost Westchurch, his £100 company was

£5,249,900 short. What could be simpler than for Magical to borrow from Ludgate and St Paul's to pay Westchurch for the shares?

There was one snag. Ludgate had net assets of £7 million. If it loaned Magical Investments more than £1 million, it would breach the rule that an authorised investment trust may not invest more than fifteen per cent of its funds in a single holding. So the loan must be made by a subsidiary, Ludgate Guarantee, which was not an authorised investment trust. However, it could only do so if its parent provided the money. This would offend against the same rule. Whichever way one turned an obstacle presented itself.

Other than to Guy. Typically, he found a tidy solution. If parent and subsidiary operated a pooled bank account, so that as one drew down on it the other replenished it, the overall balance would be nil. That way no loan account would be created. Such was Guy's view, and such was learned counsel's opinion when he sought it. Moreover, his reliable friend and lawyer Dominic Arthur, who sat on Ludgate's board and read this opinion, had no difficulty in confirming that it accorded with Guy's. Guy had grown to rely on Arthur's judgment in deciding when differences of principle might need to be resolved by compromise, or conflicts of interest by self-delusion. To be fair to Arthur, he sought no reward for his services. This laudable attitude had an unfortunate consequence, in that the Board of Trade Inspectors later expressed the uncharitable opinion that he may have been motivated by a wish to be regarded as a man of importance in the City, and had consequently failed to exercise his undoubted ability and judgment on the shareholders' behalf until too late: an opinion that may have owed more to hindsight than to sympathetic appraisal.

Faced with such unanimity, Larry Callaghan accepted that he was present when the board resolved to approve a loan of £2,750,000 by Ludgate Guarantee to Magical Investments. It would have been pointless to ask Magical's directors for security for the loan, for everyone knew that Britton Trust's assets had already been pledged to Ulster & Cayman.

Rhoda Antony was too busy to concern herself with these goings-on. She was engaged in finding a way for the delivery men to get a pristine Steinway piano into her drawing-room without dismantling it or demolishing a doorway. As the "six foot one" stood in her hall, Rhoda played a few notes on its keyboard. The mechanism was so responsive it frightened her. She looked regretfully through the drawing-room door at her beloved Broadwood. She was used to its mechanism and its tone. But there was no room for both. She checked the time on her new Cartier watch: half past two. Harold would still be at lunch; she must take the decision without him. He would want the Steinway in the drawing room, where it would look superb. It must go through the garden gate and in by the French windows. But the Broadwood would not go up the staircase. Rhoda looked through another door. Suddenly the solution became obvious. It would fit nicely in Harold's study, in place of his desk and chair. The delivery men agreed. The Broadwood was soon in place, the stool was set down before the keyboard, and up two flights of stairs and into the attic went the desk and chair. Harold would be pleased. The delivery men drank to that, as each pocketed his £5 tip. After they left, Rhoda sat at the Broadwood piano. As she played her way happily through a series of Czerny studies, she mused about curtains for her new music room.

Five miles to the south the *Sunday Telegraph*'s City editor was drafting an apology for the next edition. *Last week I wrote that Mr Guy Magnus had bought a final block of shares at 330p against his offer price of 300p.* Yes, that was factual enough. Magnus had done exactly that. The next bit was more tricky. He must be equally factual. *Mr Magnus assures me they did not.* That was true too. Now for the hard part. *It would be discourteous, and possibly expensive, to doubt his word. I would not dream of doing so.* It was painful to write so grovelling a withdrawal, but impossible to deny its gracious terms. Finally, as a newsman, it was his duty to bring his readers up-to-date, while avoiding putting himself in last week's invidious position. *The Takeover Panel has been in hot pursuit of the scent, even (oh, the shame of it) sniffing around Grieff & Hammer. They have come across a deal involving forty-two thousand five hundred shares at this price, but if as one would expect this proves to be a purely speculative purchase, there can be no possible criticism.* His duty done, the City editor stubbed his cigarette and filed his copy.

The Takeover Panel was indeed in pursuit, though the *Sunday Telegraph* had exaggerated its temperature. It was unhappy about Charteris's accusation that Guy Magnus had "looked after" a peer of the realm, and wished to be reassured that this arose from mere pique. It had questions about the highest price Guy and his associates had paid for Britton Trust's shares, and it needed to satisfy itself that the newspapers were merely gossip-mongering. Finally, it wanted to establish how Jolyon Priestley's 200,000 shares had come into

Magnus's hands. It gave notice of its intention to undertake a review of the takeover in three weeks' time.

Guy had no need to worry about his evidence to that august body. What was a merchant bank paid for, if not to do the worrying on his behalf?

On 1st November, Ulster & Cayman posted the revised offer document to Britton Trust's shareholders. The die cast, Charles Cassels reviewed the bank's position. He found that the facility of £17,250,000 had not been approved by its board. That, they agreed, was Sam Dervish's fault, for it was his duty to put on its agenda a loan he had negotiated. He had assured them it would unravel itself quickly and everything would be sold off, leaving only the profit. Cassels instructed his staff to double-check that the bank's funds were intact. Concerned that its reputation also remain undamaged, he instructed its lawyer to advise how they could best achieve this objective when they and their client were called to account before the Takeover Panel.

The lawyer proposed that they play a "pretend" game: Charles Cassels and he would pretend to be the Panel, and Guy would pretend to be … well, Guy Magnus. That way, when the real game was played the Takeover Panel would find out the real truth, or at any rate as close to it as might reasonably be expected.

A cordial Charles Cassels started the session. 'They'll start by asking how you came to bid for Britton Trust. They'll want to know when you first met the Earl of St Edmunds,' he told Guy helpfully.

Ulster & Cayman's lawyer reverted to the rules. 'When did you first meet the Earl of St Edmunds, Mr Magnus?' he asked, without waiting for the referee's whistle to start the game.

Guy thought carefully. It was the job of the Takeover Panel to ascertain whether any share deal had been carried out contrary to the rules, not to spy into his social life. If his friends had bought shares in Britton Trust without his knowledge – and they would, he was sure, swear this to be the case – he was in the clear. But if he were to be questioned as to when a friendship had started, did not that strike at the heart of an Englishman's right to privacy?

'What do you need to know that for?' he asserted his rights.

'You're going to be asked,' Cassels explained.

'When *did* you first meet the Earl of St Edmunds?' the lawyer repeated more firmly. 'Was it before or after the first offer to the shareholders on the 9th of October?'

'Shortly before. Around the end of September, I think,' Guy tried. That was when he had first met the Britton Trust board. It ought to do. Though if he remembered rightly, the earl had not been present that day. Would this make a difference? He must keep his options open.

'On what date exactly?'

'About the time I met the rest of the board.'

'You must keep a diary.'

Guy consulted it. 'I met them on 27th September,' he said.

'Was the earl present?'

'I don't think so.' Guy screwed up his eyes with the effort of trying to remember.

'Then did you meet him before or after that date?'

'Before?' Guy looked to Cassels for help. Receiving none, he repeated the question as a statement. 'Before. A few days before.'

'How many days before? Isn't that in your diary?'

Guy played for time. 'This is my business diary. My social diary's at home.'

'So you first met the earl socially?' The lawyer's interest was growing.

'Harold Antony introduced us. Harold bought shares for me from time to time. He'd been a director of Britton Trust, and he thought I might like to meet the earl.'

'This was shortly before you met the Britton Trust board?'

'A day or two before, yes.'

'Rather a coincidence, isn't it?'

'I suppose it is, rather,' Guy agreed amiably.

'You had accumulated a substantial shareholding in Britton Trust by then, some of it through Mr Antony. You had already written to the Earl of St Edmunds telling him of your intention to make an offer. I take it you talked to him about it when you met.'

'No, we didn't discuss the bid.' Guy decided to sound the lawyer out. 'It wouldn't have been proper, would it?' he enquired.

The latter made no direct response. 'What did you and the earl talk about?' he asked.

Guy thought quickly. 'We spoke in generalities. I thought I'd sound him out about the company, in case he had any information that might be useful,' he replied, springing a trap.

'And had he?'

'Yes,' replied Guy. 'It was clear he took his duty to his shareholders very seriously. I found that an extremely useful piece of information.'

The lawyer looked up the ceiling. His moment had passed, and with it the initiative.

Cassels used the hiatus to take up the questioning. 'When was the next time you met the earl?' he asked.

'The Saturday morning he sold me his shares,' Guy said firmly.

'Who asked for the meeting?''

'He did. He asked me to come round to his place. He lives not far from me, so naturally I went.'

'And you discussed …?'

'A price for the shares.'

'His shares?'

'A price he could recommend to his board and the shareholders. As I said, he took his duty to them seriously. He was extremely tough. He squeezed another 5p out of me. It was a hard bargain.' Guy looked Cassels in the eye, making clear by implication that it had been harder than the one in which Ulster & Cayman had surrendered three times as much.

An embarrassed Cassels looked at the lawyer. The latter, having recharged his batteries, took up the questioning again. 'Mr Charteris has reported that you said you had – how did he express it? – "looked after" his chairman. How might he have gained that impression?'

'I can't imagine,' replied Guy. 'Mr Charteris will have to speak for himself.'

The lawyer looked down at the notes he had been taking. 'Mr Magnus,' he said, 'may I suggest that you look at these dates again before you appear in front of the Panel? They may be confused about the sequence of events. They may want to ask you why, at a meeting you say took place several days after you had written to the earl telling him you intended to make an offer, you also say you did not disclose your intention to do so.'

Guy saw the Panel's problem, but it was not his. 'Why bother to disclose something the other chap already knows?' he asked, in a tone which made plain his disdain for anyone who asked so naive a question. 'On a social occasion?' he added. Did one have to explain that a gentleman didn't go to a peer's home for a drink and then spend the evening talking business?

The lawyer considered pursuing the question as to why, on a purely social occasion, Guy had sounded out the earl for information about his company and discovered that he had a high sense of duty towards his shareholders. Instead, he nodded at Cassels to show he was satisfied with his client's performance. Even so, he suggested that a second rehearsal take place before the hearing, in case Guy recalled anything else which would add to the Panel's reassurance.

Guy promised the lawyer he would see what he and his friends could do to help. A deferral of the hearing would be appreciated while he fixed a small matter he had put off for some time. It had become so painful he could hardly sit down. He called his doctor and told him he wanted the procedure carried out next week. He stood to take the pressure off his discomfort. God, how it hurt!

34

Guy lay on his back. Sitting up was still agony. The nurse came in regularly to reset his pillows and prop his head so he could see his visitors without his neck getting stiff. Even so, he had to crane it to look at whoever was sitting in the seat to his left. At present its occupant was Harold Antony. Jolyon Priestley perched on the edge of a straight-backed chair in front of the window to his right. The London Clinic did not consider the comfort of its patients' visitors. The Earl of St Edmunds slumped into the armchair at the far end of the room.

'Dashed awkward business,' complained the last, though not about the source of the patient's pain. If pain there was, it was his. He had been suffering from it ever since receiving Palliser's note that morning suggesting that as the Britton Trust board had never approved the Cabo do Bimbo project and it was now unlikely to proceed, it would be a good idea if the former chairman were to repay the expenses he had drawn in pursuit of the deal.

'We'll have to put our heads together and agree on a date. Then we must stick to it,' Antony told him.

'Not before the 26th of September,' Guy insisted. 'That way I can prove Charteris made it all up. "Looked after *you*?" As if you haven't managed to look after yourself extremely well without my help,' he flattered the earl.

'What it's all about, ain't it?' the earl asked the corner of the ceiling.

'I can't say I met you with the board, as you were never there.'

'What about the Saturday morning when we settled the price?' suggested Priestley. 'They know about that. What date was it?' He consulted a pocket diary. 'October 13th.'

'They're not going to believe that was the first time,' Guy demurred.

'They've no evidence for anything sooner,' put in Antony.

'I'm going to say it was the evening I came round to your place, Berry; the day I met the board,' Guy said decisively.

'What reason? For coming to me?' asked the earl out of marginal interest. He knew the real answer: one visited an earl because he was an earl.

'A courtesy visit. I'd met the rest of the board, you couldn't be present, it was the least I could do.'

'Who suggested the meeting?' Priestley took on the role of interrogator.

'You did, Harold,' Guy ruled. 'You knew us both; you'd been on the Britton Trust board; you thought it would be a good idea.'

The answer was too near the bone for Antony's liking.

'Please, Guy … I'd much rather say I don't know when you first met each other,' he pleaded, growing more nervous by the minute.

'Won't wash,' objected the earl.

'You'll have to,' Guy insisted. 'They won't believe one of us just gave the other a call and invited him to drop round for a drink. Not during a contested bid.'

'I'll have to think about how to say it,' Antony offered miserably, getting up to leave.

'You could try using words,' Guy suggested sarcastically. He was in pain, and he didn't care how much of it rubbed off on to his visitors.

When Antony had gone the earl coughed twice and raised the matter that had been troubling him far more than one on which the word of a peer should suffice. 'Expenses. This affair of ours in the Algarve,' he began.

Guy noted the use of the plural and prayed he was not being asked to intercede in a matter involving a noble heart. Priestley intervened to tell him of the Cabo do Bimbo project. It was plain that its attractions fell some way short of the glories of Gleneagles. Priestley concluded by reading Palliser's letter to the earl.

As he had no plans to add to Britton Trust's existing portfolio of assets, Guy reckoned the practical approach adopted by Palliser had much to commend it.

'Sounds like a marvellous enterprise,' he said. 'Not quite our style, Berry, but you'll probably make a fortune out of it. Why don't you do as Palliser suggests, and then it will be yours?'

The Earl of St Edmunds maintained a dignified but ominous silence.

'Any particular hurry for the money, Guy?' asked Priestley.

'How much is involved?' Guy asked.

'About £15,000.'

'Oh well, I think we could defer repayment for the time being,' Guy replied carefully. After all, the earl still had to give evidence before the Takeover

Panel. 'You weren't serious about staying on the board, were you, Berry? Could be awkward if we had to make a formal minute.'

The Earl of St Edmunds relaxed. It paid to be charitable. He reckoned his visit to minister to the sick had gone pretty well.

'Serve the bugger right!' Guy exclaimed a few mornings later.

The nurse eyed her patient coldly. In his condition it was an unfortunate turn of phrase.

'Still no movement? she asked.

Guy shook his head.

'Serve the bugger right!' Guy repeated when his next visitor had seated himself in preparation for his conference. 'See what *The Times* says about Traill Blazer: "… *still not easy to decide what kind of animal one might be buying into*". I'll say! Jon hasn't decided yet whether he's an industrialist, a fund manager or a banker. As long as nobody tells him about property …'

'I promise not to,' said Pat Crisp, smiling. Guy had a thing about Jon Traill: he was envious less of the great man's success than of the publicity surrounding it. Not that Guy wanted publicity for its own sake; but Traill was a master at using his reputation for his own ends. He could persuade the world that the stock market was a buy at the very moment he was ready to unload. Knowing how he operated had its uses, particularly if you were also long of the market and fancied raising some cash.

'That commission payment we sent your father in Jersey,' Guy turned to the business of the day. 'It was his introduction of the buyer that resulted in the sale of our Dominion shares, wasn't it?'

Crisp screwed up his eyes as he attempted to recall the transaction. One executed so many.

'Of course it was,' he said after a few seconds. 'Definitely.'

'Good,' said Guy. 'I just wanted to be sure. You know, I've been thinking about setting up an offshore trust for my holding in Magical Investments. Your father wouldn't happen to know the right people in Jersey, would he?'

'I'm sure he'd be delighted to make the introduction. Hello, Johnny,' Crisp greeted the next of Guy's steady flow of visitors as he came through the door. 'Seen about Traill Blazer? You have? Don't tell me you're short of them too. I don't know anyone who's got any left, apart from Guy,' he grinned, winking at his host.

Johnny Price waited for Crisp to depart before raising the matter that was on his mind. 'The Takeover Panel's asked me to attend the hearing,' he told Guy when they were alone. 'They're bound to ask me about the Britton shares I bought.'

'You never!' Guy feigned ignorance.

'Come off it, Guy.'

'Suppose you did. You bought some shares and you sold them. So what? You've done it before. You must have bought them because you thought they'd go up.'

'I bought for you. At 326!' It was hard to discern from Price's distress whether he was concerned more about his forthcoming interrogation or about his reputation if word of his loss went round the market.

'When City Star came in, you thought I'd have to bid more.'

'But I sold the holding to you before you had control.'

'When they withdrew, you wanted to cut your losses. I was the only buyer,' Guy explained, as if teaching a simpleton his ABC.

'You're asking me to tell lies, Guy.' Price spread his arms as if to proclaim to the world the impossibility of such an act.

'No, I'm not. You just don't have to tell them the full facts.'

'They won't believe me. They'll ask me if I know you.'

'If they ask me, I'll tell them I may have met you once or twice, I don't really know how often, but purely on a business footing.'

'What if they find out how many times I've been round at your office?' protested Price, on the verge of hysteria.

'Don't worry, Johnny, I can deal with that.'

'Harry'll tell them I did a lot of business with you when I was at Tanquerys.'

'They're not interested in Harry: he's just a former director who happens to own some shares. Neither am I: he hasn't even sent in his acceptance yet. Anyway, he's abroad.'

'They'll ask Harold Antony.'

'Brokers deal through each other. While we're on the subject, my lawyer's asking if there's any link between a contract for seven and a half thousand shares that Harold cancelled and one the next day involving a Swiss bank. What shall I tell him, Johnny? You can't throw any light on it, can you? … I thought not.'

Johnny Price asked himself how he had ever got into this mess. However, Guy Magnus's problem was more serious than his. If Guy reckoned he could keep the Takeover Panel happy, there was no point in being miserable himself.

'Come on, Mr Magnus, eat up your All-Bran. I've put some nice ripe prunes in it,' cajoled the nurse the following morning. 'You really must try harder or we'll never get you out of here.'

Guy tried, but not hard. His twin motivations, the avoidance of pain to his person and the deferral of his ordeal before the Takeover Panel, ensured that. He was soon back in bed waiting for his chauffeur to bring the day's mail. It was not difficult to run a business from a sickbed. Indeed, indisposition had its advantages. Yesterday Ludgate Investments had held its annual general meeting. In his absence no shareholder had queried Larry Callaghan when he announced that the company was making a rights issue, nor raised any question as to its purpose. No one had made the connection with the intended loan to Magical Investments: for Callaghan had said nothing about that either. In fairness to him, Dominic Arthur had accepted that there was no legal reason why he should.

The only blot on an otherwise clear landscape was the approach by a property investor who wished to acquire a quoted property company. Danny Gilbert felt that a sale of St Paul's Property would provide a timely opportunity to take some money off the table. But Guy knew that unless he planned with care, its buyer would wind up with twenty per cent of Britton Trust. Worse, if Ludgate Investments was to replace St Paul's as both lender to and shareholder in Magical Investments, its stake would go up to forty per cent. But he owned even fewer shares in Ludgate than in St Paul's. If he were to keep as much as possible of Britton Trust's profits in his own hands, he must increase his holding in Ludgate. That had been the purpose of the rights issue. But the manoeuvre required delicate handling, for it would only work if the issue were a failure.

Guy was deep in thought about how to achieve this result when Yankee Tate entered the room. He was not alone. Over his shoulder the usually affable face of Ray Munster betrayed its disappointment at not finding a magnum of champagne on ice.

'Excuse me, Sir, but I thought I'd bring my … er, um … with me,' Yankee informed him, indicating Munster superfluously.

'Stockbroker,' Munster pointed out with equal superfluity.

'I know, I know,' Guy told them both impatiently. 'Sit down, Ray. The market seems to be holding up well.' The *FT* Share Index had been steady for most of the trading account and would close at around 430. 'No, not you, Yankee.'

'Those shares, sir ...' Yankee began, standing to attention at the end of the bed. As he had forgotten all Guy had taught him other than that with one signature every vestige of a debt could be expunged, he was unable to go further.

'We've both been called to give evidence,' Munster did the job for him.

'You thought your boss was a clever chap, so you'd buy some shares in the company he was bidding for and make yourself some money. So you went to Mr Munster and asked him to buy some for you.' Guy sighed. There was no end to the line of people incapable of thinking for themselves.

'He did buy rather a lot,' Munster pointed out.

'He didn't ask to,' replied Guy testily.

Munster took the criticism manfully. 'You mean, he just told me to buy, but not how many?' he asked.

'Got it!' Guy was thrilled at the speed with which Munster caught on.

'So when I proposed that he give me discretion to buy within limits and he agreed ...' Munster continued to perform up to expectations.

'... Not knowing what that meant ...'

'... I'm afraid I went a bit over the top.'

'You'd agree to that, wouldn't you, Yankee?' Guy asked.

'I wouldn't have wanted Mr Munster to buy *without* discretion, sir. Or without limits. I'm not that stupid.'

'Of course you aren't, Yankee.' The Panel would be clear on that. 'I take it you could use that discretion to find Mr Tate a deal to make up for his unfortunate losses?' Guy asked Munster. 'Bearing in mind that your commission on a deal of £130,000 is scarcely peanuts,' he added.

Munster acknowledged that such a task should be well within his capability.

'In that case what are we waiting for?' asked Guy, picking up the telephone to order a bottle of Dom Pérignon. 'You play butler,' he told Yankee when it arrived.

'I'm glad to see you're feeling more comfortable now, sir,' said Yankee, as he twisted the wire off the bouchon.

35

While the world outside ignored the stricken patient in the corner room of the London Clinic, the object of its ignorance watched helplessly as the turbulent goings-on in the nation gathered pace. The miners banned overtime, the power engineers began an industrial dispute, the government warned of electricity cuts and reduced power in its own departments. Guy told the nurse that if it reduced power any further it would go into suspended animation, and the nurse replied that if he didn't get on with it the same would soon apply to his internal functions. As their private battle intensified the oil companies rationed petrol supplies to garages, the government urged everyone to drive more slowly and not at all on Sundays, Bank of England base rate rose to an all-time high of thirteen per cent and share prices plummeted. In such circumstances Guy was not surprised that everything came to a halt while the nation celebrated. It was, after all, the perfect time for a Royal wedding. Why, he wondered, had they not made it a three-day event?

Guy almost suffered a relapse when he saw Universal Credit's half-year results. Clive Salmon had pulled off the trick yet again. He had reported profits up over forty per cent and had rewarded shareholders with yet another dividend increase. The fall in financial stocks was a blip. Guy's own reputation as a wizard of timing was in danger of being surpassed.

He was not alone in his bemusement at Universal Credit's results. Neville Macrae had accepted its shares and loan stock offer in return for his holding in Mallard. Early in November his secretary asked him what on earth he was doing holding on to them when there was an investigation into the company's affairs. Ashamed that he had known nothing about this, Macrae sold his entire holding.

The production of a medical certificate and the consequent postponement of the Takeover Panel hearing brought about a rapid improvement in Guy's condition. He was able to leave the London Clinic in time to orchestrate the failure of the Ludgate rights issue. As the company's shares were trading at

50p, shareholders were invited to subscribe for one new share for each one they held at exactly that price. He did not have far to look for a volunteer to take up the shares left on the table.

'Why give away £50,000 underwriting commission when it's exactly the kind of deal that will suit Westchurch?' he asked his colleagues.

Meantime Guy's corporate lawyers were reviewing the circular setting out the terms of the issue. Dominic Arthur, who in addition to his duties as a director of Ludgate was an equity partner in the law firm dealing with it, made a call to Nigel Holmes.

'The draft circular says the purposes of the rights issue are to reduce the overdraft and to continue the present investment policy,' he told him. 'So that won't be questioned, one of my partners thinks you should check that Ludgate has the resources to make the loan to Magical without using the funds from the issue.'

'Guy says not to worry,' Holmes told him after checking with his boss.

Arthur soon called again. 'I know the document mentions the company's loan to Magical, but it doesn't highlight the fact that two of Ludgate's directors are also shareholders of Magical,' he pointed out.

'Guy says not to worry,' Holmes told him again.

Arthur stopped worrying.

The only cloud on the horizon was the notice from the Takeover Panel that the postponed hearing would be held on Monday, 3rd December. The Panel gave notice that it would be inviting Guy to explain the circumstances surrounding the purchases of shares from the Earl of St Edmunds and Ernest Burke, and those made at above the offer price by Messrs Price and Tate. Charles Cassels called to propose a second "pretend" meeting three days before the hearing.

'Why so soon?' asked an apprehensive Guy.

'In case we need to hold a third one,' Cassels told him.

The meeting coincided with the dispatch of settlement cheques to Britton Trust's accepting shareholders. But if Guy expected Cassels to break open the champagne, he was doomed to disappointment. The previous day a director of Universal Credit had resigned without explanation. This morning that company's shares were in free fall. When a finance house to which you have loaned a lot of money is in trouble, you are not of a mind to celebrate with a man to whom you have also loaned a lot of money and who may also be in trouble. So with no more than a cursory nod of greeting to Guy, Cassels took his seat at the head of the table and gestured to Ulster & Cayman's lawyer to begin.

'How well do you know Price?' the lawyer began without ceremony.

'What price?' Guy asked back.

'*John* Price,' the lawyer elaborated impatiently.

'John Price?' Guy thought hard. 'Oh, you mean *Johnny* Price? Isn't he one of Tanquery's clients?'

'That's the one.'

'Hardly know him.'

'Come on, Mr Magnus, you can do better than that,' persisted the lawyer.

'I may have met him once during a bid.'

'Have you met him during the past three months?'

'If he's the person you mean, he may have rung me a couple of times.'

'Come clean, Guy,' Cassels pressed. 'Haven't you seen him more recently?'

Guy hesitated. 'He may have visited me at the Clinic,' he admitted finally.

'On his own?' asked the lawyer.

Guy thought fast. The Panel would have established the link with Tanquery. 'It may have been when Harold Antony was there,' he said.

The lawyer changed his line of questioning without warning. 'What can you tell us of Mr Munster's role in all this?' he asked ominously.

'He's a stockbroker. He buys and sells shares for clients,' said Guy evasively. He knew he was on sensitive ground.

'*Was* a stockbroker,' corrected the lawyer. Grieff & Hammer had recently been suspended from trading on the London Stock Exchange. 'During the bid for Britton Trust, were you a client of Mr Munster, Mr Magnus?'

'On the contrary. He asked if he could act for me, but I told him he couldn't as I'd already appointed a broker. I said I couldn't influence what he did, but if he found any sellers I'd be a willing buyer through my own people.'

'We understand your driver Mr Ian Tate was his client. Can you explain to us how that came about?'

'What could be more natural? Ray was the only stockbroker he'd ever met.'

'Who introduced them?'

'They were both keen on cars, I think.'

'Were you keen on cars with them?'

'I do like cars,' Guy admitted. If this was where the meeting was leading, he had no objection. He would rather talk about cars than about share dealings.

The lawyer saw himself driving up a cul-de-sac. 'The recommended offer was 315p per share. Did you pay any shareholder more than that?' he changed his line of questioning.

'No.' Disappointed by the abrupt abandonment of the previous topic of conversation, Guy returned to the defensive. 'Why would I?'

'I'll ask the questions, Mr Magnus. Have you made any payment in kind to any shareholder, in addition to the 315p?'

'Payment in kind? You mean one that has to be declared for tax?'

'I mean one that must be declared to the stock exchange. An extra payment of any kind.'

'Not an inducement?' Guy sounded shocked.

'Call it a gift.'

'How can a gift be described as a payment?' Guy asked, playing for time.

The lawyer saw he had struck a sensitive point, one worth probing further. 'You can leave the legal interpretation to me, Mr Magnus. Just give me the facts,' he pressed.

'I often give my friends gifts,' Guy insisted. 'Making an unsolicited gift isn't a crime.'

'What gifts have you given?' the lawyer persisted.

Guy thought carefully. 'I think I probably gave Harold Antony a piano. Yes, I did, in fact,' he confirmed.

'A piano? What for? For acting for you? Or for selling you his shares?'

'For his wife to play. She only had a Broadwood ...' Guy started to explain, but was stopped before he reached the shortcomings of the action of the keyboard.

'Mr Magnus, I take it your company paid Mr Antony a fee for acting for you in the purchase of shares?'

'Of course.'

'How much?'

'The usual scale fee, I expect. Nigel Holmes deals with that.'

'And you paid him for his Britton Trust shares?'

'Yes.'

'How much?'

'I don't remember. It was early on.'

'You'll need to check it before the hearing. You said you gave him a piano as well. What else do you think you may have given him?'

Guy searched his memory. 'I did give his wife a watch,' he confessed in a confidential tone, as if pleading with the lawyer not to tell the lady's husband.

'You did give his wife a watch,' the lawyer repeated. 'Was it any particular kind of watch, Mr Magnus?'

'It was a Cartier,' Guy admitted.

'A Cartier? She wasn't acting for you as well, by any chance?'

'Rhoda Antony? Acting for me? What on earth makes you think that?'

The lawyer ignored the question and pressed, 'But you did give her a watch. What did you do that for, Mr Magnus? So she could tell the time?'

'She'd been very hospitable to me.'

'Do you hand out watches to every woman who's very hospitable to you? Or only to those whose husbands receive fees from you? Or sell shares to you? What are your criteria for handing out watches to women, Mr Magnus? How much did these gifts cost?'

Guy considered telling the mercenary lawyer it was not the cost of a present that counted but the thought that went with it. However, it did no harm to admit to largesse when so obliged. 'Between four and five thousand pounds,' he admitted as modestly as the circumstances permitted.

'Who paid for them?' asked the lawyer, failing to hide his astonishment.

'I believe it was Westchurch.'

'Westchurch? And what part does Westchurch play in all of this?'

Guy explained Westchurch's role as a provider of management services and underwriter of share issues.

The lawyer was none the wiser. 'You may know why a company should see fit to reward people who advise and sell their shares to a totally different company, but I'm damned if I do, and I don't expect the Takeover Panel will know what to make of it either,' he said.

Guy was saved by the entry of a secretary. She handed Cassels a note, the content of which caused him to sigh and rise to his feet.

'You'll have to go over this again in your mind before Monday's hearing, Guy. I only hope you can get your recollections in order by then. The Panel won't allow you legal representation,' he said, bringing the meeting to a premature close. It was more urgent to get back to his desk and find out what the hell was going on at Universal Credit.

Guy was in sympathy with Cassels's priorities. He too had a desk to return to. Now that Ulster & Cayman had paid for the Britton Trust shares, Magical Investments could claim ownership of the company. He wanted the resignations of Charteris, Goodman and Palliser by nightfall. He'd have the whole weekend to work out how to deal with the Takeover Panel.

One thing bothered him. He wished he knew what was on the note that had given Cassels such concern. Knowledge was power. Power to make money. The stock market was still open, and he might be missing an opportunity. If he hadn't just bought himself a company, it would have ruined his weekend.

36

The following morning Neville Macrae picked up his third cup of coffee at the very instant he reached the City pages of *The Times*. He spent the next ten minutes changing his stained trousers and nursing his scalded thighs.

Jolyon Priestley read the same article, with a not dissimilar result. Fortunately for him, he did so after placing Ulster & Cayman's cheque for £519,750 face downwards on the breakfast table so his wife could not see the amount written on the front.

Harry Griffin, sipping his breakfast cappuccino on the balcony of his apartment overlooking the port of Monte Carlo, received no cheque from Ulster & Cayman. The cheques in payment for his shares – of which there were many – had been mailed to a number of international banks for the credit of a multiplicity of nominee holdings and would not arrive until the post offices of the countries in question delivered them. Harry was not unduly concerned about the delay: it was more important that neither the Inspector of Taxes nor Sybil saw what was written on them before he showed their total to Guy.

Harry was therefore able to give his full attention to the article in *The Times* when his airmail edition was delivered. *Last night's statement by the board of Universal Credit that it knows no reason for the fall in its shares is small consolation,* he read. *No company which does not can afford to stand back and let the market invent its own reason for the collapse.*

Harry turned to the back page to look for Universal Credit's share price. Last week he had watched the shares, which at the start of the month had stood at 200p, fall from 160p to 120p. Had he not read the bank's excellent results he would have sworn Guy Magnus was leading a bear raid. What were they now? He down put the cup as his finger went down the list and found Universal Credit's name. He read the figure opposite. Not believing the evidence of his eyes, Harry checked with his still shaking finger that both the name and the price were on the same line. They were. Fifty-two and a half pence, he read again. In a single day the value of his shares in Universal Credit had halved.

Harry ran indoors and called his broker for the latest price.

'Don't worry; the worst is over,' he was reassured. 'At one o'clock they were back up to 80.'

'Do you think I should sell while the price is holding?' asked a relieved Harry.

'No need to, not while the bears are still being squeezed.'

Harry relaxed. One had to be prepared to risk the odd knock. That was what made him a successful dealer, like Guy. Technically he reckoned he was a better one, though not as lucky. In the bull market his record had been second-to-none, but when share prices fell his luck had a tendency to run out.

Harry weighed up the state of affairs at Universal Credit. If its board had no idea why its shares had fallen, he had nothing to worry about. The hot-heads would have sold out by now; the cool heads would work out a strategy over the weekend and deal, if at all, on Monday. Meanwhile he would await Guy's call and ask him whether Britton Trust had any assets over in Cannes for sale in the bargain basement. That had been a sweet deal, if ever there was one. Almost a million pounds in his pocket – £976,500 to be precise – and lunch at Maxim's once he showed Guy his share and loan stock certificates in Universal Credit.

'I'm just going out shopping for a couple of hours, dear,' Sybil interrupted his thoughts. 'I'll buy you a nice tie if I see one.'

Harry's heart missed a beat. Whenever Sybil came home with a nice tie it meant she had done serious damage saving tax in one or more of Monte Carlo's exclusive boutiques. If she was planning to buy one before she had even left home, she knew exactly what she was shopping for.

'Have a good time,' he wished her audibly. Be lucky, he wished himself silently.

He was destined to be unlucky. Sybil returned with a silk tie. Next day *The Times* told him his broker's confidence had been unfounded. On Friday afternoon Universal Credit shares had fallen to 40p before trading in them had been suspended. Now he could no longer sell them at any price. The board had announced it was in talks to *seek means of continuing the viability of the company and the security of its depositors*. Well, maybe his shares would still be worth something when they came back from suspension. But as he read on, his heart sank. *The value of a large number of shares bought with company money is now too low to provide adequate collateral.* Harry knew what that meant. Clive Salmon had been ramping Universal Credit stock. Once the bottom brick had been removed, the whole precarious pyramid had come tumbling down. The bank had no cash left. His shares and loan stock were worthless.

'Darling, I saw a lovely silk shirt yesterday, to go with your new tie,' Sybil broke into his reasoning with ominous news. 'I didn't have any money left, but I'll slip out and get it for you now if you have a couple of hundred francs on you. Incidentally, Betty Priestley called to say she and Jolyon are coming down next week to celebrate. She said you'd want to join in. It sounds as though we've done rather well. I'm so pleased, darling; I've been dying to do the place up so we can entertain properly. It isn't anything to do with Guy, is it? He must be so thrilled.'

Harold Antony read of the Universal Credit debacle with a sense of deep foreboding. He had been recommending the bank's shares to clients knowing that Clive Salmon would offer them credit. If they wanted to invest £5,000 in the stock market, Universal Credit would lend them £45,000 to go with it, so that if the shares they bought went up ten per cent, their seed-corn would double in value. As their stockbroker, he would earn ten times as much commission. Salmon had made one stipulation, not unusual in banking circles: that he must be satisfied with the quality of his debtors' collateral. However, the only shares that met his exacting criteria were those in Universal Credit. Until twelve months ago Harold's clients had respected Salmon's judgment, which was based on sound evidence: the bank's profits record and the steady rise in its share price due to consistent investor demand. However, while its profits record had continued and each announcement had beaten the board's forecast, demand for its shares had slipped away until but a few loyal friends remained. Harold Antony had foreign clients who were not yet aware of the extent of their losses.

As he considered his predicament, the phone rang. It was Guy Magnus.

'Harold, Monday's hearing: I'd like to run over your evidence with you again,' he said. 'This matter of when Berry St Edmunds and I first met. Total red herring, but we'd better get our stories straight.'

They proceeded to review them, but to Guy's irritation Antony's recollection was poor and his ability to discriminate between the relevant and the irrelevant was non-existent.

'I've been thinking about your commission, Harold,' he said when their stories still failed to tally. 'We agreed I'd pay you a penny a share. I don't think it's enough. You bought less than a million for us, which gives you less than ten grand. But the shares you bought were more important than the others. That deserves special recognition.'

Their stories soon tallied: that was how Guy could be sure they had got them right. It was Harold's turn to raise the matter which had been bothering him.

'Universal Credit. I don't understand it,' he confessed. 'Their latest profit figures were ever so good.'

'Of course they were. Clive puts next year's fees into this year's revenues.'

'How can he? No auditor would allow it. He has to back his profit and loss account with his balance sheet. Where does he find the cash?'

'Simple. The day before his year-end he swaps cheques with his friends. He credits theirs in the books but doesn't debit his own. The cheques don't clear till the following week.'

'How do you know?'

Guy decided he had gone far enough. Why admit to special knowledge? 'An educated guess,' he drawled. His only regret was that by his mentor's standards he was still a beginner in the magical art of creative accounting. Salmon must have progressed far beyond rudimentary window-dressing for one of his directors to have resigned the same week the bank's results were announced.

'What on earth am I going to do about my clients' loans?' Antony asked himself aloud, in the forlorn hope that Guy would provide him with an instant solution.

'It's too late now. If you'd asked me a week ago, I'd have told you to talk to Clive. He'd have bought the shares back from them.'

'My clients would probably have lost money at the price he'd have offered,' Antony admitted glumly.

'He'd have paid them the price that would have cleared their loans. Clive doesn't like his friends to suffer a loss on his account.'

'He could never have afforded it,' Antony objected.

'I imagine Universal Credit would have lent him the money, one way or another,' Guy said, sighing.

'It's not possible. He's a director. He'd never get away with it.'

Guy rolled his eyes heavenwards. 'You're probably right, Harold,' he said, forbearing to repeat a conversation he had recently had with Salmon on the very subject. Fortunately he had made the kind of promise you forget to keep.

'What on earth's going to happen to the bank?'

'The Bank of England will mount a rescue.'

'That sounds a bit far-fetched, Guy. Universal Credit isn't exactly Baring Brothers.'

'I'd go to bed early tomorrow night, if I were you, Harold. Monday's going to be a busy day.'

All through that weekend chauffeur-driven limousines rolled up a traffic-free Threadneedle Street and deposited their passengers at the doors of the Bank of England. By Sunday evening Sir Anthony Winchester was able to instruct Charles Cassels on Ulster & Cayman's role in the rescue plan for Universal Credit.

Did Guy Magnus ever get it wrong?

37

On Monday morning Guy came to the office early. He had a queasy feeling about the stock market, and he had an even queasier feeling about Danny Gilbert. It was as well to catch your man cold if you wanted to find out what was in his mind. Harold Antony, he was sure, would not let him down. But Danny?

'Johnny Price is going to tell the Takeover Panel he's never been to our offices,' he told him as he came through the door.

'But he has,' Danny corrected the record. 'I've seen him here.'

'Well, you're not going to say you did,' Guy told him firmly.

'If I'm asked the straight question, has Johnny been here or not, I can't tell a lie,' Danny insisted.

'If you say he has when he says he hasn't, you'll suffer for it.'

'What's that supposed to mean?' Danny asked. The conversation was taking an unpleasant turn.

'It's supposed to mean, physically.' Guy drew himself up to his full height, half a head above Danny. 'Do you understand me?' There was no mistaking the menace in his voice.

Danny acknowledged that he understood him.

Guy reckoned that Nigel Holmes and Brian Proctor would be more reliable than Danny Gilbert. Their responsibilities had significantly increased as a result of the acquisition of Britton Trust. Hand in hand with responsibilities went recompense, and where recompense led, reliability was sure to follow. Indeed, so reliable were Holmes and Proctor about to become that in anticipation he rewarded each with a salary increase from £7,500 to £12,000 a year.

But as he left the stock exchange the following evening after a hearing which had gone a day over schedule, Guy told himself he must be losing his touch. Nothing had gone according to plan. He had prepared himself for a lengthy examination into his relationship with the Earl of St Edmunds and the dealings of Price and Tate. His story was in place, as were those of Johnny and Yankee, not to mention the earl, Jolyon Priestley, Harold Antony, Nigel Holmes, Brian Proctor and, he had reason to believe, Danny Gilbert. But did they give him the opportunity to regale them with his simple tale of an underestimated genius maliciously accused by envious establishment rivals? Did they give his friends a chance to set the record straight on his dealing skills and giant-killing achievements? Did they, hell!

He felt cheated.

By contrast, poor old Berry St Edmunds received a rough ride. He stumbled from the hearing moaning about Star Chambers and misunderstandings. Guy had sat him down and gently extracted his story.

'Completely misunderstood my motives,' the earl expostulated. 'No respect. Explained I'd been trying to protect the business. No good, all that indecision and uncertainty. Had the impertinence to ask if I'd consulted the managing director of Laserbeam. Any general worth his salt perfectly capable of judging troop morale for himself. Asked why I'd been in such a hurry to sell to you when your offer still had three weeks to run. Told 'em I knew full well the chances of getting fifty per cent to go with City Star were next to nil. Cheek to ask why I hadn't stood by the board resolution. Gave the others pretty clear notice of my frame of mind, what? Man of honour!'

Jolyon Priestley was equally unhappy when he came out of the hearing. It appeared that the Panel had understood only too well.

'It wasn't fair,' he protested. 'They got me confused. They asked me when I sold my shares to Ernest Burke, without explaining why they wanted to know.'

'What did you tell them?' asked Guy, fascinated.

'I told them I regarded myself as having dealt on 1st August. That was when I signed the agreement. Then they asked why I didn't report the sale to the board. They seemed to think I might have misled my colleagues. I told them I didn't regard myself as really having sold them, as I didn't finish negotiating the price till the end of September. They asked whether not reporting the sale then might have misled my colleagues. So I explained that I didn't regard them as having been completely sold until 15th October, when I handed over the share certificates ...' Priestley stopped to draw breath.

Guy had been so rivetted by the tale that he hadn't dared to interrupt. 'Go on ...' he encouraged.

'Then they asked if I thought this affected whether or not I had misled my colleagues. So I explained that even after the sale I believed the shares remained under my control ...'

'What did they say to that?' Guy asked. He could hardly wait to hear the denouement.

'They asked whether I might not have misled myself.'

Having reached the high point of its inquiry, the Takeover Panel had relaxed. Harold Antony confirmed he was the Earl of St Edmunds's go-between with Guy Magnus, and then returned to his office to render his account for £25,000 to Magical Investments. Holmes and Proctor agreed they looked after Guy's office. As the lunch interval was approaching, Danny Gilbert was considered too inexperienced to be asked any searching questions.

After lunch it did not take the City fraternity long to reach agreement. Charles Cassels readily agreed that as the purchase of Britton Trust shares from Ernest Burke had been conditional on its shareholders' approval to the issue of its shares to Jolyon Priestley, Ulster & Cayman should have said so in its offer document. In its turn the Panel agreed that it was hard to expect Ulster & Cayman to meet such standards of accuracy if Ernest Burke had not advised it of the true position. It was unanimously agreed that the Panel should emphasise in its findings the importance of information published in offer documents and press statements being both accurate and up-to-date – in future. In such an atmosphere of trust and conciliation, Johnny Price had been asked to enter the hearing room.

'It was tricky, Guy,' he excused himself when he came out twenty minutes later. 'They asked me a straight question, so I gave them a straight answer.' He paused. 'Did I have any contact with Mr Guy Magnus during the bid period?' Guy shifted his weight on his seat as Price paused again. 'I think they believed me. They did seem rather tired,' he concluded sombrely.

Yankee Tate had been the last to give evidence. He was the only witness about whom Guy felt uneasy. Half an hour later Yankee walked slowly out of the room where the hearing was held, shaking his head.

'They believed me too, sir,' he told his master.

'Believed you about what, Yankee?' asked Guy nervously.

'That I gave Mr Munster discretion to buy, sir,' Yankee confessed, his pride dented by the admission.

'Within limits,' Guy tried to console him.

'They didn't ask me what limits,' Yankee continued to complain.

'What did they ask?'

'They asked why I thought the shares would go up. I said I wouldn't have bought them if I didn't, but I don't think that was the answer they wanted. Then they asked if I'd thought there would be a contested bid. I wasn't sure at first, but then I thought you wouldn't bother getting involved unless there was going to be a scrap, sir, so I said yes, I did. Then they asked if I sold after the other side pulled out because I thought the shares would go down. I thought you wouldn't have told me to unless you expected them to, sir, so I said yes to that too.'

Guy sensed that Yankee must be holding something back. 'Anything else? Come on, Yankee,' he pressed when his driver continued to hesitate.

Reluctantly Yankee revealed the source of his secret shame. 'They would keep asking me if … if we ever "colluded" together, sir.'

'What did you tell them?' Guy asked anxiously.

'I told them no, never. I thought they had a nerve, though. My private life's my own affair, and so, if I may make so bold, sir, is yours.'

Charles Cassels was grateful for his early release from the hearing, for he had work to do. On Sunday the Governor of the Bank of England had told Sir Anthony Winchester that Universal Credit was short of a lot of money. Let's say £25 million for starters. The Bank had decided to raise the shortfall from interested parties. I want £5 million from Ulster & Cayman, the Governor had said. When Sir Anthony protested that he did not see why his bank should be singled out for such a privilege, the Governor had given him a straight choice. Either they could do things the nasty way and let Universal Credit go belly-up, in which case Ulster & Cayman would lose its £5 million loan and its reputation for prudent banking; or they could do things the nice way and do their best to rescue Universal Credit, in which case Ulster & Cayman would lose its £5 million gift but gain honour for its public-spirited support of the nation's banking system. The prime minister wished to be kept in the picture.

When Sir Anthony told Cassels of the position, the latter asked who was to nurse the patient through intensive care back to health, and thereby supervise the safekeeping of Ulster & Cayman's funds.

'The Governor says he'll let us know by Tuesday night.'

On his return from the Panel, Cassels found a note on his desk that the chairman would appreciate it if he dropped by his office.

'Drop of scotch, Charles?' he was offered as he entered the room. Sir

Anthony had a sensitive message to relate. 'This Universal Credit business,' he said hesitantly when he could delay his news no longer. 'I believe the Governor has it in mind to invite Consolidated Finance to manage the company. Miraculous though it may be, it would appear that they're not financially involved. As they're in the same line of business, they ought to know the score.'

Cassels barely avoided choking. It was galling enough to be told that a Johnnie-come-lately outfit like Consolidated Finance was being given the responsibility of saving the face of the Bank of England, but it was positively humiliating to hear that it had lost no money in the Universal Credit debacle. Lewis White would be crowing. It was all the more important for the Britton Trust deal to come good.

'Everything go well at the Panel, Charles?'

'They seemed to appreciate our difficulties, Sir Anthony,' Cassels replied.

'Good show. Got to go over to the House and brief the Chancellor. He'll be delighted to know it's all under control.'

38

'They've got a nerve!' Guy grinned as he read *The Times* Business Diary the following Saturday. Secretly, he felt complimented. It was true, anyway. He did park his cars in chronological order. He was entitled to the odd eccentricity. He had bought Britton Trust with £100 of his and his colleagues' money, he had cocked a snook at Thruston Cutwell, Fleischmans and City Star, and the Takeover Panel was about to give him a clean bill of health. And while the Diary's author was pushing the keys of his typewriter in the freezing damp of an English December, the subject of his column was sunning himself in a deckchair on the verandah of a luxurious Caribbean villa, convalescing, he justified the trip to himself, though by now his suffering was but a distant memory. But Guy Magnus didn't need to go to the office to do a day's work. The office was wherever he was. You wouldn't get him going into one frozen by government decree to sixty-three degrees Fahrenheit or obeying a fifty mile an hour speed limit with half the street-lighting off when he could catch a flight to the sun.

Guy shaded his eyes and looked over to the kidney-shaped swimming-pool, where Don Corbishley was lathering heavy duty suntan oil over his whale-like belly and Larry Callaghan was agonising between a stack of computer sheets and the thousand page blockbuster he had deliberated over for a quarter of an hour after the flight from Heathrow had been called for the last time. Melvin Cecil was indoors supervising the cook and checking the temperature of the Montrachet. It was a propitious moment to take Larry into his confidence.

'Come over here, Larry,' he called, settling his decision for him. 'I need to talk something over with you.'

Callaghan sighed with relief and did as he was told. As Guy set out the position, he wrote it down on a sheet of paper. Britton Trust had cost £22.5 million. Ulster & Cayman had loaned Magical Investments £17,250,000 and Ludgate and St Paul's £2 million each. All three loans had been passed on to Westchurch, that from Ludgate with a generous bonus, so it could buy Britton Trust shares on behalf of Magical Investments. Even this had proved insufficient. As a result, Westchurch had been milked of its cash resources.

'Two problems, Larry,' Guy wound up his exposition. 'One, the approach for St Paul's seems to be serious. Danny wants to take some money off the table, but St Paul's has some Westchurch, and Westchurch made the offer for Britton Trust. We bought Britton for our own benefit, not to share the profits with somebody else. We have to sell St Paul's clean.'

Callaghan never counted his chickens. An approach was no more than that. But he was no more happy than Guy to give away a profit, even if it had not yet been banked.

'The loan?' he asked cryptically.

'The loan,' Guy confirmed. If St Paul's was to be clean, Magical Investments must find the cash to repay the £2 million it had borrowed from it.

'The second problem?' Callaghan enquired.

'Universal Credit.'

'The overdraft?' Callaghan asked as cryptically as before.

'The overdraft,' Guy agreed again. Clive Salmon had kept his word: earlier in the year Universal Credit had loaned Westchurch £1.3 million to buy back Mallard's stake in Ludgate. But now Universal Credit was under Bank of England control and was being run by Consolidated Finance. Lewis White was no Clive Salmon. He would insist on the overdraft being repaid on the due date.

'That could be a problem,' Callaghan pointed out unnecessarily.

'Come on, Larry, what do you think I went to all that bother for?' Guy asked. 'Press announcements, circulars?'

Callaghan guessed. 'The rights issue proceeds? You're not serious. Ludgate can't lend Magical another £3 million on top of the existing £2,750,000.'

'Give me one good reason why not. Our credibility's at stake, Larry. St Paul's may have to call back its loan to Magical at short notice. Westchurch may have to repay its overdraft to Universal Credit. The only way they can do so is by borrowing from Ludgate. When the rights issue money comes in on Friday, it will have enough cash for both.'

Callaghan was not easily shaken, but this was an exception. 'You know I was unhappy about Ludgate not disclosing the loan to Magical in the circular,' he objected. 'We said the purpose of the rights issue was to reduce the overdraft and to invest the rest in securities, not to lend it to ourselves.'

'We didn't say how much we'd reduce the overdraft by.'

'But it's what? Two and a half, three million at present?'

'That doesn't change the principle, only the amount.'

'We have shareholders, Guy. We have to inform them.'

'Don't tell me you're getting squeamish, Larry. Anyway, the shareholders would approve. They've done very well out of us, thanks to me.'

While incapable of reaching a decision, Callaghan was perfectly capable of advising caution when Guy was about to take a dangerous course.

'We sailed close enough to the wind with the pooled account,' he said. 'Surely you're not suggesting Guarantee lend us three-quarters of Investment's capital without sending a circular to shareholders? That would break every rule in the book.'

'You're looking at it the wrong way, Larry. Ludgate owns twenty per cent of Magical. When it takes over the St Paul's loan, Magical will have a rights issue. We'll organise the take-up so Ludgate's stake goes up to forty per cent. It'll double its share of Britton Trust's profits. That way everyone will be on the same side.'

Callaghan knew Guy's mind was made up; he must limit the damage. After a short tussle he won the concession that Magical could manage with a loan of £2.5 million instead of £3 million.

Guy moved on. 'You're chairman of both companies, Larry, so you'd better give the instructions to Nigel and Brian. We need to be in a position to transfer the money whenever we want,' he said.

'There'll have to be a resolution of the Ludgate Investments board,' Callaghan pointed out.

'You and I are a quorum. We'll hold the meeting here and now.'

'We can't do that. We have to give Nigel and Dominic Arthur proper notice and send out an agenda.'

'Then tell Nigel to hold the meeting over there and we'll send our apologies or proxies, or whatever else we have to do. And I want a full report on Britton Trust from him and Brian first thing on Monday morning.'

As Callaghan went into the villa to call London, Melvin Cecil emerged from it solemnly bearing a silver tray laden with four glasses and an ice bucket containing a bottle of Montrachet. 'Good man, Mel,' Guy greeted him appreciatively.

Across the Atlantic Ocean Nigel Holmes took a careful note of Callaghan's instructions on his legal pad. One, write a letter from Ludgate Guarantee to

Magical Investments replacing the previous loan facility of £2.75 million with a new one of £5.2 million. Two, hold a board meeting with Dominic Arthur to authorise the loan. Three, tell Proctor to recall Magical's £2 million loan from St Paul's. Four, tell Ken Peel of the arrangements for Magical Investments to make a rights issue increasing its capital from £100 to £500.

So meticulous was Holmes in carrying out his instructions that Magical's new loan facility was in place by Monday evening. That the loan preceded the board resolution approving it was a paradox that did not occur to him. Guy had trained him to see that it was more efficient to have the facility letter typed first and to take the resolution approving it to Dominic Arthur for signature second.

The following day Holmes walked along Fleet Street to the Inner Temple, where Arthur's law firm had its chambers. Arthur's secretary brought a large pot of coffee into the waiting-room to demonstrate how busy a lawyer Dominic Arthur was. At the end of the obligatory quarter of an hour she summoned Holmes to follow her to her boss's spacious office overlooking the river, where the absence of files on his desk emphasised how efficient its occupant was.

'Super to see you, Mr Holmes,' Arthur greeted him, rubbing his eyes to show how immersed he had been in his clients' affairs. 'What can I do for you today?'

'Guy wants us to replace St Paul's loan facility to Magical Investments with one from Ludgate,' Holmes explained when he had sat down. 'I put it in place yesterday, and I've drafted the letter and the board resolution.'

Arthur checked the documents. The paradox of the date did not occur to him either; but if there was no point in making an issue of the failure to disclose Ludgate's original loan to its shareholders, it would have been positively nit-picking to quibble about the date on a facility letter offering one of twice the amount. As Ko-Ko had explained to the Mikado on another occasion, once His Majesty gave an order, it was as good as done, and it should accordingly be regarded as having been done. Arthur had no wish to be accused of treason, let alone fall victim to a Lord High Executioner.

'I take it Ludgate Guarantee has the resources to make the loan, Nigel?' he asked.

'No problem, Mr Arthur, once the money comes in from the rights issue on Friday.'

'That's the Ludgate Investments rights issue.' Arthur recalled counsel's opinion on the pooled account and made the necessary connection. 'Does Ludgate Guarantee have the funds to make the loan without it?'

'Guy said not to worry,' Holmes reminded him.

'We told the shareholders about the previous facility, if memory serves,' Arthur recalled the broad issue, if not the fine print.

'All dealt with,' Holmes confirmed.

'Security?' Arthur remembered to ask.

'Ulster & Cayman is holding that,' Holmes explained.

'Everything seems to be in order,' Arthur said comfortably. Having exercised his fiduciary duty to Ludgate Investments' shareholders, he signed the resolution. There was a limit to the time he needed to devote to the loan when Ulster & Cayman had been content to make one three times as great. 'Give Guy my best when you speak to him,' he waved his visitor farewell.

Meanwhile, back in the Caribbean sunshine, Don Corbishley was developing his theory of investment. 'Property's the only safe store of value, Guy. Equities are on the slide. Gilts are a loser until interest rates fall, and that could take years. But property will go on rising for ever. Unless they get rid of inflation, rents will always go up.'

'St Paul's is in the market for a deal,' Guy agreed. 'What have you got on the stocks?'

'We act for institutions. They're not easily persuaded to dispose at present.'

'It's your job to persuade them. If you can't, you won't earn any fees. All I want is for you to sell to us rather than anyone else, and for the price to be right.'

'There aren't any bargains today, Guy. Everyone's in the market for quality property. At least you can be sure that whatever you do buy will prove cheap in the long run.'

'You'd make sure we bought at an attractive price if I made it worth your while to do so,' Guy said with the confidence born of experience.

Corbishley looked closely at Guy to see whether he had heard correctly.

'You know I can't be seen doing anything that might be considered unethical,' he said guardedly, unable to conceal his disappointment in that knowledge.

'Nobody can stop you sub-underwriting a rights issue,' Guy rejoined. 'If you happen to drive a hard bargain and pay a low price, that's your affair. Good luck to you is what I say.'

'What kind of a hard bargain?' asked Corbishley, more than a little interested.

'Wouldn't you regard a twenty per cent discount as a hard bargain?'

'Sounds pretty hard to me,' Corbishley was forced to admit.

'How much did you say you were going to get me for the Oxford Street property, Don?' Guy changed the subject abruptly.

'Don't worry, Guy. I promised to get you £10 million. By the time I've finished winding up the market, I expect it'll probably fetch at least twelve.'

Throughout the week the news from London grew increasingly gloomy. The stock market was in turmoil. The *FT* Index continued its free fall to 300. Ludgate's rights issue had been underwritten, so a long-stop would be in place to take up the shares in the event that an untimely statement from the Governor of the Bank of England or the Chancellor of the Exchequer unnerved the market. On this occasion the intervention of neither was needed, for the railmen's union and the prime minister did the job for them. The day after Holmes's visit to Dominic Arthur, the union announced a work-to-rule under which the railmen would work on only five days a week. The prime minister countered by announcing a rule-to-work from New Year's Day under which people would work on only three days a week. This news reached the Caribbean on Friday morning, threatening to ruin Larry Callaghan's last day in the sun. For Ludgate's underwriter was Westchurch, and his personal fortune was riding on that company's back.

That afternoon Holmes called Guy with the result of the rights issue. It had been a flop. Eighty-two per cent of Ludgate's shareholders had decided that as there were only eight more shopping days to Christmas, they would spend their money in the stores. Westchurch was left to pick up 6.5 million Ludgate shares at a cost of £3,250,000. This it did not possess.

Guy saw he would have to juggle with a number of balls, some almost empty, the rest not very full. He held his review with Larry Callaghan in the middle of the swimming pool, from where escape would be tricky.

'The result's a bit of a disappointment, Larry,' he said, showing none. 'But I suppose it was to be expected in this market.'

Callaghan knew exactly what Guy meant. 'Westchurch isn't in a position to meet its underwriting commitment,' he correctly predicted the conclusion.

'But we have a moral obligation,' Guy pronounced.

Callaghan gasped. Had he not been standing on the bottom of the pool, he might have drowned. As it was, he drew enough breath to fill a small oxygen tank.

'To do ... what?' he exhaled, thinking better than to ask Guy to explain a conversion which made the road to Damascus seem like a crack between semi-detached houses.

'To bail Westchurch out.'

'But Guy ... where are we going to find £3 million?'

'We'll place the Ludgate shares in friendly hands.'

'Friends or no friends, why on earth would anyone want to buy them?' Callaghan asked sceptically.

'Friendly hands are small hands. They'd pay less.'

'So Westchurch will take a loss?' asked Callaghan grimly. As a shareholder of Westchurch, he viewed such a prospect with gloom.

'Taking a small loss is better than going under. If St Paul's is withdrawing its loan from Magical, it'll have the cash to invest in a good thing. But you can't expect it to pay full price. It'll be taking 2,400,000 shares at 45p.'

Callaghan saw that the decision had already been taken.

'Surely you don't want whoever's buying St Paul's to have a bigger stake in Ludgate, let alone a double helping of Britton Trust?' he observed cautiously.

'But we have to find homes for 6.5 million Ludgate shares,' Guy made his priority clear.

'Who else do you have on your list?'

'You'll take 150,000 Ludgate at 40p, won't you, Don?' Guy called over to the sun-lounger.

'Sure will,' replied Corbishley on cue, with the assurance of an estate agent who has just recalculated his commission on the sale of an Oxford Street property.

'You see, we have no shortage of takers. Everyone in the know is hugely impressed with Ludgate's prospects. We'll be taking the remaining 3.6 million, along with Danny. At 30p, of course,' Guy added.

'Where on earth am I supposed to find that kind of money?' Callaghan asked. However good it was to know that he warranted a forty per cent discount, even at this price five per cent of 3.6 million shares would cost him £54,000 he did not possess.

'You have friends at Ulster & Cayman,' Guy reminded him.

Callaghan thought about his friends at Ulster & Cayman and forbore to comment. There were more pressing matters to consider. 'Westchurch will have to take a loss of not far short of £1 million,' he calculated aloud, as if this would be news to Guy.

'Eight hundred and seventy thousand, actually. A small price to pay to maintain its credibility,' said Guy, as if in agreement.

'We can hardly argue that the interests of the shareholders of Westchurch and Ludgate are identical,' Callaghan tried again. 'Not to mention Magical.'

Guy took him to task. 'Westchurch's interests are to ensure the success of Ludgate's rights issue, even if it costs money to do so, just as Ludgate's interests are to support Magical. Anyway,' he added, 'Westchurch and Magical have pretty much the same shareholders: that's you, me and Danny.'

While Callaghan readily worked out that Guy would now hold a major stake in Ludgate as well as in Westchurch and Magical, his expression showed that the knowledge did nothing to allay his concerns.

Guy sought to clarify the position. 'It's our money, Larry,' he put his view succinctly as he waded towards the shallow end. 'It's up to us how we spend it.'

By this stage it was beyond Callaghan to grasp precisely who "we" were. He ducked his head into the crystal-clear water in the hope that it would clear his mind. It did. By the time his flying white mane emerged, he had a shrewd suspicion that we were certainly not the shareholders of Ludgate Investments, who would be lending three-quarters of their company's capital to Westchurch. Nor were we the prospective buyers of St Paul's Property, who, he sincerely hoped, were more solid than that increasingly dicey company. We had a closer affinity to Westchurch; but we were closest of all to Magical Investments. This was no bad thing if that company was the borrower rather than the lender in the Ludgate circus roundabout.

But most important of all, Callaghan concluded, if Guy Magnus's interests were being protected, so in all probability were his own.

39

Guy's return flight touched down at Heathrow Airport to a dank, drizzly mid-December dawn. It had not been a pleasant experience. When awake, Guy had confidently reviewed the steps he was about to take with Britton Trust. There was some leeway between what he had paid for the company and the £30 million it was worth, but less than there would have been if Ulster & Cayman had held its nerve. Tomorrow he would call Nigel Holmes, Brian Proctor and George Ellison into his office. First he would go through the schedules his property manager was preparing. Ellison would have examined the title deeds and leases and checked Corbishley's valuations. Once Guy had confirmed his decision to sell those that were surplus to requirements – which meant anything built of brick, stone, concrete, steel or glass and standing on a plot of land – he would focus on Watson's. Nigel Holmes would have prepared schedules of its working capital – inventories, work in progress, machinery, motor cars, money owed by debtors – and how long it would take for each to be sold and the proceeds added to the cash on deposit. He would have sent Larry Callaghan a copy of each list so he could plan how to keep the taxman's fingers out of the pie. Once these assets had been sold and the loans from Ulster & Cayman and Ludgate Guarantee repaid, Magical Investments would be left with Laserbeam, the jewel in the crown, for nothing. Brian Proctor's task would be to report on the current status of its business on the cutting-edge of technology.

From time to time Guy dozed fitfully in his first class seat, his head jerking to confused forebodings. He sold: but the more he sold, the more he seemed to owe. A genial Clive Salmon morphosed into a snarling Lewis White. Gagged and bound, Dervish and de Deyler shrugged their shoulders and nodded helplessly towards Cassels. Numbers jostled for recognition in his semi-conscious mind; big numbers, but as each tried to find its place he would awaken, sweating uncomfortably, unable to recall either the quantity or its meaning.

The air hostess paid his calls even less attention than the nurse in the London Clinic. She spent the whole of the flight three rows ahead, fussing over the honeymoon couple whose late arrival had held up the flight's departure. On landing, he had to wait an age for the two to disembark before his party was allowed to follow. It took for ever for their luggage to come through. Terminal 3 was alive with all sorts of riff-raff, screaming and setting off flashbulbs. Worse, Yankee Tate was nowhere to be found. When at last the hubbub subsided and he managed to track his driver down, it was to discover that not only the weather was gloomy.

'Petrol's up 3p a gallon, Sir,' Yankee told him as he pulled away from the kerb outside Terminal 3, where he had parked the Mercedes in response to Guy's instruction. 'You'll want these,' he added, passing his master a dossier of official-looking papers which turned out to be messages from the airport police. 'They said we were in the spot reserved for Her Royal Highness. I told them I wasn't going to move, as her car wasn't as long as ours and I couldn't get into a smaller space. They didn't seem happy about it, sir.'

'I won't be happy either if you don't get me home fast,' replied Guy as he picked up the Sunday papers. A million homes had been blacked out by power cuts. The Chancellor of the Exchequer was preparing a crisis statement he would be delivering tomorrow in the House of Commons. The *FT* Share Index had closed on Friday at 305.9. That, at least, was good news. The market would be sold out. Tomorrow he would go bargain-hunting. He made a mental note to find half an hour for Danny Gilbert once he had set the other wheels in motion. He yawned. He needed to catch up on his sleep before he went into action.

By ten o'clock on Monday the cheques had all been issued. No longer did Magical Investments owe St Paul's; it owed Ludgate Guarantee. No longer did Ludgate and St Paul's each own twenty per cent of Magical: Ludgate owned forty per cent and St Paul's four; for Ken Peel had baulked at putting another £20 into the pot and St Paul's had taken up his allocation. No longer did Westchurch own almost half of Ludgate's equity: St Paul's owned a quarter, and Guy Magnus's interests almost as much. It was a merry-go-round designed to make everyone, including the potential owner of St Paul's and its portfolio of fine properties, happy.

Other than Lewis White. He called to tell Guy he wished to discuss the overdraft Westchurch had taken up with Universal Credit last March to buy back its stake in Ludgate. This very day. Guy parleyed tomorrow. The Chancellor's statement took priority, he said, even though the only way for him to discover its contents before the markets closed would be to attend the House of Commons in person or to talk his way inside the battered red despatch box. Lewis White found the appeal to his patriotism hard to challenge.

Guy had more urgent matters awaiting his attention. Holmes, Proctor and Ellison were ready with their reports on Britton Trust. Where Holmes and Proctor were Dum and Dee, the lofty Ellison was the Beanstalk.

'There's so much to tell you, it's hard to know where to start,' Holmes told him. 'Brian's been dealing with Laserbeam. George has been investigating the properties. I've been looking into Watson's. Where do you want us to begin?'

'With the properties.' Guy wanted the good news first. He had waited long enough. 'You've had Don Corbishley's valuation, George, so it shouldn't take long.'

'Well, Guy ... it wasn't a professional valuation,' Ellison said hesitantly.

'He's seen the properties. He knows which are freehold and which are leasehold, and the terms of the tenancies.'

'With lots of caveats, subject-tos and the like. He hadn't actually inspected the deeds or the leases before ...' Ellison twisted his elongated frame uncomfortably.

'What more does he need to know?'

'Well, some of the freeholds have restrictive covenants he knew nothing about. Unfortunately no one in the business knew about them either, other than the property manager, but he'd left. Some of the tenants' leases have rent review clauses that can only be triggered at specified times, and it seems he had missed some of the dates for sending out the notices. I've asked Mr Arthur to get his conveyancing people to comment, but it seems rather complicated. Of course, there's the Oxford Street property ...'

'Of course there is,' Guy agreed. 'That's the whole point.' Without it he wouldn't have bid £15 million for Britton Trust, let alone £22 million plus.

'Don's positive we won't have any trouble getting £10 million,' Ellison said proudly, as if the property were his own son and heir.

Guy spent the next half hour approving's proposals for property sales and rejecting Ellison's recommendations for the few he intended to retain. As he signed off the last decision, he turned to Holmes.

'Okay, Nigel,' he began: 'I saw from your report that Charteris, Goodman and Laws resigned with the earl, and Palliser agreed to take redundancy. Any problem paying them off?'

'We haven't settled with the earl yet over repaying the expenses of his Portuguese project, but the rest's gone pretty smoothly – almost too smoothly, in fact. Most of the head office staff went with them. That's made it pretty hard to get answers to questions, but we've kept the company secretary on pro tem.' Holmes omitted to add that this sole remaining executive spent most of his time in amused observation of how little the Ludgate Circus team knew about how businesses were run.

'What have you found?'

'Well …' Holmes said hesitantly, 'we haven't really got into it yet.'

'What do you mean, you haven't got into it? You've had three full weeks.'

'Be reasonable, Guy: Britton Trust's an accounting minefield,' Holmes began his tale of woe. 'It has over seventy subsidiary companies and joint ventures we knew nothing about. We've found over a hundred bank accounts; it's a nightmare trying to reconcile them. They're beyond their borrowing limits everywhere. The banks have been sending in demands to repay. It's been a full-time occupation keeping them at bay.'

'What about Watson's?'

'I think you ought to know we may have a problem there too,' Holmes said gravely. 'I've tried to make a reasonable assessment, but their accounting systems are in chaos. Unauthorised payments, lost documents, missing assets, you name it … I just don't know where they are …' he tailed off helplessly.

'Surely Cummings…?'

'He's where the trails seem to end.'

Guy knew he must not show panic. In his anxiety to complete the purchase of the Earl of St Edmunds's shares, he had refrained from asking himself why the managing director of Watson's had been so keen to sell at the same time. He had offered him no special deal. There was no need: Cummings had his own motives.

'Larry will get the auditors in to investigate their accounting controls and set up new books,' Guy instructed. 'Danny will look into the asset position; it'll be good experience for him. In any case, we didn't buy Watson's because we wanted to be in the oil services industry.' He turned to Proctor. 'Laserbeam?' he enquired coolly, demonstrating that he, if nothing or nobody else, was under control.

'Their systems are in pretty good shape. We know exactly what's going on,' Proctor replied more hesitantly than his answer warranted. He had been through several packets of Gauloises in the process of finding answers to Laserbeam's constant need for cash.

Guy picked up the hidden message. 'And ...'

'The business is leaking money. Heavily. Management says none of its customers have been taking orders for suits since the autumn. Apparently all people are buying now is cheap casual wear. You know, shirts, sweaters, jeans. So the clothing manufacturers have cancelled their orders for the laser cutters. Stone dead.'

'To nothing?'

'Zilch.'

As he looked down at the sheet of paper that Proctor placed in front of him, Guy's shoulders hunched perceptibly. The numbers were clear, in so far as they existed at all. And Proctor had been clear too: that Laserbeam's books were as accurate as its lasers. State-of-the-art accurate.

At half past three the Chancellor of the Exchequer rose to a mixed reception from the House. Her Majesty's Opposition, it seemed, failed to listen to Mr Anthony Barber with its customary hushed interest.

There were two matters that drew more attention from Guy, as he listened to the radio report, than from the unruly members of parliament. The first was that high taxpayers would pay a ten per cent surcharge on their previous year's surtax bills. But his interest was no more than academic, for he had never paid surtax and had no intention of joining so amateurish a club. The second was that the Chancellor described windfall profits on property development as "offensive", especially when the developer kept his new building empty in the hope that rents and capital values would rise while he did so. A new tax would accordingly be levied. At first Guy treated this with the same disdain as the surcharge, as neither was he engaged in property development nor could any of the profits he made be remotely described as offensive. However, he realised that a purchaser of St Paul's might not be as lilywhite as he. His concern increased when Larry Callaghan called to discuss the fine print of the Chancellor's statement. It transpired that he had used a dictionary not in common usage. The Inland Revenue had issued a briefing paper which stated that by "development" he had really meant "change of planning use" or "first letting". The ownership of property, concluded Callaghan, was bad news.

'I don't believe you. Barber's a Conservative,' Guy objected.

'Not today, he isn't,' Callaghan corrected him.

Guy called Corbishley's office. 'I want you to sell Oxford Street right away,' he ordered.

'Guy …?'

'I'll take £10 million.'

'You've heard the speech, Guy? The new tax?'

'What's it worth, Don? Nine million? Eight?'

'Today? Well …' Corbishley played for time. 'I'll have to get our tax boys on to it when we see the fine print, but I doubt whether it will still make sense to sell it for development that needs planning consent, let alone new tenancies. The market will need time to adjust to that. So it's back to what the current rents are worth.'

'Tell me the news, Don.'

'The good news is that the ground floor is leased to a single shop tenant with a good covenant.'

Guy didn't have to ask the bad news. Forty-odd tenants on the upper floors, all of them unreliable – he fell in to the surveyor's vernacular – covenants.

'What's it worth, Don?' he insisted. He needed the answer.

'Well … you won't lose money on it, Guy, I promise you that.'

Guy felt his stomach churn. 'What do you mean, won't lose money?'

'You'll get at least book value.'

'Book value's £4,500,000.'

'I'll get you five, Guy. Promise. Tell you what, I'll quote six. If the market holds up, we might even get a couple of punters bidding.'

If Corbishley promised £5 million, Guy told himself, a pound to a penny he'd never get it. Instinctively, he checked with the stock market. Property company shares had been marked up in after-hours trading. That told him what he wanted to know. The market never got it right.

He was in trouble. Deep trouble.

The bad news was only just beginning.

'Universal Credit's had a rough ride,' said Lewis White when Guy and Danny were seated in his office the following afternoon. 'Clive Salmon's gone on indefinite leave of absence without leaving a forwarding address. He's thought to be in California. The Bank of England's called us in to lend a hand,' he added with a false humility which Guy decided became him ill.

'And they want me to help you out?' Guy said, failing to hide a wicked grin.

'That's right,' White confirmed, the responsibility of his role causing him to miss the nuance. 'We need to recall as much money as we can. I want to discuss the overdraft facility Westchurch took up last March. What can you offer us?'

'Nothing,' said Guy incisively. 'I can't.'

'Can't? Or won't?'

'What difference does it make?'

'Not much, as you're going to have to in either case.'

'Why should I? It's a twelve month loan, not an overdraft.'

'Because of the piece of paper that's flying around.'

'What piece of paper?' Guy blinked.

'You know exactly what piece of paper it is, Guy. It's the piece of paper that says you'll do as you're told.'

Guy was stunned. He had no idea to what White might be referring. It was not his habit to put things in writing. Especially the kind of thing White might have in mind.

'That's nonsense, Lewis, and you know it,' he said angrily.

'I'm not bluffing, Guy. Either you repay the overdraft immediately or you'll suffer the consequences. You'd better go away and think about it.' White made as if to stand.

Guy had heard it all before. He stood as if to leave.

'If it weren't for Danny, and I happen to have a soft spot for him, you wouldn't even have had the courtesy of a meeting,' White went on, putting out his hand in a gesture of commiseration. 'I'd have told you to repay the money, and if you didn't, that would be the end of it. I would simply produce the piece of paper, and you'd be forced to pay up.'

Something in the tone of White's voice, in the look of his eye, told Guy to change his mind. On a day such as this, the risk was not the kind he relished. It was one for Yankee Tate, and he was no longer inclined to trust even his driver's luck. As for himself, he was ready for home.

'Give me a week,' he capitulated. Then he thought again. 'No: that's Christmas Day. Give me till the year-end, Lewis. Don't worry, you'll have your money back. It's not as if we really need it.'

When his visitors had left, Lewis White smiled quietly to himself. He would have dearly loved to know the contents of the piece of paper Guy Magnus had been so worried about.

The truth was that Guy knew the contents no better than he did. But by now he had become so overwhelmed by the precariousness of his position that he simply wanted time to plan his strategy.

Of one thing alone was he sure. He was going to need money, lots of money; as much money as he could lay his hands on.

He must gather in his assets before he was beaten to the draw.

40

'Ahem. Is everyone here? Shall we begin, then?' Larry Callaghan called the board of St Paul's Property to order in his typically consensual manner.

'For God's sake get on with it, Larry,' Guy ordered autocratically. He was in a different position from the others. Nigel Holmes, Brian Proctor and George Ellison sat around Larry Callaghan, their faces turned attentively towards his end of the boardroom table, awaiting his instructions. But they were directors, subject to the authority of the chair. He was not a director.

Still recovering from jetlag, Guy had slept poorly in the uncomfortable knowledge that his purchase of shares in the Ludgate Investments rights issue had left him illiquid. He had been right to remind Larry Callaghan about the friends they had at Ulster & Cayman. That morning he had reminded Sam Dervish, too. He had also reminded him of another matter, as a result of which Dervish had acknowledged that he was as impressed with Ludgate's prospects as everyone else, and that the shares Guy, Larry and Danny had taken up represented excellent security for loans. Even so, the words of the Chancellor of the Exchequer and Lewis White had reinforced Guy's resolve to gather together his resources.

'Shall we take the resolutions on the sale of the company first?' asked Callaghan.

'I'm not happy with the balance sheet,' Guy objected. 'There's too much cash. We should mop some of it up before we sell.'

'Our buyers seemed happy enough about it when they checked the assets,' George Ellison told him. 'We did have a bit of a barney about our stake in Ludgate going up to twenty-five per cent, and some of the legal enquiries on the properties need further checking, but I think our answers will satisfy them. They didn't raise any objections to the cash, though.'

'St Paul's has no Bijou,' Guy pointed out.

The directors turned to him attentively. The name was one they had heard from time to time, spoken with awe. It was a company in which only Guy and his most intimate friends held stock. For Bijou's secret was this: where another company might make a scrip issue so as to widen share ownership and become more marketable, Bijou would undergo consolidation. Guy would merge ten shares, even a hundred shares, into a single share. That way a holder of fewer than a hundred shares would end up with none at all. Effortlessly, without additional investment, his personal equity in the company would increase. Each Bijou share was now worth, said Danny Gilbert, – and Danny was often a reliable source of information in such matters – a minimum of 25, perhaps even 30. No, not pence, pounds. No, not on the stock market, for they were too rare and valuable a commodity to be quoted; but NAV. Net asset value.

The directors knew that what Guy said was true. St Paul's had no Bijou. They suspected the omission was about to be rectified.

'In fairness, I could make some available,' Guy confirmed their suspicions.

'We may need to consider whether such a purchase would have to be declared,' Callaghan observed cautiously.

'To whom?' asked Guy, his tone making his disagreement clear.

'To the shareholders.'

'Whose shareholders?'

'St Paul's.'

'No need. I'm not a director of St Paul's.'

Callaghan conceded the point. 'Do we have an independent valuation?' he moved on, marking off the point on his checklist of fiduciary duties.

'Thirty-five pounds a share,' Guy asserted firmly, sliding the company's latest balance sheet along the table.

'As at 30th September, Guy?' Callaghan queried gently as he glanced at the figures, scratching the bald part of his head. His role was to exercise benevolent restraint on his master, not to harass him.

'They're the latest available figures.'

'But ... the Chancellor's statement?'

'What does the Chancellor know about property valuation?' Guy was more than usually scornful.

'George?' If Callaghan hoped the ruling would be taken from him, he was doomed to disappointment. George Ellison remained unhelpfully silent, his eyebrows raised in query towards Guy.

'As we're both present, I want to convene a Westchurch board meeting,' Guy announced, the absence of Danny Gilbert being of mere academic interest. 'I've been so busy I haven't had time to consider Nigel's and Brian's shares – the ones they bought last January. I reckon they've doubled since then, thanks to their hard work. That makes them each worth – what? – £5,000? Times are hard: want to cash in, boys?'

While Holmes and Proctor nodded eager assent to both questions, George Ellison's eyebrows remained raised. He too would dearly love to cash in. As one of Ludgate Guarantee's merry band of debtors, the result of his purchase of a hefty parcel of St Paul's shares in a more bullish phase of the stock market, he was less disinterested than his colleagues in the value of that company. For some days his doubts as to whether its sale would really take place had grown. After yesterday's events in Parliament they had sunk without trace – to be replaced by the certainty that it would not. Today no one in his right mind would buy a property company. Valuations of St Paul's and Bijou were purely academic. Extracting himself from his loan was not.

'No, not you, George; you'll get your chance when we sell St Paul's. Minute it, Nigel,' Guy gave Holmes an unfamiliar instruction.

Holmes took a moment to orientate himself, decided that his notepad was a Westchurch, headed it appropriately and drew up the form of words. Callaghan checked that everyone approved – not that he was in any doubt that they would – and that company bought in its shares from Holmes and Proctor for cancellation.

'Westchurch meeting closed,' Guy ruled. 'We were doing St Paul's, weren't we, Larry?' Callaghan acknowledged that St Paul's was indeed what they had been doing. Ever-sensitive to eyebrows stuck in the raised position, Guy continued, 'I wish to record our appreciation to George Ellison for his outstanding efforts in the negotiations on behalf of the shareholders. Incidentally, George – I know this isn't exactly St Paul's business, Larry, but we're all in this together – you'll be happy to know I've put aside some Britton Trust warrants for you. Back to you, Larry. How do you want to play my Bijou shares?'

'Unanimous, I think,' Callaghan declared, taking the sense of the meeting and adding his vote to those of his colleagues. Guy abstained from participating in the decision of a board of which he was not a member; but in truth he had already seen which way the wind was blowing. St Paul's Property now had some Bijou.

The sale of 3,000 shares, even at £35 apiece, was a drop in the ocean; but as Yankee drove him along an unlit Embankment, Guy told himself he had at least made a start. As they passed a newsagent his eye was caught by the evening newspaper billboard. *New Companies Bill Defines Insiders*, he read.

It'll never work, he told the back of Yankee's head.

Christmas 1973 was a time when such goodwill as was on offer was thinly spread. Ignorant of the seasonal tradition of goodwill, the Gulf States announced that they had doubled the price of oil. Knowledgeable of seasonal weather conditions, the miners offered to make up for the shortfall in fuel if their wages were given similar treatment. The Takeover Panel, having allocated its small amount of goodwill to Guy by reporting that it had found no evidence of collusion between him and his friends, had none left for the Earl of St Edmunds and Jolyon Priestley, whom it roundly condemned for selling him their shares.

George Ellison was right about one thing. As there was no goodwill left for the owners of property companies, the sale of St Paul's Property failed to take place. The company accordingly had no need to remain clean and was able to reinstate its loan to Magical Investments. Larry Callaghan pointed out that this meant Ludgate would not have to lend Magical quite so much.

Guy already had plans for St Paul's cash balances. His promise to Lewis White had to be kept.

'Nobody else has the money to lend Westchurch so it can repay Universal Credit,' he enlightened Callaghan.

Callaghan saw the light. Immediately after Christmas, St Paul's advanced Westchurch £1.3 million, and Westchurch repaid its debt to Universal Credit. As a result, St Paul's freedom of manoeuvre was severely curtailed. In the past, if one company in his stable needed funds, there was another which had an excess or could offer an unused facility. But now the Ludgate Circus had to deal with the cash flow of Watson's and Laserbeam, both of which were in strongly negative mode, at a time when its own liquidity was much reduced. It would willingly have done so from the sale of surplus properties were there any more takers for property than there were takers for property companies.

But there must, Guy told himself, be a buyer for so prime a freehold as Watson's property at Euston. On New Year's Eve he told Ellison and Holmes to prepare a report of their marketing recommendations. On the first business day of 1974 he sat in his office, its curtains drawn, its radiators burning full blast, its chandelier blazing alone in the darkened Square Mile, engrossed in a report in *The Times* that the developer of the Centre Point office tower had attacked the government's attitude to vacant property as "the unacceptable face of ignorance".

'Guy, about the Euston property …' the portly Holmes interrupted his thoughts in a semi-whisper. 'We didn't realise until after we saw you the other day, together …'

Ellison, a head taller, took over, his voice trembling.

'We'd been working separately, you see …'

'Then we wondered …'

'We're not exactly sure, but …'

'Spill it!' Guy insisted impatiently.

'I'm afraid we … you …' Ellison made the admission with as much impartiality as he could muster, 'Ken Peel reckons its value must have been included twice.' Seeing Guy's bemused expression, he barely dared to continue: 'You see, it's in my valuation of Britton Trust's property assets …'

'Of course it is,' Guy agreed.

'And I think it's probably … in my valuation of Watson's too,' said Holmes, sounding close to tears.

Had it known its way to the office, Guy's heart might have skipped a beat. As it was, his head spun. He stared at the schedule placed in front of him. It was because the figure was so large and so obvious that they had all missed it – he, Larry, Danny and everyone at Ulster & Cayman. Of one thing he was certain: Britton Trust did not own two properties at Euston, each worth £5 million.

Guy rose and went down the corridor to the toilet. As he washed his hands he stared into the mirror. The face of ignorance stared back.

Where normally he would spend less than ten seconds on such a simple matter, Guy wrestled with the problem of Westchurch for almost a minute. Having repaid Universal Credit £1.3 million, the company had no cash, heavy borrowings and owned a quarry. The net result was that it owed £350,000 more than it owned, and it had no resources with which to trade out of its deficit.

Westchurch was strapped to the ground.

But where Guy's usual instinct was to surrender such a dog to its creditors without a minute's – and often without even the aforesaid ten seconds' – hesitation, in this case he allowed his calculations to run on. Westchurch was, after all, three-quarters his. This fact, and the sea-change his attitude to personal liquidity had undergone in the past two weeks, gave it a special value, one not to be lightly surrendered. For a company that owned a valuable quarry must, he told himself, be worth at least the par value of its shares. The par value of Westchurch was £100,000. And he could certainly make use of £75,000.

'I wonder how much Westchurch's quarry is worth,' he remarked non-committally to George Ellison on a Monday morning later in January. He had developed the habit of making non-committal remarks on Monday mornings, having found time to practice them over the weekend. The Ludgate Circus had become accustomed to the start-of-the-week ritual.

'Ooh …' Ellison hesitated professionally, unsure which of the many kinds of valuation Guy wished him to adopt. Historic cost, current use, open market and discounted cash flow competed unsuccessfully for his commendation. 'Say, oh, it's in the books at £500,000, isn't it?' he sat on the fence.

'I didn't ask you that, silly. If that was all I wanted to know, I'd have asked Nigel. What's it *worth*?'

Ellison saw he was being asked to aim higher. '£1 million?' he hazarded.

'And the rest,' Guy said with confidence. 'It's worth a million and a half of anyone's money. But let's use your figure as a basis, George. That makes St Paul's net asset value £150,000, doesn't it?'

Ellison saw the merit in Guy's calculation. 'I suppose it does,' he agreed.

'That's what Brian thought. We're holding a board meeting of St Paul's to make an offer for it. Larry and I won't be voting, of course.'

Ellison saw merit in that, too. Larry Callaghan shouldn't vote if he had an interest, albeit only five per cent, in the result. Guy shouldn't vote because – apart from his interest – he wasn't a director of St Paul's, though that hadn't stopped him putting up his hand at its board meetings whenever he felt like it.

'How much will St Paul's be offering?' he asked, so he could document the decision he was about to take.

'Danny and Larry have agreed to accept £100,000,' Guy told him. 'I know it's a one-third discount on a conservative net asset value, but they didn't want to take advantage of their special position. I would never have recommended them to sell at as low as par value, but I suppose I'll have to go along with it.'

Wearing different shoes Ellison might have argued that the price reflected a barely discernible discount on an inflated valuation of a hole in the ground, but he knew who had paid for his custom-made size twelve black Oxfords.

'Seems fair enough,' he said, but with sufficient hesitation to set off a warning light in Guy's acute brain.

'Larry will be holding the board meeting in ten minutes,' Guy told him. That was how long their conversation had lasted. Brian Proctor shouldn't take as long. Especially when he was told how much Ellison reckoned Westchurch was worth. Proctor bowed to Ellison's expertise in property valuation, just as Ellison bowed to Proctor's expertise in fire sales of plant and machinery.

Brian Proctor came to Guy's proposal well-prepared. He had been in an advanced state of preparation ever since he learnt that the value of his Westchurch shares had doubled. He quickly jotted down Guy's proposal in the form of a minute, ready for transcription into an agenda item. If he was good at one thing, it was saving time. *The board resolved (Mr Callaghan not voting),* he wrote, *that an agreement be drawn up for the purpose of acquiring Westchurch Limited, and that Mr Ellison and Mr Proctor satisfy themselves as to the value of the assets owned by the company.* He passed it to Guy for approval.

'Why include George?' asked Guy.

'I thought – well, he's a director.'

'So's Nigel. He's much better qualified to deal with the other assets. And insert the words "as quickly as possible" in here,' Guy ordered, marking the text with an arrow. Why should he wait a moment longer than necessary for his £75,000?

Guy's assessment was spot on. When the St Paul's board was told of the offer for the sale of Westchurch by its owners, Holmes showed no surprise at their generosity. Generosity was coming into fashion at the Ludgate Circus. He had just witnessed a worrying example. For Larry Callaghan had become increasingly nervous about his shareholding in Magical Investments.

'I've come to a decision, I think, Nigel,' he confided. 'You see, as Ludgate now has such a large interest in Magical, and I'm still chairman, I think, perhaps, bearing in mind the possible conflict of interest, I was wondering …?'

'You're not thinking of resigning?' Holmes asked, trembling at the prospect of the possible alternatives. Guy's current attitude to assuming the chair of public companies could be set down in two monosyllables. No way. That left Dominic Arthur, perish the thought. Or Nigel Holmes.

'No, I don't think so,' he heard to his relief. 'Unless Guy has other plans. But I was wondering whether I ought to let Ludgate have my interest in Magical.' Callaghan peered uncertainly over his spectacles in the hope of finding an answer to his dilemma in Holmes's eyes. Seeing a similar uncertainty there, he added quickly, 'At the price I paid, of course. Fourteen pounds, I think it was, altogether. You don't have to agree if you think it's too high, Nigel: I'm not after a profit.'

Guy made his next proposal to Holmes and Proctor together. 'I've decided to sell 100,000 St Paul's. Ludgate owns twenty per cent. If I were to unload my shares onto the market, I suppose ...' He left the consequences unstated. His subalterns knew their duty.

'You don't think Ludgate ought to buy them, to protect the value of its existing investment?' asked Holmes, his notepad at the ready.

'What do you think, Brian?' Guy enquired of Proctor.

'I don't see why not,' Proctor replied thoughtfully. 'Although it would have to be at the proper price.'

'I've thought about that. Sixty-five pence.' Coming as it did from the Ludgate circus's expert in share valuation, the figure went unchallenged.

Proctor scribbled fast, but on this occasion his colleague finished first.

'*Mr Proctor informed the meeting that Mr Magnus had offered to the company 100,000 shares in St Paul's Property Limited at a price of 65p per share,*' Holmes read out his resolution.

'Mr Holmes informed the meeting,' Guy corrected, adding after a moment's thought: 'that an opportunity had arisen whereby the company could acquire ...'

'But if there is a connection with the seller, we have to issue a public statement,' Holmes justified himself.

'They aren't owned by me personally,' Guy pointed out unnecessarily. They rarely were. 'They belong to Bijou,' he added confessionally.

Holmes treated this revelation with the special respect owing to the name. 'Of course, if you weren't a shareholder of Bijou ...' he suggested helpfully.

'The trouble is, Larry's got a few Bijou too,' Guy said regretfully.

'Larry's got a few Bijou too,' Proctor echoed. 'That's it, then,' he added unhappily. Callaghan would insist on making a public declaration of his interest.

'That's it, then,' Holmes added his own echo. 'Anyway, it would take the holding to over fifteen per cent of our assets. We'd have the usual problem with authorised status.'

'What's wrong with the usual solution?' asked Guy derisively.

'That's it, then,' Proctor agreed, as he completed his corrected version of the minutes of the board meeting he and Holmes were about to attend. He might have finished second, but the winner had been disqualified.

For his part, Guy also had to settle for second-best, for even though Larry Callaghan was unable to veto the transaction, he did insist on declaring it. But it was important that the precedent had been established. After all, Bijou still owned a large chunk of the equity of St Paul's, and as long as it needed to raise cash it would remain a seller of its shares. And Bijou did need to raise cash, to pay Guy for the 2.4 million Ludgate shares he had bought from Westchurch after the rights issue. For prudence dictated that while these remain under his control, they no longer be registered in his name.

Having established the principle that Ludgate was a buyer of St Paul's, the only matter requiring consideration was how many Bijou shares it could afford.

'How much cash does Ludgate have?' Guy asked Holmes.

'Three hundred and fifty thousand,' Holmes told him when he had checked.

'In that case it's buying ...' Guy made a rapid calculation, '630,000 St Paul's from Bijou at 55p. Tell Harold Antony to put the deal through the market.'

Larry Callaghan accepted that these were proper transactions, for Bijou did not discriminate by buying Guy's shares alone: it bought his as well. Nor was Danny Gilbert left out. He watched bemused as the share certificates and cheques flew around the office and Guy gathered in his assets. The Ludgate Circus seemed to have turned into a magical fairground in which a carousel handed out cash prizes to every rider, each of whom in his turn spent his money on a never-ending series of faster and more dizzying rides until ...

Until the cash ran out.

41

He would not go to the office. The office reminded him of a world of decaying business and unconsummated deals, collapsing markets, mounting debts and unsympathetic bankers. Each day a report from Holmes or Proctor or Ellison brought news of shrinking assets, falling sales and demands for cash, ever more cash, from Britton Trust. It was a commodity none of his companies any longer possessed.

In any case, the office was wherever he was. He could work just as easily from home. There he was free to work out his strategy for survival without a secretary who kept an over-accurate diary, a switchboard girl who logged his calls or a paper trail that followed his dealings. There he could take solace in his paintings and Mahler, in caviar blintzes and slightly chilled Dom Pérignon.

It was only a matter of time, Guy told himself, before Ulster & Cayman realised Britton Trust was a busted flush. Sam Dervish had asked him to set out a worst-case scenario. He had requested him and Danny to draw up statements of their personal assets. He had insisted that Ludgate Investments document the guarantee Guy had promised, in proportion to its holding in Magical Investments.

Despite Guy's precarious mental state, the instinct for self-preservation died hard. 'I never did promise you one,' he tried first.

'You most certainly did,' Dervish challenged him.

'I couldn't have. I have no authority to give the company's guarantee without board approval,' Guy tried again.

'You told me you'd ask for it.'

'I wasn't able to persuade the other directors to agree.'

'Which other directors? I thought you were in charge,' Dervish pressed.

'Dominic Arthur's a lawyer. He's extremely cautious about that sort of thing.'

Dervish appeared to accept that defeat, but then asked whether the rest of the money had come solely from Ludgate or partly from St Paul's. Guy assured him that Ludgate had loaned Magical Investments the full £5 million.

'We're in trouble over Ludgate's guarantee,' Dervish told de Deyler later that day. 'There's nothing in writing. If they won't give it to us, we can't shoot them.'

'Bloody fools in City, forgetting a thing like that,' de Deyler shook his head, mystified. 'We'd better check whether its loan to Magical Investments was properly authorised. Was there a board resolution, full knowledge of shareholders? If not ...'

Though not party to this discussion, Guy saw his exchange with Dervish as a straw in the wind. What if the bank were to pull the rug and call in his guarantee? Where did they think he was going to find £17 million? All he needed was time. Time to turn assets into cash, cash into thin air. Then what could they do, when they discovered that everything he owned, everything he loved, was within these four walls? He made a tour of his paintings, promising himself they would never touch so much as a frame or a picture-light, a hook or a wire. He went down to the cellar and stroked a bottle from his collection of Château Pétrus, with at least one representative of each post-war vintage, swearing that no hand but his would uncork a solitary bottle. Even if ... he scribbled a few notes on his leather-clad notepad. It was essential Dervish and de Deyler get the right picture ...

The next stage required him to lift his boycott of the Ludgate Circus. The following afternoon he sat with Danny Gilbert reviewing the latest figures from Britton Trust for his report to Dervish. The worst-case scenario was Hiroshima. The best was an away draw. He set out a picture of withdrawal from the battlefield with his troops in reasonable order in spite of substantial losses.

'It's essential they get the right impression. You'd better send this to Sam,' he told Danny, passing him the handwritten figures. 'Be in early on Monday, would you? I've arranged for my personal lawyer to come in. He's going to draw up my service contract.' He left Danny to carry on wading through the mass of reports from Britton Trust telling of its impending doom.

Be in early! Danny was incensed. Was he not in early every day, on his own, doing his best to mitigate the damage at Watson's, at Laserbeam, at the other Britton Trust subsidiaries? Service contract, my arse! Honey-pot, more like.

'I want to contingency plan. We must be ready for them if they call in our guarantees,' said Guy next morning. Robert Lord, his personal lawyer, and Danny Gilbert sat with notepads perched on their knees. 'I mean, we're not exactly made of money, you and me, Danny. What have I got as my reward for five years of enterprise and hard work? A house, a few pictures, a modest shareholding in my companies, and bank loans and a claim from the tax inspector that'll wipe them all out. When they see I'm not worth bankrupting, they'll leave me alone. Rob, I want you to draw me up a service contract as joint managing director of St Paul's Property. Twenty-one years at £20,000 a year, inflation-proofed. I'll need a flat in town and first class travel: how else am I going to live properly? And a Bentley and a chauffeur; I can't put Yankee out on the street, and he's already moaning about being seen around town driving a Merc.'

'If you don't settle, they'll bankrupt you and take most of what you earn. You'll be barred from being a company director,' Robert Lord snivelled feebly. He was used to dreaming up schemes for offshore trusts, not incorporating lucrative emolument packages into contracts of employment.

'Grow up, Rob. I don't want problems, I want solutions,' said Guy. 'You can make me general manager, can't you? It's my assets I need to protect, not my job title. I'm going to sell Melvin Cecil a lease on my house. And my St Paul's shares – in return for preference shares redeemable at the company's option. That way they won't have any value and Ulster & Cayman won't be able to touch them. You should take precautions with your St Paul's shares too, Danny.'

'I'd rather take my chances,' Danny declined, not without a tinge of regret.

'You have other assets, Guy,' Lord whined, ready to learn more.

'I won't let them touch my paintings. Even if I have to sell them to St Paul's,' Guy revealed the next stage of his plan. 'I've spent over £750,000 on them,' he justified his stance.

'You'll be lucky to get away with it,' Lord said unhappily. 'You'll risk being adjudged to have disposed of assets in the knowledge that you were insolvent. That will invalidate the dispositions. Do your bankers know how bad the position with Britton Trust really is?'

'I sent them a paper last Friday setting out the likely losses,' Danny confessed before Guy had a chance to shut him up.

'You did what?' Guy asked with exaggerated incredulity. 'What losses? No, don't tell me. Better I know nothing about it. As far as I'm concerned, everything's on course. The property market's holding up nicely, I hear.'

He asked Larry Callaghan to take the early train from Norwich next day so they could have an hour together before the Ludgate board meeting. Subdued, he admitted to Larry that things were not going all that well at Britton Trust.

'Laserbeam's a black hole, Larry. Cash is running out from the business like there's no tomorrow. We can't fill the gap with property sales; the market's as flat as a pancake. It's a total disaster area,' he told him. 'If it carries on much longer, the bank will call in my guarantee.'

'That's terrible, Guy. What are you doing about it?'

'I'm doing whatever I can to protect myself.'

Callaghan sat in silence for a few minutes, deep in thought. 'You don't actually *know* how bad it is,' he said at length, making a statement rather than asking a question.

'Of course not,' Guy confirmed.

'You mustn't report anything to the meeting that could imply that you did. It would go in the minutes. You'll have to find some way of reporting satisfactory progress.'

The matter was one Guy had not considered. He was pretty sure he had never seen a board minute. Minutes made no money.

'Nigel?' he asked.

'Nigel takes the minutes,' Callaghan corrected him.

'No problem, then.'

'Even so, you must be careful.' Callaghan thought again. 'I'm not affected by the guarantee,' he said. 'I might be able to help you more if I distance myself from the problem. Then I'll have no conflict of interest.'

'In what sense do you have one?'

'Maybe I shouldn't have approved some of the board's decisions. I mean, Ludgate Securities bought shares in Bijou without independent advice. I'm a director of one and a shareholder of the other. I wonder whether someone may not think there was a conflict of interest. Perhaps if I were to resign from Ludgate?' Callaghan thought aloud. He was beginning to sound almost decisive. It was an ominous sign.

'You can't abandon me now, Larry!' To lose his father-figure on the very day Dr Spock told parents he had been wrong all along would be to suffer the worst kind of double jeopardy.

'Ludgate Securities, not Ludgate Investment. Nigel can take my place. Maybe I shouldn't be on any subsidiary boards,' Callaghan continued. He had no need to expand on the point. The action was in the subsidiaries; the parent companies merely gave formal approval to their boards' decisions. 'It might even be better if I got rid of my holding in Magical,' he made final the breach between duty and friendship. 'I've been talking to Nigel about whether I ought perhaps to sell it to Ludgate, at par,' he suggested, though in fairness the recovery of his £14 investment was not the overriding factor. 'This conversation never took place,' he ended, taking the firmest decision of his life.

'Any movement on property sales, Danny?' asked Guy on his next visit to the Ludgate Circus. It was the Monday after the Ludgate board meeting.

'Not a bite. George says the market's flat as a fart. Where the hell have you been, Guy?' Having spent the past month trying to hold a fortress under siege, Danny felt entitled to lodge a protest. 'We've been needing to take decisions. You might at least have phoned in.'

'The kind of decision I need to take can't be dealt with on the phone. I have to go liquid, Danny. Really liquid.'

'Don't we all?' Danny couldn't have agreed more, but saving his own skin was not at the top of his agenda. Trying to staunch the flow of blood at Britton Trust was. Guy's absence had had the same effect as a surgeon abandoning the operating theatre as soon as he had made the first incision. 'Listen, Guy, you're clever enough to sort out the position if only you set your mind to it and roll your sleeves up.'

But Guy was not listening. 'The Britton Trust property in Gray's Inn Road that Don Corbishley valued at a million and a half. What do you reckon it's worth today, Danny?' he asked.

'Conservatively? The rent roll's a hundred thousand a year, so say a million.'

'It can't be worth anything like, or you'd have sold it by now.'

'That's because we're asking £1.2 million, on your instructions. If you lower your sights we'll stand a better chance of getting it away.'

'Money's costing eighteen per cent, Danny. Who's going to buy £100,000 of rent at a price that needs £180,000 a year to finance?'

'A tax-exempt fund with cash in its pocket?' Danny suggested.

'If someone made us an offer of £500,000 cash, what would you say?'

'I'd say bollocks,' Danny replied firmly.

'I want you to agree it.' Guy was equally firm.

Danny had no wish to be threatened again with violence. 'You'll never get away with it,' he tried after a prolonged silence. 'Nigel and Brian will have to sign the contract.'

'They'll do as they're told if I make it worth their while. Twenty five grand each in a Swiss bank is not to be sniffed at.'

'You can't be serious, Guy.' Used to his boss's methods, this time even Danny was shocked.

'You and I are both in the same boat, Danny. The bank's going to go for our assets. We have to stick together.'

'I couldn't, Guy. Absolutely couldn't.'

'I need help, Danny. I've got to raise as much cash as I can. How else can I pay back my guarantee?' Guy tried, failing to convince even himself.

'It's more than my life's worth.' Danny's refusal was final. He knew exactly what Guy would do with the money.

'I'm going to have a nervous breakdown, Danny. I can feel it.' Guy fled from the room.

Danny shook his head and returned to his paperwork. He could no longer concentrate. He went down the corridor to the toilet. As he washed his hands he looked in the mirror, the mirror that had shown Guy Magnus the face of ignorance. Staring back at him he saw the face of knowledge. It was a burden he was not yet ready to bear. He would not be twenty-two until Monday.

He needed help.

Lewis White heard Danny Gilbert through without interruption. Danny told him he was getting into the office on time and beavering away trying to sort out the mess, while Guy was in a blue haze, funking everything, salting his assets away, having a nervous breakdown, going abroad. What was he to do?

White felt sorry for his protegé, but he knew he must put his sympathies aside. Danny needed advice, sound advice that would see him through to the end of his career.

'You're going to have to go to Sam Dervish and tell him everything you've told me and throw yourself on his mercy,' he said when the tale of woe had ground to a halt.

'I can't do that, Lewis. I wouldn't know how to handle it. Where am I going to find £17 million? They'll take me to the cleaners.'

'They'll settle with you. They don't want it to get out that they took your guarantee for that kind of money. It'll make them look stupid. It'll cost you in the short run, but you'll have to take the loss on the chin. It's the only chance you'll have of ever starting again.'

'You wouldn't come with me, would you, Lewis?'

'Of course I will, Danny. And if you need a good lawyer to parley a settlement with them, I'll find you one.'

Having found themselves passing the same elevation of Norwich Castle for the third time in half an hour, Guy left Yankee Tate to find somewhere to park the Mercedes and crossed the city centre on foot. His frustration at the usurpation of motorists' rights by the new breed of pedestrian shoppers, out in their thousands as a result of the three day working week, was partly assuaged by the character of the streets and the quaintness of their names. He skirted one end of Back of the Inns and found himself in the thronged and inappropriately named Gentleman's Walk. Passing the Christmas windows of Jarrold department store and the turning into Lobster Lane, he headed down a cul-de-sac towards a terrace of Georgian buildings. He had no need to check the number; he had read it countless times on Larry's letterhead.

The receptionist told him to go up to the first floor, where Larry welcomed him at the door of his office. From its window Guy had a view of the River Wensum; had he twisted his neck he would have seen the spire of the cathedral.

'Larry, we need to review my tax position,' said Guy.

Sam Dervish and Sidney de Deyler heard Danny Gilbert through with the occasional terse comment. It was not their style to feel sorry for others, let alone for themselves. Life was too short for sentiment. It might contain enough hours for damage limitation, but they were realists enough to doubt even that.

'Twenty-five grand, he offered?' de Deyler commented at one stage.

'Fine paintings they must be,' Dervish remarked at another.

'Live like a prince, eh?' de Deyler observed without a trace of envy as Danny enumerated the terms of the proposed service contract.

'Guy Magnus a clever bloke: you can say that again,' Dervish agreed with Danny's assessment.

'I can't do it all myself,' Danny concluded. 'Britton Trust's far too big to handle on my own. You must put somebody in to run it. Guy could, but he's never at the helm. All he's interested in is taking his assets out of the country where you can't get hold of them. Everyone's beavering away, but there's no one to say yes to this, no to that. If no one comes in to run it, things are going to go pear-shaped.'

'Put a man in, you say?' Dervish repeated thoughtfully. He glanced along the table at de Deyler, who shook his head. 'That would look terrible. If we put someone in now it would look really bad, what do you think, Sidney? Lewis?'

De Deyler changed the shake of his head to a nod. Lewis White grunted non-committally. Supporting Danny meant not taking sides.

'Then what do you want me to do?' asked Danny, exasperated.

Dervish and de Deyler pondered the problem.

'I think the best thing you can do, young man, is to keep on doing what you're doing and stay in touch with us and keep us informed about what's going on,' said Dervish at length. He exchanged glances with de Deyler and picked up a message from his lips. 'Gone to see his accountant today, you said?' He turned to White. 'If Mr Magnus has been trying to stash his personal assets away, it won't hurt if young Mr Gilbert lets us have a note of what he thinks they are, and how much he thinks they're worth – will it, Lewis? You'd better send us your own statement at the same time,' he addressed Danny again.

'So the Inland Revenue could justify a claim for £750,000?' Guy summed up. He and Larry Callaghan were discussing his capital gains tax liability.

'As I say, it may be a lot less. It depends on any losses you can crystallise and offset against the gains between now and 5th April,' Callaghan replied.

'I'm not a seller of my shares,' Guy said firmly.

'You can "bed and breakfast" any that stand you in at a loss.'

'Of course I can, Larry. I probably will. But if you were to write to them asking for confirmation that that's how much money they want from me, they'd agree, wouldn't they?'

'They'd be over the moon.'

'So if you were to put it in writing, you could state categorically that as things stand I have a tax liability of £750,000?'

Callaghan hummed and hawed, but eventually agreed to that too. 'But take care: you don't want that kind of document lying around where the Tax Inspector can see it,' he said. 'He might just want to pass on a copy to the Collector of Taxes.'

'You don't think I'd allow those worms to get their hands on my money, Larry? I need something to show to Sam Dervish and Sidney de Deyler when I meet them tomorrow.'

Callaghan sighed, called in his secretary and dictated the letter.

'By the way, I'll be declaring an increased interest in Ludgate,' Guy said when he had finished, as if he were telling Callaghan the time. 'Three and a half million shares: twenty-five per cent of the equity. I thought I'd give you advance notice, as you're the chairman. I'm not intending to mount a bid,' he added dryly.

Callaghan had learnt never to show surprise at Guy's revelations. 'You've bought back the shares you sold to Bijou last week? Was that wise?' he asked.

'I've restructured my interest in Bijou,' Guy corrected him. 'I've increased it to over a third, so I have to declare the interest in Ludgate as if it were my own. Don't worry, Larry, I've taken precautions. They won't be able to touch my Bijou.' He failed to specify whether he was referring to the Inland Revenue or to Ulster & Cayman, but Callaghan expected neither to have been left out.

'I've been thinking further about my own position,' Larry said. 'I've been wondering whether I shouldn't be resigning as chairman of St Paul's Property. Just in case anyone suggests there might be a conflict of interest between that and my chairmanship of Ludgate Investments. Just in case,' he repeated.

'You're not thinking of resigning too?' Guy asked Yankee Tate half an hour later. His driver had been complaining bitterly about Norwich's one-way systems.

'With 600,000 unemployed?' asked Yankee. 'Mind you, sir, if the train drivers keep on striking, there's bound to be more demand for car drivers.'

42

The review of Britton Trust's assets was finally complete. Each company and each property had been subjected to detailed analysis, to decide which was going to be sold and which was not. The first list had been long, the second short. Asking prices had been discussed, agreed and minuted. Dervish and de Deyler had been accompanied by a team of assistants, lawyers and accountants. It could have been worse, Guy supposed: Charles Cassels might have been present. He had sent his apologies: that morning the Bank of England had announced the formation of a "lifeboat" committee of banks and financial institutions to provide expertise and support to any secondary bank that found itself shipping water. Sir Anthony Winchester wished to review Ulster & Cayman's position so he could give the Governor – not to mention the Chancellor when he bumped into him tonight outside the division lobby – the appropriate assurances.

When Ulster & Cayman's plethora of advisers finally left Guy and Danny alone with Dervish and de Deyler, Guy was free to voice his overriding concern. 'We're going to need help from the bank for working capital, Sam,' he began. 'While we're waiting for offers to come in and deals to go through, we have to pay the bills,' he elaborated in a tone which implied that the plenary meeting had been a mere public relations exercise and the senior players must now get down to practical matters.

'With a little patience, the property market is bound to improve,' replied Dervish, showing even greater optimism than Guy. He looked along the table to de Deyler. On receiving the customary scowl he added: 'But we want to see some constructive moves from you, Guy, before we agree to help any further.'

'Cassels is getting jumpy,' de Deyler elaborated. 'He wants to meet again on Monday to review progress.'

'But we've just reviewed it,' Guy protested.

'He thinks it's time we talked through certain financial aspects of the deal.'

'Does he have anything particular in mind?'

'He's pressing us on Ludgate's guarantee. I've explained your position, but he's still unhappy. Also, he wants to talk to you about your personal situation,' Dervish said, choosing his words carefully.

'My personal situation? Sam, I thought we had an understanding.'

'An understanding?' Dervish shrugged. 'Charles didn't say nothing about no understanding to you, did he, Sidney?'

'Not to me, Sam, no,' replied de Deyler, shaking his head.

Charles Cassels's implacable expression the following Monday morning brought to Guy's mind Detective Inspector Jack Slipper of Scotland Yard. He felt a visceral sympathy for Ronald Biggs, the news of whose arrest in Rio de Janeiro had broken over the weekend. Was there nowhere left for a man to hide?

'If we're to keep our heads above water, you must provide us with enough working capital while the asset sales go through. Don't forget, your interests are the same as ours. If we go under because you fail to back us, you won't look at all good,' Guy warned Cassels. He turned to Dervish for agreement and received a blank stare in response.

'We're not putting in another penny unless our interests are fully protected.' Cassels's stiff response belied his smooth demeanour.

'You have the security of the Britton Trust shares.'

'Would you have any objection to our having a man on the board to protect our interests?' asked Cassels.

'And have him block us whenever they don't coincide with ours? You must be joking,' replied Guy scornfully.

'You just said our interests were the same. Is that your only objection?'

'Isn't it enough?'

'We'll nominate someone from outside the bank. Not to run the business, just to countersign the minutes on asset sales and policy decisions.'

Guy needed the bank more than it needed him. 'Will you release the proceeds of the Kingston property to us?' he changed the subject. The first Britton Trust property to be sold would bring in £1 million but under the terms of the agreement the receipts would be credited against their loan.

'Can't you borrow from your own companies?'

'The directors would never agree to it unless they were secured. You hold all the security.'

'You've borrowed unsecured from Ludgate Investments already. Was that its own money, or was it borrowed money?'

'Mostly its own,' Guy replied. He knew he must take care. 'Of the £3.5 million it loaned Magical, it borrowed £700,000,' he gave the first plausible figures that came into his head. 'That's right, isn't it, Danny?' he demanded, glaring at his young colleague.

Danny had been sitting in sullen silence at Guy's side. He decided that denial was not worth a further threat of violence. 'Seven hundred thousand,' he agreed.

'The loan was from a company controlled by you.'

'Controlled by me?' Guy looked up innocently.

'You must have shares in Ludgate. How many do you actually have?'

'Very few, personally. I do have 2 million St Paul's,' Guy admitted. 'But that's only twenty-two per cent of its capital. It hardly amounts to control. Anyway, St Paul's didn't lend us any money in the end,' he explained.

'I was asking you about Ludgate Investments, not about St Paul's. What was your influence on Ludgate that persuaded it to lend money to Magical Investments?' asked Cassels, not so easily put off.

'Influence? I may be a director, but there are others on the board.'

'What exactly are your shareholdings in Ludgate?'

'Legally, none. Technically, I suppose I have an indirect interest via my personal trusts and my holdings in other companies.'

Cassels was losing patience. 'What are their holdings, then?'

'It's is a very complicated set-up. I'm not sure how I could use it to exercise any influence on the company.'

'But it is a public company, and it did make an unsecured loan to Magical Investments to fund its offer for Britton Trust,' Cassels persisted.

'That was a commercial decision. The board approved the loan, and the shareholders were advised in the rights issue document.'

Cassels changed tack. 'What rate of interest does Magical pay Ludgate?' he asked.

Guy spotted the catch. To admit the truth, that the rate was higher than Magical was paying Ulster & Cayman, would be embarrassing. But if he lied that it was lower, the terms would be deemed uncommercial. He must tread warily.

'The same as to you,' he said. 'It bears the same risk if things go wrong.

The difference is that Magical owes Ludgate less, and Ludgate hasn't the resources you have to lend it more.'

Cassels fell temporarily silent. Keeping up with Guy Magnus's explanations was giving him a headache.

'Ludgate Investments and St Paul's Property have an interest in keeping Magical going,' Dervish came to his help. 'If they want us to give more help, they must both give us a guarantee. You can't expect us to stick our necks out any further without one.'

Cassels returned to the fray. 'Who's paying the interest on our loan? Where are you finding the money?' he asked Guy.

'It's being rolled up until the end of May,' de Deyler answered for him.

'In that case, who's going to pay it when it falls due? As things stand, you won't be able to. Don't forget, you have to pay interest on Britton Trust's own borrowings as well. You won't get any change out of £5 million a year, £100,000 a week.'

The statement gave Guy neither surprise nor comfort. He had made the calculation more than once himself, without finding a solution.

'The problem won't wait till the end of May,' he said. 'If you don't support us now, we'll go down by the end of the week. Together,' he emphasised. 'You must release the million from the Kingston sale to enable us to keep going, or someone will put in a receiver. Then you'll lose control of Britton Trust as well as us.'

'I suppose we might consider it,' Cassels said after a moment's thought. 'There'll have to be a condition. Both of you must provide us with the statements of wealth we've asked you for. Complete, with no omissions.'

'If you and your colleagues give us your full cooperation, I'm sure everything will be resolved satisfactorily,' added de Deyler, showing the trace of a smile for the first time.

'What price should I put my St Paul's shares in at, Guy? Fifty pence?' asked Danny the following morning. He was sitting opposite Guy drafting his statement of assets. It was a matter to be taken seriously.

'Forty,' Guy replied. The *FT* Share Index had just fallen below 300.

'Ludgate bought Robert Lord's holding for 65p,' Danny reminded him.

'You want me to let my friends down?'

Danny had reconciled himself to the knowledge that his refusal to perjure himself in front of the Takeover Panel had cost him any chance of joining that exclusive band. More important was Guy's attitude towards his foes, of whom he reckoned he was in danger of becoming one. And he had 500,000 shares in St Paul's. Any fall in their price hurt.

'They must have come a bit off the top,' he said miserably, 'but surely they're not worth less than 50p?'

'Don't you see, Danny, that the less you're worth, the less Ulster & Cayman can make you pay?'

Hope and desperation competed for Danny's attention. At one end of the scale it would be unwise to put too high a price on his St Paul's shares, though when he bought them Guy had granted him an option to sell them back to him at 50p. At the other end, if property values continued to fall through the floor the shares could become worthless. He settled on a range of values: 20p, 30p, 40p; £100,000, £150,000, £200,000 – let Dervish choose. Then he deducted the overdraft he had taken up to buy them. He was no longer a rich young man.

On the other side of the desk, Guy had carried out a similar task. He passed Danny the result of his labours, as if to invite comment. Danny accepted the invitation and perused the list. Eight hundred thousand pounds, he read, for his two million shares in St Paul's. A hundred thousand for his house in the country. A round half a million for his paintings and other works of art. Thirty-five thousand for his vintage cars. There was no mention of the Chelsea house, or of his shares in Bijou.

'Your paintings?' Danny asked, to show his keenness rather than in any sense of criticism. 'Didn't you tell me St Paul's was going to buy them from you for £750,000?'

'That was the buying price,' Guy responded.

'And this?'

'This is the selling price.'

'They said they want us to include everything,' Danny continued his investigation as gently as he could.

'This is it. I've had to sell off my other assets. My Bijou shares, my Chelsea house.' Guy waved his arm in an easy-come, easy-go manner. 'The market's been so rotten, I was lucky to find a buyer.'

Danny wondered whom Guy could possibly have found to buy his shares. He would have taken a hiding on the house, too. He raised his eyebrows.

'Melvin bought them from me,' Guy had to admit.

By now Danny's eye was on the last two lines of the statement. Guy had deducted £750,000 from the total. It seemed he owed a lot to St Paul's, and even more to the taxman. As a result, the bottom line of his net asset statement had fallen to £650,000.

'Seven years' capital gains tax,' Guy said ruefully. 'I thought I could hold them off indefinitely, but they're finally catching up with me.'

Guy Magnus was a rich young man – but he was no longer filthy rich. For all Danny knew, Melvin Cecil was probably richer.

43

These were times that called for cautious appraisal before embarking on irrevocable action; yet supposedly rational men were capable of behaving with extraordinary impetuosity. On 7th February the prime minister called a snap general election in the hope that the voters would take his side against the miners he was so demonstrably incapable of controlling. The only advantage Guy was able to discern was that the political uncertainty might take the City's eye off his particular ball. This was more than outweighed by the damage the return of a Labour government would do to the stock market.

Private Eye had a better measure of the times when it hinted with uncharacteristic reticence that the assets against which Caliban had borrowed £20 million might be a trifle down in value. They knew damn well they were, and more than a trifle, Guy told himself bitterly. It was not his fault that the secondary banking sector had chosen this of all times to collapse, that he had found administrative and financial chaos at Britton Trust, that Ulster & Cayman was losing its nerve. When the bank had committed its funds and set its name to the bid, its directors had licked their greedy lips over the surplus he had uncovered. They must take their share of the blame if the deal had gone sour. He was not responsible for Oxford Street property halving in value overnight. Or that suddenly no one would buy businesses that lacked reliable books, or properties whose titles were not properly documented, from owners who were trying desperately to keep their bankers at bay. The mess at Britton Trust must be sorted out before the sale of its assets could be implemented. Only when it was would he have time to deal with tax planning and reorganising its appallingly managed subsidiary companies.

And now Charles Cassels was talking of calling in his guarantee, and asking for further and better particulars of his personal assets. He must buy time. Time either for the deal to come right, or to take steps that if it did not, he would not go down with it. Before they next met he would set out his analysis of the position in writing. He would tell Cassels everything – except what he could do with his personal guarantee. Cassels had better work that out for himself.

'Thank you for your letter, Guy; most helpful. And for sending us the additional information we asked for.' From the sarcasm in Cassels's tone it was apparent he had found nothing in the figures Guy had provided that was of any assistance at all. Guy inclined his head in acknowledgement. 'I want to examine the financial position of Britton Trust in further detail,' Cassels continued. 'You say in your letter that its borrowings were £2 million higher than you had been led to expect.'

'Brian Proctor is au fait with the details: he's in day-to-day control of the money, while I focus on the policy decisions.' Guy's tone conveyed the seriousness with which he was handling the management of the business. In the absence of Dervish – though de Deyler was present, if so far silent – he intended to treat Cassels as a mere nuts-and-bolts man.

Whilst pretending to listen attentively to Proctor's answers to the banker's enquiries, Guy reserved his concentration for the questions. They told him how Cassels's mind was working. From time to time he would turn to Guy and ask the price he expected a particular asset to realise, and Guy would tread the narrow path between an optimism Cassels would not credit and a pessimism that might cause him to pull the rug from beneath their feet without further ado.

But nothing prepared Guy for the bombshell Cassels exploded when his questions came to an end and he moved smoothly into summing-up mode.

'I appreciate that the original rationale was to realise the surplus properties to repay the borrowings, and to retain Laserbeam,' he said. 'Unfortunately it has become clear that this is no longer a realistic option. We need to re-evaluate our strategy.' He hurried on, 'I happen to think we should seriously consider finding a buyer for Laserbeam.' There was a palpable silence as he waited for the response. 'It's losing money, and it may well command a premium over net asset value,' he continued when none materialised. 'It has an exciting technology. There could be serious interest from the United States.'

The blood rushed to Guy's head. Cassels had been happy enough to agree to the basic concept of the deal: that everything was for sale to repay the loans except the crown jewels, which he and his partners were to keep as the reward for their enterprise. Now the bank was demanding total liquidation. That would leave them stripped bare. He had every justification for the steps he had been taking: if the bank would not support him until the agreed objective was achieved, why should he help it to recover its lost millions?

'Well, there's food for thought,' he drawled laconically when he had taken control of himself.

De Deyler was quick to spot the change in his mood. 'May I say how much we appreciate the difficulties you face, Guy. The old management left you a real dog's dinner. We at the bank want a profitable outcome to this affair just as much as you. We'll do what we reasonably can to help you, won't we, Charles?'

For a moment Cassels betrayed his frustration; then his merchant banker's imperturbability returned. 'Of course we will,' he confirmed.

This was no time to heal the rift on the opposition team, Guy decided, but one to take advantage of it.

'Come on, Brian, we've spent long enough socialising,' he said, putting his papers into his brief-case. 'It's high time we went back to work.'

Work meant the board meeting of Ludgate Investments. It was time to bring his colleagues up to speed on progress with the reorganisation of Britton Trust and the discussions with Ulster & Cayman. Larry Callaghan had an interest in both, and Dominic Arthur needed to be reassured that Ludgate Guarantee's loan was secure. And the fall in the company's share price must be arrested.

'Guy, would you like to give the board your report on Britton Trust?' Larry Callaghan began. Then he turned to Dominic Arthur, seated on his left. 'Dominic, you recall that Ludgate Guarantee has a minority shareholding in and an outstanding loan to Magical Investments, the principal shareholder in Britton Trust?'

Dominic Arthur nodded sagely. Seated at the far end of the table, Nigel Holmes minuted the state of the board's knowledge.

'May I remind the board,' Guy began, 'of my previous report of satisfactory progress with the reorganisation of Britton Trust. Since then our surveyors have completed their appraisal of the properties. We're highly satisfied with the values they've put on them. It's too soon to say whether they will achieve all the asking prices we've set, but they've already done so for the Kingston property. If this is repeated for the remaining properties, there'll be no cause for concern about our investment in or our loan to Magical.

'However, I have to report that when I met Ulster & Cayman's directors last week their attitude had changed radically. They seemed to have forgotten the agreed concept of the deal, which was to sell the surplus properties in order to repay the loans, so as to end up with the Laserbeam business for nothing. If we follow their line and sell the operating businesses with their properties intact, the prices will be based on earnings, not asset values. As earnings have been poor, the value we realise will be less.' Guy looked round at his colleagues' solemn expressions. Satisfied that the bad news had had its required sobering effect, he turned to the good. 'Naturally I explained the importance of dealing with matters as we originally agreed. I'm pleased to report that at a further meeting this morning they accepted this. Mr de Deyler reaffirmed the bank's intention that the deal be profitable to all parties, and said it would give us its full support in dealing with the short-term liquidity problem we inherited from the previous management.'

At the head of the table, Callaghan remained inscrutable but calm. On his right, Dominic Arthur sighed contentedly: how very agreeable to be a director of such a soundly run public company! He had heard anecdotal evidence of others where management was out of control.

'I should like at this stage,' Guy went on, 'to circulate a draft statement to be included with the interim results we will shortly be sending to our shareholders. As you may know, there have been rumours in the market that the reorganisation of Britton Trust has not been going well. This has affected our share price, which has fallen sharply. It is the board's duty to scotch these rumours. As the chairman knows, I have increased my own shareholding. If the shareholders were aware of this, I'm confident that the price would stabilise at the proper level. The statement I have drafted tells them of our belief that the current price presents an attractive buying level, and that we are increasing our holdings accordingly.'

'*Are* increasing, Guy?' Larry Callaghan raised an eyebrow.

'*We* are increasing?' Arthur queried, barely audible.

'I bought 12,000 the week before last. I can't say *have* increased as I haven't settled yet, so I don't have the stock certificate. The collective "we",' Guy corrected Arthur, to the latter's visible relief. 'Whatever the wording, it must be in the shareholders' interest to be told of our confidence.'

Callaghan proposed that Guy ask Ulster & Cayman for its view of the draft statement. But when he did so, much to his annoyance the merchant bank advised the directors to make no reference in the interim statement to his increased shareholding.

One week later the board of Ludgate Investments was again in session. Guy was in fighting mood. The value of the company's shares must somehow be shored up. Where one plan failed, he must try another. What better way to show the board's confidence, he argued, than to pay a dividend to the shareholders?

'How can we afford to pay a dividend when we're squeezed for cash?' asked Callaghan.

'We can't let the shareholders down. If we pass the dividend, the market will draw the wrong conclusion,' Guy insisted. As the holder of twenty-five per cent of the equity and the prospective recipient of a dividend of £25,000, he felt entitled to take on the mantle of defender of his fellow-owners. 'One and a half pence per share should lead them to the right one.'

'A dividend of one and a half pence net will cost the company £140,000,' Callaghan persisted.

'It's fully covered by earnings,' Guy declared grandly.

'Interest received seems rather high,' Callaghan observed after perusing the draft accounts. 'Do you have a back-up schedule, Nigel?' Holmes passed him one. 'This shows an accrual of £250,000 interest from Magical Investments,' he continued. He peered at Guy. 'If I had reason to believe we were going to receive it before we have to pay the dividend, I'd have nothing to argue about.'

'It's due at the end of May,' Holmes informed him. 'By then it will amount to ...' he calculated rapidly, '£475,000.'

Callaghan made a strategic withdrawal. 'We can't send the accounts out as they stand without giving the shareholders more information,' he argued. 'We can't keep on hiding a loan to a company in which a director has an interest.'

'Hide an interest? No, we oughtn't to do that,' agreed Arthur.

For Guy this was an unwelcome turn. Callaghan's confidence that he was taking the proper line was reinforced by the knowledge that as he no longer had shares in Magical Investments, he could take an objective view. More seriously, Dominic Arthur was showing signs if not of independent thought, of being influenced by Callaghan rather than by Guy.

'We don't have to say who Magical's shareholders are,' Guy searched for a way out. 'We disclosed Ludgate's interest and that Larry and I were directors in the rights issue document when we gave details of the original loan. All we have to say is that the facility is now ...'

'Five point two million and that accrued interest has been included in the results,' Callaghan completed.

Dominic Arthur had been silent for some time. Though this was by no means unusual, Guy sensed that trouble was brewing. He was relieved when the result of the cogitation was revealed.

'Don't you think Ludgate Investments has a disproportionate share of Magical's equity?' asked Arthur, 'Bearing in mind that its loan of £5.2 million is unsecured, and that its equity investment is only, er ...'

'Two hundred pounds,' Holmes reminded him.

'Good point,' Guy agreed. He was not for arguing about the scale of Ludgate's participation in what was looking increasingly like a worthless shell. 'In confidence, the board of Magical Investments has been considering the possibility of increasing its share capital. Perhaps Ludgate would care to subscribe?'

Callaghan stared at the ceiling. This was a moment to avoid commitment. Though he no longer had an interest in Magical, nor had he any wish to provoke a clash with Guy. However he felt bound to say something, even if only so he could then step aside.

'It may not look right if you set the terms on your own, Guy. As it's Dominic's idea, may I suggest that he be authorised to take up the cudgels with you on Ludgate's behalf?' he proposed.

'Seconded,' said Guy quickly, before a full-scale debate could ensue.

Dominic Arthur removed his glasses from the bridge of his nose, then replaced them at a more traditional angle. He had been delegated by the board to negotiate terms with Guy Magnus. He would be no pushover.

44

Would he resign? Would he stay put? As the financial crisis developed and the *FT* Share Index plummeted, Guy reviewed the issues and reached his conclusion.

He would stay put. He was bound to. He was a Conservative.

After a three day hiatus the prime minister decided otherwise and resigned. A new – that is to say, the old – prime minister returned to Downing Street at the head of a minority government. The miners' leaders accepted a pay offer from a pipe smoker that they would have refused from a piano player, and the Share Index continued its plunge towards a seven-year low.

'Our properties will sell as soon as the political situation stabilises and the institutions come back into the market,' Danny Gilbert assured Valerie East in the conference room of Ulster & Cayman's head office as the crisis approached its climax.

Valerie East was the executive deputed by Cassels to tidy up the mess at Britton Trust while he got on with running the bank. She was a no-nonsense Cambridge University first class graduate who had passed her job interview ahead of her male competitors and had since climbed higher than even her directors had expected, on merit. Her black-rimmed spectacles and dark brown hair pulled back into a tight bun belied the fact that with the former removed and the latter let down she cut a more than attractive figure. But in the office, the glasses and the bun remained firmly in place.

East had just made a note to report back on the chaotic state of Watson's books and the pressure this imposed on selling properties to raise cash. The next task she set herself was to verify the note made by Cassels at his meeting with Magnus five weeks ago: that Ludgate Guarantee had borrowed £700,000 of the £3.5 million it had loaned to Magical Investments. She did not recall having seen either figure in the documents. Surely Ulster & Cayman had loaned Ludgate and St Paul's Property – wasn't it a couple of million each? And had not each taken up twenty per cent of Magical Investments? If the bank had loaned Magical eighty per cent of the money to buy Britton Trust, was it too far-fetched to suspect that Ludgate and St Paul's might each have passed on its loan to Magical to provide the remaining twenty per cent?

She called the Ludgate Circus to check with Nigel Holmes.

'Not St Paul's,' Holmes corrected her. 'Surely you knew? Ludgate took over its loan. You see, when Magical issued another £400 of equity capital, most of it was allotted to Ludgate; its equity share went up to forty per cent. St Paul's didn't take up any, so it's down to four per cent ... Why? Would you expect to be allotted new equity if you no longer subscribed to the loan capital? ... Altogether? Well, altogether Ludgate's loan to Magical is £5.2 million ...'

Valerie East nodded slowly to herself. It was obvious, really. And neither Ludgate nor St Paul's had given Ulster & Cayman a guarantee.

Her bank's money was as good as lost.

'Let's take the original figures as a base, Guy.' Charles Cassels consulted Valerie East's notes. He and Guy were meeting to review the status of the security for Ulster & Cayman's loan. 'When you bid for Britton Trust, it was on a property valuation of £38 million, though there was an inherent tax liability of £8 million if they were realised at full value. In addition, the value of Laserbeam was estimated at £8 million, and that of Watson's at £5 million. That's how you arrived at £43 million for the net assets. Agreed so far?'

'Agreed.' Guy saw there was no point arguing.

'And on the other side of the balance sheet the company had liabilities of £21 million. You paid £22 million, so give or take a million of sundry assets and various costs, the deal barely broke even?'

Guy agreed again. The tax liabilities would never have to be paid, but there was no purpose in arguing for the sake of it now, when there would be plenty to argue about for the sake of survival later.

'Now let's look at what the company is really worth. The properties? A third down? Twenty-five million?'

'That's unduly pessimistic. The property investment market is only off twenty per cent. Provided you support us so buyers don't treat it as a fire sale, we should get £30 million. At that level the tax liability will come down to less than £5 million.'

'Laserbeam?'

'It's worth what we said it was,' Guy insisted. 'It's a marvellous business.

We could put it in at £7 million, I suppose, to be really conservative,' he conceded adopting a responsible tone. 'But I refuse to have it sold off cheap just because Stephen has a bee in his bonnet. He doesn't have your long-term vision, Charles.'

Cassels acknowledged the compliment. He knew it to be true. He also accepted the valuation.

'Watson's?' he asked, looking Guy in the eye.

Guy returned his look, poker-faced. 'The books are in a bit of a state but the underlying business is sound,' he said.

Cassels drew a deep breath. He was about to raise a sensitive issue.

'I'm told you double-counted the Euston property. It was in the property valuation and also in the company valuation.'

'*We* double-counted,' Guy corrected him. '*You* are our financial advisers. You had a duty of care.'

'*They* were double-counted,' Cassels compromised. 'We still have to take £5 milion off the value of the business.'

'Only three and a half,' Guy argued. 'Don't forget the reduced tax liability.'

'Which means,' Cassels calculated, 'that the net assets available to repay our loan are worth no more than £13.5 million.'

Guy was unsurprised. He had reached the same conclusion six weeks ago. 'We weren't alone in expecting the gearing to go with us,' he included his financial advisers in the same breath as he excused himself.

'All the same, it leaves the company £4 million short of its borrowings. You have a commitment to repay half of our loan at the end of May, plus interest that's been accruing at sixteen per cent. You'll have to find £10 million. You haven't a cat's chance in hell. There'll be nothing left for Ludgate Investments, either.' Cassels knew from Valerie East's notes not to bother to include St Paul's Property.

Guy sensed the time was ripe for a display of contrition. 'I want to be frank with you, Charles,' he replied. 'I know Ludgate has lost its money and I know what I did was unwise and ill-judged, but it was all done within the law and in good faith. We genuinely thought we would make a killing on Britton Trust, and so did you. Don't forget, I backed the deal with my own money, and I gave you my personal guarantee. No one has lost more than me – relatively,' he qualified his assertion. Regardless of what the bank succeeded in extracting from him, he had lost every last penny of his £200 equity stake in Magical Investments. 'I could do with your advice on one aspect;' he switched topics before Cassels had time to contradict him: 'surely I'm not under an obligation to disclose the position to Ludgate's shareholders before I have a chance to put things right? It must be in their interests that we dispose of the properties in an orderly manner?'

'Exactly how much did Ludgate lend – has it lost?' Cassels asked, knowing the answer.

'Over £5 million,' Guy replied, this time truthfully. It was imperative that Cassels recognise his basic honesty, his desire to put things right.

'Out of what total capital?'

'Seven million,' Guy added truthfully again. Ludgate's balance sheet value had been higher last autumn, but since then its share portfolio had fallen in line with the market. 'It means the net asset value per share is down to about 15p,' he answered the next question before Cassels could put it. 'It was 45p in the interim accounts.'

'What are the shares changing hands at?' Cassels asked.

'Seventeen-and-a-half,' Guy admitted, more galled that the market saw fit to mark down Ludgate's shares than cheered that it underestimated the damage suffered by the company's investment in Magical Investments.

Cassels hid his concern. Guy Magnus had something of a reputation in the City. If he were to expose himself to charges of improper conduct, and Ulster & Cayman were to be publicly associated with him as his financial advisers …

'I'll have to take legal advice,' he replied. 'I take it you're fully aware of your own position – regarding your personal guarantee?'

Guy knew the next few moments were crucial. If he struck the right balance between injured supplicant and cooperative defendant, with a judicious seasoning of implicit menace, he might yet survive.

'I've been working flat out with you for the past six months, Charles, and all I see for my pains is a court order in bankruptcy in which I declare a deficiency of umpteen millions pounds. It's hardly fair,' he protested. 'Or practical, for that matter. After all, you need my help to sort everything out. I want to cooperate as far as I can, but how can I do my best with this hanging over me? You're putting me in the position of a man forced to dig his own grave knowing that when he's finished he's going to be shot and shoved into it. I'm not complaining, Charles – I've no right to – but I hope you'll give my position some consideration.'

'You mean fire blank bullets? You know I can't do that, Guy. If you raise less from the disposals than we loaned you, we'll be bound to recover the balance from you under your guarantee.'

'You know I haven't got £17 million, Charles.'

'Perhaps not, but you must be wealthy enough to pay the difference.' Cassels riffed through the pages of his file until he found Guy's statement of affairs. 'You don't expect me to believe that this list sets out the sum total of your personal fortune. You live like a millionaire. You must have other investments, more than one house?'

'All pledged, except for the 2 million shares in St Paul's Property. Come on, Charles: you must have known I'd be geared up. You don't think I could have grown my assets so fast without borrowing against them, do you?'

Cassels saw his quarry slipping away unless he remained firm. 'I can't let this go, Guy,' he said. 'Either we reach a realistic agreement now on how you're going to meet the shortfall, or we're going to have to call in your guarantee at the end of May.'

'Where will that get you? If you call it in, you'll bankrupt me.'

Cassels resolved to play the game hard. 'If that's what it has to come to, so be it,' he said.

'In that case,' said Guy slowly, 'I shall have to talk to my partners.'

Cassels spotted the menace in his tone. 'Your partners?' he asked carefully. Danny Gilbert's guarantee was worth little and Callaghan had given none. In any case, Guy was in charge. 'You never have to talk to anyone,' he pointed out. He looked into Guy's eyes and saw something that troubled him. 'Which partners?' he asked instinctively.

'That's a question you'll have to ask *your* partners,' replied Guy, putting his papers into his briefcase.

After Guy left, Cassels sat alone drafting a note of their meeting. It required discretion if it was to be circulated amongst his colleagues. My partners? he muttered to himself. He did not hear the door open.

'I thought you'd want to know we've received an offer for Watson's,' Valerie East broke into his reverie.

'How much?'

'Six hundred thousand.' After a pointed pause, she added, 'Subject to a retention.'

Cassels raised an eyebrow. 'Tell me the worst,' he demanded. 'How much?'

'The whole amount, of course,' she said mordantly.

'Conditional on … ?'

'Clarification of the tenure of the Euston property.'

Cassels hung his head. 'Anything else?' he asked, anxious to hear all the bad news at the same time.

'Not yet.' Valerie East shrugged, as if to say she wasn't sure it made good use of her time trying to predict what was going to emerge next from this particular can of worms. 'Oh, I suppose you should also know they've appointed Kenneth Peel chairman of St Paul's Property.' She shrugged again and made her departure, heels clicking sharply on the parquet floor.

Cassels returned to his report. He wondered how Sir Anthony Winchester would react to the news about his former partners. He did not have to wonder about Stephen Cornelius's reaction. Stephen was no fan of Sam Dervish – nor of Sidney de Deyler, for that matter. Stephen would be delighted.

45

'Right, Nigel, what's on the agenda?' Ken Peel opened his first board meeting as chairman of St Paul's Property Limited. He stroked his newly grown and only partly successful moustache. The absence of both Guy Magnus and George Ellison suggested it would be a formal affair: reports, resolutions, no other business. The papers littering the space in front of Holmes said it was his show; the shiny table top in front of Proctor that he was there to make up the numbers. He looked round the table to see whether anyone would mind if he lit up, but concluded they would.

'As the board is aware,' Holmes began formally, 'this company owns just under thirty per cent of the issued share capital of Ludgate Investments, and Ludgate owns a third of us. What you may not know is that we also hold just under thirty per cent of the issued share capital of Bijou Limited, and that in January Bijou bought 3.2 million shares in Ludgate ...' He paused to pass his colleagues a schedule setting out the shareholdings of each company in the others. 'So as you see, the three companies have a ... a mutuality of interest.' He looked up to check that the message had gone home. He need not have bothered, for the others were accustomed to Guy's use of cross-holdings to keep his corporate empire under control. 'In order to finance its purchase of Ludgate shares,' he went on, 'Bijou took up a loan facility. Unfortunately,' here his tone became less confident, 'due to the state of the stock market the value of this stake has, ah ... diminished, and Bijou has had to repay some of the principal. That is where we come in. It seems ...' he hesitated to give himself time to choose the right words, but the only ones which sprang to mind were the unvarnished truth: 'It seems it was this company that advanced Bijou the money to repay Ludgate.'

'On what basis?' Peel asked, sighing audibly. Younger than his colleagues, he was given to sighing audibly in the hope that this would indicate a sceptical maturity. By "this company", Holmes could only mean St Paul's. The absences were easily explained.

'Guy promised that Bijou would have a substantial rights issue to raise the money to repay us,' Holmes replied unconvincingly.

'So where's the problem?' asked Peel, knowing instinctively that there must be one.

'It's felt that a rights issue is no longer appropriate. The view is that funds should be provided by way of a further loan.'

Peel guessed that the view Holmes was quoting was Guy's. Proctor had been in the Ludgate Circus long enough to know why.

'As bad as that?' he remarked without emotion.

'Things do seem to have deteriorated rather since the proposal was first made,' Holmes admitted. He handed each a second sheet.

Proctor was first to complete his analysis. 'A net liability situation,' he commented infelicitously.

'We've considered other possibilities,' Holmes went on unhappily. 'At one stage we thought of buying Bijou's holding in Ludgate, but that would have given us over fifty per cent and we'd have been forced to make a cash offer for the rest. Then,' Holmes added quietly as if to reveal a confidence, 'Guy offered to sell us his holding in Bijou for £1. But that would have given us sixty-six per cent of Ludgate and put us in exactly the same position.' At some stage or other, Proctor thought, Guy would have considered every conceivable combination of cross-holdings. 'Guy gave his guarantee to the original loan, of course.' Holmes shrugged his shoulders to indicate that the dubious comfort of this guarantee had not been passed on to St Paul's. 'So we're left with two choices,' he summed up. 'Either we continue to advance Bijou the money it needs …'

The room fell ominously silent.

'Or?' Peel prompted him.

'Or we demand repayment of the existing advances.'

'Resulting in …? asked Peel, guessing the answer.

'Resulting in a creditors' liquidation of Bijou.'

Peel looked to Proctor for a comment.

'Does George know about this?' the latter enquired.

'Guy's going to tell him. George wants to talk to him about his St Paul's shares. He's given me formal notice that he's planning to sell 350,000.'

Peel wondered what sort of deal Ellison was striking with Guy. A creditors' liquidation of Bijou would hardly be part of it.

'Suppose we were to advance Bijou the money it needs, what security could it offer?' he asked.

'Security? Actual security?' Holmes answered one question with another.

'Well, we can't just keep advancing money without anything.'

'Loan notes?' suggested Holmes half-heartedly.

'Unsecured?' Peel shook his head. St Paul's must have better than Guy's promise to pay.

'I'll talk to Robert Lord,' Holmes offered. 'He's running this one for Guy. I don't expect Bijou has a whole lot to give, but he may be able to come up with a formula.'

'I hope to God he can. I don't imagine any of us would much like to be around if we had to go the other route,' remarked Proctor, the voice not so much of wisdom as of experience.

Proctor had matters other than asset-shifting on his mind. Not only had the cash flow from Britton Trust dried up; but by the time he met Valerie East a few days later, the tide was fast flowing the other way.

'Our financial position has become extremely critical,' he told her gravely. 'If you don't provide a cash injection, Laserbeam and Watson's will go under within weeks, if not days.'

Valerie East had a different agenda. Her investigations had told her Britton Trust's head office was costing over £5,000 a week.

'You'll have to cut central overheads to the bone,' she said. 'You can't afford to keep running as you are.'

'We're cutting into the fat all the time. I'm working on a reorganization. If we close the head office down and work out of our own place, just Guy, Danny, Nigel, me and our secretaries, we can reduce costs to £2,000 a week.'

'That's only scratching the surface,' she objected. 'Each of the businesses has a serious liquidity problem. We can't keep adding to the loan account.'

'Perhaps you could ask your directors whether Ulster & Cayman would be prepared to take an equity participation in return for a cash injection.'

'In what?' Valerie East pulled a face. 'In Britton Trust? In Magical Investments?' It was apparent that neither was her first choice as a sound stock.

'I only asked,' sighed Proctor. All they needed was one lucky break. Even if they had to go to the Shetland Islands to find it, he told himself optimistically.

'Don't try to put yourself into Larry's position, George,' Guy remonstrated with the managing director of St Paul's Property. 'He doesn't have enough of an interest in the company to be objective.'

George Ellison did not need to be told of the disadvantages of objectivity. He had a substantial interest in St Paul's Property. It was not just the value of his 350,000 shares that concerned him, albeit they were worth only a fraction of the £200,000 he had paid for them; it was the way he had financed the purchase. He had borrowed the money from Ludgate Guarantee. At the time Guy had promised he could repay the loan by selling half the shares when the price doubled. That prospect was now as unlikely as a Labour tax cut, and Guy's promise was worth as little as his shares.

'How objective are you asking me to be?' he enquired disingenuously.

'I want you to show your optimism,' replied Guy. 'If St Paul's can't buy its own shares, the least it can do is buy shares in a company that has a holding in it.'

'Such as Ludgate Investments,' Ellison guessed.

'Not directly. St Paul's already holds nearly thirty per cent of Ludgate. We'd have to make an announcement. I was thinking of Bijou,' Guy disclosed.

A stake in Guy's most private of corporate vehicles! There must be a catch.

'But doesn't Bijou own a lot of Ludgate?' Ellison asked hesitantly.

'Of course it does,' Guy said proudly, as if the holding were one he had built up as a prelude to a takeover bid rather than one he and his associates had acquired to salvage a failed rights issue.

'How much Bijou would we be buying?' Ellison asked warily. He had heard on the grapevine that Bijou had borrowed heavily to buy the Ludgate shares, and that Guy had promised it would hold a rights issue to raise the money to repay its debt; but he had his suspicions about that.

'I could spare, say, thirty per cent.'

'I don't suppose I could see a balance sheet?' Ellison asked without much hope.

To his surprise, Guy passed him a sheet of paper. The Ludgate shares had been included in the assets at cost. Ellison mentally calculated that at the current market price the drop in their value was greater than the figure on the bottom line. That meant Bijou was worth less than nothing.

'Everything works if St Paul's lends Bijou half a million,' Guy explained.

'What about security?' asked Ellison naively.

'Bijou will issue convertible loan notes. I'll still hold a large enough interest to want them repaid. If anything goes wrong, I'll be watered down and St Paul's will take control.'

Ellison understood. St Paul's would take control of Bijou if it proved to be worth less than nothing. It was time to return to his principal concern.

'About my St Paul's shares?' he asked. 'I owe Ludgate Guarantee a lot of bread for them.'

'If you were to offer them at a reasonable price, I don't see why Ludgate shouldn't make a further investment in St Paul's,' came the thoughtful response.

'At cost?' Ellison enquired hopefully.

'It seems a reasonable basis.'

'And the interest on my loan account?'

'You've been a loyal servant to the company.'

'St Paul's to lend Bijou half a million, you say?'

'That should do the trick.'

The flight to the Shetland Islands had been turbulent enough, but had been made worse by the pilot's skill in warning of each change in atmospheric pressure some time after its occurrence. Danny Gilbert stepped out of the aircraft's door in two minds as to whether to take the boat back. His face was hit by a blast of freezing air. He pulled the collar of his Crombie overcoat around his icy chin, but it made no noticeable difference. He negotiated the ladder-like steps to the runway and raced across it as fast as his freezing legs could carry him. He had forgotten his gloves and reckoned he gained the safety of the prefabricated terminal building of Lerwick's airport only a couple of seconds ahead of frostbite. Brian Proctor followed in his wake, preceded by a cloud of foul-smelling smoke.

'Where can I find a cab?' Danny asked the first uniform he saw.

'Ye cud try the taxi rank,' the helpful man offered. 'It's just oot the door.'

Danny braved a gust of arctic air. 'Can you take us to Watson's dock?' he shouted above the gale at the driver of a car drawn up outside the entrance.

'Ye can want an' I can try, but we'll no get onywhere yellin' at each ether,' the driver replied, eyeing him gravely. 'Ye may as well step inside the car and try agin.'

'It's on the west coast of the mainland,' Danny informed him when he and Proctor had gratefully taken their places on the strips of torn cloth that passed for the back seat. Proctor unfolded an Ordnance Survey map and pointed to a red circle where land met sea.

'I'm glad it's on the mainland. But ye'll find nae docks thereaboots,' said the taxi driver, shaking his grizzled head. 'They're on the ether side.' He did not specify a point of the compass, merely one of general principle.

Danny had not flown to the Shetland Islands to be told this. He was on a mission to verify the valuation of the wharf belonging to Watson's North Sea oil-rig servicing operation, not to argue about its geographical location. The company report showed that it supplied the rigs with mud for drills, and with food and water for the crews. It was shown in the Watson's balance sheet as a £1 million asset.

'I've seen the title deeds,' he insisted. 'This is where it is,' he pointed. 'At any rate, this is where we want to be taken.'

The taxi driver started his car and drove out of the tarmac field that stood for an airport. When they arrived at a T-junction, Danny saw a sign to the right for Lerwick. The car turned left. There was no name on the signpost to indicate the name of the town towards which they were heading, presumably because no town was there. They motored for about twenty minutes along a single-track road, passing the occasional half-surprised sheep and a lonely crofter's cottage but meeting no opposition. The road finally came to an end where the sea began and the car shuddered to a halt. The driver turned to the back seat as if to say that if this was how they wished to spend their money, it was all right by him.

The two colleagues opened their doors and got out. The howling of the gale was now matched by the shrieks of gulls and the lash of spuming waves on defenceless rocks. Above them the dark scudding clouds promised an early drenching. Before them they witnessed a scene less of devastation than of construction site anarchy. Sections of a former concrete wharf were strewn around in the churning sea like so much confetti, partly submerged, partly sticking up out of the water, with rusting iron spars emerging at random from their sides.

'Shit!' exclaimed Danny.

'You can say that again,' commented Proctor.

'Shit!' Danny obliged.

'They say a big English firm bought the land. Verra cheap,' said the driver when his fares had climbed back into the car, their cheeks tingling from the raw salt air. He nodded his head in approval of such high-minded thrift. 'I dinna ken why they decided to put their pontoon here, though. That yon's the Atlantic Ocean. The ether docks a' face the North Sea, sheltered frae the prevailing winds. Some days it gets a wee bit fresh aroon here,' he made his point with due gravity. 'Their pontoon sank in a storm,' he came to a doleful end, the nod turning into a shake of the head over the queerness of folk and the ways of the Lord.

46

'You might at least congratulate me,' Guy complained sulkily.

'Congratulations,' said George Ellison without enthusiasm. While he had not lost his job since the sale of his shares and the elimination of his debt, he could not help asking himself whether that would not have been the more favourable outcome. It was one thing to be managing director of St Paul's Property, but quite another to be its joint managing director. Especially when his newly appointed colleague in that office had just completed negotiating a vastly more generous remuneration package than his own.

'Don't forget I have a far more expensive lifestyle to fund than you,' Guy tried unsuccessfully to console him. 'Twenty grand a year isn't going to fill much of a hole in my budget, even if it is inflation-proofed.'

'I don't suppose I could have a five year contract too?' Ellison asked forlornly.

'I don't suppose so,' Guy agreed.

'Or six weeks holiday a year?'

'You couldn't afford it. Where would you go, on your salary?'

'Okay, okay; then how about a new car, like yours?'

'I can't have Yankee driving around in the sort of car you're used to, George. Do you want me to put him out on the street and take the tube to work?'

'Joking apart, Guy, I could do with some help with my mortgage too.'

'I need the flat for my job. What if Ulster & Cayman were to take my house from me? Surely you don't expect me to commute from the country or live in Brixton?'

Knowing nothing of Guy's ownership arrangements, Ellison capitulated. As he no longer had a financial interest in St Paul's Property, it made little difference to him if its revenues were being used to pay for his new colleague's lifestyle.

Guy turned the discussion to matters of business. 'If we're going to share executive responsibility, I suggest I handle the securities side and you carry on looking after the properties,' he said. 'Though as joint managing director you ought to be aware that I've sold my holding in Bijou.'

As the securities side of St Paul's Property consisted entirely of its holdings in Bijou and Ludgate, companies Guy had been managing, Ellison might be forgiven for feeling he had lost little by the change in his job description. However, the news Guy had given him sounded ominous. If he had sold his holding in Bijou, who might the new shareholder be? One who would take a less helpful view of the need to repay St Paul's the £500,000 it had advanced Bijou against its unsecured loan notes? He raised a querying eyebrow.

'To a company I have a majority holding in. Dominic Arthur's people have the details,' Guy completed his exposition.

As the London spring burgeoned under the pink and white of its cherry and apple blossoms, an architect was jailed for seven years for corrupting a council leader who was hit for six, the England football manager was fired, Jon Traill offered to buy back the Dustbin Trust and an industrial court fined the engineers' union, whose leaders announced that its members would strike rather than pay up. Amid the spate of retribution Guy reluctantly accepted an invitation to attend a May Day meeting at Ulster & Cayman to explain how he was going to meet his financial obligations. Accompanied by Larry Callaghan and Brian Proctor, he found Cassels flanked by a guard of unsmiling executives.

'We thought you might like to begin by updating us on progress at Britton Trust,' Cassels began.

On the grounds that asset sales had been negligible and the end of May was growing ever closer, Guy was short of encouraging material.

'Production at Laserbeam has increased by twenty per cent since we took over last December,' Proctor tried to help.

'How about sales?' asked Cassels, barely concealing his scorn.

'It's meant that it's been somewhat strapped for working capital to finance its growing inventory,' Proctor elaborated. Guessing from the numbing silence that he had failed to give the full picture, he added feebly, 'And work in progress.'

'Sales are not yet in line with production,' Callaghan gave it in his place.

'I'd like to introduce Mr Long,' said Cassels tersely, making it plain that while he had heard Callaghan well enough, it was time to move on and at a fresh pace. 'He will be taking over the management of the Britton Trust businesses with immediate effect, assisted by the gentlemen at his side. I take it that their appointment meets with your approval, Guy? And that when our loan repayment falls due at the end of the month, Mr Callaghan, Mr Holmes and Mr Proctor will stand down from the board?' Guy glumly nodded assent. 'Good. In which case the Ulster & Cayman board may give favourable consideration to not calling in its loan and to allowing the interest then due to be rolled up. On condition, it goes without saying, that Ludgate Investments takes a similar view.' He looked again at Guy and, receiving the signal he sought, went on, 'The main hope that the loans will ultimately be repaid rests with the Inland Revenue accepting the tax schemes you propose. In the meantime, I take it we're agreed that the less said in public, the better.'

'You mean, as far as the Ludgate Investments shareholders are concerned?' Callaghan asked uneasily.

'As far as any shareholders are concerned.'

'Are you sure that wouldn't be the wrong thing to do?' asked Callaghan. 'You don't think ...?'

'I don't want to think,' Cassels admitted. 'We have a potential disaster on our hands. We have a debt approaching £20 million on our books and collateral of less than £14 million – if we should ever manage to realise it. The last thing we want to do is jump up and down and proclaim to the whole wide world how clever we've all been.'

Suddenly Guy felt better. The threat of revelation was showing signs of becoming a powerful weapon.

'I hope you have your partners' agreement to keep the information to yourselves,' he said benignly. He was gratified to note that Cassels appeared to find his chair somewhat less comfortable.

It was the turn of the board of Ludgate Investments to discuss the status of its loan to Magical Investments.

'Dominic, do you have a progress report on your negotiations with Guy about the company's equity stake in Magical?' Larry Callaghan enquired from the chair.

Dominic Arthur hesitated. He had put a series of suggestions to Guy on how Ludgate might increase its holding to reflect the scale of its loan investment in Magical. He had yet to receive a reply.

'I'm hopeful of being able to report back in the not-too-distant future,' he tried without conviction.

Guy stared vacantly at the window. Did they not see that even if Magical were to double its equity capital that would add a mere £500 to its resources? To be meaningful, an investment must be either an increased loan, which he doubted the Ludgate board would approve, or a share subscription of such magnitude as to dilute his own holding to the verge of extinction.

'I'm waiting to hear from financial advisers,' he said in a neutral tone which gave no clue who these indolent people were or which party they were advising.

'Shall we move on, then, to the main item on the agenda?' Callaghan suggested: 'At the risk of repetition, the company has made an equity investment in Magical Investments of ...' he looked to Holmes for the amount.

'Two hundred pounds.'

'Two hundred pounds. And a loan investment of ...'

'Five million two hundred thousand pounds, plus accrued interest at eighteen per cent, currently some four hundred and ...'

'Quite so. For which the prospect of repayment is doubtful and security is negligible, due to the prior claim of another party. Which means that the company has lost £5 million out of a balance sheet of £7 million. The question is, are we obliged to send the shareholders a statement reporting the position? Dominic?'

Dominic Arthur lowered his horn-rimmed spectacles to the bridge of his nose to survey his audience. 'Company directors are under an obligation to advise their shareholders of any transaction in which they have a personal interest,' he stated.

'We told the shareholders about the loan in the circular,' Guy reminded him. 'And we told them we were directors of Magical.'

'But not that we had a financial interest,' Callaghan pointed out.

'And to report to them any matter that materially affects the financial status of the company,' Arthur continued, treating Callaghan's objection as of no more than peripheral significance.

'We've taken advice from Ulster & Cayman,' Guy told him. 'They advised that the directors are bound to consider the effect on the shareholders of publishing such a statement.'

'Ulster & Cayman are not this company's financial advisers,' Arthur pointed out.

'They gave an independent view.'

'Did they put it in writing?' asked Arthur.

'I took a handwritten note,' Callaghan told him. 'I must admit there's some merit in their view. What would the stock exchange say if we were to announce that we've lost three-quarters of our assets and can't get back a brass farthing until the secured creditor has been repaid? Britton Trust is probably in breach of its loan stock covenants too. It would have a queue of creditors from here to the Virgin Islands.'

Guy grew impatient. Callaghan was shooting at the wrong target. It was time to clinch the argument.

'Which directors attended the board meeting which authorised the loan?' he asked, his eyes fixed on Dominic Arthur.

Arthur reviewed his opinion. A company of which he was a director was in danger of telling its shareholders that all was not well, when its financial advisers had advised that it might benefit them not to have that information. If the shareholders' interests would be damaged by an admission of the truth, ought not the directors to keep the knowledge to themselves? Even if his colleagues' frailty – perhaps even his own, though less culpable, fallibility – were thereby concealed?

'On the other hand, directors do have an overriding fiduciary duty to act in the best interests of their shareholders,' he intoned the revised litany. 'Having taken the matter under advice, they could be sued for any damage that arose as a result of acting contrary to it.'

It was a persuasive argument. Anxious not to be seen pressing his view on his colleagues, Dominic Arthur abstained from voting until all other hands had been raised. Then he made the consensus unanimous.

'Lend Bijou another £200,000? You must be joking,' Proctor protested.'

Guy could hardly believe his ears. The biggest residential landlord in the land was about to become its biggest bankrupt, an industrial property developer was going belly-up, the company which had bought Farranwide Properties from Ulster & Cayman was short of £50 million, and Brian Proctor was bleating about petty cash. He, Danny and Larry had saved the Ludgate rights issue out of their own pockets. It had been understood that they would be repaid as soon as alternative finance was in place. When a lender had been found, he had offered Bijou as a home for the Ludgate shares and himself as a guarantor for the loan. Now he had talked Bijou's creditors into accepting £200,000 in lieu of £250,000, on the ground that a bird in the hand from Guy Magnus was worth a colony of moles down a mineshaft. But Bijou had no money to repay even £200,000. Uniquely among the Magnus stable of companies, St Paul's Property still had.

'I've never been more serious in my life, Brian,' Guy replied. 'You should consider yourselves lucky I negotiated a discount. If Bijou doesn't repay its creditors, the walls will come tumbling down, St Paul's will lose its loan notes, and who'll have egg on their faces then?'

Brian Proctor and Nigel Holmes looked at each other. Guy was right. They had put their names to the £500,000 loan St Paul's had made to Bijou. It had seemed the proper thing to do.

'What would we do about security?' Proctor asked.

Guy knew from the question that the game was almost won.

'The Ludgate shares were good enough for them,' he replied. 'Why should they be any less good for St Paul's?'

'Guy's right,' Holmes agreed, backing the man who paid his salary. 'Three million two at 14p comes to £450,000. That's more than enough cover for a loan of £200,000.'

'You'd better hold a board meeting to approve the loan,' Guy clinched the argument. 'Obviously I won't be voting, as I have an interest in Bijou, but I'm sure you'll do the right thing, Brian. Nigel, will you draw up the facility letter?'

Charles Cassels stared gloomily out of his office window and asked himself why he had allowed Callaghan and Guy's pair of clowns, as useless as they were to him nameless, to remain on Britton Trust's board for so long. As Valerie East had warned him, the company's accounts made horrible reading. In the six months prior to the bid from Magical Investments, Britton Trust had lost £1 million. Now its auditors had reported that Watson's financial controls were non-existent, Laserbeam's costing records were a shambles, and Britton Trust had to take an additional loss of £1,400,000. And Ulster & Cayman had become its effective owner at the very moment the government announced the continuation of its freeze on business rents. No one in his right mind would be buying property today.

Guy Magnus must pay up. He, Charles Cassels, would see to it that he did. And that his so-called partners paid up as well.

47

It was in the nature of Guy Magnus's business empire that while some board meetings were actually held, others were simply deemed to have been taken place. Nigel Holmes saw no need to call a formal meeting of the board of St Paul's Property to approve Bijou's new loan facility; he had merely to agree the matter with Brian Proctor and make an appropriate entry in the minute book. At the next meeting the minute would be read, or rather be deemed to have been read. Regardless of semantic niceties, Bijou would by then have drawn down the money and the minute would later be dated shortly before that important event.

The board minutes of Ludgate Investments and its subsidiaries show that one or other must have been in virtually constant session, either in fact or in spirit, during the first week in June, and not merely to clear the decks before Royal Ascot, the Lord's Test match, Henley and Wimbledon swung into their stride. To avoid upsetting Ulster & Cayman, the directors resolved not to claim the interest due from Magical Investments at the end of May. They also resolved to tell their shareholders of the loan; for Dominic Arthur was entitled to yet another change of mind, recognising that *Private Eye* had already told them what *The Times* had not. If Ludgate's shareholders were happy to learn that their forty-three per cent stake in Magical Investments had cost only £215 – cheap at the price compared with their loan of £5,200,000 – they said nothing. No doubt they were taken aback by their chairman's statement that a long term plan had been evolved for the management of Britton Trust, that their company's loan facility to Magical Investments had been extended, and that even without taking into account the value of its stake in Magical, Ludgate's net worth was not far short of 14p per share.

Whether or not drafting this statement required the Ludgate board to meet, there can be no doubt that on the same date the Magical Investments board did. How else could Danny Gilbert have refused to approve the minutes of the meeting of 1st April?

'You can't put my name down as having attended a meeting that never took place,' he objected. 'April Fool's Day ends at noon.'

Danny's intransigence was unfortunate, for Larry Callaghan had asked for the minute of his resignation from the Magical Investments board to be backdated to that day. Guy obliged by crossing Danny's name off the minutes and substituting that of Kenneth Peel. This was timely, for Peel was also about to resign. Britton Trust's loan stockholders were in nuclear fission over a six-month extension to the company's accounting period and the fact that Magical Investments had filed no accounts since its incorporation, and Peel no longer wished to be under the fallout. He sold his shares to Ludgate for the same £25 he had paid for them, and the board accepted his resignation at a meeting attended by Danny Gilbert – or so the minutes were subsequently to record.

But before that date Danny had left the Ludgate Circus for the last time, in circumstances so memorable that he could not have mistaken the timing. As he emerged from the toilet one morning Guy's personal lawyer was waiting for him.

'For God's sake, can't a man even take a crap in peace?' Danny demanded.

'Not any longer in this building, you can't,' replied Robert Lord, taking his arm in a vice-like grip. 'Guy wants me to see you off the premises personally, and that's what I'm going to do.'

'I want my P45 before I go,' Danny insisted.

'We'll send it on.'

'I'm entitled to my personal files.'

'Put them on top of your desk. I'll check them through, and if they have nothing to do with the business I'll post them to you with your P45.'

'I'm not going anywhere until Guy meets his obligation to buy my St Paul's shares back from me. He gave me a put option at the price I paid: 50p. It's a legally binding contract.'

'If he pays you, you'll only have to pass the money on to Ulster & Cayman.' Lord tightened his grip on Danny's upper arm and marched him down the corridor and past the kitchen door.

'You might at least let me say goodbye to Fiona.' The latest occupant of the kitchen had gone as far as to allow Danny to clasp her buttocks while his tongue was down her throat, but not so far as to give him her telephone number.

'You'll have to write her a thank you letter.'

Danny gave up. He had lost his job. He had lost his money. He had lost his innocence. He hadn't even gained a cook. And he was still barely twenty-two years old.

Charles Cassels scratched his head as he struggled to follow the trail of transactions set out in Valerie East's report, while its author sat silently at his side.

'Kindly explain these dealings to me, Guy,' Cassels demanded, passing the report over the table. It was galling for an experienced merchant banker to have to admit to himself, let alone to his colleague or his visitor, that he was confused.

'Which dealings? Oh, those.' Guy was plainly bored. 'Just a tidying-up exercise.'

'What about the transfers of shares in St Paul's Property?'

'There's nothing substantive in them. It's purely a reorganisation of my affairs, to provide dealing liquidity. I don't know why you bother.'

'We bother because of your personal guarantee, Guy. You hold 2 million shares in St Paul's Property. We're entitled to know what the company is up to, in case we have to call them in.' Cassels was growing impatient. 'What's on earth's going on?'

'Going on? How should I know? St Paul's Property is a private company. It has its own board of directors.'

'Of which you are one ...'

'Only appointed a few weeks ago ...'

'And the principal shareholder.'

'A minority shareholder. I don't have control.'

'Look here, Guy, I don't want things to get out of hand, but you're making life extremely difficult for me with my colleagues,' said Cassels, trying to hide his exasperation. 'We'd rather not be put in a position where we have to bankrupt you, with all the costs and complications that would involve, but if you flatly refuse to cooperate with us we'll have no alternative.'

'I am cooperating with you, Charles. I'm doing my best to make some money so I can repay you in full, but you won't let me have the working capital I need to keep dealing. That's why I have to manoeuvre funds from one pocket to the other.'

'Our job is to mitigate our losses as far as we can, not to compound them. The Britton Trust deal has gone wrong enough already. We're not in the business of throwing good money after bad.'

Guy had no answer to that. 'Tell me what you want me to do and I'll do it,' he said humbly.

'You keep promising to let us have a detailed up-to-date statement of your affairs, but it never comes. Time's running out, Guy.'

'But I've told you what I have. A house, a few pictures, my cars, the shares in St Paul's Property and a bill from the Inspector of Taxes. If the scheme I've entered into to offset my losses works, he won't get a bean. But if it doesn't ...'

'He gets it all, and we get nothing,' Cassels finished for him. 'It's not good enough, Guy. I need to know the full picture – how much each asset is worth and what the tax liability may come to. Let's start with your house in the country.'

'Fifty to sixty thousand?' Guy tried, more question than statement.

'You put it down before at a hundred thousand.'

'The market for second homes has fallen flat. Seventy-five at best.'

'What about your art collection?'

'It's just a few pictures I happened to buy.'

'We want every single one listed, with a certified valuation.'

'That would cost me one per cent. What's the point of wasting £5,000?'

Cassels was quick at the arithmetic: 'The statement of affairs you gave us last January said they were worth three-quarters of a million, not half a million.'

'Six hundred thousand at most in this market.'

'The cars must be down to £20,000,' said Cassels sarcastically.

'That's the trouble with investing in things you love,' Guy agreed. 'If only I'd stuck to buying and selling shares.'

'And what will your tax bill amount to if your scheme fails?'

'Oh, at least £500,000.' As relaxed about his liability as he was about his assets, Guy forgot to increase it and applied a matching discount instead.

'This is no joke, Guy. I want a proper up-to-date statement of your affairs, certified by your accountant, in Valerie's hands within the next seven days or we're going to have to reconsider our whole position.'

'Is that a threat?'

'Take it in whatever way you wish.'

'Are your partners in agreement with your approach?'

'My partners?' enquired Cassels. 'Oh, you mean my boardroom colleagues? I don't imagine Mr Dervish or Mr de Deyler will be much bothered either way. They've notified the board of their intention to resign their positions with the bank and to devote their future energies to their family and charitable affairs. I think that was how they expressed it.'

So what? thought Guy. Their resignation was as good as an admission of guilt. The threat of revelation was assuming nuclear proportions.

'I have to say I'm extremely upset,' Larry Callaghan told Valerie East the following afternoon. He had agreed with Guy that as his accountant he would speak first. Guy's solicitor, seated on his left, would be held in reserve. Guy, on his right, was to play aggrieved and dumb. Very, very dumb.

'I'm sorry to hear that,' she replied perfunctorily. 'Might I know why?'

'Mr Magnus tells me that Mr Cassels expressed his dissatisfaction yesterday over the management of Ludgate Investments and St Paul's Property, which are none of his affair. He then threatened to make a formal demand on Magical Investments, a wholly separate entity, and to put it into liquidation. I presume he would then call Mr Magnus's guarantee and force him into bankruptcy.'

If Callaghan was angling for a denial, he was due for a disappointment. Valerie East had no intention of falling for that one. She took a more sceptical view of the affair than her directors. Whichever way you sliced the loaf, Guy Magnus owed Ulster & Cayman a lot of bread. He must be made to repay it.

'Those are among the options open to us,' she confirmed.

'Not if we're to believe the assurance given to us by Mr Cassels,' Callaghan objected. 'He stated categorically that he would not bankrupt my client.'

'On the clear understanding that Mr Magnus gave us his full cooperation and that our position was not prejudiced in any way,' she corrected him. 'In any case, the purpose of yesterday's meeting was to clarify the situation regarding the transfers of shares in Ludgate and St Paul's. Mr Magnus's personal position came up later. Mr Cassels simply wished to make it clear that the time for prevarication was over. We want a clear and complete statement of Mr Magnus's affairs so we can assess our position and decide on a course of action.'

'I'm not sure that …' Callaghan began.

'I don't want there to be any misunderstanding,' she told him bluntly.

Callaghan needed to call on reinforcements. He turned to the solicitor on his left for a view.

'As a lawyer, I cannot advise my client to disclose all his personal affairs,' the latter obliged.

'In that case you'll leave us with no option but to take formal action under his personal guarantee,' responded the banker.

Guy had used his chosen silence to think. Valerie East was living proof of his credo that while the fools of the City rose to the top like cream, the brains sank like sodden tea-leaves. It had taken four full-size idiots to lose Ulster & Cayman £20 million, but if he was not careful one tough-minded middle-ranking female executive might win back a sizeable part of it at his expense. He was not about to underestimate Valerie East's tenacity simply because she was an attractive young woman. He gave a whispered instruction to Larry Callaghan.

'On the other hand ...' Callaghan said slowly, in a tone mixing wisdom with compromise, 'as an accountant, I think it perfectly reasonable for a bank to be provided with the fullest possible information on the assets and liabilities of its customers.'

'We'll give you seven days,' she stated uncompromisingly.

'Fourteen, please, if you will bear with us. My assistant, who deals with the detail of Mr Magnus's affairs, is on leave.' Lest he appear over-decisive, Callaghan put in a further proviso: 'It's understood of course that this is subject to us having an up-to-date position on St Paul's Property?'

Valerie East frowned. Was Callaghan prevaricating? 'What has St Paul's to do with Mr Magnus's personal statement of affairs?' she asked.

'If we don't know how much the company is worth, how are we supposed to value his shares?'

'Put in your best estimate,' she suggested.

Callaghan turned uncomfortably to Guy for further instructions.

'What if we say 25p?' he suggested when he received them.

'Why not? We can always adjust the figure later.'

'We'll have the management accounts for March out by the end of June. You'll be pleased to know that the company has realised enough cash to ensure its profitable survival.'

As if the issue were ever in doubt, thought East. 'I shall look forward to receiving a copy,' she said.

Callaghan had one more card to play. 'I'm sure you don't need me to tell you the consequence of putting Magical Investments into liquidation,' he said deliberately. He paused. 'I trust you appreciate the position on the tax losses,' he went on when he saw he had gained the banker's full attention. 'You realise they could be worth up to £1,500,000?'

'If we ever generate the profits to absorb them,' she pointed out.

'Tax losses can be sold.'

'At a discount. Don't worry, Mr Callaghan, my directors are fully aware of the position. I'm sure they'll take it into account when they consider their options. Which they will do just as soon as they have a comprehensive and satisfactory statement of affairs from Mr Magnus. By the end of the month, you say.'

As he rose to leave, Guy passed close to Valerie East. 'Lunch, Val?' he whispered in her ear. 'The Savoy? We need to talk this through one on one. I'm sure we can find a solution together.'

'Miss East to you, Mr Magnus,' replied the banker severely. 'And I don't lunch.'

Two weeks later Valerie East stared in disbelief at Callaghan's letter. Marked strictly personal and confidential, its contents, it stated, were not to be copied, nor revealed to anyone in the bank without the prior written consent of Guy Magnus. Not to Cassels, nor to his colleague Stephen Cornelius, nor even to Sir Anthony Winchester MP. She telephoned its author.

'Why bother to send it to me if I can't show it to anyone?' she asked impatiently. 'It's no use at all on those terms. Apart from that, it says you're unable to give an opinion on the valuations of your client's assets. I may as well send it straight back and recommend my directors to appoint a liquidator this very afternoon.'

There was a long silence as Callaghan absorbed the message.

'I was afraid you might take that view,' he said eventually.

'A fortnight ago you told us the assets of St Paul's Property were mostly in cash and its shares were worth 25p,' she held on to the initiative. 'Your letter says they're only worth 15p.'

'That's Guy Magnus's best estimate. I can only go on what he tells me.'

'So the man worth £650,000 is suddenly only worth £250,000? Has the pound in his pocket devalued so far in two weeks?'

'That's what he says.'

'We won't wear it, Mr Callaghan. He'd better become rich again as quickly as he became poor, or he may find himself sleeping under Waterloo Bridge with all the other paupers.'

'I'll pass on the message. I don't suppose you want to show my letter to your colleagues, then?'

'In the strictest of confidence Mr Callaghan, I already did. I take it you're prepared to give me your personal assurance you won't pass that information on to your client?'

As she put down the telephone, Valerie East slowly shook her head. She made a written record of the conversation and dictated a note of her recommendations to her secretary. She sent Charles Cassels a typed copy.

A week later she was summoned to the chairman's office. 'Very well done, Valerie. Very sound indeed, your recommendations,' Sir Anthony Winchester congratulated her. 'Though I fear we may want to postpone acting on them for the time being. Other considerations,' he added enigmatically. If Ulster & Cayman was about to issue a statement that it would be making a provision of £17 million against bad debts due to the difficult financial climate, it would hardly be politic to take a step that would implicitly attribute this action to a single transaction. After all, they had just announced the resignations of Sam Dervish and Sidney de Deyler and the sale of their shares in the merchant bank. And the Chief Whip had said the Leader of the Party had no desire for further ammunition to be handed to the other side while the political situation remained on a knife-edge.

Wisdom dictated that the dust be allowed to settle. Later they would look again.

48

Outside there was an eerie silence. In the real world, if the House of Commons can be so described, Sir Anthony Winchester MP's youngest fellow-member lost as much in a Canadian share deal as the fortune Guy Magnus admitted to; the world of literary fiction was to be the winner or the loser, depending on the taste of the reader. Across the seas the quasi-fictional events surrounding the presidency of the United States approached their climax. The equally capricious *FT* Share Index fell to a succession of lows; by mid-August it was below 200. But none of this bothered Guy.

Inside his own world there was also little to discomfort him. The Ludgate Circus was at peace. When Bijou drew down £250,000 from St Paul's against the facility of £200,000 authorised by the board, there was no Ken Peel or Danny Gilbert to protest. When Ulster & Cayman injected £2 million into Britton Trust to keep it afloat, no one from the bank troubled Guy for his view. So he bought a new Bentley, filled its capacious boot and took a circuitous route to the Côte d'Azur.

Bad news awaited him. Harry Griffin apologised profusely, but the *Gay Dog* was no longer at his beck and call. Casey Long, the manager appointed by Ulster & Cayman to supervise the disposal of Britton Trust's assets, had been making enquiries about the cabin cruiser. On being told it was being used to facilitate communications between the south of France and the Algarve, he had instructed that it be taken out of the water and put on the market. Moreover, an aggrieved Harry had been asked to settle his expense account with Britton Trust. It was insinuated that his bills for flowers, shirts and a trip to Deauville had in some unexplained sense not been authorised.

'Everyone knew that was how I drew my salary after I left England. What do they expect me to do with my Diners Club bill? Pay it myself?' Harry complained to Guy as they scoffed lobster at L'Oasis in La Napoule.

Guy was not of a mind to sympathise. 'Your turn, Harry,' he said when the bill was presented. 'I had to pay for your shares. You must have had the best part of a million from me.'

It was apparent to Harry that Guy had forgotten their bet. There was no point reminding him of it. That they were not in Paris, and that, exceptional though its cuisine was, L'Oasis was not Maxim's, was of no significance. There were more compelling reasons. Harry had lost enough on Universal Credit to hurt, though not enough to offset his profit on Britton Trust. And he had gone non-resident too late to avoid being taxed on last year's capital gains. So, having failed by a whisker to show his million at the moment of settlement, he had to make the last £250,000 all over again. He had then treated each fall in the stock market as a buying opportunity. In consequence he had come to envy those who, like Guy, had nothing to put on the table.

'My turn,' Harry agreed.

On his return home at the end of August, Guy was not surprised to be told that Charles Cassels wished to renew his acquaintance. The phoney war was coming to an end. His secretary told Cassels he was fully engaged for a month. On hearing the response, she managed to find an early cancellation in Guy's diary. At the appointed hour Guy was shown into Cassels's office by a secretary whose face seemed familiar.

Sharon avoided Guy's eye. She had every reason to do so. For having at last achieved her heart's desire, a position with a willing partner, she had agreed to accompany her new boss on a business trip to New York. During the flight Cassels had learnt more about Harry Griffin and his friendship with Guy Magnus than any former confidential secretary had a right to disclose. Within minutes of their arrival at the St Regis Hotel he had raped his travelling companion – or would have done had Sharon not proved so willing an accomplice that she prevented the crime. To her chagrin, the transgression had not been repeated after their return to London. Such are the rewards and the penalties of conducting the pillow-talk before the disillusionment.

'My colleagues and I are not prepared to wait any longer,' Cassels told Guy without observing the customary courtesies. 'We've taken our medicine in public; now we want our pound of flesh from you.'

'If I had £17 million in the bank, it would be yours, Charles, you know it would,' said Guy agreeably; 'but I haven't. The tax people won't accept my capital losses and Danny Gilbert's suing me over a put option he says I gave him. He's a fool: he knows I can't pay even if he wins. If he pursues his sordid vendetta, it's only going to line the pockets of his lawyers.'

Cassels had been finding it as difficult to reach a settlement with Danny Gilbert as with Guy, not because Danny was unready or unwilling, but because he was unable. The value of his shares in St Paul's Property had been diminishing daily. At the current price of 10p, they were worth £50,000. But he had borrowed to buy them, and if that was all he could obtain for them, his fortune would be reduced to a few thousand pounds. When Cassels refused to accept this as a basis for releasing his guarantee, Danny had issued a writ requiring Guy to meet his obligation to buy the shares back at 50p so he could settle with Ulster & Cayman at £200,000 and walk away a whole man. Cassels knew that getting such a sum from Danny Gilbert would be a thousand times easier than squeezing a drop of blood from Guy Magnus; but if he could get nothing out of Guy, would Danny's lawyers fare any better?

'You should settle with Gilbert,' he tried without conviction.

'And pay him money I owe you?'

'He has his option in writing. He won't drop his suit, and he'll win.'

'It won't pay him to pursue it.' Guy outflanked him. 'He'll only have to pass whatever he gets from me on to you.'

The trouble with Guy Magnus, Cassels knew, was that he had worked it all out and was already two steps ahead. He made a final attempt.

'If I can do anything to help settle your differences ...'

'Well, I might be able to find him a buyer at 10p – I'm not saying I can – but if I did, it would have to be on the basis that he drops his claim. Can I rely on you to persuade him that would be in his best interest?'

'I won't commit myself now, but I'll give it serious thought,' Cassels responded carefully. 'Now, to return to your own position. We don't want to behave unreasonably, but your statement of affairs shows a net position of a quarter of a million. It's a pittance, considering the scale of our losses, but I might be prepared to recommend it to my colleagues as a basis for settlement. Anything less and we'll have no alternative but to pursue our rights under your personal guarantee.'

'I can't write you a cheque for £250,000, Charles. My assets aren't liquid. Anyway, if you do put me into bankruptcy, the tax man will come first and you'll get bugger-all.'

'And you'll never be allowed to deal again. You're simply going to have to find ways and means of raising the money. What about the house in the country?'

'I've been meaning to tell you. It isn't mine. The deeds are in Melvin Cecil's name. The house in Chelsea's mine, but as you know it's mortgaged.'

Cassels drew a deep breath. If what Guy told him was true, it was the reverse of what he had previously said. But it would be too late to do anything about it. As the bank had not called on his guarantee, he could not be accused of fraudulently disposing of his assets while knowing he was insolvent.

'Sell your St Paul's shares,' he tried. 'At 10p they'd realise £200,000.'

'If I can find a buyer. Two million is a lot of shares to sell.'

'You have your pictures. You could sell them.'

Guy felt a chill run down his spine. His collection of contemporary British art was on the way to becoming the most outstanding in the land in private hands. It was his duty to preserve it, for himself, perhaps even for the nation. He must take care with what he said.

'I've already taken steps in that direction, but it'll take time,' he said truthfully.

'We must have them as security until they've been sold,' Cassels insisted, his sixth sense warning him to be watchful.

'Don't worry: my house is very well protected,' Guy assured him. 'I've had the windows barred and the best alarm system fitted.'

'If we allow them to remain where they are,' Cassels gave an inch to keep a yard. 'We must have a comprehensive schedule and a bar on movement other than on consignment to an approved dealer. Even then we must be kept advised.'

'Nothing will be removed from where it is at present until I've met my obligation to you,' Guy promised.

'We must have our interest registered with the selling agents and all proceeds set against your account until the quarter of a million has been reached.'

Guy saw he must avoid such a commitment if he was to remain in control.

'Unless I manage to raise the cash first,' he made the qualification.

'That goes without saying. I have to make the proviso that this is all entirely unofficial and subject to the formal approval of my colleagues. And we'll need to talk to Danny Gilbert again, to complete the picture.'

'When you've done so, would you put it in writing so I can have my solicitor look it over?' Guy asked.

'Of course I will,' Cassels confirmed, relieved to have reached so close to agreement without serious argument. 'I'm sure we'll be able to sort everything out amicably,' he added. 'So much better than having to take unpleasant steps.'

That, thought Guy, was undeniable. As he rose to leave he noticed a letter awaiting signature on Cassels's desk. Sam Dervish and Sidney de Deyler's names had been blanked out from the list of directors on the Ulster & Cayman letterhead. They had been spared a mention during the meeting too, he recalled.

As Sharon showed him out, Guy recalled where he had seen her before. He needed to keep tabs on how Cassels was thinking.

'You're looking fabulous, Sharon. Sure you haven't done something with your hair?' he asked. 'Tell you what: I happen to be in the market for a secretary who's more than just a pretty brain. Let's slip over to the Savoy and have a bite of lunch in the restaurant, for old times' sake.'

Sharon considered her duty to her employer. She also took account of her disillusionment. She thought too about the Savoy Restaurant.

'I'm due an afternoon off,' she said. 'Take me to Walton's.'

'What difference does it make what price you get from Magnus?' asked Valerie East. 'You'll have to pay it over to us anyway.'

Danny Gilbert's lawyer knew that the banker was passing on a message from her masters. It was his task to turn it into a cast-iron agreement.

'Are you saying that the amount you'll settle for depends on the amount my client gets for his shares in St Paul's Property?' he asked.

'You could say it's a fair bet,' she conceded.

'So if I sue and get 50p, you'll want a quarter of a million; but if we agree to settle for 10p, you'll accept £50,000?'

'You've got the message.'

'Magnus must be in trouble,' remarked Danny's lawyer.

Cassels had not fallen for Guy's ruse. *Your pictures will be placed on deposit with us. We will realise them together with you until £250,000 has been raised*, he had written. Guy stroked his Henry Moore sculpture abstractedly. He looked round his bare walls. Ulster & Cayman could no longer lay their hands on so much as a loose flake of impasto. Now he must find a way to sell his shares in St Paul's Property – if such an animal as a buyer for them existed.

At least the message had got home to Danny Gilbert. Danny had ignored the advice to take steps to protect himself, silly boy. He had agreed to pay over the entire sale proceeds of his St Paul's shares to Ulster & Cayman, so it made no difference how much or how little he was paid for them. It made no difference to his own position how much he paid Danny either, because of the steps he had taken. So it was worth getting the burden of Danny off his back, wasn't it?

Guy decided to wait a week before replying to Cassels. Then he would write that there was a strong argument for saying he had been released from his obligations. He would let him sweat on that. Then, when Cassels put it to him, as he undoubtedly would, that they ought to resolve the matter decently as between men of honour, the merry-go-round of negotiations could begin again.

He was in no hurry.

49

Sir Anthony Winchester MP was furious. He had been upset when Labour won the year's second general election, and irritated when Universal Credit had showed no signs of recovery as a result of the lifeboat's attempts at resuscitation; but that his directors had failed to nail Guy Magnus to the mast made him incandescent with rage. With his anger came loss of memory, for now that the political future of the country had been settled and neither the Leader nor the Chief Whip was showing any interest in how he solved the bank's financial problems, the "other considerations" of which he had spoken to Valerie East no longer applied.

With loss of memory came impatience. 'I can't imagine what can have persuaded you to ignore Miss East's recommendations. These pictures: what exactly are they, Valerie?' he demanded.

'We can't tell from the statement of wealth, Sir Anthony; but if they were worth £750,000 last February, they must be pretty special.'

'Why haven't we got hold of them, then?'

'Magnus gave me his absolute assurance they were safe where they were and wouldn't be moved,' said Charles Cassels. 'I took the view he was taking a frank and realistic approach to his problems. I didn't see the point of getting his back up by removing them from his walls while he was still co-operating with us.'

Cassels looked down at the floor. Valerie East stared up at the ceiling. Sir Anthony had no doubt why.

'When you've got a man by the balls, you don't let go to get a better grip,' he instructed, applying the Chief Whip's political philosophy to the world of banking. Valerie East felt the blood rush to her face. She hoped that in this case her chairman was being more figurative than literal.

'We must take Magnus for every penny he's got,' said Cassels, showing his appreciation both of the lesson and of the need to please his chairman.

'You've got the message,' said Sir Anthony. 'May I suggest you do so before he takes a leaf out of that crook Salmon's book and does a runner to California?'

Guy was slower to learn, or perhaps less willing. He, and they, had settled with Danny Gilbert. The experience had hurt his ego.

'I may have £50,000 less to give you, but you have the same £50,000 in cash from Danny. You should be over the moon. You've swapped a promise for cash,' he told Charles Cassels at their next meeting.

'Let's talk about you, Guy, not about Danny,' Cassels riposted. Ulster & Cayman had no intention of being the second bank to negotiate a £250,000 debt down to £200,000. 'We're not prepared to wait any longer for our money. We want you to deliver your paintings to us.'

'I'm sorry I'm no longer in a position to deal with them,' Guy said candidly.

'What do you mean?'

'Exactly what I say. All I have left is my 2 million shares in St Paul's Property. They're worth £200,000. That's all I have to offer you.'

'But you gave me an assurance about your paintings,' said Cassels, going pale.

'Not to move them,' Guy agreed. 'Which I've kept.'

'Where exactly are they?' Cassels asked hopefully but in vain.

'Exactly? They're in exactly the same place they were when we last spoke. As I told you, they're extremely well-protected.'

'This is monstrous, Guy.' It was Cassels's turn to be angry and impatient. When he had told Sir Anthony of Guy's frank and realistic approach to his problems, he had overestimated his frankness and underestimated his grasp of reality.

'Don't worry, Charles; my St Paul's shares should be good for 200 grand.'

'If the market will pay 10p a share for them.'

'Well, they're all I can give you. You'd better make your mind up whether you want them or not. A lot of starving Chinese children would be only too happy to be given the chance to own 2 million shares in a public property company.'

'We'll have to take a charge on the shares and hold the certificates until they're sold and your debt has been fully discharged. I'm not going to have you turning round and telling me they're held in a very safe vault.'

'Let's get one thing clear, Charles,' Guy took back the initiative. 'I don't want there to be any misunderstanding. When I say I'll give you the proceeds of 2 million St Paul's to meet an agreed liability of £200,000, that's the absolute maximum. If I get less than 10p for the shares, you'll have to accept it. You see,' he pleaded, 'I have literally nothing else to give.'

Every last penny, Sir Anthony had insisted. And he would have it. But Cassels knew he must still tread carefully. Guy Magnus would not think twice about selling shares cheap if he stood to lose nothing by doing so.

'We must have the last word on whether an offer for them is accepted,' he said.

'That's fair enough. Get your lawyers to send mine a draft agreement,' said Guy, offering Cassels his hand. 'I won't let you down, Charles; you know that.'

It was hardly his fault, Guy told himself, that the lawyers were so dilatory. Each time his solicitor sent him the draft agreement he would find an obvious error, and back to the other side's lawyers the document would have to go. Another couple of weeks would pass while they prepared a further draft and sent it to his lawyers, when the whole time-consuming process would start again.

Guy spent the intervals between draft agreements preparing for the future. When the general election went the wrong way, he had placed a wager on who would lead the Tories into the next one. The knives would be out for Edward Heath. He rather fancied the odds against Willie Whitelaw, and took them. Not for him the gamble on a 50/1 outsider: the Tory Party would no more pick a woman named Maggie as its leader than Ludgate would recover its loan from a company named Magical.

For that was his next task: the Ludgate board must resolve to write off the loan. Unusually, he found himself surprised; for Callaghan, Holmes and Arthur were all content to agree to this, though on differing grounds: Callaghan, that a possible former conflict of interest required him to leave the decision to others; Holmes, that Guy was present; and Arthur, that, as he understood it, the matter was a commercial rather than a legal one, was it not?

The delay in agreeing the terms of Guy's release from his personal guarantee coincided with a continued fall in share prices. For all he had sworn to Cassels that he would not let him down, he could not but feel that *force majeure* had intervened and they must face its music together, perhaps in the coming year if the financial situation improved and the financial markets took heart.

Cassels had a different timetable in mind. The disappearance of Lord

Lucan after the discovery of the body of his children's nanny was mirrored when a former Labour minister went absent without leave after a dawn swim in Florida. The latter event occurred on the same day *The Times*, referring to Jonathan Traill's latest venture, commented that the temptation was to say thank you and wave goodbye. Cassels knew Sir Anthony would regard him as careless in the extreme to fall for a third vanishing trick, so when the terms of the agreement had not been finalised by the end of November, he instructed his lawyers to issue a fourteen day ultimatum.

Guy was not to be pressurised. He proposed that they meet on the fifteenth day to talk over their differences.

'The problem's more obvious than the answer,' he explained when he and Larry Callaghan sat down with Charles Cassels and Valerie East for what turned out to be the last time. 'However hard we've tried, it's proved impossible to sell my St Paul's shares at 10p.'

'What can you get for them?' asked Cassels, growing uneasy.

'With the Index heading for one-fifty? I suppose they have a theoretical value of about 5p.'

'Theoretical?' Cassels prepared himself for the worst.

'There's simply no market for them.'

'What's the net asset value of the company – per share?'

'Thirty-two pence,' Callaghan provided the information.

'That's after the assets have been written down to rock-bottom,' Guy added. 'As you must have learnt by now, we always prefer to take a conservative view.'

'If your shares aren't going to fetch more than £100,000, where are you going to find the balance?'

'I've told you, I can't. I'm going to have to ask you to reconsider the terms of my release.'

'What do you have in mind?' Cassels asked before he had time to think.

'Suppose we were to start with a notional figure of £100,000 ...' Guy began, alert to his opponent's weakness.

'I've told you we won't take less than £200,000,' Cassels tried to recover the ground that had already slipped from under his feet.

'But £100,000 is the most I can offer,' insisted Guy.

'We've done the best we can. Compared with what we've lost, it's a more than generous settlement. You must have other assets you can sell.'

Guy sensed the need to offer, if not something more, at least something else. His thoughts went to the only immovable object he still possessed. Ulster & Cayman couldn't possibly want that. However, it was worth a shot.

'I do own a sculpture,' he made the gratuitous admission.

'Worth?'

'It's been valued at £20,000. It's a Henry Moore.' Guy could have gone further and asked whether, if a work of art was worth less than £20,000, Cassels thought he would touch it, but preferred the course of discretion.

Cassels had reached the point where he was prepared to clutch at any straw Guy offered. Moreover, it seemed realistic to assume that any sculpture by Henry Moore was worth more than the paper of one of Guy Magnus's corporate vehicles.

'That still leaves us £180,000 short,' he commented.

'I've been thinking about my St Paul's shares. If you were to take them in lieu of my liability and hold them, instead of trying to sell them on the open market ...'

Cassels rejected the suggestion after a moment's thought. 'There's a difficulty in that,' he said. 'If we own more than ten per cent of a company's stock, we have to make an announcement to the stock exchange.'

'Why should that be a problem?' Guy probed this new weakness.

'To be frank, we can do without the publicity,' Cassels admitted.

Larry Callaghan had been dividing his time between listening intently and calculating rapidly. He whispered into Guy's ear.

'Let me see if I can help you,' Guy adopted a conciliatory tone. 'Suppose I were to sell you only 800,000 of my St Paul's shares.'

'What would be the advantage of that?' Cassels could see the disadvantage: it would be hard to persuade Sir Anthony that any asset should be left in Guy's hands.

'It's less than ten per cent of the company, so you won't have to announce it. Also, it will be easier to sell than twenty-five per cent. And if I keep the balance, it will give me the incentive to make money for us both.'

'But we don't want to make money with you any more, Guy. We've already been through that learning experience. What would we want another round for?'

'I'm simply pointing out that I'd have just as much interest as you in making the shares worth more.'

'And if we don't achieve your valuation?'

'Ten pence each will give you £80,000,' Guy ignored the objection. 'Plus you would have the Henry Moore at a valuation of £20,000,' he said. He consulted Callaghan briefly and then took the high ground. 'If there's a shortfall, I shall accept the moral responsibility for making up the difference.'

An audible snort escaped from Valerie East. Cassels ignored it. Directors did not display personal feelings. They negotiated with grace. If they did not like what they heard, they sidestepped politely and proceeded coolly to the next point.

'The bank has heard what you say and reserves its position,' he made the formal pronouncement. 'I shall consult with my colleagues and come back to you in writing.' He stood to shake Guy's hand for the last time.

Callaghan frowned. Cassels had found a polite way to reject compromise.

Valerie East scowled. Her boss had found a convenient way to prevaricate.

Guy smiled inwardly. His proposal had not been turned down outright. It was the only one left on the table.

50

Harry Griffin relaxed contentedly in the back of the cab as it made its way in fits and starts through the lunch-time traffic of the 16ᵗʰ *arrondissement*. If he had any regret, it was that Guy wasn't paying the fare. Nevertheless, lunch at Maxim's was in the bag. It was his suggestion, though he had taken care not to use the word "invitation": unfinished business, he had replied enigmatically when Guy had asked whether he had a specific purpose in mind.

Harry patted his briefcase, whose contents had arrived in the morning post. He gazed out of the cab window at the blossoming chestnut trees which lined the avenue Victor Hugo; but he saw none of them. Instead, his reflections took him back to the summer's day he and Guy had shared almost two years ago.

The Board of Trade Inspectors had never broken his story, though God knew they had pressed him long and hard. Had they managed to subpoena the mosquito on the deck of the *Gay Dog*, he told himself, it would have told them that it all began like this.

'Got your Diners Club card handy, Harry? You owe me lunch. Twelve months, we agreed, didn't we?' Guy had chortled merrily that scorching late June morning in 1973, as he shoved his airmail edition of *The Times* under Harry's nose and pointed to the front page report that Elizabeth Taylor and Richard Burton had announced their separation. They had, they explained, loved each other too much. The moment Guy had read of the gift he had made the bet with Harry. Now it was time for the pay-off. 'I rather fancy the Moulin de Mougins. No need to book – Vergé knows me well. I'm always going on about his silly sauce spoons.'

On the next mattress Harry had glanced at the headline and grunted. He should have known better than to wager with Guy Magnus on anything but a game of chance, and even then to own the dice; but somehow he was always sucked in. Still, he reckoned, the news might help. The spoils of victory would put Guy in benevolent mood.

'You win, Guy,' he admitted, scratching at his damp chest.

Guy shielded his eyes from the midday sun and surveyed the scene. On the horizon he made out the faint outline of the Île de Lerins; closer by the Boulevard de la Croisette, lined by its wedding-cake hotels and apartment buildings; higher up the pine-clad hills from which orange-roofed villas competed for a share of the view. Nearer still the deep blue of the Mediterranean was sprinkled with breeze-filled sails and crisscrossed by the wakes of speedboats. And luxury cabin cruisers like theirs. Harry had mumbled something about borrowing it from a priest, but so long as the *Gay Dog* lived up to its name, who gave a toss who owned it? Guy rolled on to his stomach so his long back could fry next.

Harry wondered whether the time was ripe for his revelation. He scanned the back of Guy's head in a vain attempt to elicit a clue to its owner's mood. It was hard to stay patient when you had something important to tell; but it was critical to give no hint of the pressure he was under. When Guy spotted a vulnerable prey, he would spring on to him like a panther. So the disclosure must emerge casually, at the psychological moment.

'Come on, Harry, spill it,' Guy said suddenly. 'You didn't bring me all the way from London just to celebrate the anniversary of our coup.' It was four years almost to the day since Harry had brought him the Mallard deal. 'It's not Sybil – you're too stupid to leave her. Some men can't live without a woman. You just can't live without Sybil. You'd kill yourself if she wasn't telling you how much of your money she'd saved at Harry Winston. So it's not about Sybil. Business. It's about business, isn't it, Harry?'

Harry grinned. 'Business it is,' he conceded. He loved Guy in this mood. You'd lost before the battle had even begun.

'Well, then, it's Britton Trust. You've lost your shirt on everything else. Since you merged CHIT into it you've had nothing left to play with but your balls. Don't tell me that's going sour on you too? Britton Trust, I mean.'

Harry thought fast. He was already on the wrong foot; how to step on to the right one? It would be churlish to avoid the question altogether.

'As a business? Or as a deal?' he batted the question back down the line.

'You tell me,' Guy batted it straight back at him.

'The business is fine. Expanding nicely, plenty of good deals, you know how things are nowadays. When you buy a company the properties are always worth more than you expect – they've been undervalued, there's marriage value in the leases, development potential, a special purchaser the surveyors have ignored. That's what we found when we bought Watson's. When the Britton portfolio is revalued – I really shouldn't be telling you this, Guy.'

'How much?'

When Guy asked a direct question, albeit in a manner so casual you could never be sure how keen his interest was, it was hard to avoid giving a direct answer. Harry sensed that this was a moment to take care: to give enough, but not all, away.

'I can only guess,' he replied. 'It's the way they talk. The new management's conservative as hell – must be cautious, mustn't count our chickens, what if this, what if that? It's pretty clear there must be a gold mine there, though.'

'Then what's your problem?'

'Don't think I'm not grateful to you, Guy, for putting me into CHIT; but things have changed. Britton Trust's ten times the size CHIT was when I put my money in, but my stake's been watered down by all the mergers. I'm not sure I want it any more. I've been wondering whether I shouldn't cash in my chips and look for the next play.'

'Why give in, Harry? Make the company the next play. Do something with it, for God's sake.'

'Wouldn't I, if only I could? You should hear what the others say whenever I make a proposal. That's why Andy and I are resigning from the board. It's going to be announced at the end of next month. Didn't I tell you?' Harry feigned surprise at his discourteous omission.

'You're crazy! Just when it's time to make your shares worth as much as possible, you talk of quitting. How does Harold feel about it – and Archie?'

'Harold's had enough too. When we merged, we agreed to give Charteris and his colleagues equal numbers on the board. They outmanoeuvred us. They got this Palliser chap in to keep an eye on the books while Jolyon wriggled around. All he ever does is moan about our expense accounts. Jolyon may be a snake, but at least he's our snake. The noble earl's supposed to be an independent chairman, but we thought he'd be our man. Now he just blows with the wind, and Archie Laws refuses to take sides. So it's not our business any more. It's too late to do anything about it now,' Harry ended lamely.

'*J'ai soif.* Make yourself useful, Harry. See if you can get the cork out of my Corton-Charlemagne without using your thumb for a change, you clumsy oaf.' Guy needed time for thought. He watched his host's squat body cross the deck and his curly dark brown hair disappear down the steps to the galley. Two minutes later the head reappeared, followed by two hands holding slender glasses whose pale yellow contents were clouded by a fine layer of condensation.

'How many times have I told you not to over-chill white Burgundy,' Guy moaned. He took a sip and rolled the liquid slowly over his palate. 'Kills the bouquet, let alone the flavour.' He sat back in his deckchair and stared at the sky. It was time to play it cool.

Harry grinned and said nothing. When Guy was in this mood, his mind was on something else.

Guy decided that further intelligence was best extracted over the dining table. He gave his glass a twirl and held it up to the light.

'Too hot in the sun for decent Burgundy,' he complained. 'Can't taste the acid finish. Get out your wallet, Harry; I'm developing an appetite.'

The prow of the *Gay Dog* was soon cutting across the calm waters of the bay towards the port of Cannes, where Yankee Tate awaited their arrival in his master's new electric-blue, stretched-body, six-door Mercedes limousine. While Harry had been collecting Guy from Beaulieu-sur-Mer and piloting the *Gay Dog* across the waters of the Mediterranean, Yankee had taken the drier, but in his case no less hazardous, route from Monte Carlo to Cannes, scouting the corniches of the Cote d'Azur for teenage girls wearing halter tops and short skirts or less and seeking transport. The balmy air, the proximity of his passengers' knees to the gear shift and the language difficulties had combined to produce odds much to his liking.

Yankee negotiated the steep bends up the foothills of the Alpes Maritimes with such panache that Harry, seated on the passenger side where he could see the oncoming traffic except when Yankee leaned across him to do likewise, promised himself he'd buy Sybil an eternity ring if he survived. He reckoned the odds against this were as long as one of Yankee's accumulators.

'I had to keep overtaking, sir, to see where I was going,' Yankee excused himself as he pulled up outside the doors of the Moulin de Mougins.

As they took theirs seat among the restaurant's exotic sub-tropical plants, Guy returned cautiously to the subject of Britton Trust.

'You say it's worth ten times as much. As much as what?' he asked.

'Figure of speech,' Harry smiled inwardly. Guy was on the hook. 'There are ten times the number of shares, before you start looking at what they're worth.'

'How many in issue?'

'About six and three quarter million.'

'What's the price in the market? I haven't been following them recently.' Guy perused the mouth-watering specialities on the à *la carte* menu as he waited for the number of which he was only too well aware.

'Two hundred pence, give or take.'

'So, market value £13.5 million,' Guy mused. 'Net asset value?'

'Double?' Harry replied tentatively, more as a question than an answer.

Guy masked his reaction until he had given his order for Terrine de rascasse au citron and Langouste royale au poivre rose.

'So, £25 to £30 million, eh?' he mused. 'Worth it?'

Harry guessed it was time to slow down. 'Not in the present board's hands,' he said. 'They'd have a job making it worth £20 million.'

'And you hold?'

'I've already cashed some in,' replied Harry, determined not to elaborate.

'But you still have some left,' Guy picked up the inference.

'I'm riding with a few,' Harry confirmed. 'To be honest, Guy, we're reckoning on a bid to take us out. I wouldn't go for it, though, not if I were you,' he warned hastily. He knew Guy regarded warnings as challenges. 'It's too large and too risky, even if there is a pretty fancy surplus sloshing around.'

'What's so risky about it?' Guy was not ready to challenge the insult that the deal was too large for him until he knew more about the downside.

'You'd be fighting the big boys. Consolidated Finance has bought a stake. A million shares, last time I heard. I reckon Lewis wants to put the company into play. We may not squeeze the last penny, but we should get one more turn.'

'In that case, where's the downside?'

'Too many shares in the boardroom. That means Lewis won't bid without a board recommendation, but he won't get one at a price he's willing to pay – not once the directors have a property revaluation. My guess is Consolidated Finance will end up taking a turn from one of the bigger players. Lewis reckons one of them will pay ransom money for his stake. He's probably not wrong. Crying shame, though, missing out on that fat surplus.'

Since the sale of Mallard six months ago, the enforced inactivity had begun to play on Guy's nerves. He was fretting for a sweet deal, but in the present market sweet deals were increasingly hard to come by. His instinct told him there was a healthy turn to be made out of Britton Trust. But his old friend Harry Griffin wasn't about to sell his part of the action at a price which left the profit for somebody else, let alone for his old friend Guy Magnus. To

Harry friendship meant paying more, not less, even if you were the friend who put him into the deal in the first place. Still, it was worth a try.

'If the numbers are as you say and you don't want to hang around, I suppose I might consider giving you the same price as Lewis,' he said carefully, more as a comment than an offer.

Harry knew his response was critical. His rejection must sound categoric if Guy was not to lose interest.

'Sorry, Guy,' he said. 'I'm not that desperate. There's bound to be a full bid. I'd rather wait till Lewis sells and then go for the main chance. Britton Trust won't go down for less than 300p.'

'But you said it's worth four?' Guy asked for confirmation.

'To five,' said Harry in the tone used by politicians when they speak of cautious optimism. It wouldn't do to deprive a pal of his share of happiness in your good fortune, especially if he might want to make his own at the same time. 'No harm in you having a punt on a few, I don't suppose,' he added without enthusiasm. 'You probably won't lose out. Since Lewis took off the weak holders, the market in the stock's been pretty tight. You may pick up a parcel from Harold or Andy if they lose patience.'

Guy pondered. This was 1973, not 1972. As the government stuttered from one unworkable form of wage and price controls to another, from rail strikes to foreign exchange crises and ministerial resignations over indiscreet assignations with call-girls, the stock market had been falling steadily. This was no time for a punt: if you bought shares for the turn, you were three times as likely to hit a bad week as a good one. The profitable way to deal was to short stocks that were following the market down, and buy them back when you had to deliver. The only game worth playing long was property. But the best way to buy property at a discount – for Guy never bought anything that was not at a discount – was to buy a company that owned it. Like Britton Trust. Harry reckoned its assets were worth four to five quid a share, and they stood at only two. Well, if Harry Griffin couldn't cut the mustard with the company, Guy Magnus would. It was time he showed which of them had the Midas touch. But he must take care: Harry had never been shy about making a few bob out of his friends. Before he took irrevocable action he must check Britton Trust out. Not with Berry St Edmunds, but with Harold Antony.

Harry read Guy's hesitation and struck. 'If you should think of buying a stake and need funding, Ulster & Cayman may be interested,' he said. 'Their Mayfair office is pretty flush from the Farranwide sale. They're keen to lend on anything with property. If you need an introduction, tell Sam Dervish I gave you his name.'

Guy knew of 'Whirling' Sam – who in the City of London did not? But first he must set wheels in motion. That meant a speedy return to his suite at La Reserve in Beaulieu-sur-Mer. London might be an hour behind, but the stock exchange closed at half past three.

'Your bill,' he said predictably. 'My petrol,' he added, as if in justification.

Yankee Tate dropped Guy at his hotel before taking Harry on to Monte Carlo. As Guy strode towards the entrance Harry wound his window down.

'Take care not to give me my first million,' he shouted after him. 'It'd mean paying for my lunch.'

'Fat chance of that!' Guy yelled back, pulling a face. 'You owe too much.'

Harry returned to his apartment in Monte Carlo, where he mixed himself a gin and tonic and pondered for a while. Then he put in a call to Jolyon Priestley. He put in a further call to Harold Anthony. Then he had a brief word with Andy Oakes. He forbore to speak to the Earl of St Edmunds on the grounds that it was better for Harold Antony to do so for him; and in any case there was too much painful ground to cover with the earl.

Two pounds fifty a share, Harry calculated: that would give him a million four. Guy was right about his debts, of course – but even taking account of his £500,000 loan, he was only 100 grand light. Another 20p and he'd be home. One million pounds! There to be earned – and hidden, please God! from Sybil.

Since then almost two years had passed. With the benefit of 20:20 hindsight, Harry was able to fit most of the pieces into the jigsaw. Though he had known nothing of Guy's call to Danny Gilbert, he guessed it had not taken long for his friend to change into his swimming trunks and go down to the pool, where he would have had an exchange of views with Ray Munster, his most friendly stockbroker.

'Why don't I have quiet a word with Mark Penney-Stockes?' Munster would have suggested. 'He's not connected with you. I'll tell him not to disturb the market.'

And now, Harry told himself, as his cab drew up in front of Maxim's and the doorman gave him the nod of recognition he accorded without discrimination to all the restaurant's guests, he was about to collect his reward. Now, for the very first time, Guy Magnus was about to pay for lunch with Harry Griffin.

51

Guy had been quick to agree to their rendezvous. At the time of Harry's call, Paris seemed an infinitely more agreeable place than London to break bread and chew the fat with an old friend. The wolves from the Inland Revenue had been baying at the door of his Chelsea home, and the vultures from the Board of Trade had been circling around the Ludgate Circus in the vain hope of picking over the entrails of Britton Trust. It would spoil the funeral, he had told Dominic Arthur if there were no murderer or corpse to greet them. So at the crack of an early spring dawn he had slipped silently behind the driving wheel of the Rolls-Royce he had decided was more appropriate to his new status than the Bentley, switched on the ignition, and a few hours later stood on the deck of the cross-channel ferry, waving goodbye to the white cliffs of Dover and setting his face towards the fresh breezes of the English Channel. He had spent that evening relaxing contentedly in the apartment Melvin Cecil had rented by the Bois de Boulogne the previous autumn. His companion-in-exile had at first argued cogently for San Francisco – for the cabernet sauvignons of the Napa Valley were reputed to be on the way up, whereas Bordeaux had suffered four poor years out of five – but Guy had referred him to an article in *Private Eye* which had reported that while Caliban had become poorer Melvin Cecil seemed to have grown richer, and told him he could afford both.

He had moved on to the Circus Maximus, he told Harry cheerfully the following day as he took his seat opposite him, surveyed le tout Paris and began his tale. An hour and a half later, replete with a double portion of Beluga caviar, Saint Jacques à la nage and a third glass of Corton-Charlemagne, he paused as he approached its denouement.

'So what exactly did they do to you?' asked Harry, stuffing a fork loaded with caneton aux pêches on to his salivating palate.

'They carried out their threat. They took me for every penny I had. Charles wrote to me, just as he'd promised. The letter arrived by hand next morning.

Their final offer, Charles said.' Guy paused again, savouring the moment. Harry was well and truly on the hook. But he must go on. 'I was to acknowledge a debt of £150,000. In return, the bank would release me from my guarantee.'

'A hundred and fifty thousand!' Harry repeated. 'What about the rest of the £17 million?'

'*Mon petit cadeau*. He must have known it was my birthday. My thirtieth, as it happened.'

'They can't have thought it was all you had. You've made millions.'

'I owe a lot of tax, Harry.'

Harry was not to be put off the scent. 'Come off it, Guy: you told me you'd avoided more taxes than your father ever collected,' he objected. 'Don't tell me you've changed your habits just so he can become proud of you.'

Guy saw no benefit in further deception. 'They obviously had no intention of calling on my guarantee,' he replied. 'Bankrupting me would have been a public admission of failure.'

'So you paid £150,000 and walked away?'

'Not exactly. I had no cash. I was to reduce the debt by selling them 800,000 St Paul's shares at 5p apiece.'

'Leaving, if I'm right,' said Harry after a pause, 'a balance of £110,000.'

'You are. And I was to throw in the Henry Moore for £20,000, leaving £90,000. If they sold either for more, my debt would be reduced accordingly. If they sold for less, it would be increased.'

There was a more protracted hiatus as Harry extracted a lump of wax from his left ear with his little finger, the better to follow Guy's tale.

'What did you reply?' he asked at length.

'He had been candid with me, so naturally I returned the compliment. I told him that the value of St Paul's might in fairness be as low as 2p a share, so in the agreement my debt should be recorded as £114,000 rather than £90,000. He must have been touched by my honesty, as he said that as this was rather a lot of money, I would be allowed to repay it in instalments.'

'And you agreed,' Harry guessed.

'I agreed,' Guy confessed, shrugging.

'And made a first payment,' Harry guessed again.

'Naturally. I handed over the shares and the Henry Moore.'

'And the rest? The £114,000 ...?'

'Was to be regarded as a debt of honour.'

'A debt of honour? From you, Guy?' Harry was incredulous.

'Interest free. To be repaid if and when I was in a position to do so. The agreement specified that I was not under any legal obligation to pay. It is, of course, a legally binding contract. We both signed it. Such is the manner in which matters of this nature are resolved between gentlemen,' Guy added sardonically, making it clear that as far as he was concerned that concluded the matter.

'For £17 million! I don't believe you,' Harry shook his head in wonder.

Guy feigned affront. 'Charles had faith in me, Harry, even if you don't.'

'Such is the manner in which matters of this nature are resolved between fools,' Harry plagiarised.

'Fools? Me a fool? Well, I suppose I was a bit,' Guy conceded. 'But in the world of the City,' he quickly excused himself, 'I was a boy, and they were grown up men.'

'And Danny?' Harry asked.

'Danny's a baby. He paid up.'

As their cheese plates were removed and they awaited the delivery of Maxim's celebrated Tarte Tatin, Harry turned the conversation to the financial opportunities currently available to the discriminating international investor.

'I reckon the Bourse offers better prospects than London or New York. Will you be looking for another shell?' he asked hopefully. He knew that Guy needed another play, and soon. A recent report in *Private Eye* had informed him that his companion had sold the market short when the *FT* Share Index sped up through 200 and had had to meet his commitments as it passed 300 – or would have to if he wished ever again to deal on the London Stock Exchange. Whereas Harry, ever the optimist, had gone long of the market when the Index turned at 146 early in the new year and had stayed with it until last week, doubling his money. Now that he qualified as a tax exile, the only significant deduction against his profits would come from Sybil's infallible sense of direction and her highly developed shopping French. He had a powerful suspicion that at that very moment the tills of the rue du Faubourg Saint-Honoré would be ringing merrily to her tune.

'Another shell? You must be joking. I've collected enough shells to fill a bucket, and what d'you think they got me?'

Harry scratched his chin. Was this one of Guy's riddles? 'Tell me,' he said.

'Nothing but a bucketful of seashells,' Guy replied.

Harry nodded. 'Like Caligula,' he observed.

'Like Caligula,' Guy agreed.

'Didn't a seagull shit on him while his men were collecting the shells?'

'The other way round this time, I fancy,' Guy smiled to himself. Then he added, 'My favourite Roman emperor. He always had the answer.' For a moment he was lost in thought. 'Until they killed him,' he added ruefully.

Harry paused while the dessert was set before him. He allowed the powerful scent of apples and cinnamon to seduce his nostrils, and then asked, 'You know why it went wrong?'

Guy looked quizzically across the table. Harry didn't usually play the philosopher.

'You tell me,' he demanded.

'You broke your own rules. You fell in love with the deal. You dated on your first screw.'

The only time, Guy admitted to himself.

'You not, I gather. A propos,' he said straight-faced, 'Sharon asked me to give Sybil her love.'

Harry grinned. 'You have plans?' he tried again as he savoured a delicious mouthful of caramelised apple. It never hurt to know what Guy was up to.

'I'm working on them,' Guy said enigmatically. Then he decided it would do no harm to have Harry on board again as a punter. 'St Paul's is having a rights issue. It needs to raise £250,000.'

'At what price?' Harry's dealing instinct looked for the turn.

'High enough so no shareholder will want to subscribe. Ludgate already has thirty-seven per cent of St Paul's, so I'll gain control. It's got a quarry. Dolomite. Pilkingtons use it to make high grade float glass. It was mortgaged to finance a development, but I reckon I can persuade the lender to take the building off my hands and release the charge. Then I'll sell the quarry to Pilkingtons for a fortune, and ...' Guy shrugged.

Harry could see why a lender would want to release a mortgage from a company in which Guy Magnus had an interest. He was less confident that St Paul's other shareholders would do as well from the deal. Guy's capacity for invention was inexhaustible, his propensity for manipulation incorrigible. A healthy slice of the fortune would end up in his hands. Which reminded him – Guy had kept him on the hook; it was his turn to repay the compliment.

'That unfinished business of ours, Guy. You remember?' he changed the subject as their empty dessert plates were removed.

'You want your free lunch.'

'That's right,' Harry smiled in triumph. 'Your turn to pay.'

'In my financial state? You must be joking.'

'A deal's a deal, Guy. I can show my million. One lunch at Maxim's on you, *s'il te plaît.*' Harry opened his briefcase and passed a sheaf of stockbrokers' settlement statements across the table.

Guy examined the papers cursorily. 'This is yesterday's date,' he observed as he came to the last page.

'Of course it is. I knew we were having lunch today.'

Guy took a folder from his pocket, the logo of Sotheby & Co embossed on its cover, and handed it to Harry.

'A professional valuation. One million and twenty-five thousand pounds. Check out the date,' he chuckled. 'Geneva, August 1974, I think you'll find.'

Harry perused the contents. 'Still in your possession and unpledged?' he asked, knowing the answer. Guy would have protected his paintings with his life.

'Still in my possession and unpledged. Apart from the Henry Moore. You don't trust me?'

'On this, yes,' Harry conceded, handing back the folder. Guy was invincible too, he was forced to admit to himself. No one stayed ahead of him for long. He knew exactly what he would find in Guy's apartment. 'My turn to pay,' he agreed without resentment. As a lunch companion, if nothing else, Guy Magnus never failed to give value for money. He called the head waiter and asked for the bill. But he failed to do so before Guy had ordered a bottle of the finest vintage of Dom Pérignon on Maxim's list – they ought to celebrate their respective successes, he said.

'Your place for coffee?' Harry suggested.

As they sat in silence in the salon of Guy's apartment, sipping their espressos and Armagnac, Harry was human enough to feel a slight twinge of guilt over his part in the affair.

'Any regrets?' he finally broke the silence.

Guy glanced instinctively round his new domain. Britton Trust, Magical Investments, Ludgate – all gone, worthless. But his collection of paintings remained secure, fixed to the walls. Even so, the gap in the middle of the floor was beginning to unsettle him.

'Just one,' he confessed.

Harry stared at Guy, puzzled. Then he caught on.

'The sculpture? You'll get over it, Guy,' he said. 'You always do. And you do at least have the consolation that it's turned out to be the most expensive Henry Moore in the world.'